The Pupil

THE
PUPIL

ROS CARNE

CANELO

First published in the United Kingdom in 2020 by Canelo

Canelo Digital Publishing Limited
31 Helen Road
Oxford OX2 0DF
United Kingdom

Copyright © Ros Carne, 2020

The moral right of Ros Carne to be identified as the author of this work has been asserted in accordance with the Copyright, Designs and Patents Act, 1988.

All rights reserved. No part of this publication may be reproduced or transmitted in any form or by any means, electronic or mechanical, including photocopy, recording, or any information storage and retrieval system, without permission in writing from the publisher.

A CIP catalogue record for this book is available from the British Library.

Print ISBN 978 1 80032 030 7
Ebook ISBN 978 1 78863 967 5

This book is a work of fiction. Names, characters, businesses, organizations, places and events are either the product of the author's imagination or are used fictitiously. Any resemblance to actual persons, living or dead, events or locales is entirely coincidental.

Look for more great books at www.canelo.co

Printed and bound in Great Britain by Clays Ltd, Elcograf S.p.A.

For

Nathan and Tommy

Part 1

April

Chapter One

Mel

Success is an aphrodisiac. Mel pulled out her phone and called Paul's work number. 'Another triumph.'

'I'll read that as another criminal on the streets. So much for legal ethics. Where are you?'

'Isleworth. On my way to the tube. I don't need to go into chambers.'

'The thing is, Mel, I can't really get away.' It was as if he had slammed a door in her face. 'What about tomorrow?' he asked. 'I could grab a couple of hours.'

'Jacob's back. Plus, I'm in Northampton all day.'

'Sounds like we'll... listen, I need to shoot. Three o'clock seminar. Mel? You there?'

'Traffic noise. It's difficult to hear.'

'I'll call you later.'

She slipped the phone into the side pocket of her bag and headed northwards past school playing fields and dull suburban houses towards the Great West Road. The day was grey, dry, and windless, neither warm nor cold, the sun no more than a faint glimmer through clouds. Disappointment would subside. How could she expect Paul to adapt his schedule without warning on a Tuesday afternoon in term time? Ringing him had been a spur of the moment thing, a longing to share the thrill of victory. She wasn't one of those women who fell to pieces at their lover's absence.

As she fell into the comforting rhythm of the walk, her whirling mind slowed. The phone call had been a mistake. She usually waited for him to contact her.

The houses between the Crown Court and the tube were mostly bow-fronted semis with clipped hedges and low walls. She could imagine Paul in such a house, though his would be bigger, glassier, with kitchen and loft extensions. Of course, she would never see the family home which he and Caro had bought soon after the dinner party seventeen years ago where Mel and Paul had met for the first time.

Mel was still with Claude then and they were planning their own family home, though that dream was to crumble a few years later. There were two other couples at the party, but their names or faces had become lost in time. Even Caro had become a blur, though Mel still recalled her gentle, pale blue eyes and flustered manner as she struggled with the burnt Osso Buco in between sprints up and down the stairs trying to get the children to sleep.

In the large kitchen the rest of them had speared the charred meat, drank a lot of red wine and argued. Mel couldn't remember what they'd argued about, only that she had felt outnumbered, and unsupported by Claude. She had sensed Paul watching her and had never forgotten the expression on his face, the power of his deep blue eyes as he turned to her in agreement and said, 'You are not alone.'

Three years ago, Claude long gone, she had run into Paul in the Temple. He told her he often used the short cut from Waterloo to his office at the University of North London where he worked. Walking through a well-tended garden was much pleasanter than struggling with crowds on the Strand. They went for a coffee. She talked. The pressures of work. Her need to hold her life together for her son. He listened. Afterwards, she wondered if she had talked too much. But, two days later he rang to say how much he had enjoyed seeing her again, inviting her for a drink. He didn't mention Caro.

'That sounds great,' she said.

When she put the phone down her heart was beating hard. But she felt no guilt. Paul was what she needed at this point in her life. No one would know. No one would get hurt. Sometimes, when Jacob was staying with Claude, she and Paul would meet in Mel's flat, though there was a niggling discomfort at his presence after they had made love, awkwardness over their cups of tea or glasses of wine. She wanted him, but not in this place. They were better off somewhere neutral. There was a sweet-sour detachment in their hotel encounters which enhanced their intensity. Paul would never move into her life to find fault with her slovenly habits and her moody teenage son.

The sun emerged from its sheet of cloud. When she started at the Bar, she little realised how much of her time would be spent tramping around London's fringes, seeking out-of-the-way courts. The courts were fewer and larger now, the directions easier, thanks to mobile phones and Google maps. But she had enjoyed those backstreet expeditions, her battered Court Guide tucked into her rucksack, working out obscure bus routes or parking spots. Nowadays she used a wheelie bag, but that end-of-the-day feeling was unchanged, the mid-afternoon lull that preceded the next set of instructions.

At least the trains were frequent, and today she would be travelling against the rush hour with the luxury of nothing immediate to prepare, no one to report to, and a good thriller on her Kindle. Never mind Paul. She would do the right thing, hurry back to chambers, listen to other people's war stories, talk rugby with Andy, her clerk. It was time she showed her face.

Coming out at Holborn tube an hour later, she cut through Lincoln's Inn Fields, then across the Inn to the Temple. More than twenty years after she had first seen the place, it could still work its magic, particularly on a bright spring day after a successful afternoon in the Crown Court. Walking past the weathered brick, the arching fountain surrounded by neatly trimmed lawns, the pale tight buds of the lime trees, she breathed the scent of newly cut grass, the sense of renewal deep within the city's turbulence. Whatever went wrong in her personal life, she had this.

Bridge Court Chambers was bustling with tenants coming in from court, picking up papers for the next day, solicitors accompanying clients for conferences. Mel swept through the clerks' room, past the pigeonholes, which even in this day of electronic communication remained a focal point, shouted 'Hi,' to the clerks and bounded up the stone stairs to her room. It was cramped but light, with three desks. Two were piled high with other people's papers, the third and best placed faced out across the Temple Gardens.

In these days of hot desking she could no longer regard it as her own, and it was currently occupied by a beautiful Asian woman. Her glossy hair was drawn back into a large clip, and so fine and symmetrical were her features, so perfect the hairline, that she had no need of the loose strands which most women, Mel included, used to soften the outlines of their faces. Alisha was staring intently into a laptop, flipping the pages in the thick Lever Arch file beside her. Mel viewed her with detached admiration. It would be easier to like Alisha if she had been prepared to let down her guard in private. Chambers gossip hinted at a difficult husband, a gambler. Alisha's Hindu parents reportedly disapproved. Mel had learnt all this from her friend Georgie and felt a little piqued that she herself had not been chosen as a confidante.

'Hello, stranger.'

'Hi, Alisha.'

'How d'you get on?'

'Fine.'

What else could she say? In the last five days she had slain the prosecution witnesses, guided her client through his shaky evidence, rescued him from a powerful cross-examination and finally soared in her closing speech. She'd been at her best.

Standing up in court she had been oblivious to the outside world, focusing only on the evidence she needed to handle, her own well-prepared tactics, the thrill of battle. The judge's summing up had felt weighted towards the prosecution and the wait for the verdict was as ever, nerve-jangling. But against all odds, they had won. That her client was clearly guilty, and would no doubt go out and mug another innocent passer-by was something she preferred not to think about.

Mel typed up her Attendance Note, a brief outline of what had gone on in court that morning, the hours divided between preparation, conference and the trial itself. She would pick up her next set of papers and work on tomorrow's brief at home. She was eager to get back to see Jacob. He'd be starting his exams soon and she needed to be around for him. Just as she was about to leave, she heard Alisha speak. Her words hit Mel like a sudden, destabilising blast of wind.

'When's your new pupil starting?'

'What new pupil?'

'Natasha. She's already been here six months with the Civil Law team. Now it's our turn. You must have seen her around. Fair, straight hair. Striking-looking woman.'

'I don't think so.'

'Talk to Andy. As far as I recall, he said she's starting with you.'

Two minutes later Mel had dumped her brief, endorsed with the jury's verdict, together with the Attendance Note, in Andy's tray and was standing at his desk.

'Hi, Mel.' Andy continued to stare into the screen in front of him. 'Northampton tomorrow. Meet the client at 9:30 a.m. You OK to get there?'

'I'm used to early starts. What's this about a pupil, Andy?'

'Natasha. She's starting tomorrow. I'm sending her to the High Court with Jess. After that she's yours.'

'Nobody told me.'

'She was supposed to be Georgie's but he's in Birmingham for another three weeks. Plus, it's your turn.'

Mel was aware of that. It was five years since she had last had a pupil, an overenthusiastic young man who used to hang around for hours asking irritating questions at the end of the day when she needed to get back home for Jacob.

'She'll come along to your Patel case in the Principal Registry. I've sent her copies of the papers. She seems pretty on the ball.'

'Fine.'

It was not fine. There would be no more empty afternoons. No more drifting around London suburbs, planning hook-ups with Paul. Pupils were keen. They stuck to you like limpets.

Chapter Two

Natasha

Natasha walked fast, cutting a swathe through the Oxford Street crowd. She looked straight ahead, blurring her focus just enough to avoid confronting the sad inelegance of the English shopper. Women stepped to one side. So did most men. Occasionally a bully would try to face her off and she would make a quick decision, having good antennae for danger and stepping aside at the faintest whiff. There was no point in risking an unwinnable argument. Face-off was a game and she liked games. It was why she had decided to become a barrister, and why she was striding through the West End this bright April morning, about to shoplift a respectable outfit for her first day in Bridge Court Chambers.

Most sensible people would have told her she was an idiot to try a spot of thievery on the day before starting her second six months of pupillage, risking a criminal record and the certain destruction of her fledgling career. Not to mention the waste of £40,000 in fees and expenses, five years of study, a score of exams and twelve interviews. All for the sake of picking up a few items of clothing which, given the size of her debt, she might as well buy. But she was bored, and she needed a kick. She was good at shoplifting and it always gave her a thrill.

She chose Marks & Spencer, despite being thirty years younger than most of their customers. The staff were lazy, only the really pricey stuff was tagged, there were no security guards on the door, and the cameras were usually out of action. She had dressed carefully for the task. Neutral grey shirt and jeans, light jacket, hair neatly clipped back, minimal make-up.

'You look nice,' said Luke as she was preparing to leave their flat. She had been changing the battery in her insulin pump, replenishing the stock of glucose tablets in her handbag. 'Not going to work then?' He was used to her dark suits. Even if she sat in chambers all day, she was expected to wear court gear in case she had to accompany her pupil supervisor over the road to the High Court. She knew what Luke was thinking. If they were both at home, why not take a break in bed around midday? Sex with Luke was always good, and it was particularly satisfying when the rest of the world was on its treadmill. But Luke would always be there, or for as long as she wanted him, whereas today's expedition was special. It would be her last. Once she started in court, everything would change. No more shoplifting. That was the plan.

'Just shopping. Gotta look smart for court.'

'You're always smart.'

'New job, new suit. I'll be on my feet in court any day.'

'You'll be brilliant. Terrifying.'

He grinned, and she was pleased. Nothing he said indicated suspicion, though he must realise she had more cool clothes than could realistically be bought on her income. Pupils at Bridge Court were expected to exist on £14,000 a year. He'd confronted her once and the row had been horrible. Since then he had stayed silent about her shopping hobby. He wanted her more than she wanted him and that meant accepting what she was. There had been one unpleasant incident when she had gone a step too far with a man at a party and tested his patience. After that she had been more careful. She could have any man she wanted for sex, but not many, like Luke, who would care for her and support her. It was not, she told herself, that she needed him. She could easily manage alone. But she was fond of him and had come to rely on him. It was the only relationship she'd had that had lasted more than a few months.

She had met Luke two years ago at a time when she was bored with cooking alone and having no one regular to go out with. He had turned up, in the traditional way, at a party. He was a social worker, but she could forgive him that because he was the most beautiful man she had ever seen, thick wavy hair the colour of polished oak, long straight nose, deep brown eyes. Yet he had none of the confidence that one might expect would accompany such an appearance. His movements were tentative and his speech slow and uncertain, as if he had to think hard before deciding what to say.

She pecked him on the cheek, leaving him disappointed, and swung out of the door of the former council flat in Brixton which, for the last two years, had been their home.

Marks & Spencer was quiet, the stock dreary. She bought a brown sweater in the sale for Luke to wear to work and picked up a large store bag, which would come in useful later. She quickly checked the positioning of the mirrors and cameras. The layout of the store was familiar, and she had frequently kitted herself out with gloves, scarves and tights. Jackets were straightforward. She clattered through the rack; charcoal grey with velvet trim and matching skirt looked ideal. Best of all, there were no security tags. She added them to an armful of random stuff. The girl by the changing rooms simply ushered her into Room 7 without bothering to count the items. Seven was lucky. She tried on the jacket and skirt. Perfect. She stuffed them behind the sweater in the store bag, waited a few minutes and then left the cubicle, handing back the other things. None of them was quite right, she said with a practised smile. The girl nodded and proceeded to hang them on a rail as Natasha headed slowly for the exit.

Shoplifting was like lying, most effective when linked to honesty. If they stopped her now, she would say it was an accident, she'd no idea she'd put the items in the bag. She'd started to feel dizzy and confused while she was trying on the clothes. She was type 1 diabetic and must have let her blood sugar fall too low. If she could just sit and eat some glucose tablets and a cereal bar she would be fine. She was so very sorry. The excuse had come in handy on a couple of occasions, but she didn't need it today, she simply walked out of the back of the store, smiling inwardly as the rush hit, the physical pleasure of small-scale criminality.

The rush was already fading as she zigzagged the Soho streets. She checked her phone. It was 12:45 p.m. Just as she suspected, there was a message from Ricky, if he really was Ricky, on Tinder.

Hi, Lola. You on your way?

Give me ten minutes, she texted.

Waxy O'Connor's was two streets away. It was a cavernous Irish pub, large enough to permit Natasha to scrutinise her prey without the unwelcome intimacy of The French House or The Ship. If Ricky looked hot, she'd introduce herself. Lola's online portrait was sufficiently like her own. If less than hot, she'd ignore him and enjoy her lunch. They made an excellent crab sandwich in Waxy's. If he confronted her, she'd smile and tell him he must have made a mistake.

There he was, just as she suspected, swiping his phone, darting glances towards the door. He'd said he was an architect, in a long-term relationship, looking for a sexy, independent woman under thirty for the occasional hook-up, maybe more. She turned back to her crab sandwich. There was no way he was five foot eleven, and he was at least ten years older than the photograph. Bloody cheat. She had no intention of talking to him anyway. Witnessing male trepidation was always fun. It would take someone very special for her to take it further. It was just a game.

A year ago Luke had cooked her favourite Chinese duck, opened a bottle of expensive wine and asked her to marry him. He wanted children and he wanted her to be their mother. She had felt an icy shiver, tried to calm herself with slow breathing and finally, in answer to his pleading, reminded him how hard it was for her to commit. Touching on the chaos of her own childhood, she told him that he more than anyone should understand the dangers of intergenerational damage.

He had tried to reassure her, held her close, whispered that all would be fine. But the conversation had unsettled her. Far from the romantic ending he had hoped for, she had pulled away, saying she needed time alone, leaving him on the sofa watching Formula One. She had gone to the bedroom and tried to ground herself by surfing Tinder. An hour later she had resurrected Lola, the fake identity she had adopted years ago when she first came to London. Lola even had her own Facebook profile. She was pretty, just under twenty years old and within a few months she had gathered more than fifty friends her own age.

From the corner of her eye she glimpsed Ricky. It was clear he was fed up with waiting. He looked at her briefly and she thought she detected a flicker of suspicion. She looked away. He stood up and walked out. She finished her apple juice and crab sandwich, paid her bill, left a generous tip for the waitress, picked up her stolen goods and set off for the tube.

Chapter Three

Mel

'So, the deal is, you just sit there and listen.' Mel concluded her few words of instruction to the new pupil.

'Say nothing?' Natasha looked incredulous.

'Exactly.'

'Even if I can help?'

'Especially if you think you can help. Speak to me later, ask anything you like, only not in front of the client.' Was Mel imagining it or was that disdain in Natasha's arched brows and crooked smile?

'So, this morning… Was it…?'

'That was helpful. But, if you're left alone with the client, stick to pleasantries.'

'I'm terribly sorry, I…'

'Forget it,' replied Mel.

Natasha moved to the tall window, lowering the blind to shut out the shaft of afternoon sunlight that gleamed across the cold glass of the conference table. Then, with the grace of a dancer, she sat, setting out her papers and her laptop, and waited.

The day had got off to a bad start with Mel arriving late for the Principal Registry, the main family court in Central London. It had been a mistake to drive her son to school, though at the time it seemed an opportunity for twenty minutes' uninterrupted conversation. Traffic had been heavy and slow, conversation had been desultory and largely one-sided, culminating in Jacob turning up the volume of some ranting, incomprehensible radio chat show when she had tried to introduce the topic of revision.

Neither said another word until they reached the school gates at which point, he mumbled, 'Thanks, Mum,' in response to her cheery, 'Have a good day, darling.' She set off for the nearest tube station and after a ten-minute search for a parking space, managed to wedge her tiny Hyundai between a couple of monstrous four-by-fours.

The journey from East Finchley station was longer than her usual route from Finsbury Park. There were no spare seats, the train stopped twice in tunnels and the crush in the carriage meant there was no chance to take a final flick through Mrs Patel's financial statement. They pulled into Holborn station at 9:45 a.m. She'd asked Mrs Patel to be there for 9:30 a.m. and the case was listed for 10:30 a.m.

Mel raced down High Holborn to the Principal Registry, a large square building at the top of Chancery Lane. There was a long queue at the security desk just inside the front door and it was close to ten o'clock when she stepped out of the lift onto the fourth floor where the hearing was due to take place. The usher told her that Mrs Patel was with her representative in one of the small conference rooms.

'What representative?' asked Mel. Did the usher mean her solicitor, who might turn up to reassure the client and would be none too pleased about his barrister arriving half an hour late?

'Her barrister, Miss Baker.'

'Miss Baker's not her barrister, she's my pupil.'

'Well, she signed her name here.' The usher showed Mel a list of the morning's cases. There, next to the name of the client and in a box marked Counsel was written in neat cursive script, Miss Natasha Baker.

Mel felt a rush of irritation. Natasha might be a qualified barrister, but she was still just a pupil. She had no right to put her name on the list as Counsel. Mel crossed out Natasha's name and put down her own. Then, after a moment's hesitation, she wrote Natasha's name underneath her own. The judge would need to know who was in court.

Mel found the conference room at the end of a long corridor. Through the glass she could see Mrs Patel, a large woman in a bright green dress and heavy gold jewellery. She was talking with apparent animation to a much younger woman in a smart charcoal grey suit. Mel recognised the younger woman immediately. She'd seen her around chambers but hadn't connected her with the name. Natasha looked far too mature, too poised to be a pupil. Her thick mid-blonde hair was swept elegantly off her face and pinned high at the back, and she sat facing Mrs Patel, calm and confident, as if she had been doing this job all her life. She appeared to be listening intently, typing on her laptop while referring occasionally to the neatly annotated paper statement which lay on the table beside her. Mel was desperate for a pee but that could wait. The important thing was to meet her client and take control.

'Mrs Patel, good morning. I'm so sorry I'm late. Good morning, Natasha.'

'Hi, Mel,' said Natasha.

The greeting felt unduly casual given they had never met before. Mel knew she should have arranged a meeting with Natasha, talked through what was expected of them both in the pupil–supervisor relationship. But it had all happened so suddenly. There had been no time. The meeting would have to be postponed.

'So, we'd better get started,' said Mel. 'We're on in half an hour.'

'I'm sure Miss Baker can explain,' said Mrs Patel. 'She has been taking detailed notes, offering helpful suggestions. I may consider some slight compromise with my ex-husband, brute though he is.'

'Great. Thanks, Natasha.'

'No worries, Mel. And I had a call from Andy. He said he couldn't get through to you. Unfortunately, the solicitor can't make it this morning.'

'I see. Lucky you were here, then. Mrs Patel, I'm sorry to say that we'll need to go through the same material again.'

'But I've already told your assistant everything.'

'I'm afraid there's no other way, Mrs Patel. Miss Baker is not authorised to address the court or negotiate with the other side.' As she spoke, she caught her pupil's eye and remembered that this was Natasha's second six and so in theory she *was* authorised to address the court and negotiate with the other side. 'At least not unless she has been instructed,' she added. Natasha smiled, and looked from Mel to Mrs Patel. Her blue eyes glittered.

Mel spent the first five minutes listening to Mrs Patel's fury at her husband's failure to disclose ownership of three apartment blocks in Karachi.

'He bought them ten years ago. I've seen them. He showed me when we were on holiday in Pakistan.'

'Do you have a photograph?'

'I had lots. He deleted them from the camera.'

'Address?'

'No. Is that a problem?'

'I'm afraid it is. Mr Patel denies ownership of the blocks and unless we have documentary evidence we won't get very far. Have you ever seen papers relating to the blocks?'

'Oh yes. They were in my husband's safe.'

'And now?'

'He took everything when he left.'

The usher popped her head around the door.

'Counsel in Patel?'

'Yes, I'm Melanie Goddard.'

'The other side wants a chat. He's been here since nine. Mr Diggory-Brown's representing.'

Mel's throat felt dry and she unscrewed her bottle of water. 'Digger' was a rising star who lived up to his name, a supremely confident young man with hair as sleek as a wet mole. It was ridiculous to be unnerved, but something about Digger desta- bilised Mel. She told herself he was no more than a typical posh boy, but he had a brain that soaked up evidence and a Machiavellian head for tactics. In the robing room he oozed charm, but he never stopped working. Every friendly enquiry had a subtext.

'I wonder if you can give us ten minutes.'

'I'll tell him.'

Ten minutes were insufficient to get much out of Mrs Patel in addition to making the essential trip to the Ladies. Her client refused to drop the allegation about the apartment blocks, so Mel would have to put it. Though it was unlikely Patel would crumble and admit something as critical as undisclosed property. Mel had run losers before, but it was galling to have to do so on her new pupil's first day.

Negotiations commenced. Neither husband nor wife was prepared to compromise and at the stroke of eleven Mrs Patel was on the stand. Without firm evidence, there was no way Mrs Patel would get what she wanted, and the evidence wasn't there. You didn't choose your cases and Natasha needed to understand this. Witnesses rarely collapsed under the shaft of cross-examination, however sharp the advocacy.

Mel calculated there was no need to spend long questioning Mrs Patel, given that her situation was set out in her financial statement. For one thing the judge wouldn't allow examination in chief on every document set before the court and, more significantly, Mel simply hadn't had time to run through every point in the conference. But when Digger put to Mrs Patel that she received unexplained credits and directed her to the precise page and line in the raft of bank statements, Mel realised she had miscalculated. She should have pre-empted him. She listened helpless as, one after another, her client's financial misdemeanours were laid bare before the court.

It was always easy to blame yourself after the event, but how much could she have done? She could have studied the papers more carefully, spent longer in conference, questioned her client more closely about the allegations. If Mrs Patel hadn't insisted on fighting the apartment blocks point there would have been more time to strengthen her own defence. Some cases were unavoidably jinxed, but Mel knew she could have put up a better fight. Above all she should have abandoned Jacob to his Xbox, ignored the incomplete biology homework and left him to make his own way to school.

Natasha disappeared during the lunch adjournment saying she needed to pick something up at Boots.

'Fine, I'll be in the conference room,' said Mel.

She was irritated. The role of a pupil was to shadow her supervisor, not to disappear off to the shops. Though she could hardly object if Natasha urgently needed toiletries or a prescription. Hadn't someone said she was diabetic? Mel had little idea what that involved other than a careful diet and regular doses of insulin but there might be some special medication. She sat with Mrs Patel and her sister for twenty minutes, avoiding all but the most general references to the case and then left them with their sandwiches, returning to the robing room to run over her cross-examination of the husband. She avoided eating in front of clients. She'd packed a chocolate bar and that would do for now. She would grab something on the way back to chambers.

Natasha turned up five minutes before they were due in court with a casual, 'Hi, Mel. How's it going?'

Now was not the time for a lecture on Bar etiquette but she looked at her pupil in a way she hoped Natasha would understand, and made a mental note to explain a few ground rules when the time was right.

As she stood up to question Mr Patel, Mel felt a pang of hunger coupled with a tremor of anticipation. She ought to have gone out to buy something. That was what Natasha must have been doing. They should have gone together, got to know each other. It wasn't as if those last sixteen minutes of preparation had been any help. Her papers were already flagged where she could reasonably challenge the witness. Areas of questioning were itemised in her notebook, together with page references. But as she looked down at her scribbled biro marks, she knew her notes were too general. There were days when you needed detail and this was one of them.

She set off gently, asking him about his successful business, appealing to his pride. He was doing well, making good money, rather more money than you would expect for someone who ran a corner shop. But he had an answer for every point. This was going to be difficult; Mrs Patel's allegations, even if true, would be hard to establish.

Working her way to the killer question, Mel asked about Mr Patel's property investments.

'I own a house, if that's what you mean. Not like my wife. She owns three.'

'That's not correct, is it, Mr Patel?'

'It certainly is. She didn't deny it when Mr Diggory questioned her.'

Mel challenged him on the Karachi properties, but Patel wouldn't budge. Just as she had anticipated.

She was conscious of Natasha behind her, listening to every word. It was good for her to see the real thing. Success in court didn't come easy and it was nothing like TV drama.

She must have paused a moment too long, because before she could lob her next question, Mr Patel added, 'Like I said, I own a house. My home. Since she chucked me out that is.'

Mel kept plugging away. The bank accounts, the share certificates, the sports car. Mr Patel never faltered.

Searching for her next question Mel noticed, to one side of the lectern, resting on the polished wooden ledge, a small piece of folded paper. It had not been there earlier.

'Mr Patel, may I ask you to turn to page 169 of Bundle B?'

He flipped through the pages of the Lever Arch file.

'Thank you. Now if we look down the page you will see regular credits of £1,450 per month into your bank account. Could you explain that, please?'

'Certainly, that's my salary from the shop. It's set up as a company. I pay myself a small wage, as you can see.'

After a few more ineffectual questions Mel sat down. Her unfocused gaze lingered on the piece of paper, presumably a question from Natasha, still resting on the ledge. She put down her pen and reached for it, pressing out the fold and reading the pencilled note. 'Bundle B, page 267.' Reaching for Bundle B, she turned to page 267 and there they were: a further string of unaccounted credits.

'Mr Diggory-Brown?' The judge was speaking. 'Do you have any re-examination?'

'No, madam.'

She could at least thank God for that.

'You may return to your seat, Mr Patel,' he said.

Mel jumped up. 'Sir?'

'Yes, Miss Goddard?'

'I wonder if I could put a couple of further questions to Mr Patel?'

'This is most unorthodox.'

'I apologise, sir. Two points were omitted in my cross-examination.'

The points were put. Mr Patel had an answer for each one. Mel reminded herself it wasn't the fault of her questioning. It wasn't always possible to destroy a lying witness. But the reminder was little comfort. Her cross-examination had been weak. Having it witnessed by Natasha on her first day as a pupil was an additional humiliation.

Her closing speech was as fluent and persuasive as she could make it. There was nothing more she could do. Mr Patel walked off with an order for a substantial lump sum payment from his unhappy wife. Her brief conference with Mrs Patel after the hearing was an unpleasant experience. Mel tried to explain that there were no grounds for appeal. Then she handed Mrs Patel the paper she should have given her at the outset, explaining the terms of instruction and methods for making a complaint.

Chapter Four

Mel

They crossed High Holborn and reached chambers with moments to spare before the next client conference. Natasha had been charming on the walk back, but there was an edge to her that Mel found discomforting. In her experience pupils were usually eager, ignorant and immature. Most were easy to read and a little too desperate to please. This one was a few years older than average with an unusual degree of self-possession. These were egalitarian times and Mel did not expect servility. But she was taken aback by Natasha's walking into chambers in front of her. A pupil would be expected to allow her pupil supervisor to enter first.

The conference made up for the appalling performance in court. Mel was careful, reassuring, measured, and Vicky – formerly Victor – Brightman spilled out everything her barrister needed to know. Private *Children Act* cases had almost dried up since the last round of Legal Aid cuts, but thanks to a whip round in the trans community Vicky had obtained funding to challenge arrangements for her three children, and the case looked as if it would run to a contested hearing.

Natasha was silent throughout, taking notes on her laptop. The notes were emailed to Mel immediately afterwards, together with a full transcript of the morning's proceedings in court. Her self-assurance might grate, but her efficiency and attention to detail would be useful. Mel could see how she must have impressed her previous supervisor. There was a glowing report from him in her pigeonhole. She decided to wait before mentioning the report to Natasha.

'So, Natasha, how did you find your first day?' she asked after Vicky Brightman and her solicitor had left.

'Brilliant. Like, totally brilliant.'

'I'm afraid I didn't put up much of a show at Uxbridge.'

'What could you do? The case was a loser.'

Mel realised she had expected a compliment, flattery. Pupils didn't usually have such firm opinions.

'Well, I'm heading to the tube. Which way do you go?'

Mel was relieved to learn it was the other side of the city. They were about to depart when Andy put his head round the door.

'Hi, Mel. Got a return from Paula. She's stuck in a long care case. I know it's late, but we didn't want to interrupt you earlier. Can you do Barnet Family Court tomorrow at 2:30 p.m.?'

'What is it?'

'Domestic violence.'

'You know I don't do injunctions.'

'Yeah but… Marcus doesn't want it to go out of chambers. The solicitor's new. We're hoping for more work from them. If we return it, some other chambers will pick up their work. They're a good firm. We can't afford to ignore this kind of thing.' Marcus was the senior clerk. In effect, the boss. Andy had a point. Solicitors were like GPs, barristers more like specialist consultants. At least that's how they saw themselves. The trouble was solicitors were doing more and more of the work usually confined to barristers. Sometimes it felt as if barristers were a dying breed. But somehow they staggered on. Mel knew that Bridge Court couldn't afford to let work go elsewhere. Even if she didn't want the brief herself, she owed it to her chambers. 'You've got nothing in the diary,' Andy added. That was true, though she had a pile of paperwork to catch up with and a new care case to prepare for Monday. She was torn. She needed a day off court if she was to have any time for Jacob at the weekend. And she longed to see Paul.

'Not much of a fee of course but the solicitor says it's complex. Could lead to more work. Sorry, Mel, but it's worth keeping them sweet.'

Natasha was packing her shoulder bag. 'I could do it,' she said.

Andy sized up the new pupil with veiled scorn. He caught Mel's eye. In theory, Natasha could indeed do it.

'Have you organised your Practising Certificate?' asked Mel.

'Of course.'

'Insurance?'

'Marcus told me chambers did that.'

'That's right, Mel,' said Andy.

It was clear from the irritating note this morning that Natasha was smart. Her notes were meticulous, and she appeared to have boundless confidence. Chances were she would do a good job, possibly even an excellent job. And it would be so good to see Paul. He had said he would be free tomorrow. For a few brief, uncomfortable moments it was as if her pupil and her clerk were reading her mind. Andy tapped his foot lightly on the polished floor. It was six thirty. He was keen to get away.

'OK, if you feel confident, Natasha. Why not? You've got to start somewhere.'

And when Andy looked doubtful, she added, 'Don't worry, Andy. Natasha will be fine.' She looked at Natasha who flashed an unsettling smile.

'OK if I stay on here to work? I may need to use the library.'

'Sure,' said Andy. 'Make sure you shut the door properly when you leave.'

Mel remembered the excitement of her own first brief. There was every reason to encourage her. The more work Natasha landed the less she, Mel, would have to bother with her.

'Good luck then. Let me know how you get on. Night, Andy.' She turned down the corridor and swung through the heavy wooden door. Lifting her wheelie bag down the stone steps, she set off into the fading light towards Holborn station.

–

The tube was packed, as usual. She alighted at Finsbury Park, feeling like she had been wrung through a mangle, shaking out the creases as she strode up the long sloping tunnel to the barrier. Then into Seven Sisters Road, under the old railway bridge, and right into Fonthill Road lined with wholesale clothing shops.

The W3 bus was waiting. It was late enough to get a seat and she collapsed into a comfortable stupor as they weaved around the dusty brick houses. It was a short walk from the bus stop to the front door and she was looking forward to crashing on the sofa with the first glass of red wine and a mind-numbing dose of *Coronation Street*. But the car was not parked outside the house as usual. And then she remembered. That morning she'd driven Jacob to school and taken a different route to court. She'd left her little Hyundai in East Finchley station car park.

Chapter Five

Natasha

She was alone in the book-lined conference room on the fifth floor. It was cool and quiet, conducive to concentration. She took out her kit and checked her blood sugar. 7.4 was fine but she was feeling faint and shaky. She was probably just tired. She'd been up at five to study the Patel case. Not that Mel appreciated her effort. Keeping track of glucose levels while running a demanding job was not easy. Her eyes shifted from the digital display to the fingers on her left hand, rough and calloused from numerous pricks with her lancet. What she really needed was a flash glucose monitor. She'd still have to do a finger-prick test for driving, but mostly she'd be able to rely on a portable reader. She could even use an app on her phone. No one would notice the sensor on her upper arm because she could pick up the reading through clothes. It would be a huge relief. She'd get one when the money started rolling in.

Taking a deep breath, she untied the red ribbon, unfolded the stiff back sheet in front of her and glanced through the instructions. Her first brief. She felt a tremor of excitement. She could do it well; she knew she could. At Bar School, she'd come near top in advocacy exams. Now for the real thing.

Her client was the defendant, excluded from the family home. He hadn't been informed about the previous hearing and had simply received an order, delivered by hand, telling him to get out. He was accused of non-violent abusive behaviour, undermining his wife's confidence, refusing to let her go out, cutting her off from family and friends. There was a GP report recording the wife's depression. The husband denied most of the allegations and had offered an undertaking if his wife let him return. Natasha hoped she would refuse so she could try out her cross-examination. There were further complications. The couple had a one-year-old baby. According to the health visitor there were signs of serious neglect and the local authority was contemplating care proceedings. A copy of their letter was included in the brief. Natasha took in its cold official language and shuddered. This was the world she had left behind at ten years old. But even at ten she had been conscious of the language, 'Unable to cope', 'inadequate', 'safeguarding', 'the welfare of the child'. And her knowledge of that world had landed her the pupillage. There was money in it for lawyers. The shudder subsided. It was a physical reaction and she had learnt how to control her physical reactions. She took a deep breath. The threat of care proceedings must be the reason why Andy said the case was complex. If she impressed the client tomorrow it could lead to further better paid work. She refolded the pages and stuck them in her shoulder bag.

–

The flat was filled with the aroma of onions, tomatoes and garlic. Luke was cooking lasagne.

'Hiya, how was your day?' he shouted. She closed the door behind her and walked down the corridor to the kitchen.

'Great. Got my first brief.'

'Fantastic. What's it about?'

'Some bloke kicked out of the house for being controlling. You want to watch your step.'

'Me? I couldn't control anyone. Certainly not you.'

She threw off her jacket. 'So, what about you? Sorted out your no hopers?'

'I wish.' He turned his head towards her, nudging the vegetables in the frying pan, adding, 'Don't I get a kiss?' She pecked the side of his neck and he turned a little, saying, 'Mustn't let it burn.'

'I need a shower.'

'Don't you want to hear? You asked about my day.'

'Give me ten minutes.'

She could tell from the locked-in voice, the concentration on the frying pan, that Luke's day had not been good. His days rarely were. He was a social worker, after all.

'They're not bad people,' he would say. 'Just never had a chance.'

She would disagree.

'They fucked up.'

'It's not as simple as that.'

'They have choices, don't they? They don't have to hit their kids.'

'Sometimes they… there are forces we can't always control. Christ, Tash, you of all people should understand.'

She did understand. That was the reason she wasn't going to have any kids herself, the reason why she wasn't going to have that conversation tonight.

In the bathroom she removed her clothes and folded them neatly on a chair. She ran the shower, unhooked the old tubing from the set on her abdomen and stepped under the warm water. The knots in her head unravelled. There had been a moment this afternoon, alone in the conference room, when she'd felt the terrors of the past return. It was that letter from the local authority. The welfare of the child. She remembered the time when that's all she was. The child. Not Natasha, not Tash, not anybody's special person. Just 'the child'. She buried the thought. She was good at burying thoughts. And now she was home and safe. Luke was here for her. He was sometimes glum. He might get irritated with her. But he accepted her, believed in her, thought her better than she was, and she knew he would stay with her. He might be upset; he might disapprove. But still he would love her.

She washed and rinsed her hair and stepped out onto the wooden mat, wrapping herself in the fluffy towel that had been warming on the rail. As she filled the reservoir on her pump, she could hear the voice of Leonard Cohen on the sound system. She attached the tubing, peeling off the old set and inserting the new one just above her left hip.

'You ready?' he called.

'Five minutes.'

She dressed and waved the dryer around for a couple of minutes so that her hair was bouncy and thick, the way he liked it. Back in the kitchen, Luke was laying the table, dressing a salad.

'Your phone's been ringing,' he said.

'It's not important.'

'Sounds persistent.'

She checked the name on the phone. Eleanor. 'It's my sister. My adoptive sister.'

'Aren't you going to call back? It could be important.'

'She left a text. Ed's ill.'

'Your father? Are you going to visit?'

'No.'

'You should go.'

When the anger came, it came like lightning. Despite all she had been thinking in the shower, at that moment she wanted to destroy him. 'Don't fucking tell me what I should do.'

'I'm sorry... I...'

'Don't, OK?'

A pause. His eyes retreated into his face.

'Tash?'

She could sense her heart pounding and feared she would hurt him. 'What now?'

'Do you think you should go and see someone?'

'What someone?' she snapped.

'You know... a therapist.'

'Fucking get off my back, Luke. Fucking leave me alone.'

She walked out of the kitchen into the sitting room and onto the little balcony that faced out across the car park to the trains. The city was ablaze with lights. Planes descended, their wing tips twinkling; overground trains flashed by towards Peckham and Canada Water. Their movement soothed her. Briefly she wished he was elsewhere. His concern was a burden she needed to shed. She couldn't let him squash her.

She wasn't about to visit Ed. She'd broken off from her adoptive family years ago. She'd been an outsider when she was with them so why go back now? All those early teenage years when she'd struggled to deal with her diabetes, tried to fit in with the people who'd taken her in. She'd been a good girl. No drink. No booze. Still they had picked on her. For her long silences, her refusal to join their stupid games. Her brothers Olly and Jamie called her 'Sticko' because she was skinny, until she was fourteen when they started making rude comments about her tits and bum. Her sister Eleanor called her 'Little Swot' because she was clever. They all laughed at her accent. Her parents hadn't a clue what she had to put up with. She'd tried telling them, but it was always Natasha's fault.

'You've lied to us so many times, how can we believe you?'

At sixteen, after getting her nine GCSEs, she'd left home, moved to London, found a room in a shared house, worked in shops, pubs and clubs, eventually for an escort agency. The escort work saw her through college and university and the first year of part time Bar School. It came to an abrupt stop when a client had tried to yank off her pump as soon as she removed her clothes. She'd sunk her teeth into his arm and run off.

Soon after that, she'd found Luke, and everything changed. She never asked herself what was happening or why. It wasn't about love. Though the sex was good. It worked for her and it was what she needed now. He had offered her a place to stay rent-free and she'd given up the escort work to concentrate on her studies. She tried to be nice to him. But she needed freedom.

Breathing steadily, she looked out towards the tracks. No, visiting Ed was not on. There was too much happening at work. She was making her mark and couldn't afford to relax.

'Supper's ready, Tash,' called Luke, as if nothing had happened.

'Thanks. Coming.'

Chapter Six

Mel

Apart from the occasional soft tread from the floor above and the low buzz from the light bulb in the hall, the flat was quiet. Mel put her head round Jacob's door. He was seated with his back to her, draped in a towel, hunched over a computer, headset locked around his ears. Coloured lights flashed across the screen. The curtains were closed. He was six feet from her, but he seemed very far away.

'Hello, darling.' No answer. She tried again, louder. 'Jacob?' Still no answer. She walked forward and wedged her body between his and the screen.

'Mum!' There were a hundred ways of saying 'Mum'. This was the two-syllabled reproach.

'How long you been wasting your time with this?'

'Hand-eye co-ordination.' he said, watching a running figure as a hawk eyes a mouse in the grass.

'Homework?'

'Waiting for you.'

'That's rich. Why aren't you dressed?'

'What is this? Fucking cross-examination?'

'Please don't swear. Sorry, I'm a bit late. Conference went on.'

'S'all right.'

'Plus, I've got to go out again.'

'What's for supper?'

'I'll make some pasta.'

She retreated to her room. She had managed to straighten the old flowered duvet before rushing off that morning, but the space that should be comforting looked sad and unloved. She should get a cleaner. It would give her someone to tidy up for. She kicked off her too-pointed shoes, tore off the dark jacket and shirt and stepped out of her pencil skirt. Everything felt tight. Her body had swelled in her uniform. It protected her like armour, but she was never quite herself inside. She yanked off her tights and threw on jeans and an old shirt, feeling sweaty but too lazy to shower.

The interior of the fridge was not promising: a few scraps of cheese, a Tesco pizza, numerous half-full jars of sauce and a third of a bottle of Chilean Sauvignon. She scouted further in the salad drawer and discovered an onion, a tad slimy on the outside but perfectly edible within, a fingernail clove of garlic. At least there'd be some good olive oil. She would chop and slice in silence, mend her frazzled brain.

Once, on Alisha's recommendation, she'd tried a Mindfulness Meditation course. The course leader had been a tired-looking middle-aged woman, with delicate features, wispy blonde hair and big earrings. Something in her small grey eyes spoke of suffering. She'd advised Mel to imagine each thought as a leaf, floating down a river. Mel's river soon became blocked. At least this way you had something to eat.

'What time are you starting tomorrow?' she asked. Jacob had stirred himself and was now dressed in artfully torn jeans and a T-shirt bearing the logo, I TRIED TO BE NORMAL ONCE.

'Dunno. Late. There's Art.'

'So, you'll be back around five?'

'I guess. You're doing it again.'

'Just checking. I like to know where you are. I'm your mum.'

'Thanks. I'd forgotten.'

'Saturday I'm going to see Granny. Want to come?'

'Gotta work.'

Jacob and Isabel used to be the best of pals. Mel had a file of photos, Jacob on the slide, Isabel beaming at the base; Cornish holidays; Monopoly on rainy days; Isabel in her sixties leaping about the beach with a Frisbee, playing with the boy as she never had with Mel. Then Jacob hit twelve and the games stopped.

'We could do something Saturday night? Maybe a film?'

'I'm going to a party. You know, Nikita. Don't look like that.'

'I'm not sure about Nikita.'

'Just 'cos his dad's an arms dealer.'

She remembered Nikita's mother, Yelena, with her purple claws, hair like candy floss, eyes a-glitter with a palette of pink and turquoise.

'It's not Nikita personally. Of course not, he's just a kid.'

'Just a kid.'

'It's… I'm sure they're nice people but I came to pick you up once when you were only thirteen and the parents had gone away some place and the house smelt of dope.'

'So?'

'Jacob, you were thirteen. Too young to smoke dope.'

'I'm sixteen now.'

Chapter Seven

Mel

It was almost nine p.m. when she set off for East Finchley station, the sky a deep cobalt blue fading to faint charcoal in the west. She had slung on a fleece but quickly realised she was under-dressed for the cool spring evening. There was no one at the bus stop so it was likely she had just missed a bus. Rather than wait in the cold for twenty minutes, she continued on foot, enjoying the soft bounce of her trainers, the ease of walking with only a light handbag. Exercise was the answer. She should try to get to the gym. If it had been earlier, she would have taken the old railway path that cut down between straggly trees and bushes from Alexandra Palace to the tube station. But she was not looking to buy or sell either drugs or sex, so it seemed wiser to use the pavement.

Unlike many of her acquaintances she had no fear of walking in the London streets at night. She faced directly ahead, strode fast and with purpose and had never had any trouble. She would get to the car park by nine forty, jump in the car and be back by ten. Then a long bath, a book or a TV drama on the iPlayer. She would skip the news. It was too depressing.

A few pedestrians passed her, workers trudging home, a mother and baby in a pram, a group of youths. A couple of kids about Jacob's age swerved around the corner on bikes without lights. A stray dog crossed her path to snuffle in the gutter. An urban fox stood silhouetted by a street lamp against a dustbin.

It was as she was walking underneath the old railway bridge that she sensed the presence behind her, footsteps echoing along the Victorian brickwork. She increased her pace. Soon she would get to where there were shops, restaurants, bright lights and people. She avoided the temptation to look back. It would be a perfectly innocent Londoner going about his or her business just as she was. There was no reason to fear. She must keep walking as fast as she could without breaking into a run. The footsteps were speeding up. She was coming to one of the entrances to the railway path, a small metal gate and steps rising from the road to the rough vegetation that fringed the cutting. On one side of the steps there were overgrown bushes, on the other, a small patch of guerrilla garden. Whoever had been behind her was still there.

The arm around her neck was firm, determined. When she tried to scream there was the sensation of rough wool, a large gloved hand on her mouth. She could smell hot, sour breath and thick sweat. She tried to bite through the wool till her teeth hit something firm that must have been flesh.

'Fucking bitch,' squealed a young male voice and the hand dropped away. She kicked out and her trainer made contact with a leg. She was about to shout but before the sound came out there was pressure on her back and she was propelled through the gateway to the wooden steps that led up to the cutting. Someone pushed her to the ground. It was soft from last night's rain but there were scratching stones, the weeds were coarse, and nettles stung her face. Despite her fear, part of her wanted to laugh. It was ridiculous, like something from a film. She heard a car go by, voices from the street. She was less than twenty-five yards from the nearest house. But she was pinned to the ground and could hardly breathe, let alone shout. When she tried to lift her face a hand behind her clamped her down. She felt for her bag. It was gone. They had ripped it off. She tried once more to raise her face but again the hand pushed her down, though she managed to twist her neck to one side to gasp air.

'Keep quiet, you bitch,' said the voice.

She could see no one, but she was conscious of two, maybe three of them behind her, holding her down. Boys, men, she didn't know, didn't care; it made no difference. A fourteen-year-old, younger than Jacob, was as likely to stick a knife in, rape her, as a thirty-year-old.

'Stop it,' she shouted, realising she was echoing her mother whose strident upper-middle-class tones always sprang up inside her in moments of tension. It sounded weak and stupid, as useless as the efforts of a junior teacher in a room full of adolescents. The hand pushed her face down again and she was choking on earth and stone.

'I said, keep fucking quiet.'

The hold was loosened, and she was silent. She felt the hand again, gloveless now, under her shirt, round the top of her jeans.

'Leave her, GJ,' a different voice now, deeper, calmer. 'She's older than your mum.' And the barrister in her, not quite extinguished, made a mental note, *GJ*.

The pressure eased, and the hand fell away. She continued to hear their murmured voices though not what was said. For a few moments it was as if she were as far away, watching the actions play out in a film: the woman on the ground, the ruffians holding her down, mumbling among themselves. Then she saw something flash in the half-light, what looked like a small kitchen knife. She shifted her head to look at the face above her, just visible beneath his hoodie. He was about seventeen or eighteen, neither black nor white but somewhere in between, with regular, gentle – almost feminine – features.

And she wanted to say, 'Why? Why you? Why me?' But he continued to hold the knife and she dared not say it and the question remained unanswered.

'Cunt,' he spat. It was his parting shot. He turned, and with his faceless companion, disappeared, two long dark figures running up the steps to the path.

She remained in the dirt, unable to move. She was not badly hurt, scratched a little and probably bruised, but she had been felled, trashed, hurled to the ground like a piece of rubbish. The terror which she had kept at bay now struck and she was trembling, cold, immobilised. But she was here, she was alive, she was unharmed.

She tried to stand but her strength failed her, so she lay and waited. It was cold and dark, and she could hear the cars and then a bus. People talking on the streets. She could have called out, but something stopped her. She pulled herself up to all fours and crawled towards the wooden steps, letting herself down backwards until she reached the railings where she managed to haul herself upright.

Dazed, she attempted to focus. She was free and unharmed, but she felt invaded by the brutality of the contact, seeing stars as if she had been concussed. At first, she clutched the railings for support but when her legs would no longer hold her, she half slid, half eased herself down to the pavement. Instinctively she felt for her bag although she knew it was gone. Her old friend, her ancient cheap handbag, gone, together with her phone, her wallet, her Oyster, her cards, her keys.

Tools of her life. At least they would have no way of knowing where the car was. She reminded herself how much worse it could have been. They had snatched a bag. It happened every day on London streets. She had been lucky. Nothing was broken. In a minute she would stand and walk home. But she was conscious of rising anger and a battering inside her head.

Among the random thoughts there rose the image of a middle-aged woman with tired grey eyes and wispy hair and Mel heard a sad voice chanting, 'Breathe in, breathe out'. Mechanically, she started to do just that: in and out. Her whirling thoughts subsided, and she was out on the ocean, an unmoored vessel with neither motor nor sails. Navigation aids, oars, they too had been stolen. She was ten minutes from home, but the horizon was a thousand miles around her. She sat on the cold pavement and waited.

When the man came up to her, she had no apprehension. She couldn't make out his features in the dark, but his voice was gentle, accented and sincere.

'May I help you?'

'Thank you. I'm OK.'

'You are hurt.'

'No, no, not hurt. I'll be fine.'

'I could take you to hospital?'

'No, like I said, I'm fine.

'We will go to the light.'

And he helped her up with a cool insistence she was unable to resist, leading her by the arm towards the dull glow of the street lamp. He was middle-aged, neatly though casually dressed, only an inch or two taller than her, with sorrowful dark eyes, grey black hair, heavy brows and a strong broad face, at once fleshy and furrowed. He too could be a mugger, though now she had nothing he could take. He could be a rapist. But she doubted it. He was a kind stranger who had stopped for her and she wanted to weep at the sweetness of it. Holding her by the shoulder, he inspected her with detached professionalism.

'No damage. I think you are good. But there's dirt on your face and scratches.'

'They threw me down.'

'They are animals, worse than animals.'

'Are you a doctor?'

'Not a doctor. But I understand such things.'

'That's good,' she said, not knowing what she meant.

Then suddenly, apropos of nothing he said, 'I am Palestinian.'

'Oh,' she said. She hadn't asked where he was from, but it was something he needed to say, perhaps even some connection with what she had endured. Had he fled war and occupation? His powerful Arab features broke into a smile. She sensed understanding, even compassion. He asked nothing of her, simply greeted her as a fellow human being, a fellow survivor.

'Would you like me to call the police?' he asked.

'I'll call them later. Right now, I need to get home.'

'Where do you live?'

'Close. It's OK. I can walk.'

'I will walk with you.'

'Really, it's OK.'

'It is not OK. I will come with you.'

He was determined, like her attackers, but careful, where they had been careless. A voice in her head added 'good where they had been bad'. But had they been bad? She had defended boys like that and she knew they were never wholly bad.

'Show me,' he said.

As they walked, he told her his name and how it was spelt: Sami. She wanted to ask him about his story but sensed it could be too momentous for her to respond to adequately. So, for most of the way they walked in silence. They reached the door. Should she ask him in? What was the etiquette?

'Your husband is here?' he asked.

'No. My son,' she replied. 'He's sixteen,' she added, as if she were trying to warn him off, though that was not what she intended. And before ringing the bell she added, 'What I said just then, about them throwing me down. Please don't say anything to my son. I don't want to frighten him.'

'I understand,' said Sami.

She rang the bell. Jacob opened the door. She almost told him off for failing to use the chain but stopped herself and said, 'This is Sami. He helped me. I was mugged.'

Jacob stared at her, then at the strange man standing next to his mother. She read a chaos of reactions in his face. It was surprised, transparent with anxiety. The person he relied on had proved vulnerable.

'What happened, Mum?'

'I'll tell you.' She turned to Sami, thanked him. 'You've been very kind. I won't forget it. I've interrupted your evening. Do you have far to go?'

'No, not far.'

She was curious. Did he have a family, children? But it was not her business.

'Wait a moment, please,' she said. He stood at the door as she went into the flat and picked up a pencil and page from a notepad. She wrote down her mobile number.

'Here,' she handed it over. 'If you need ever help, I'm a lawyer.'

Was she making a mistake? She wasn't there to solve everyone's problems. And why should she assume he had problems? He might be anything, a professor, a diplomat, a banker. She could hear Alisha's voice. 'Don't tell them you're a barrister. Don't hand out your number. You'll just get hassled.' This was different. She wanted to show her appreciation and if he did need help she could always refer him to the right people. That was all. He took the paper, folded it, placed it in a pocket and said, 'Thank you. I hope you feel better soon.'

'Goodnight,' she said.

He smiled and nodded slightly. 'Goodnight.'

'Night,' said Jacob.

—

Once inside she bolted the door and put on the chain. She would need to have the locks changed, would need to cancel her cards, ring her phone provider.

'Want to tell me?' asked Jacob.

'In a bit.'

He went through to the kitchen, began to heat some milk, setting out two mugs. She walked in and looked at him. He was reaching for the hot chocolate, focusing on what he was doing. She came up behind him, put an arm around his waist and gave him a hug. He was taller than her now, had been for almost a year. His body was solid, unfamiliar. She felt afraid that she might be losing him. He turned. 'Sorry, Mum.'

'Why sorry?'

'You had a rough time.'

'It could have happened to anyone. And I'm all right now.'

'You've got blood on your face.'

'Just a scratch. I fell over. They pulled off my bag and I fell over under the bridge. But it's OK – I'm not really hurt.'

She knew that tears were rising behind her eyes, could see that he too looked like he might cry, though she suspected some struggle to stop it. Perhaps he felt he needed to be strong for her. She held him close.

They sat together on the sofa, with their drinks, feeling each other's warmth. They didn't speak, didn't need to. There was too much to say and nothing to say. They skipped the news.

'Choose something nice,' she said, as he searched through the recorded programmes.

'How about *Planet Earth*?'

How well he knew her. He set up the programme and settled back with her on the sofa as the familiar voice took them to a world beyond the human. They sipped their hot chocolate and sank deep beneath the oceans. She was still trembling as she felt the warmth of Jacob's body beside her.

Chapter Eight

Natasha

The applicant in the witness box looked angry rather than depressed. Natasha decided to temper her questions accordingly. A delightful shiver ran through her body as she stood up to speak.

'You say he criticised you.'

'Yes, all the time.'

'That's incorrect, isn't it, Mrs Driver?'

'It bloody isn't. He never let off.'

'You fabricated this story to get him out of the house.'

'That's not true.'

'You wanted him out of the house, so you could bring in your lover.'

There was nothing but the husband's word to go on here, but it was part of his case and needed to be put. Besides, winding up the wife would be a good tactic.

'That's rubbish.'

'No one witnessed this so-called criticism.'

'How could they? He was sweet as pie when there were people around.'

'Mrs Driver, you're a strong woman.'

'Was a strong woman. I'm a wreck now.'

'You give as good as you get.'

'I don't know what you mean.'

'Not only were you yourself critical of Mr Driver, but on several occasions, you lashed out at him.'

'Bullshit.'

'What you call criticism was nothing beyond the usual marital disagreement.'

'More bullshit.'

The judge intervened. 'Mrs Driver, please refrain from using foul language in court. It does little to assist your case. A simple "yes" or "no" would serve you better.'

'Sorry, Your Honour, but she's talking crap.'

'Please proceed, Miss Baker.'

'Your husband has already apologised for upsetting you.'

'So?'

'He is prepared to overlook your behaviour in the interests of your daughter.'

Mrs Driver was red-faced and shaking.

'Don't you bloody bring my daughter into this.'

It was going well. She might not have destroyed the evidence, but she had angered the witness. The judge could see this wife was no helpless victim. He allowed the husband back into the marital home, ordering him to confine himself to a separate living area. It was a crazy solution, but her client was delighted.

'Thanks, Miss Baker, you did a great job. I'll get my solicitor to ask for you if I need another brief.'

'Let's hope you don't,' said Natasha, smiling and shaking the client's hand. 'But if you do need help, she'll know where to find me.'

Or would she? The tenancy interviews were two months away. Andy had told her they were looking for people who could bring in the work. It sounded like the client would be giving a good report to his solicitor, and Andy would be sure to ask.

–

The following day she was shadowing Mel on an Interim Care application for a Miss Felicia Gonzalez who had a child called

Pedro. She spent most of the two hours at court sitting with the unhappy Felicia as Mel ran in and out of the conference room, negotiating visiting arrangements for Pedro with the social workers. They were only in front of the judge for five minutes. It was disappointing. She'd had more fun watching commercial disputes with her other supervisor.

Mel looked tired and there was a red mark on one side of her eye. Natasha decided not to mention it, even when she had to grab Mel's arm to stop her walking in front of a bus on the way back to chambers.

'Sorry, I wasn't concentrating,' said Mel when they reached the other side of the Strand.

'Are you all right?' asked Natasha.

'Yes, fine.'

Mel's face appeared twisted, as if she was in pain and Natasha suspected she wasn't fine at all. Then she told Natasha she needed to pop into Carphone Warehouse to pick up a new phone.

'I'll join you in chambers in half an hour. You might find a desk in the computer room.'

A few minutes later Natasha was back in chambers, but she had no idea what she was supposed to do. Mel seemed to expect her to learn just by following her around. And now, when they should be talking through the afternoon's hearing, she had disappeared to sort out a phone. It wasn't exactly incompetent, but it was certainly disorganised.

Her Civil supervisor, Gerald, had been a dominating man but at least he'd given her clear instructions. Unlike Mel, he'd always asked her for her comments at the end of a conference. She took out her laptop and looked over an Opinion she was preparing for him. Fifteen pages of closely reasoned legal advice for a solicitor whose client had suffered serious spinal damage after negligent surgery. She had spent most of the weekend researching the law. Luke brought her snacks and cups of tea, but she could tell he was pissed off when she told him she couldn't go out. He needed to realise her work came first. Not that she'd be paid much. Gerald would get the full fee and give her half if she was lucky. Still it was work.

When Mel turned up almost an hour later she simply nodded at Natasha and switched on one of the desktop computers that lined the wall below the window. Out of the corner of her eye Natasha could see she was going through emails.

'Did you get your phone?' asked Natasha.

'Yep. Sorted,' said Mel without glancing up from her screen.

It was five o'clock. Natasha had finished work on the Opinion and wished she could go home but there were no set hours, pupils were expected to wait till their supervisor made it clear it was time to go.

She looked about her. The room was just below ground level, the only view consisting of rectangles of light through the barred windows, occasionally crossed by passing legs in dark trousers, wheelie bags or trolleys loaded with Lever Arch files on their way to the Royal Courts of Justice. No pictures, no plants, not even law books to break up the monotony. Not what she had imagined when she'd been offered a pupillage in the Temple.

Natasha liked books. She was one of the few students at Bar School who looked up paper law reports instead of googling. She had loved the quiet of the university library, the soft footfall on parquet, the occasional cough and rustle of paper, the scent of leather and wood polish. Law reports were puzzles and she was good at solving puzzles. One of the other tenants popped her head round the door and asked if they would both like a cup of tea. It was Jess, the woman who'd taken her to court on her first day. She was staring hard at Natasha who remembered that making tea was her job.

'I'll make it,' she said, jumping up and going to the tiny galley kitchen. When she came back five minutes later, Jess was sitting next to Mel with her arm around her shoulders.

'It's nothing. I'm being stupid,' Mel was saying.

'No, you're not.'

'I'm a bit shaky. But basically, I'm fine. I mean, not hurt.'

'You shouldn't be here. You shouldn't be in court,' said Jess.

A man's bulky frame filled the doorway. He was clutching a small laptop and a bundle of papers. His waistcoat was loose across his chest. His collarless shirt was unbuttoned round the neck and a mist of sweat wafted across the room.

'Hi, Georgie,' said Jess, 'I thought you were in Birmingham.'

'Case collapsed. I argued abuse of process and no case to answer.'

'There goes your trial fee,' laughed Jess.

'Some of us have ethics, Jess. I am not prepared to prolong a case unnecessarily. Anyway, the guy deserved to get off. The police behaved like thugs.' Then turning to Natasha with a big smile he said, 'How do you do, I'm Georgie.'

'Hi, Georgie, I'm Natasha.' Mel should have introduced her, but she seemed totally out of it.

'Mel's pupil,' explained Jess.

Georgie turned to Mel. 'So, what's this about a mugging?'

'I'm OK.'

'You should take time off.'

'You know that's not possible. Anyway, I was fine this morning.'

Fine? Mel had done a lot of running backwards and forwards, but the woman's kids were still in care. Plus, she'd nearly killed herself and Natasha on the way back to chambers. Nobody had said anything to her about a mugging.

'You've been looking stressed,' said Jess. 'I mean before the mugging thing.'

'We're all stressed. This is the Bar,' said Mel.

'Give yourself a break. I would,' urged Georgie. 'Hang out with Jacob. Binge on Netflix.'

'I've got too much on.'

Jess glanced at Natasha. 'Natasha can do the easy stuff, can't you Natasha?' she said.

'I'd be happy to.'

'There is no easy stuff,' said Mel.

'OK. OK. The clerks can sort that out. They won't let it go out of chambers,' said Georgie.

'It makes sense, Mel,' added Jess. 'You need a break. Drink your tea. I'll walk to the tube with you.'

–

Natasha was alone. She was packing up to go when she noticed the Bridge Court logo lit up on the computer Mel had been using. She walked over and glanced along the icons at the bottom of the page. Word was still running and so was Chrome. Mel must have forgotten to log off. A helpful gesture would do no harm. She pulled out her phone. As she brought up Mel's number, she tapped on the Chrome icon and Mel's Inbox flashed across the screen. Her supervisor was even more careless than she had imagined. She skimmed the list of senders. Solicitors. Unfamiliar names. But one of the them jumped out.

She knew the guy. Paul Freedman. He was a lecturer at North Bank. At least fifty, he'd seemed desperate to look younger with his tight leather jackets and jeans, cosying up to students in the pub on Friday nights. She'd taken his politics and law option in her final year. He'd come on to her, inviting her back to his office on some pretext of lending her a book she might find interesting. Then he'd kept her there, sounding off on politics for a good half hour before asking her out for a drink. She'd only taken one module in his department and he wasn't marking her dissertation so there would have been no point in going. Saying no was easy enough. She told him she didn't go out with married men. He grinned. Nice smile. She had almost changed her mind.

Natasha typed Freedman's address into the Sort box and pressed the Find icon. A string of communications popped up.

Dates, times, places. Hotels. Restaurants. She carried on reading. What a fool. Didn't he realise Googlemail was about as private as Facebook? She was surprised: she'd have expected Paul to go for a younger model. Though Mel was not unattractive, with good cheekbones, bright hazel eyes and a wide smile, on the rare occasions she chose to display it. Her dress sense was non-existent. Her court jackets didn't fit and her handbags were cheap rubbish. But men were probably less interested in clothes than women liked to imagine, and no doubt they were drawn by Mel's full breasts which she flaunted in clingy silk blouses. Her curly brown hair was always coming loose from whatever was pinning it back, giving her a rumpled, fresh from bed look. Natasha, whose own hair was dead straight, felt a stab of irritation as she pictured it.

There was a printer in the corner of the room. Natasha printed off a couple of emails, then added Paul's address to her own Google contacts. She rang Mel.

'Mel, sorry to bother you. Can you speak?'

'I'm about to get on the escalator. Reception's not that good.'

'Only it's… just… I was using the computer to print my stuff and I noticed you hadn't logged off.'

'Oh shit. Right. Could you just…'

'I thought there might be work you wanted to save or…'

'Thank God you rang. Would you mind saving and printing my Attendance Note on Gonzalez, the Interim Care hearing? There's an icon marked Care on the desktop. It should be there. Unless it's still open. I don't remember. Jess came in and I got… well, you know how it was. Just print it off and give it to Andy. Tell him I'll sign it when I come in.'

'No problem. Anything else?'

'No… I'm losing you…'

Natasha could hear the racket of the station announcements down the phone and then silence as Mel hung up. She tucked the printed emails into the pocket of her bag, closed Googlemail and opened the Attendance Note for the case of Gonzalez. There it was, setting out the time spent in negotiation and the final terms of the Interim Care Order. She glanced at the clock. It was six o'clock. Two of the clerks were still at their desks so she could hand over a hard copy immediately. Her right hand rested lightly over the mouse, guiding the cursor towards the print icon. But the cursor seemed to be moving of its accord, drifting across the words on the screen away from the print icon to the small x in the top right-hand corner of the page. Natasha watched with detached curiosity as the cursor continued to hover over the small x. Suddenly she realised she wanted to be at home, she needed to get out of this grim building. And with that thought her finger clicked on the mouse and the Attendance Note disappeared. She logged off and shut down the computer.

Chapter Nine

Mel

Mel stepped onto the escalator. A gust of hot air swirled around her, the stink of soot and steel seared her lungs. It was hardly worth giving up smoking. She settled on the moving metal stair and the stink became a medley of aftershave, body odour and cheap perfume. Then she was back into the moving crowd, onto another escalator and finally the platform. She realised she had not told Natasha to log off. But the girl was no fool. That was why she had rung Mel in the first place.

The following morning, Saturday, she picked up her car from East Finchley station, and spent the afternoon with her mother, leading her around the new boutiques which dotted Dulwich Village. Isabel might be seventy-eight but she still wanted to look good and regularly added to her wardrobe of floating, patterned tops and loose trousers. Her need for elegance provoked in Mel a paradox of admiration and disdain. Unlike her mother, Mel hated shopping.

On Sunday Mel spring-cleaned the flat, scouring kitchen surfaces as if she were destroying an enemy. She fretted about Jacob who'd come back late again last night and left the house to see friends in the afternoon. She made him promise to take the long way around from the tube and avoid the walk under the railway bridge. Then there was Paul. She rarely spoke to him at weekends. She would wait for him to call. When he did she'd be careful about what she said. Part of her wanted to collapse on him and tell him everything as she'd told that sweet

Palestinian dentist who'd picked her up off the pavement. But she never collapsed with Paul. He admired her strength and independence. She had no idea how he would react if he found her in pieces.

On Monday she drove Jacob to school then treated herself to a visit to the local bookshop. After lunch she pottered in her tiny garden. By Tuesday she was desperate. She rang Andy.

'Anything in the diary for tomorrow? I don't want my work to go out of chambers.'

'Don't stress yourself, Mel. Natasha's covering the family cases. She did well on your Financial Provision hearing this morning. There's not much crime around just now.'

'Right.' It was not right. It was wrong in every way. Financial Provision hearings were complicated, difficult, well paid. It was unusual to let a pupil take them on. Why had she allowed herself to take time off? 'How about the rest of the week?' she asked.

'I thought you were taking a week off.'

'I never said that.'

'Then you better chat to Jess.'

'Why Jess?'

'Mel, I'm only following instructions. Plus, I should tell you, there was a problem with Gonzalez, the Interim Care on Friday.'

'What about Gonzalez?'

'Your solicitor never got a call.'

'I called him after the case. I always do. Anyway, I emailed the Attendance Note.'

'He says not.' She couldn't answer him. Was it possible she had forgotten? Her memory of that day was confused.

'It's not like you to forget, Mel. Anyway, I asked Natasha what had happened and she gave me details so I called the solicitor myself. Plus, I never got the printed copy of the Attendance Note. I'll need that for billing.'

'There was definitely an Attendance Note. I asked Natasha to print it off and give it to you.'

'Well, you'll have to sort that with her. Like I say, I never got it, nor did the solicitor.'

'I'm sorry, Andy. I guess I was a bit distracted with the mugging. I really can't explain it. Listen I'll come in tomorrow.'

'Jess reckons it's better if you take a week off. Give us a call on Friday. I'll tell you what there is in the diary.'

She sat down and stared at her coffee. The air in the flat was heavy with silence. This was not good. It wasn't like her to make mistakes. Not this sort of mistake. There were always moments in a case when you could do better, when you came back afterwards rethinking your cross-examination, kicking yourself for asking one question too many. But not administrative mistakes. Those were the mistakes that made you unpopular with your clerk and your clerk was the key to everything. A chill ran through her.

She waited till later in the day when Jess would be out of court and rang her on her mobile.

'What's this about me taking a week off?'

'Hang on, Mel. I'm in the middle of something,' Mel heard voices, movement, and then Jess was back on the line.

'It's fine now. I'm in the corridor. Didn't want the others to overhear.' Why not? What was going on that Jess needed to speak to her in private? 'Shoot,' said Jess.

'You spoke to Andy. He wants me to take a week off.'

'We all thought it would be best. You've been driving yourself, Mel. The mugging was traumatic. I don't think you realise how that can affect you. You need to rest and learn to delegate. Listen, it's nothing formal. But I had a word with Jeremy, and we decided it would be best if you left things to the rest of us for a couple of weeks.'

'A couple of weeks? Andy said one week.' Worse and worse. Jeremy was head of chambers. How had things got so bad that Jess felt she needed to speak to him? 'What about Natasha?'

'She seems to be picking up work. I've arranged for her to talk to Georgie or myself if there's a problem. I don't want to make you feel worse, Mel, but you've been a bit snappy with other members of chambers. It's a clear sign of stress. There've been one or two comments from other barristers. You've not been your usual competent self. Is everything all right at home?'

'Comments from who?'

'I really can't say. It's hearsay and probably just gossip. You know what it can be like in chambers. Everyone worrying about losing work. I'm only telling you because I'm your friend and I'm concerned for you. I'm sure it's nothing. But you don't want to give people ammunition.'

'Give me names. This isn't fair.'

'Just give yourself a break and come back refreshed. Is everything all right at home?'

Mel thought of her worries about Jacob, her difficult mother, her distant lover. But barristers don't show weakness. And many people's domestic lives were far more troubled.

'No one likes to be mugged,' she said.

'Exactly. Have you been to the police?'

'I'll go tomorrow.'

'If they offer victim support, take it. These things can take their toll.'

'Goodbye, Jess.'

She didn't want to hear any more.

That afternoon she went to the police station, but the only person known as GJ on their books was at least ten years older than the sweet-faced boy who had run his hand under her shirt. Photographs were produced. None of them fitted. The police didn't seem concerned. There were no serious injuries. When the officer asked why she hadn't come in earlier she explained she hadn't felt strong enough. It sounded lame. She could imagine what he was thinking. The police had terrorism and stabbings to deal with. One more mugging wasn't worth the expenditure of resources. She was offered victim support. She said she would think about it.

Paul rang on Wednesday. He had a free afternoon. But there was an assumption in his announcement which grated and she felt herself biting her lip before offering him a much edited version of her mugging. He was sympathetic but there was a distant edge to his voice she had never noticed before. Then, for the first time, she lied to him, told him she was busy.

On Friday she rang Andy to ask about the following week. She was wanted for a pre-trial hearing at Snaresbrook on Monday morning and he would email over the papers.

'ABH,' he explained. 'It's come in from a new solicitor. He asked for you. We said you might be stuck on a part-heard case. But we'd get back to them by lunchtime. Better not to say you were unwell.'

'Thanks for that, Andy.'

'Conference at nine thirty. Case of Stevens. He's in custody. I'll email the papers over. No worries. Natasha's out of court, so she can come along.'

'Fine.' It wasn't fine. Mel wished her pupil would simply disappear.

Chapter Ten

Mel

Snaresbrook Crown Court is a Victorian Gothic pile situated at the end of the Central Line. Defendants arriving by van see nothing of its grey castellated splendour, fifteen acres of parkland and landscaped lake. From prison vans they would be led in handcuffs through the holding area to the cells, small windowless cubes, where stark white light displayed graffiti and ominous brown stains on cracked cream walls. Mel had never been in a Snaresbrook cell. But her clients were graphic in their descriptions.

The interview room was just big enough to fit four metal chairs around a grey rectangular table and was illuminated by a single glaring strip-light. Natasha, who'd arrived at the court a few minutes before Mel, followed her into the room and sat down. She opened her laptop, took out her copy of the instructions and waited. Her hair was tied back into a knot, accentuating her sharp features and her wide, clear forehead.

The guard brought in Conrad Stevens, a lightly built man of thirty-two. He hadn't yet made a statement and Mel would need to work out his defence. He was charged with assaulting his girlfriend, Lily Parsons, who'd sustained a broken arm and a black eye. Stevens had told his solicitor that he never intended to hurt Lily. If her arm was broken, he reckoned it was because she had brittle bones. They'd had a row. She could be violent herself, and he might have pushed her in self-defence. He'd given the solicitor a photo to show a bruise on his leg where he said she had kicked him. He didn't know why she had fallen. They'd been in the kitchen. Maybe the floor was wet.

The prosecution had provided a photograph of the injured Miss Parsons. It might have been a pretty face. It was hard to say, given the state of her right eye, which was closed, purple and puffed. Her other eye appeared blank and almost colourless. Her hair was brown with pink streaks, long and lank. Her right arm was in plaster. Mel couldn't help feeling this was not the first time Lily had suffered physical abuse.

She told Stevens that she'd seen the pictures and heard what had happened in a note from his solicitor. She understood there'd been a row and needed to hear his story in more detail.

What followed was confused, rambling and contradictory. Mel took down the odd note as she listened, conscious of Natasha tapping away beside her. Lily had been flirting with some men in the pub. She'd had too much to drink and Stevens had brought her home, taking her into the kitchen for a coffee. Then she'd started on him, accused him of treating her like shit.

'She went fucking crazy. Said I never let her do anything. Like I was trying to control her. As if. No one can control that woman. I never hit her. She was standing by the knife rack. I'm not that stupid.'

'Miss Parsons said you grabbed her arm and twisted it behind her back. Then you threw her to the floor.'

'Fucking liar.'

'She says you then pulled her up and hurled her against the counter.'

'More fucking lies. I never hurled her anywhere. Might've pushed her. Like I said she was winding me up, provoking me.'

'I'm afraid, Mr Stevens, provocation is no defence.'

'You telling me to go guilty?'

'I'm not telling you anything. Your plea is your own choice. I can raise provocation, but only if you plead guilty. If you decide to plead not guilty I can't advance provocation as a defence.'

'What do you want me to do?'

'It's not a matter of what I want. If you have a defence I'll put that to Miss Parsons. Then you'll give evidence and the court will hear your version of events.'

'What do you mean if I have a defence?'

'Before we decide on plea I need to know exactly what happened.'

She was handling this badly, explaining procedure in too much detail, failing to get his story out. It was poor practice, sending them round in circles and she was conscious of Natasha sitting next to her, taking down every word on her laptop. As a pupil, Natasha was the most junior member of the defence team, yet Mel couldn't dispel a disquieting sense that roles had been reversed, that Natasha was the one doing the supervising. Stevens had gone quiet. His eyes darted round the room and rested on Natasha.

'You heard me. What do you think?'

'I can't really…' Natasha started.

'Miss Baker is here to listen and take notes,' interrupted Mel. 'She and I will discuss your case later, but it is easier for all of us if we don't confuse the situation with two points of view at this stage.' She nodded at him. 'Do go on.'

Stevens' story involved another man, text messages between that man and Lily, flirting in a pub. The interview room was hot and her client's voice was flat and slow, mildly soporific. Mel had not slept well last night. She'd woken early, worrying about Jacob. His GCSEs were starting at the end of May, but he had taken to going out more, staying out late. On Saturday he had rung from a friend's house telling her he planned to sleep over. It was midnight and safer to stay out than walk back alone from the tube. She'd asked to speak to the friend's parents and been told they were asleep. What could she do? After one glass of wine too many she had no wish to drive across London to pick him up, if he was indeed where he said he was. This morning she'd left him huddled in a dressing gown at the kitchen table. He had a timetabled class at nine a.m., but she wasn't going to risk being late by driving him in again.

Conrad Stevens' voice droned on. Then there was a slight change of tone and Mel realised she'd been drifting. She clicked back into the moment.

'Then she gets up off the floor and goes and sits down. I'm not about to hang around and have her shout at me, so I'm off down the pub.'

'So, even though she was injured, you chose to leave her,' said Mel.

'How'd I know she was injured? Like I said, she got up off the floor. Next thing she's sitting on a chair.'

'And before the fall, you say she threatened you. Is that right?'

'I told her to mind her mouth. She was accusing me of all sorts.'

'What kind of thing?'

'Shagging one of her mates.'

'Is that true?'

'What's it matter?'

'If it's true it could support your case. It gives her a motive for threatening you.'

'Yeah, I suppose. Mind you, I don't want to look like a bastard in court.'

'Better to look like a bastard than go to prison.'

She could hear her own voice rising. Was it irritation? She had never messed up like this in conference before. Stevens was not an easy client. But then clients were never easy. He might not be very articulate, but he was no fool. They carried on, Stevens giving contradictory versions of the events, Mel trying to pin him down.

'So why didn't you call an ambulance?'

Natasha glanced up then returned to her notes.

'I already told you. I thought she was all right. I went down the pub. Had enough of her fucking games. When I got back she'd disappeared. Mad bitch.'

'It would be better not to call her names in court.'

'It's what she is.'

'I suggest you refer to her as Lily.'

'She fucking provoked me.'

'Mr Stevens. We have already been over this point. Let's get back to the injuries. Something must have propelled her pretty hard to cause them. Was it you?'

'I thought you were on my side.'

'Did you hit her?'

'No way.'

'Push her?'

'Might've done. She bloody pushed me.'

'The injuries need to be explained.'

'Like I said, she fell over. I thought I was innocent till proved guilty.'

'True. But Miss Parsons has made certain allegations. We need to answer them.'

'Then fucking answer them. You're my brief. I told you what happened. I'm not pleading guilty. I'm not going inside. I got kids. I got a job. My employer's keeping it for me while I go through this court crap. You got to get me off.'

'Your plea is your decision, Mr Stevens. I can advise you. But I can't mislead the court. We need to prepare a statement. It doesn't have to be very detailed. But it has to give some idea of your case.'

'So, what you advising?'

'You need to stick with your story. And in five minutes I need to tell the judging what you're pleading.'

The trouble was she was increasingly unsure what his story was. She should be taking him through it, point by point but she had allowed her mind to wander. Fatal. She had lost the thread.

'Tell 'em I'm not guilty. And bloody get me out of here.'

'I'll do my best to get you bail. Of course, you'll have to undertake not to go near your girlfriend's flat.'

Mel glanced at her watch. Ten twenty-five. They were on at ten thirty. She put her head round the door and called the guard. She promised Stevens she'd do her best to get bail, reminding him he didn't have to say anything this morning except tell the court he intended to plead not guilty.

–

The hearing went by as anticipated. Conrad Stevens pleaded not guilty. Bail was refused, and the case was listed for two days in three weeks' time. Mel's head was banging. She had handled this badly. Maybe Andy had been right, it was too early to come back to work. The client was all over the place, but she should have controlled him. She still didn't have clear instructions. And Natasha had been listening to every word. First the Patel case, now this.

They walked in silence to the robing room. Natasha still hadn't said a word. Mel threw off her wig and gown and bundled them into her wheelie. She shook out her hair and brushed it back to life. Then she turned to Natasha who was waiting beside her.

'How d'you think it went?' she asked. She was apprehensive about the reply but she couldn't ignore her pupil.

'Hard to say,' replied Natasha. 'Is it OK if I send over my notes when we get back to chambers? Or do you want them now?'

'Later will be fine. But I'd like to know what you think. He wasn't an easy client.'

'True. Only when he said Lily was by the knife rack. I thought you might have asked more about that. I mean, given he's relying on self-defence.'

Mel allowed herself a moment's thought. It was a good point but she didn't want to get into discussion.

'Possibly.'

She was wondering whether she should say more when Natasha added, 'And the advice on plea. I thought that was supposed to be left to the end.'

Mel felt a stab of irritation at this young woman, fresh from Bar School who thought she could do so much better. She felt like grabbing those delicate shoulders and shaking them. Let Natasha try sorting out a difficult client a week after she'd been chucked on the ground and threatened with rape. She said, 'Ideally yes. But it can be tricky when a client asks at the outset.' And when your mind is wondering and you're only half-present.

'I guess it can be.' Mel was endorsing her papers and tucking them into her bag when Natasha spoke again. 'One more thing. When Stevens said he thought Lily was going to kill him...'

But he hadn't said that. Or had he? Could it have been when she was thinking about Jacob? She looked up at Natasha whose face was blank and inscrutable as ever. 'I don't recall him saying that.'

'Perhaps you missed it. I wondered why you didn't pick up it. Was it because you were worried about him changing his instructions again? Anyway, I've written it all down.'

'Excellent.'

She zipped up her bag and reached for her anorak. It was all she was prepared to say. She couldn't remember Stevens saying anything like that but she wasn't going to admit she had missed it. Natasha might have made it up. She wouldn't put it past her.

'I'm not sure how you're going to work out a defence statement from all that,' added Natasha.

'Oh, we'll keep it general.'

Mel was ready to go but Natasha was still packing her papers and laptop into her shoulder bag. Then she sat down and took out a large black wallet. She unzipped it and removed a small gadget with a display screen, a strip of paper and a white plastic object, which looked like a fat pen. She stuck the paper in the gadget and pressed the pen thing against her finger. A drop of blood appeared, and she smeared it on the paper strip. She glanced at the screen before packing everything away. All this was done with cool deliberation and Mel couldn't help staring. Natasha's hands were smooth, pale and manicured, only the tips of her fingers looked calloused and discoloured. From the constant pinpricks, Mel presumed.

'Don't you find it a hassle? Having to check all the time?' she asked.

'It's OK. I'm used to it,' said Natasha, putting the gadget away and getting out one of her energy bars. 'I'm planning on buying a different system when the cheques start rolling in. Are you going back to chambers?'

'Yep. Need to put a face round the door occasionally.'

Mel was standing by the door of the robing room, ready to go but Natasha, who hadn't moved, said, 'Give me a couple of minutes.'

Mel felt a twinge of irritation that her pupil, who should have been her shadow, saw fit to keep her supervisor waiting. Next, Natasha unclipped her hair, brushing it back and swirling it up again, this time in a looser style, using a big tortoiseshell clip. The style suited her. It was softer while still highlighting her long neck, delicate jaw and neat ears. Mel was about to ask about the finger pricking and this new system she planned to buy, conscious of how little she knew about this condition which her pupil lived with from day to day. But the questions felt too big and she didn't want to start that conversation now.

She watched as Natasha got ready. If you inspected hard you might focus on her blemishes, the slightly crooked mouth, the tiniest hint of a bend in her slender nose as if it had once been broken. But the overall effect was arresting, near symmetry with a seductive hint of imbalance. Her eyes were a deep turquoise blue, almost unnatural in their brilliance. And then Mel realised. They were indeed unnatural. When she first saw Natasha in the interview room at Uxbridge Family Court the eyes had been a pale blue grey. Natasha must be wearing lenses. Mel had no idea of their real colour.

'Ready,' said Natasha.

They set off together across the reception area to the front door, down the stone steps, along the long path lined with huge dark rhododendrons. There were no more questions about the case and Mel was disinclined to revert to a difficult topic. It started to rain, and Mel pulled up the hood of her anorak. Natasha, who was wearing an expensive-looking belted rain-coat, offered to share her umbrella.

'No, it's fine. The tube's five minutes down the road.'

They walked on, Natasha's presence beside her an invisible stain on the morning air. The diabetes business gave Natasha a vulnerability that ought to have called out Mel's sympathy, if not compassion. Instead it left her cold, even irritated. It must be a bore, but it was not a reason to like her. Anyway, it was hard to like someone who had just seen you at your worst. It was much easier to dislike this woman with her neat hair, her smart understated clothes, her obviously expensive handbag. Every-thing was fine with Natasha, no cracks in her shiny surface, only those calloused fingertips, and Mel had missed the moment.

They arrived at the tube, Mel drenched and exhausted, her pupil still full of energy in her dry, well-cut coat. As they waited in silence for the train Mel remembered she had said nothing about the missing Attendance Note. She'd been meaning to ask Natasha about it, but she been focusing on Stevens and the moment hadn't arisen. In fact, there were a few things she'd like to ask Natasha.

'How about a drink after work?' she suggested. 'We were supposed to have a meeting at the outset but somehow there was never a right time.'

'OK,' replied Natasha, though she looked surprised.

'Great. I've got a few papers to attend to in chambers and expect you have too. Five thirty at Daly's any good?

'Five thirty it is.'

The train came roaring into the station. They sat side by side in the empty carriage as it hurtled back towards Chancery Lane.

Natasha took out her iPhone and tucked a wireless headphone behind her ear. It must be a good quality system. Mel could never hear anything through her own earbuds in the noisy tube. She pulled out her Kindle and looked at the thriller she'd started a couple of weeks ago. She was still struggling to follow the plot. The words swam across the page.

Chapter Eleven

Natasha

'It's always been my ambition,' she said, 'ever since I was a kid.'

'You were brought up in care, right?' said Mel.

'Till I was twelve. Then I was adopted. How did you know?'

'It was on your application. You must have thought it relevant.'

'I don't know if it's relevant. I just... well, I don't hide it.'

It had got her the pupillage. Natasha knew that. She hadn't mentioned the adoption on the application form. Just written that she'd been in care for ten years on the box marked 'other relevant considerations'. She might as well get something out of those miserable years. Alisha told her they had been looking for another ethnic-minority candidate. Georgie had persuaded them they shouldn't overlook well-qualified white women from disadvantaged backgrounds.

She and Mel were tucked into a booth at the back of Daly's Wine Bar on the corner of Essex Street and the Strand. The place was surprisingly empty, perhaps because it was a warm evening. She would stay for one drink. A run in the park would be good, but Mel had asked her to join her and you needed to keep your supervisor sweet. Natasha was keenly aware that Mel hadn't warmed to her in their first two weeks. It was time to turn things round.

So, over a glass of expensive Chardonnay, she spoke about her diabetes, how she'd discovered it at twelve, around the time of the adoption, the weight loss and repeated infections, the mood swings and exhaustion which everyone had put down to adolescence, that hot day at school when she'd collapsed and been rushed to hospital. She told of the doctor with the long face who'd talked down to her as she lay on the hard bed attached to a drip, her confusion at the diagnosis. Mel nodded. Natasha did not describe the feeling in her stomach as she sat in a fluffy dressing gown in the room off the children's ward, staring at teddy bears and plastic toys, listening to warnings about possible blindness, kidney failure and amputations. Never mind that such outcomes were rare and could be prevented by careful management. All she could remember now was her insides turning, her fury that she had been picked to go through this nightmare.

She'd stayed in hospital for three days as the nurses explained about insulin and blood glucose and showed her how to measure her levels and inject herself. She had a terror of injections and after constant begging, they'd let her have a pump. It was horrible, stuck to her body all day like a leech, and she still needed to prick her fingers with the lancet. But it was better than jabbing herself with a syringe before every meal. Back home, her adoptive parents were too anxious to be any help, her mother was already sick and her new brothers and sister, though curious at first, quickly lost interest. In the end it was her social worker, Susan, with her plump, pink cheeks and ragged blonde hair, who had saved her.

'You're strong, Natasha, a fighter. You're not going to let this thing beat you.'

'It's not fair.'

'Life's not about fairness. It's about making something of yourself and you're going to do that. There's stuff you can't control and stuff you need to control. You know which this is.'

Something had clicked in her and she started to heed the nurse on the diabetes team. Later she had joined an online support group. She never contributed to the group, but she read the posts and watched the clips. They knew nothing about the silent Natasha Baker, but for years they and Susan were her only friends.

'That must have been really hard, I mean as an adolescent,' said Mel, after listening to Natasha's edited version of her diagnosis.

'I had a good social worker,' said Natasha. 'If it hadn't been for her I'd probably be blind by now. Or dead.'

'How do you feel about it now?' asked Mel, taking a big gulp of her Chardonnay. Natasha shook her head and smiled. She had no desire to feed Mel's crude curiosity.

Mel had got to the bottom of her large glass and was looking at her. Clearly the head shake had not satisfied her. She was waiting for more detail.

'It's not very interesting. Not much to say. I was an average teenager. Bit of a goody-goody. Another drink?' Natasha asked.

'Why not?'

'I'll get it.' Natasha went to the bar, quickly caught the barman's eye and asked for another large Chardonnay and a fruit juice. She had checked her glucose levels in the Ladies just before the wine. They were fine, but she needed to get back for supper soon. She would have to miss her run. When she got back to her seat Mel was scrolling her phone. She looked up as Natasha returned with the drinks.

'Jacob's home alone. Mustn't stay too long.'

'Do you have a photo of your son?'

'Sure.'

Mel proudly produced one of a smiling, well-dressed teenager, taken at a family wedding.

'Good-looking boy.'

'Yes, I suppose he is.'

'Looks like you. How old is he?'

'Sixteen going on twenty-five.'

'Must be fun.'

'Can be. He's got GCSEs coming up, but he spends most of his time on Fortnite. That's why I need to be around.'

'Cool. I love Fortnite.'

'You play computer games?'

'Sure.'

Mel smiled. She looked pretty when she smiled. 'Another generation.'

'That's me. Just a kid.' Natasha felt herself smiling back.

'Still, you want to join the Bar. Doesn't it all seem a bit outdated? I mean our funny traditions. Wigs and gowns and dinners and the Inns of Court. Queens Counsel and silks. Who knows how much longer we'll be here? You might have qualified as a solicitor.'

'Yeah, everyone said there were more opportunities as a solicitor, more contact with the client. That wasn't what I wanted. I wanted to stand up in court. That seems like the point of it. I know I can do it – do it well.'

'I'm sure you can. I'm sure you will.'

Natasha felt herself being scrutinised. That was all right. She could deal with scrutiny.

'That domestic violence case. I was like on a complete high. OK, I confess, I love winning. And I can't wait to address a jury.'

'I was like that. Listen, Natasha, let me give you a bit of old lady's advice. Don't rush it. Learn the nuts and bolts, particularly the ethics. There are a lot of grey areas out there. You don't want to come unstuck. The briefs will come. You're doing well. Maybe you should specialise in Family Law. Think again about crime. There's no money in it.'

'Everyone tells me that. I don't need loads of money.'

'Really?' Mel was looking pointedly at Natasha's designer handbag.

'OK, I like nice things. But I'm good at saving.'

'You do like nice things. I was admiring your earrings.'

'Present from Luke,' she said. 'He's really generous.' That last bit at least was true.

She had picked them up in the shop at the Rijksmuseum in Amsterdam, their first weekend away together when they'd dragged themselves out of their sweaty hotel bed to look at some old masters. The earrings were copied from a Vermeer that Luke loved. He'd told her she looked like the model, so she'd tried them on. The assistant was totally dozy, and Natasha just walked out with them dangling from her delicate earlobes. She and Luke had a massive row, but she wasn't about to take them back and Luke wasn't about to report her to the Amsterdam police. After that she kept her shoplifting to herself.

Mel lowered her voice, 'There's something I want to ask you.'

It was coming, and Natasha had her answer ready.

'What happened to my Attendance Note? You know, the day you called and said I hadn't logged off the computer.' Mel was looking at her intently now.

'Oh Mel, I'm really sorry. I should have told you. I looked in the file like you said. I couldn't find it anywhere. I tried both the drives. Maybe you didn't save it? Or was it on a USB? I mean, you might have forgotten. You were in a bit of a state.'

'The Attendance Note was there. I'm positive.'

'Shit, I must have missed it.'

'It's not there now.'

'What a bore. You must have deleted it by accident,' said Natasha. 'Though I suppose you've got the endorsed brief. I've got a full note. I can let you have that.'

'That's not the point. The clerks needed it. They keep a record of everything, time spent, results of the case. The solic- itor expects to be given it immediately.'

Natasha wondered why Mel hadn't rung her to check. Prob- ably because she was so out of it. Mel was still talking.

'You know what it's like at the Bar. There's not that much work to go around. Oh I know everyone looks busy. But that's the way it is. Feast or famine. You'll find out. Keeping the clerks sweet is crucial.'

'I have been keeping the clerks sweet.'

'So I've noticed,' said Mel. The implication was clear and Natasha didn't like it. It reminded her of her sister, the same envy tangled up in cruelty. 'Sorry, I shouldn't have said that,' said Mel quickly.

'That's all right,' said Natasha. But it wasn't all right. The words could not be unsaid. The mood had changed in an instant.

'So, about the Attendance Note, did you delete it?'

'Of course not. Why would I do that? Like I said, I couldn't find it. I assumed you must have handed it in or sent it over already.' Natasha put on her best concerned voice. Unlike Mel, she could be nice when niceness was required. 'I should have rung you again to let you know. Only I didn't want to disturb you. What with the mugging and everything. I'm so sorry. Is there anything I can do?'

'These things matter, Natasha. Getting a tenancy's not just about being good on your feet. People need to know they can rely on you. I'm not sure if I can.' There was no attempt to mend the breach she had forced between them. 'Anyway, I must get back to my boy.'

Mel might make no effort, but Natasha would. 'I'd love to meet him sometime,' she said.

Mel looked surprised. Natasha felt she might have said the wrong thing.

'Not very likely. He barely sees his own mum these days.' And with that Mel gulped down the rest of her wine, stood up and picked up her bag. 'Are you in court tomorrow?' she asked.

'Yes.'

'Well, let me know when you've got a window and you can shadow your pupil supervisor.'

Natasha forced a smile and stood up. What did Mel expect? She should be glad her pupil was doing well. But it was clear she was only irritated by Natasha's success. Before she could say goodbye Mel was out of the door.

After dinner that evening while Luke was watching *The West Wing*, Natasha went to the bedroom and switched on her laptop. She scrolled down her contacts till she found it, Paul.Freedman@northbank.ac.uk. She typed.

> Hi Paul, Remember me? I was on Politics and Law
> a few years ago. Guess what? I got a pupillage
> with your mate Melanie Goddard! How cool is
> that? Hope you're OK. Thanks for all your help
> on the course. Maybe meet up sometime. Natasha
> x (Baker)

She was about to send it when she stopped. She'd leave it in Drafts. Wait for the right moment. In the meantime, there were other ways of getting back at Mel. She closed the page, opened Lola's Facebook account and searched for Jacob Goddard. Nothing. Then she remembered Mel's ex-husband, Claude Villiers. Mel and Jess had been chatting about him in chambers the other day. He was some big shot criminal silk.

She typed in Jacob Villiers. And there he was, floppy brown hair framing the face of an angel, only this time in a torn T-shirt, holding a pint of beer. She clicked on the name and tapped in a friend request from Lola Tondowski.

She went to join Luke to watch the rest of *The West Wing*. It was good to lie back on the sofa and feel the comfort of his arm around her shoulders. After the show she went back to the bedroom to organise her work for the morning. She clicked on her Facebook page. Just as she had hoped, her request had been accepted.

Part Two

June

Chapter Twelve

Mel

The city lay under a haze of heat. The streets were bright with white shirts, coloured dresses, pink and brown flesh. Lawyers were the exception. Some of Mel's colleagues favoured short-sleeved black cotton shifts and sandals, but she hadn't the nerve to appear in court in anything less formal than a jacket and skirt or trousers, complete with tights and high heels.

She'd been glad of her jacket that morning in the air-conditioned atmosphere of the Principal Registry. But as she emerged into the dazzling light, heading down Chancery Lane towards Fleet Street, the afternoon sun bore down on her.

Her head was filled with thoughts of Jacob. His exams would soon be over. Was today his last? She couldn't remember. The timetable was stuck on the kitchen notice board, but she'd forgotten to check this morning. She worried about what he would do over the long summer break. Claude would take him away with Jo and the kids for a couple of weeks in July or August. But for the rest of the time he'd be lolling about in his room, playing computer games. He'd mentioned temporary work at a music festival. Some of his mates were going. But Mel had told him he was too young to spend weeks on his own camping in a field full of twenty-year-olds high on drugs. He'd glared and said nothing. For days they'd barely spoken. Mel thought of past holidays, she and Jacob, clinging together, screeching in delight as they whizzed down the water slide at Center Parcs. She couldn't imagine going away with him now. What would they talk about?

Before crossing the main road, she glanced at her watch. One o'clock. When had she last taken a proper lunch break? Her head was still buzzing with thoughts of her son as she queued for a sandwich and bottle of water at Pret. Minutes later she was heading for Inner Temple Garden.

A group of French tourists were being led down the narrow passage from Fleet Street into the Inn. Mel's French had ceased at A level, but she could just follow the guide's explanation of the centuries old history of the four Inns of Court, originally staging posts for the Knights Templar during the Crusades, then the workplaces of lawyers.

She squeezed past the throng towards the garden. In Shakespeare's time it was an orchard, stretching to the banks of the Thames. Now it was a formal space with lawns and gravel paths, an oasis of quiet, wedged between the traffic-clogged arteries of Fleet Street and the Embankment.

Before she learnt the reality of the barrister's life, Mel used to imagine late afternoons sauntering on the Long Walk, discussing legal tactics with learned colleagues, contemplating, with leisurely interest, the fate of her clients. She soon realised the fancied afternoon saunter was more likely to amount to a snatched twenty minutes. But it was nonetheless with a rising heart that she made her way to Kath's bench.

Kathleen Maloney had been Mel's best friend. They were close in age and had studied law together in the Nineties. Unlike Mel she was tall, blonde, willowy, a true beauty. Yet Mel felt no envy, acknowledging the radiance that reflected on her when they were together.

Both women preferred to woo than be wooed, and they liked to do it as a pair. Fired by alcopops and the pure thrill of the hunt, they would track their favourite musicians after gigs. Stalk the best-looking lecturers. They looked out for each other. When Mel's drink was spiked, Kath confronted the man who provided it, threatening him with the police, bearing Mel home in a taxi. Underneath her soft exterior she had a will and mind of steel.

Sitting on Kath's bench now, those days of fun flashed back to her. They were two ambitious, academic young women who both knew that time would pass and that the real life of careers and families would commence. They were the lucky generation. Well-paid, meaningful work; attractive, helpful men, beautiful, clever children – they would have it all.

They lived close to each other in north London and when they took time off to be with their baby boys, they were constantly together. They both returned to work at the same time, putting their children into the same expensive private nursery and sharing childcare at weekends so each could prepare for court on Monday. The attractive men, Claude and Justin, were indeed helpful, but the women had recognised early on who would be doing most of the caring. They did not complain. They knew it wouldn't be easy. And as their mothers kept telling them, they had it all.

It started in her arm. They were on holiday together in the Peloponnese, all six of them, lapping up sunshine by the pool on the terrace of their rented villa. Ben and Jacob were two years old, toddling about on reins. Mel and the men were practising their diving, when Kath screamed, 'I can't hold them.'

She had lost her grip on their reins and the little boys were hurtling towards the water. Justin pounced on the pair of them with the speed of a cat on its prey. They could all see Kath's face, tight with pain. The men were casually sympathetic. Was it a twist? Tendonitis? A sprain? Perhaps she had overdone the diving? But from the first Mel suspected more. Three weeks later she saw her friend on her feet for the last time in the lobby of chambers, her right arm in a bandage, her beautiful features scrunched in agony. By the time of the first scan it was too late. The tumour in the bone had spread. Kath was young and fit, and cancer loved her. Ten months after their Greek holiday, Mel was standing with Claude and Justin by her best friend's grave.

It was Mel's first experience of the death of a contemporary. With the loss of Kath, she lost a chunk of herself.

Thirteen years on, she still missed Kath. She had no sisters. Kath had been her other half, as close to her as a twin. There was no one she could share with as she had shared with her.

Her colleagues had bought the bench in her memory. Sitting there now between the banks of flowers, the edges of their velvet petals crinkling in the midday sun, Mel was transported to earlier times when she and Kath had chatted about the world, love, friendship, families, work, men, their glorious futures. There had been no calculation, no unsought criticism, no anxiety about who said what or why. Life was richer, more brightly coloured for their conversations. There had been other friends, but no one to match up to Kath. Was it because barristers, however generous and well meaning, were always in competition for work? However powerful your bond with your colleagues, essentially you were on your own.

The tenancy interviews were to take place that evening. Mel had not forgiven Natasha for deleting the Attendance Note then lying about it to make her supervisor look inept. The last two months had done nothing to dislodge her antipathy. Natasha was efficient; she already had more independent work than would be expected of a second six pupil. And she made it all too clear she didn't need Mel's guidance. Mel would need to be strong if she was to prevent her pupil becoming a tenant.

–

As Mel arrived back at chambers from her lunch on Kath's bench her phone rang and Paul's name flashed across the screen. So, he was back from holiday with his wife.

She listened to his message. He needed to see her. It had been too long. She could ring him that afternoon on his mobile.

Peremptory as usual. As if she had spent the last three weeks aching to see him. Which would once have been true. But was no longer. His long body still entranced her. But something had shifted for her. The shock of the mugging had been a lesson.

A stranger had rescued her. Jacob had sat her on the sofa and made her drink hot chocolate. Paul had been out of bounds.

Georgie's face popped around the door from the kitchen.

'What's up? Bad day in court?'

'Court was fine. I was listening to a message from Paul.'

'So he's still around.' He affected surprise but she knew he was disappointed. Georgie had made his views clear. Mel could do better than Paul.

'I will end it. But I need to… you know how things are. I need the right moment.'

'How about dumping by text? I'll write it for you.'

'Fuck off, Georgie.'

'Maybe you need a replacement?' He smiled. 'Though I fear hetero men are not my speciality. Coffee?'

'Sure.'

She nodded. He poured fresh coffee into the machine and asked, 'So, what d'you reckon to Natasha? She's favourite for the tenancy.'

'I don't like to predict these things.'

Fifty applicants had been whittled down to three. The two others were a confident, elegant black woman and a brilliant young man who was also a wheelchair user and wanted to build up his Civil practice.

Georgie switched on the coffee and said, 'Come on, you know her better than any of us, you must have a view.'

'I try to be open-minded,' said Mel.

'What the fuck's that supposed to mean?'

'It's not always been easy.'

'Everyone else likes her.' Georgie was looking at her hard as he spoke. He knew Mel didn't like Natasha, but he had never accepted her suspicions. Mel didn't want this to come between them.

'So it would seem.'

'Why so cagey? She's a known quantity. Bloody good advocate. Solicitors eating out of her hand. The clerks all love her. Clients love her.'

The thought of clients loving Natasha made her want to puke. It was even worse than the thought of Paul swanning round Central Park with his wife. But she wouldn't argue with Georgie now. He would only challenge her, ask for evidence of Natasha's supposed wrongdoing and she would save that for the meeting. So much of it was hunch and instinct and lawyers weren't interested in hunch and instinct. She threw out a stupid comment, 'She's white.'

'Oh, for Chrissake, you don't go along with that quota crap.'

'Just kidding. No, it's just… I have reservations.'

'Such as?' asked Georgie.

'She interrupts in conferences.'

'All the time?'

'Once or twice. Until I told her not to.'

'Pupillage's a learning curve. A steep one. Anyway, the bright ones all do that. Hardly a reason for a veto. So, what is it?'

'I'll tell the meeting, Georgie. OK?'

She took her coffee and went to her room. There was work she needed to get on with, but she couldn't stop thinking about Natasha and what she, Mel, would tell the meeting later. There were things she would mention and things she wouldn't, like her irritation when she heard Natasha on the phone, chatting up that new solicitor and landing a lucrative care case as a result. Like the way she worked the room at the chambers' party. Ambition was fine. Some people were just too blatant.

Chapter Thirteen

Mel

Mel scanned the familiar faces ranged around the polished table. She had known them all for years, battled against them in court, taken on their returns, read their garbled attendance notes. She knew their domestic arrangements, their sexual orientations, their family backgrounds. Yet, apart from Georgie, it seemed to her that none of them knew her. She loved the world of the Bar, the individual responsibility, the freelance life, but as she sat there waiting for the meeting to start, she found herself wishing for a more collaborative existence.

Jess was chairing the meeting. She had insisted that Mel, as Natasha's pupil supervisor, should attend. Jeremy, head of chambers, had sent his apologies and said that he would happily abide by any decision they made. And now Jess explained that the second woman candidate had been snapped up by another set of chambers. 'So, the choice is Nigel or Natasha. Marcus, what do you think?'

As chief clerk, Marcus had no vote. But his opinion was critical. 'I say we take them both. How often do we get two candidates of this quality? Nigel will bring in the money on the Civil side. But we need to expand our Family base. Natasha's committed to that. She can take on criminal cases too if necessary. She's good news.'

'Georgie?' asked Jess. 'You've been in court with her. What do you think?'

'Most of you already know my view,' said Georgie. 'Natasha is just what chambers needs. We co-defended last week. You'd think she'd been in the business for years. The judge was impressed. She floored the prosecution witness, gave a brilliant closing speech. There's no argument, as far as I can see. What's not to like?'

'Must you use that dreadful expression?' interjected Julian.

Julian Goodhart, QC, was the oldest member of chambers, well into his seventies but showing no sign of retiring. Mel had co-defended with him and had been amazed at how judges let him pursue the most outlandish submissions of no case to answer, or abuse of process. His knowledge of law was encyclopaedic, his manner theatrical, his vocabulary both entertaining and baroque. In his time, he had defended alleged IRA terrorists, radical Islamists, rapists and paedophiles, all with elaborate old-world courtesy. He had an extraordinary record with juries. Mel looked at him fondly. He was of a dying breed.

'Thanks, Julian, a reminder we must all keep our language up to scratch. Do you have anything to say about Natasha?' asked Jess.

'She seems a very nice young lady.'

Paula Hatfield, a leading member of the Bridge Court feminist caucus, narrowed her eyes but made no comment. Julian's performances in court for almost half a century absolved him from criticism.

She spoke. 'In my view Natasha would be a huge asset. I've not been in court with her, but I've done one of her returns. The client was deeply disappointed not to see her. Plus, she's got the right background, worked her way through uni.'

'Working class,' said Georgie.

'As long as she's not Oxbridge,' muttered Mel staring at the table.

'Oxbridge is not the point,' he countered. 'She was brought up in care. It shows strength of character.'

Georgie's determination to support Natasha felt painful and disloyal. Mel said nothing. Brought up in care was a slight exaggeration given that Natasha was adopted at twelve. But she let her colleagues wallow in her pupil's social background. How they loved to talk.

'I'm going to stop you all there,' said Jess at last. 'The meeting seems generally in favour. Mel, you're her pupil supervisor. May we hear from you?'

Mel, who had been trained never to put forward a submission without supporting evidence, felt the silent scrutiny of the meeting. She recognised the rush of cold air, the beating heart of excitement that comes at the start of a difficult cross-examination. This time she was in the witness box.

'I don't think we should take her,' she said.

'Why not?' asked Jess.

'She's not right for us. Oh, she's a good lawyer and from what I'm told, an excellent advocate. But we need someone we can rely on, a team player. Bridge Court is more than just a bunch of talented people.'

'That's a bit vague. What have you got against her?'

'OK Jess, I don't want to make allegations that can't be substantiated,' began Mel, conscious that starting with a negative was unhelpful. Her speech was prepared, but the sharp eyes of her fellow lawyers unsettled her as she continued. 'She's been a difficult pupil. Of course, we look for confidence in our applicants, but Natasha's a little too confident. And I'm not 100 per cent convinced of her professional ethics.'

'Wow, that's serious,' said Paula.

'Your evidence for that?' queried Jess.

Mel had suspicions, but there was only one thing she could rely on. The Attendance Note. She reminded them of the mugging, the afternoon she had been advised to go home and take time off. She explained how she had forgotten to log off, how she had asked Natasha to save her work, print off and hand in the Attendance Note.

'Only she never handed it in. I'm pretty sure she deleted it.'

'That's ridiculous. Why would she do that?' asked Paula.

'I'm afraid I can't explain why. All I can say is that the Attendance Note was not there when I next logged on. I asked her to hand it in, but she failed to do so. Of course, I can't prove she deleted it. I can only say what happened.'

'Hang on a minute, Mel, you weren't well that day. You'd suffered a trauma. At best you were distracted. Could you have deleted the note yourself, inadvertently? We all do it. No big deal,' Jess said.

Mel felt her body stiffen. Everyone was watching her, waiting for her reaction. Her throat was dry and she reached for one of the bottles set out along the table and poured herself a glass of mineral water. After taking a sip, and allowing herself a long slow breath, she began to speak. But despite vowing to stay calm she could hear her voice rising in pitch and volume.

'Are you saying I deleted my own Attendance Note?'

It was Paula who replied.

'You have just accused Natasha of doing it. Isn't it far more likely you did it yourself?'

Jess had said much the same thing, but her comment had arisen out of concern for Mel's wellbeing. Paula's question felt like gloating and there was no way Mel could respond other than with words she would regret. 'By accident of course,' added Paula with a sickening smile. Mel had heard enough.

'Are you suggesting I'm losing my mind?' she snapped.

'You were not yourself that afternoon,' countered Paula. 'We could all see it.'

Mel couldn't even remember Paula being in the room at the time. It was too much.

'Oh, for Christ's sake, Paula!'

Her hand was on her glass and she had a violent urge to chuck it at the irritating woman on the other side of the table, who seemed to be loving her moment of triumph. The room fell silent. The urge was controlled but Mel was conscious of eleven pairs of eyes awaiting her next move. She loosened her grip on the glass and took a deep breath.

It could have been worse. She could have thrown the glass. But it had been bad enough. What was most damaging was that her outburst had been witnessed by Marcus. As chief clerk he was responsible for bringing the work in. He was the last person she needed to see her vulnerable and emotional. She spoke again. This time her voice was low and steady.

'That's what Natasha said.'

'There you are then. Did she log off?' Paula asked.

'Someone did. I was off for a week. Listen, even if she didn't delete it, she should have explained why it wasn't handed in. She had my number. She should have called me.'

'Why would she delete your Attendance Note? It doesn't make sense.'

'That's the unanswered question. She's unpredictable, hard to read. We need people who are trustworthy, open,' said Mel. Natasha was probably too busy chatting up the clerks and trying to steal other people's work. She was a mischief maker. Mel knew she was right even if she didn't have proof.

'Well, if that's all there is,' said Jess.

Julian looked up. 'May I point out that this meeting was due to finish at 6:30 p.m. I wonder whether the matter could be put to the vote.'

'I agree, Julian,' said Georgie. 'I must say it's looking difficult. If Mel has a problem with the woman I don't see how we can take her. We have always said that new tenants need to fit in socially as well as professionally. Other chambers have had splits and differences. Bridge Court has always had a collegiate feel and unlike others, we are still here, despite difficult times for the Bar. If there's tension between a pupil and her supervisor there's likely to be further tension if that pupil becomes a tenant. There'd always be an issue.'

'Fine,' said Jess. 'We'll go for a decision. Unless anyone has anything more pressing to say?'

The silence was heavy and long, broken by Paula. Her eyes were on Jess, but Mel felt it as a personal attack on herself.

'I must say I am very uncomfortable about making a decision on unsupported allegations,' she said.

'Thank you, Paula,' said Jess. 'I am sure none of us are comfortable but that is the situation in which we find ourselves. May I remind you all that this is not a trial. It's a decision about who will be best for chambers. There's bound to be an element of subjectivity. As Marcus has already suggested we can afford to take both, we'll vote on each of them separately. All those in favour of Nigel.'

Thirteen hands were raised.

'Against?'

No hands were raised.

'Natasha? All those in favour?'

Paula and Jess and two others raised their hands.

'Against?'

Mel raised her hand and, to her surprise, saw Julian and Georgie raise theirs.

'Abstentions?'

There were six. Barristers were not natural abstainers. Mel realised she had created both a stir and a precedent.

'That's it, then,' said Jess. 'Nigel has it.'

'I'll ring him,' said Georgie, adding, 'who's going to tell Natasha?'

'I'll do it,' said Mel.

Chapter Fourteen

Natasha

Natasha pushed open the door to the flat. Leonard Cohen was crooning away as usual. As she tossed her bag and jacket onto the sofa, she could smell onions, garlic, meat, a casserole simmering in the slow cooker. Luke would be in the bedroom, typing up case-notes. She peeked round the door. There he was, staring into the screen, head bent forward, deep chestnut hair short enough to expose a tiny patch of pale neck, long enough for a hint of soft curl around the ears. She enjoyed watching him without being seen.

He had a face to lead a medieval army, but he had chosen a profession with a different kind of heroism. As a social worker he would be gentle and self-effacing. Natasha had experience of that tribe and most of those she met had been kind but controlling. Luke wasn't like that. She was sure he would listen to his clients, show his compassion, though she couldn't help feeling he was wasted in the job, trudging around housing estates, advising the poor on how to improve their lives when what they needed was money and jobs.

He was a genuinely good man. And however badly she behaved, he stuck by her. She might find it hard to love, but at least she was learning to be loved.

She wished she had his capacity to feel. Sometimes it rose in her, an inkling of concern, but then it would vanish, a tiny seedling shrivelling in the sun for lack of water. Feelings might start in her, but they never grew. She would never have real friends as other people did. She had read several books on the subject. One piece of practical advice was that if you behaved tenderly to another person you would start to feel tenderness towards them. She was trying it out with Luke, tiptoeing forward and kissing the back of his neck.

'Hey, buddy,' he said, swinging round, beaming. His American slang made her laugh. 'I heard you come in.'

'Why didn't you say?' she asked.

'I like to pretend. I like it that you come up behind me when you think I don't know you're there.'

'That's unfair.'

'I learnt it from you. So, how was it?'

'Good. It was OK.'

He clicked the mouse and started to shut down the computer.

'Just OK?'

'I need a shower first.'

She undressed, removed her pump and stepped into the hot jet, letting the day wash away. The tenancy interview had gone well but she was unsure about Mel. She was angry with herself for deleting the Attendance Note in her first week. It was almost two months ago now but Mel had never believed her explanation and the relationship had not recovered. At least she hadn't sent that email to Paul. It was still sitting in her Drafts folder.

Natasha didn't know why she behaved this way. She'd be on the crest of something good, a job, a friendship, an apology, when some force took over and she would sabotage whatever had been about to happen.

Stepping out, reaching for a soft white towel, she began to rub herself dry. She was thinking about her adolescent years. How, instead of asking for more pocket money, she had stolen from Janet's bag. How she had become the rude one, the naughty one. When her brothers teased her about her skinny arms and legs, her wild hair, she attacked them with fists and teeth. They were cowards, never fought back, only snitched on her to Ed. She was locked in her room for hours. Once, but only once, Ed hit her, smacking her hard across the face. She had never forgotten, never forgiven. She threatened to ring Social Services, but her sister Eleanor had intervened.

'Don't do that. They'll take you away and stick you in a care home. Anyway, Dad's sorry. He said so.'

She calculated. He wouldn't dare do it again and she was better off where she was. She stopped fighting. But no one would stop her doing what she wanted. And now there was Luke, her constant protector.

Poor doting Luke. From the start, she had tested him. She was living in a tiny bedsit and he had invited her to share his flat in Brixton soon after they met. Two days before she was due to move in, at a crowded party, she had met Elliot, a rangy American with floppy brown hair and long-lashed blue eyes. His gaze transfixed her. He wanted her, and she liked to be wanted. While Luke was drinking and chatting, Elliot had taken her hand, led her upstairs into a bedroom and placed a chair against the door. There she let him remove her clothes, standing naked in front of him as he removed his. He said nothing as she silently detached her pump and laid it on her clothes. There was no shame or anxiety, only the deep mutual understanding that this was something they must do. They had kissed at last, deep slow kisses, his tongue inside her mouth. Still without speaking they lay down, his smooth dark chest swaying over her, the silk of his cock against her thigh, lust in his brilliant eyes. There must have been forty people in the house, but she and Elliot were alone in the world. Their bodies fitted. As he nudged against her, pleasure rippled to her toes. Sex was good with Luke but there was an edge here, an excitement she had never known. Twenty minutes later he got up and dressed.

'Wait a few minutes,' he said. They were the only words he ever addressed to her. He removed the chair and went downstairs.

She did as she was told. There was a mirror in the bedroom so after dressing she was able to tidy her hair and her clothes. She didn't dare take a shower. Not here, not in someone else's house. She barely knew her hosts; they were social workers, friends of Luke. When she reached the bottom of the stairs, she saw Luke waiting for her. The look on his face told her that he knew what she'd been doing. Would he hit her? Tell her it was over? Instead he said, 'Let's go.'

They walked to the tube. Neither spoke. She wondered whether to say, 'I'm sorry.' But she wasn't sorry, didn't regret those twenty minutes with Elliot.

Luke said, 'If you don't want to move in...'

'But I do.'

'OK.' He paused. 'There's one thing.'

'Yes?'

'Don't ever do that again.'

'I won't.'

'That's good. Because if you do, I...' Luke hesitated. Some instinct had prompted her to test him and she waited in silence for his response. 'I don't know what I would do.' He had passed the test. Just. She never apologised.

Natasha remembered those words as she stepped out onto the bath mat, Leonard Cohen still wailing through the bathroom door.

Her phone was ringing as she stepped into the bedroom. She saw the name on the screen and answered.

'Mel?'

'I'm sorry, Natasha.'

'I didn't get it.'

'I'm afraid not.'

'Why?'

'There were lots of good people. It was a really difficult decision.'

'There was me and Nigel. You could have taken us both. Marcus reckoned you would.'

'I'm afraid it's not up to Marcus.'

There was a pause. Mel said nothing. She could have explained. But Natasha knew why she didn't explain. It wasn't just the Attendance Note. Mel had disliked her from the start. She had never wanted a pupil, particularly one who was quick, who could see through her waffle. Oh, Mel could talk the talk. She could be nice to clients, work out the legal issues. But put her on her feet, give her someone tough to cross-examine and she would fall apart. Natasha had seen it. Mel didn't want another tenant on her patch who was better than she was. Younger, sharper, who would steal her solicitors, take her work. That's why she voted for that bloke in a wheelchair. Mel's practice was looking thin. She was never around when the work came in. Not like Natasha who stayed in chambers every evening till the clerks went home. She knew from those emails where Mel was spending her afternoons when she pretended to go home to work on papers.

'I'd like feedback.'

'OK. I'll pass that on.'

'So, what now?'

'You've still got three months. They might let you have a third six months if you don't find anywhere else. What are you doing tomorrow?'

'I'm in Westminster Magistrates' Court.'

'Well you seem to be getting plenty of work. You could always squat.'

Natasha didn't want to squat. Barristers were self-employed so technically they could work anywhere. But traditionally they clubbed together in chambers where they employed clerks to bring in the work. As a tenant she would have had status, a say in the running of chambers, a secure foothold. As a squatter she would be a nobody, available for work but with no base on which to build a practice. Squatters never lasted long. The tenants could kick her out any time. And a third six as a pupil was even worse. There would be no reason for the clerks to put her forward if they knew she wasn't staying. New pupils would move into her territory to be nurtured by Andy and the other tenants. People might be friendly; they might pretend to support you. But when you were no longer any use to chambers, they wouldn't bother. Mel had destroyed everything.

'Listen, I have to go. Jacob's just had his biology exam. I haven't had a chance to talk to him. We'll speak soon.'

'All right.'

As if everything was just the same. Which, Natasha supposed, it was; the same shitty, badly paid trudge around the courts of Greater London, waiting for someone to give her a crumb of work. She had played the game, chatted up people she despised, worked all hours for less than the minimum wage. Everyone thought barristers were well paid. She could make three times the money in escort work.

She put down the phone, sat on the edge of the bed and stared at the wall. She had worked so bloody hard. If only they had given her a male supervisor, none of this would have happened. Men didn't take offence at the tiniest hint, didn't set up cabals and cliques. Chambers were no better than school. The girls had always been tricky, shifting like silverfish. Natasha had preferred hanging around with boys. You didn't have to keep proving yourself. She felt something rise within her, the same something that in her childhood turned to bites and punches.

Natasha knew from experience that the mood wouldn't pass unless she did something active. She used to try to blame her diabetes, but it wasn't that. She shook out her hair, reattached her pump and checked her blood glucose. It was low, and she ought to eat, but a run would help to calm her down. She could stop if she felt unwell and she would take her phone. She put on her shorts and a T-shirt and went into the kitchen where Luke was standing over the stove.

'I'm going for a run,' she said.

'But I'm just about to put it on the table.'

He watched her as she opened a drawer, took out a glucose gel sachet, ripped it open and swallowed the contents. 'Keep it warm for me,' she said. Then, as he gave her his hurt, worried look, she added, 'I'll be fine. Once round the park. Twenty minutes.' With that she darted out of the front door and down the stairs.

The cool evening air brushed her cheeks, her bare arms. She breathed the scent of rain dripping off trees from an earlier shower, the hot spell finally broken. The air was heavy with lime and plane and horse chestnut. Under a grey sky streaked with the pale silver of twilight, she ran, past the neatly planted beds, down the gravel path to the playground, past the pond and canal, around the bandstand. The park was almost empty – just the odd jogger, a few dog walkers. She could hear the hum of traffic on the main road, the occasional scrape and roar of a plane across the sky. She felt the rhythm of effort, the comfort of repetition, the gradual loss of thought in movement. She could have gone on for an hour, but she needed to get back to eat.

In the flat she took another quick shower. She checked her levels. Just in time. She was beginning to feel faint. In less than five minutes she was clean, dry and dressed at the table with a glass of apple juice, facing Luke's concern.

'It's fine, Luke. Don't worry.'

'But I do. You take too many risks.'

'It's my body.'

'I live with it.'

'Your choice.'

He said nothing. Just looked. She knew the pain she gave him, but she couldn't stop herself. He might have read every book and website he could find on the subject, but he could not know what it was like to live with type 1. He sometimes said it came between them like a difficult child.

'My child,' she had said.

'No, our child. We're in this together.' She shuddered as he spoke. It was as if he were trying to steal something from her.

But she stayed silent. She had made her decision about Luke. She wanted him around more than she wanted to be alone and if that meant compromise she would compromise. If he crossed a line she would be gone, and he knew that.

The casserole was good, but she needed to be careful not to eat too much, too fast.

'Is it OK?' He still looked anxious.

'It's fantastic.'

They ate slowly, silently. Luke took a second helping. He said, 'I heard you on the phone.'

'I'll get something. It'll be fine.'

'Of course you will.'

Empty words. He had no idea how hard it would be. If she was to get a tenancy elsewhere, she would need Mel for a reference. She thought about the email to Paul Freedman. She still hadn't sent it. Nor had she deleted it. It might work in her favour. Mel wouldn't want the world knowing about her private relationship. A reference in return for silence could be a perfect bargain. And even if Mel didn't care, Freedman would. Natasha remembered the way he came on to her at uni. Like he was entitled. Just because she was a student and he was a lecturer, he thought he could get away with anything. It was time he learnt to behave himself. She remembered the photo of the pretty woman on his desk the one time she had been to his office. It certainly wasn't Mel. Stupid man. He ought to be more careful with his emails. As for Mel, a good reference would cost her nothing. In fact, if Mel wanted to see the back of Natasha it was the best thing she could do.

They carried on eating in silence. That was one of the many things she liked about Luke. He didn't feel the need to punctuate every gap in the conversation, didn't try to invade her thoughts.

They finished their food and cleared the plates into the kitchen. Luke was stacking the dishwasher and wiping down the surfaces.

'Want to watch anything?' he said.

'Maybe later. I've got a bit of work for tomorrow.'

He gave her his sympathetic look. 'Your colleagues are a bunch of fools. You work non-stop. You're smart; you're beautiful. They're crazy not to take you.'

'Yeah well, I guess they must have their reasons. Like Mel said, there are lots of good people out there.' Luke moved towards her, placing both hands on her waist and smiling into her eyes. She pecked him on the cheek and shifted away. He would have stopped everything to take her to bed at that moment and she loved the way he wanted her. But the anger towards Mel was building inside her again and there was something she needed to do first.

Back in the bedroom she turned on her laptop. She opened the Drafts folder on her email page and scrolled back to April. There it was: the message to Paul. There wasn't much in it. She wondered why she'd been so careful. It was not like she was accusing anyone. If it gave either of them a moment's discomfort, all to the good. She moved the cursor to Send and tapped her mouse.

Then she took out her phone and opened Messenger, scrolling through the old texts till she found what she was looking for, her young Adonis, Jacob Villiers, a beautiful not-so-innocent kid, up for a bit of internet flirting. The messaging had been fun, and his latest photo was suggestive. He was stripped to the waist and had towel draped around his groin. His hair curled over his ears, his dark eyes looked huge and his skin was pale. He must have been holding the phone himself because the features appeared slightly distorted. But he was still a lovely adolescent boy. He reminded her of a painting she had once seen. She loaded another Lola picture, eighteen years old, blue-grey eyes, carefully tousled blonde hair and come-to-bed smile.

Hi, Jacob she wrote. *Lola here.*

She was sure Jacob would remove the towel if she asked him to.

Chapter Fifteen

Mel

Mel gazed through the open French windows across the tiny garden to the night sky, a swathe of deep orange behind a silhouette of Victorian roofs and chimney pots. She was lying on her back on the old chintz sofa, head propped on her hands against two cushions. The air was still and warm. The sofa was a dear friend, beloved despite the wine and tea stains hidden among the swirl of pink roses. The brown piping had frayed, the sides of the arms had been shredded by Mozart the cat, but if Mel must wait, this was where she would prefer to be.

Mozart was no longer with them. He had slunk out through his cat flap one evening, never to return. Jacob, then twelve, had begged for another pet. Mel had stalled. She had never liked cats, not even Mozart with his cool disdain for all things human. Claude had brought him home in a rucksack. Mel remembered her dismay as she saw the little black and white nose peeking through the canvas.

'Someone for you to love,' Claude had joked. Two months later he left her.

There had been no replacement. A dog would be impossible, and she could not countenance a creature in a cage. Jacob grew older and less bothered about animals, and now there was a terrible emptiness in the flat, no one and nothing to remind her of her own existence. Tonight, even a goldfish would have tempered the ache of solitude.

She glanced again at her watch. It was just past midnight. If Jacob stayed out beyond eleven he was to ring her. She checked her phone. Had she missed a call? No. The sound was on, the phone charged and there would be no problem with reception. She opened her text messages. Nothing. She looked at Instagram, WhatsApp. Twitter, Facebook, Gmail. Unlikely that he would use any of them to tell her his whereabouts, though they were links of a sort. There was one reassuring note on Facebook informing her that Jacob Villiers was 'attending an event near you'. Her first reaction was relief – at least he was not dead. Then she remembered that it only meant he'd accepted an invitation. It wasn't live. He could be anywhere. She'd heard of parents installing trackers in their kids' phones so they could check on them. But much as she longed to know, she wouldn't go that far. Anyway, Jacob would refuse. And phones could be stolen. It might have been stolen now. Jacob could have been mugged. Or worse. He could be lying bleeding in a gutter at this very moment.

She heaved herself up and reached for the half-empty glass of Pinot on the low table beside her. Once again she dialled his number, but it was his voicemail that clicked in. She ended the call without leaving a message.

She waited. As a girl, she had waited for her mother. Isabel Goddard was an actress who, for most of Mel's childhood, had played a pivotal role in a long running soap. During the day there had been rehearsals and filming. After coming home from school and letting herself into the empty house, Mel would pour herself an orange squash and stretch out on the first-floor landing with its clear view of the front garden. There she surrounded herself with biscuits, books, magazines, reading and nibbling through the blissful suspension of late afternoon, waiting for the sound of the key in the lock.

On arrival Isabel would stand in the hallway. Now it was her turn to wait as Mel abandoned her pleasures to run downstairs and hurl herself against her mother's tall, unyielding body. Even at home Isabel Goddard carried herself with regal detachment. In her small way she was a star. To Mel she was the brightest in the sky.

Mel's father had disappeared when she was six, reappearing at Christmas and birthdays for the next ten years. He had married again and now lived in Spain. He rarely flew over to see them and Mel had no desire to see him. Mistakes travelled down generations. She gulped her wine. How was it possible to hold a family together nowadays? Three quarters of Jacob's class had separated parents.

She glanced at her watch. Twenty-two minutes past one. She must have drifted off. A second wind had hit, and she knew she would not sleep again while Jacob was out. She was due at Feltham Family Court in seven hours' time to meet the client in a contested care application. Her cross-examination required more work. But she was too tired to focus. Jacob was never this late on a week night. Should she ring his friends' parents? There seemed to be nothing else she could do.

'I'm afraid I can't help, Melanie,' said Jonathan's mother, Clare. 'I've no idea where Jacob is. Jonathan's asleep in bed. Do you have any idea what the time is?'

'I'm really sorry,' mumbled Mel. 'It's just that I'm anxious.'

'I wouldn't worry. He'll be back.' Clare put the phone down. She tried other numbers, Kim's father, Hannah's mother. Then Mel called the only other person in the world who would drop everything and drive across London to pick up Jacob at this hour.

'He'll be fine. It's his last exam. He'll be celebrating.' Claude might be sleepy, but he spoke with the usual iron certainty. Was it his last exam? Wasn't there one more next week? She couldn't remember. She could hear Jo's voice murmuring in the background.

'How do you know he'll be celebrating?' Mel asked.

'Leave off, Mels. I'm in the Court of Appeal tomorrow.'

He was always in the Court of Appeal when she needed him. 'I think I should call the police.'

'Don't be daft. They'll tell you to go to bed.'

'He might be hurt.'

'I'm telling you, Mels, they won't give it a thought. It's the end of the exam season. There are thousands of sixteen-years-olds on the streets after midnight.'

She put down the phone without saying goodbye. She had come to hate what she had once loved, his freedom from doubt. She would wait ten minutes then call the police. She didn't need Claude's approval. The police might indeed tell her to go to bed. If that was the worst they could do, she had nothing to fear. She stood up to go to her desk. Her legs were unsteady. This was ridiculous. She'd had two glasses. Or was it three?

The door of his room was ajar. Mel swung it open, hit by the smell of unwashed socks and sweat, laced with the tang of cheap deodorant. She hovered. He was her son. This was his territory. She would have been furious if Isabel had invaded hers. But when, on rare occasions, she had cut a swathe through the clutter to tidy up, Jacob had seemed indifferent. Not because he had no secrets, surely. More likely that, as a child of the millennium, his darker secrets were stored in a cyberworld she could not imagine, let alone enter.

Mel switched on the centre light. Clothes were strewn over the floor. There were books too, magazines, fantasy and sci-fi scattered between mugs half-full of cold tea, chocolate wrappings, empty crisp packets. She picked up a T-shirt, sniffed it, dropped it, hesitated. What was she looking for? Only the essence of the boy who should be here. She surveyed what he called his desk, an old door resting across two trestles, seeking some clue as to where he might be, who he might be, this child who had become a stranger. A couple of chemistry textbooks, covered in yellow and green highlights, scraps of paper and post-it notes covered in doodles, scribbles, names, telephone numbers.

She stopped, conscious of the ambient hum of London traffic. Was it her imagination or had cars become quieter? A sudden burst of rock music pummelled the air, thrumming across the gardens. She leant down and picked up the T-shirt for the second time. She would take it to the laundry basket.

She looked at the scraps of paper on his desk, telephone numbers, girls' names, Hannah, Maud, Lola. Then she looked at her watch. Ten minutes had passed since she'd spoken to Claude. It was time to call the police.

As she headed for the phone in the hall, she heard the scratch of metal on metal. His key in the lock. Relief washed through her. She waited.

He stopped in front of her. Something about him was drawn away from her, inward, as if he didn't wish to meet her. She detected a new crop of spots on his forehead. His hair looked greasy, uncombed.

'Sorry, Mum. I thought you'd be in bed.'

'I was worried.'

She noticed his right arm was held across his stomach, the hand and wrist tucked inside his cotton jacket.

'I need the loo,' he said.

He strode past her into the bathroom. She heard the tap running and waited a little before walking in behind him. He was standing at the sink with his back to her. She took a step forward to see what he was doing. The water was pink with blood.

It was a cut, about half an inch long. As he lifted his arm from the water she could see the white edges of the wound, the open flesh. Her stomach turned as it always did when she saw blood, anyone's blood. She reached for the towel and held it towards him.

'Here,' she said.

Without a word he extended his arm, let her wrap it. Staring down as the scarlet seeped into its fluffy whiteness.

'Hold it,' she said. He obeyed, and she dived into the cupboard to get lint and gauze. Her first aid training was rusty, but she remembered enough to fashion a rough bandage and stem the bleeding.

'You're going to hospital,' she said.

'No, not hospital.'

'You need stitches.'

'I'll be fine. It's tiny. It's not deep.'

'Deep enough.'

'Leave off, Mùm. I'm all right.'

'It needs to be checked. You don't want a scar.'

'I don't care. Anyway, it's tiny.'

'Was it a knife?'

'Doesn't matter.'

Something unyielding settled inside her, the tough persistence of cross-examination.

'I said, was it a knife?'

'Maybe.'

'For Chrissake, Jacob. You can't just… You've been attacked. We need to go to the hospital. We need to tell the police. We need to report it.'

He turned and faced her and she saw the hard certainty of his father, the man who wouldn't be argued with, the man who could make his own submissions, had his own cross-examination ready to hand.

'No, we don't. We don't need to report it. I'm fine and I won't let you take me to the hospital.'

She knew this Jacob. It was the teenage version of the three-year-old who had screamed for thirty minutes when she tried to put on his shoes.

'OK,' she said. 'We'll try a different tack. We'll sit down have a cup of tea. You can tell me what happened.'

'I need to sleep.'

He was right. She too needed to sleep. It was after 1:30 a.m. and she needed to be up at six to prepare her cross.

'What happened, Jacob?'

'I'm going to bed.'

'Did you hurt someone?'

'I said I'm going to bed.'

'Jacob, I need to know. Who hurt you? Did you hurt them? What happened?'

'No, you don't need to know. You don't need to know anything.'

'Jacob…'

'I'm not your property.'

He walked past her out of the bathroom and down the corridor to his room. She followed and stood staring at the closed door, listening to him move about until there was silence. The cut would heal. There might be a scar, but it was small and looked clean. She felt the gulf between them. She couldn't hold him, couldn't control his life.

Chapter Sixteen

Mel

The alarm went off at 5:45 a.m. Still in her pyjamas, she made herself a cup of tea, skimmed once again through the social worker's statement and refined her lines of cross-examination. By 7:15 a.m. she had showered, thrown on her court gear and a pair of trainers and was sprinting out of her front door to the tube.

Worry about Jacob clouded the journey from Finsbury Park to Hatton Cross; the wound, his secrecy, her frustration, all nagging like a rotten tooth. For the first half hour she'd been standing squeezed between commuters, hanging from the overhead rail, avoiding eye contact, her bag on the floor between her legs. But as the train pulled away from Knightsbridge she found a seat and was able to look over her papers. At one point she sensed a neighbour glancing at the typed script. He was about twenty years old, stick-thin, wearing paint-stained jeans and a faded brown T-shirt, unlikely to be involved in the hearing. Instinctively, she shifted to block his view.

On the bus to the court, more thoughts about Jacob filled her head. She pushed them away. She had a job to do and she would do it well.

The West London Family Court is a solid rectangle of two-tone brick and grey tinted windows, set back from the A312 behind a car park, trimmed with low hedges. As she walked down the broad walkway to the sliding glass doors and the security desk it seemed to Mel she could have been in any country in the world.

She queued at the entrance desk, allowing her bag to be searched and her person to be frisked by a hatchet-faced security woman with cropped brown hair. She pondered how it would be to have a proper job, one where you went to the same place every day, had your own office, your own desk, plants on the windowsill, your name on the door, paid holiday leave, set hours.

Like Paul, she thought, remembering their frantic coupling, in the North Bank University Politics Department, crushed against a pile of stacked boxes. The top half of his door was frosted glass, but if you stood behind the bookshelf you could not be seen from the corridor. She recalled balancing on one foot as the stack of boxes behind her threatened to collapse at any moment, after which there was some complicated shifting, both she and Paul ending up, cramped and half-clothed, on the carpeted floor beside the desk. Throughout their glorious contortions there had been the thrilling awareness that anyone, at any moment, might knock on the locked door.

The security woman brushed down Mel's body, looking for hairspray, lens cleaner or any other weapons a barrister might attempt to smuggle into the Family Court.

'Right,' said the woman, 'you can go through.'

Mel turned towards the robing room, halting briefly in surprise to see the skinny young man from the tube journey, seated on a hard chair in the reception area. She offered a faint smile. Either he didn't see her, or he decided not to react. Whatever the reason, there was little chance he was involved in the same case.

She was wrong. The young man turned out to be Ezra, feckless father of five-year-old Mason, whom she was endeavouring to have returned to his alcoholic mother. Ezra was twenty-one years old. He had never looked after Mason and it was clear from his monosyllabic evidence that he had neither the desire nor the capacity to do so now. Mel was reassured. The last thing on Ezra's mind would be reporting her to the Bar Standards Board for reading court documents on public transport.

It quickly emerged that the local authority had failed to obtain the required evidence. Mel managed to expose every shortcoming. After that it was easy to persuade the District Judge of the merits of removing Mason from his apparently capable foster parents to the care of his irresponsible mother. Her spirits lifted as she strode out through the sliding glass door to the walkway. In the bright summer sunshine, the municipal architecture had a new stylish appeal.

For two hectic hours she had not thought about Jacob, but she was thinking about him now. It was after midday and he would surely be awake, though not necessarily out of bed. She must speak to him. Yet she feared what she might discover. When she was busy she could contain such fear. With any lull, the fear jumped out.

There was no one at the bus stop. She pulled out her phone and tapped on Jacob's number. No reply. But he would see she had called. She zipped the phone into the side pocket of her bag. When the bus arrived, she jumped on and found a window seat from which she could gaze at the grey suburban landscape gliding by in the summer heat. As the bus was pulling up at the station she heard the ringtone. She looked at the name on the screen. Not Jacob, but Paul.

'Hi Mel.'

'Hello.'

'Can you talk?'

'I'm about to get off a bus.'

'Are you going back to chambers?'

'Yes.' She needed to show her face. Her diary was looking sparse.

'Call me when you get there.' He sounded peremptory. 'I'll be in my office. There's something I need you to look at. I've had an email. I'll forward it. Ring me when you've read it.'

It sounded ominous. Had Caro found out? In some ways it would be a relief.

She waited till she was alone in one of the downstairs rooms, before opening the email. It was from Natasha.

Hi Paul, Remember me? I was on Politics and Law
a few years ago. Guess what? I got a pupillage
with your mate Melanie Goddard! How cool is
that? Hope you're OK. Thanks for all your help
on the course. Maybe meet up sometime. Natasha
x (Baker)

She stared at the screen. Was Natasha crazy? She rang him.

'I read it,' she said.

'How does she know we're friends?'

'You must have told her.'

'Well, I didn't. I barely know her. Did you?'

'Of course not,' Mel shot back.

'You see her every day. You must have got to know her.'

'In a way.'

'So, did you mention me?'

'I don't recall.' As she spoke it came to her. The Attendance
Note. Accessing Mel's computer. Natasha's inevitable trawl
around Mel's otherwise uninteresting cyberworld. There were
one or two messages no lover should put on email. Mel knew
her instincts had been right. For no good reason she added, 'She
didn't get the tenancy.'

He said, 'I don't give a fuck whether she got the tenancy or
not.'

A pause. She knew what he was thinking, the words he
wouldn't say because to speak that thought would blow the two
of them apart. 'But you give a fuck if she wrecks your marriage.'

She wouldn't tell him about the likelihood of Natasha
accessing her emails. He would freak. 'She and I we went for a
drink. A few weeks ago. I don't remember exactly when. She
told me she was at North Bank. I may have mentioned you.
What does it matter now, anyway? It's not like she says much.
Nothing she shouldn't know.'

'But why tell me?'

'She probably wants an excuse to write to you. Maybe she
fancies you.'

'She doesn't.' She refrained from asking how he knew. 'I hope she doesn't cause trouble.'

Of course she would cause trouble. It was what Natasha did. Why they couldn't offer her a tenancy. She was about to speak, about to tell him that Natasha had nothing to gain from wrecking his marriage when the door flew open. Georgie and Jess burst in, deep in conversation.

Mel pointed to her phone, Georgie uttered a loud, 'Oops,' and Mel walked out into the corridor.

'Sorry, Paul. Too much racket here.'

'Are we going to meet?' he said.

'I don't know.'

He'd been absent when she needed him, when she'd been sitting in the dark on a wet pavement, and when she'd been lying awake in the small hours, worrying about her son's wound. Did he think of her as he boarded the plane to New York with his family? Did she exist for him outside the bubble of their private world?

'I'm free now,' he said.

His low voice stirred her as it always had.

'Let me ring Jacob,' she said. 'He's been in a bit of trouble lately.'

'What sort of trouble?' he sounded genuinely concerned. Might she speak to Paul, pour out everything, share her untold fears?

'I'll tell you later.'

There was no reply from Jacob's phone. Nor from the land-line in the flat. It was two p.m. He had been asleep when she left, but she remembered he was going into the sixth form college to speak to staff about next year's A level options. She left a message telling him she'd be back by six. She called Paul again.

'I can't get through to Jacob. He'll be at the college.'

Jess from emerged from the room into the corridor, raising her eyebrows in interrogation and making drinking gestures as she walked past Mel towards the tiny kitchen. It crossed Mel's mind that she hadn't talked to any of her colleagues since the tenancy meeting. She flashed Jess a quick smile as she shook her head and moved further down the corridor where no one could hear her.

'Where do you want to meet?'

What would he suggest? Last time it had been a coffee bar, echoing with the clatter of cups, strident voices and background disco.

'Can you come to my office?'

'Your office?' She remembered the tumbling boxes, the frantic contortions as they copulated half-standing, half-sitting, against the thin partition wall. 'I'm not sure.'

'If you'd rather not, that's OK. We could meet in a pub.'

She wanted him. She looked down the now empty corridor and a voice emerged. Her own, shocking, surprising.

'What about the Premier Inn?'

Chapter Seventeen

Mel

His curly grey hair was inches away on the pillow and she could hear his soft breath mingling with the hum of the air conditioning. He moaned, turning to face her, flopping an outstretched arm across her breast. After their lovemaking he had, unusually for him, drifted into sleep and now she watched him, studying his fine, angular face. Despite the name, he didn't look Jewish. He had once told her he took after his Irish Catholic mother, with her long straight nose and the hint, now more than a hint, of bags beneath his green-brown eyes. The shadow of stubble on his cheek touched some unmet need in her and she leant over and kissed him. He stirred and mumbled something incomprehensible.

She looked away to the room around her. The walls were off-white, punctuated with neutral flower prints, the closed curtains a plain loose weave that filtered the afternoon light. The air smelt of cleaning fluid and air freshener. Everything was horribly familiar, the television, kettle, sachets of tea and coffee, the tiny fridge and dull wooden furniture. The place had a hard, unbreakable feel. Whatever you threw at it, nothing would change. She turned back to Paul, nuzzling up to his fragile human warmth beneath the bedclothes.

He shifted, letting his hand drift down her body to her thigh. It had been more than a month since they had shared a bed and their first moments had been tense and disjointed. Strangers would have met more easily. But now she waited, unhurried, eyes closed as he emerged from his private dream to launch her on a wave of pleasure. This second time he was gentle, slow, holding back till she was ready.

Afterwards, they lay together in silence in the half-light. Minutes later, she had no idea how many, he said, 'Thank you.'

'For what?'

'For seeing me. For putting up with me.'

She didn't know how to reply. Then, before she could speak, he said, 'Do you think she'll say anything?'

His question was a cold draught from the world outside. He must have sensed her stiffen because he said, 'Mel, are you OK?'

'I'm thinking.'

But she had no control over the thoughts that tumbled about her like falling debris. That he could bring her to this hotel, stroke her to ecstasy, then ask the one question that showed where his heart lay. He was a frightened man. She looked again at the face that minutes ago had seemed so appealing. How quickly it could change. The fine lines were strained in apprehension, the eyes freighted with anxiety. He had not asked about Jacob and she had not said anything. That story would remain untold.

But it was she who had suggested the hotel, she who had made her wants so brutally clear. A few minutes ago, she had clung to him in lust. Now she wanted to scream and throw things around this horrible room which had been so perfectly designed to withstand the destructive outburst of a hysterical woman.

She pulled away, stood up and moved to the bathroom, conscious of his eyes following her naked body as she walked. After less than a minute under the hot jet of the shower, she stepped out onto the soft white mat and began to dry herself.

'Are you all right?' he called through the open door.

'Sure, I just need to get back.' She picked up her things and went back into the bedroom to dress.

He was standing naked by the bed. 'You're angry with me,' he said.

Please, she thought, don't start, we both know how it is. While he was in the bathroom, she quickly dressed and looked in her bag for cash. He preferred not to use a card or cheque and she insisted on going halves. She placed the money on the table.

When he emerged from the bathroom and saw the notes, his face tightened with discomfort. He tried to protest, and she shook her head slowly. 'No, Paul. We've talked about this before. This is how it is.' Then, while he was dressing, she said, 'I don't think she'll say anything.'

But she had no grounds for the prediction. It was no more than an attempt to reassure them both.

'But why now?' he said. 'You said she just missed the tenancy. The timing feels significant.'

She knew what Paul was thinking. What had Natasha got to lose? But she said nothing. They walked out of the room and down the stairs to the hotel foyer. She stood back as he handed over the cash. Once she had offered to use her card to avoid him embarrassment: a few painful moments at the reception desk after their two-hour session, her lover hovering by the exit. Since then Paul had always made the payment.

They walked out together into the heaving rush hour that surged around the Kings Cross gyratory. The air was thick with fumes, gritty on her throat. Sometimes they stayed in a country house hotel, sometimes pubs. Once they had been for a weekend to Paris. But wherever they stayed it would always end in the same bleak misery of separation.

He kissed her cheek and she kissed him back. She knew he would head for the tube.

'I'll take the bus,' she said and turned away. They made no plans to meet again.

Chapter Eighteen

Mel

The flat was empty when she let herself in at six p.m. Jacob had texted to say he would be back at seven for supper. She wondered why he was so late when all he had to do was pick up some information at college. But he was almost seventeen, he had friends, he had a life. Yet he seemed so innocent. No sign of drugs. And that wound on his arm was practically a badge of heroism. She thought of her afternoon with Paul, wondering if her son had inherited his mother's instinct for secrecy and deviation.

She poured herself a red wine, sat on the sofa and pulled out the post from her bag. There were the usual uninteresting circulars, announcements from the Inn, appeals for money, an invitation to guest dining night. One intrigued her, a long thick cream-coloured letter stamped Crown Prosecution Service. She couldn't imagine why they would be writing to her. There was a vague feeling she might have done something wrong, but she knew enough to be sure that any misdemeanour would not be addressed by a typed letter to her workplace.

It was a reference request for a Miss Natasha Baker who had applied for the post of Crown Prosecutor. The letter invited Ms Melanie Goddard to log onto the website where she could fill in the appropriate form. Natasha must have applied some weeks ago despite looking for a tenancy at Bridge Court. Anyone would do the same. Her pupil was just a young woman looking for work. But the thought of her as a prosecutor was even worse than the thought of her as defence barrister. She reached for her phone and called Natasha's number.

'Hi, Mel.'

'Hello, Natasha. How are you?'

'Fine. Busy. How can I help?'

'It's about the reference. For the CPS.'

'Oh, that yes. Is it a terrible bore? It's just they, well, they asked for my pupil supervisor.'

'I thought you wanted to be a defence barrister.'

'I do. But you know how it is. I need to find something, so I thought just in case. As it turned out, it's lucky I applied. But if you don't want to do it...'

'It's not that.'

'Thanks, Mel. I hope it's not too time-consuming. I know these reference things can be a pain.'

'Not a problem. It's part of my job as pupil supervisor. How are you feeling? It must have been a blow failing to get the tenancy. You should know you had a lot of support.'

Mel could imagine how Natasha might be feeling but she couldn't help wondering what she would say. Would that shell of confidence eventually crack?

'I'm sure you tried your best. So, is there anything you want to know? I mean for the reference?'

There was no getting out of the reference. Her colleagues already questioned her judgement about Natasha. Refusing to write a reference would beg more questions. And it would need to be a good reference. Candidates were entitled to see them, and a bad reference would only cause further trouble. Mel decided she would make it brief, fair on Natasha's competences, of which there were many, but not overenthusiastic. Whether or not it would be good enough to get Natasha into the CPS was not her concern. It just needed to be good enough to get her out of Mel's life. Yet Natasha intrigued her. She might as well admit she was fascinated by this elegant creature who moved like a cat and for whom other human beings were simply a means to an end. Why had she written to Paul? Mel needed to know her intentions.

'How about meeting for a coffee?'

If Natasha was surprised she didn't let on. 'Next week?'

'Well, I was thinking at the weekend. I'll be in south London on Sunday. My mother lives in Dulwich. That's not far from you, is it? We could meet at the Picture Gallery. Do you know it? It's nice. There's a cafe there. We could have a chat. More relaxed than chambers.'

'OK. What time?'

'About four thirty? Might be a bit crowded but I'm sure we'll find a place. We could even take in the exhibition.'

There was a pause at the other end and for a moment Mel wondered if she had gone too far.

'OK. Only I don't want you to make a special trip. Is there anything I can tell you on the phone?'

'I'll be in Dulwich anyway. It's been a few weeks since we last met up, and I'm still your supervisor. I'll need to do a report.'

'Sure.'

'So, four p.m. at the cafe. Keep your phone handy in case.'

'I'll be there.'

'Great. Bye, Natasha.' As Mel shut down her phone, she realised she was trembling. What was happening? Why did this coffee feel like a step too far?

Chapter Nineteen

Natasha

Natasha hung up and opened Lola's Facebook account. She'd been messaging Jacob when Mel rang and she wondered if he'd picked up on her latest picture, the one in the blue dress under the palm trees. It was ten years old, but he wouldn't know that.

It was Friday evening. Just after six. Where would Jacob be at this hour? Did he have a girlfriend? Would she be keeping an eye on his messages? Teenage girls were smart, they had a nose for cheats. They wouldn't be trusting like Luke.

And what if his mother checked his phone? But Jacob wouldn't have picked up the chat thread if he sensed he was being watched. And if he was being watched, what could Mel do that she hadn't already done? It was not like Natasha was doing anything criminal. She might even use the texts and photos to wangle a decent reference. She scrolled down the messages. Jacob had already replied.

You're beautiful. I'd like to see more of that tan. Got a bikini shot?
She tapped in *Sure*.

Natasha had never learnt to swim or even worn a bikini. She didn't want people commenting on the pump. But she had a picture ready, one of the fakes she'd used on Tinder. He replied immediately.

Hot
U? she typed.
I already sent one.
Take off the towel?

I'm not sending U a naked pic. U could be a bot.

I'm not a bot she typed.

Prove it.

Ask me a question. Any question.

No reply. Was he thinking? Or had he just given up?

He reminded her of someone, but she couldn't recall who. She was struggling to find a name, a place, when she realised her lips were tingling, she was starting to sweat, and the familiar black spots were floating across her vision. She swiped the reader in her arm. The new kit was a massive improvement but even a Flash Monitoring System wasn't proof against a hypo. The reading was too low, and she needed to act fast. The spots were swelling into blobs, some of them merging to form snakes. She minimised the page, picked up her reader and went to the kitchen for a Coke.

She drank half the can, hating the way it repeated on her, rushing up her throat and nose, but she was out of glucose tablets and she knew this worked. The symptoms were subsiding but now she was feeling nauseous, so she sat on a stool and waited. One thing type 1 had taught her was patience. She looked about her. The work surfaces were wiped down and the plain white breakfast plates had been washed, dried and returned to the cupboard. She appreciated that. Often, she had to leave earlier than Luke to get to suburban courts and his fastidiousness made it easier to come home to their small flat. But however clean and neat, however modern the lines and freshly painted the walls, the flat was still pokey. Natasha had already decided that when she got the CPS job they would look for somewhere better. One of those Edwardian semis on the edge of Dulwich would be ideal, close to where she was meeting Mel on Sunday.

She knew the Picture Gallery well, though she had pretended she didn't, unable to resist the minor deception of feeding into the other woman's prejudices. If Mel was too stupid to realise that someone who went to the wrong university might like beautiful things, why bother to explain?

Once again, she swiped the sensor. Her blood glucose was up but she was still feeling sick, so she sat on a bit, waiting for her body to settle. Yes, Dulwich would be perfect. A step up from Brixton. She imagined the house they would buy. They would get builders in to gut the place, make a decent kitchen extension, French windows onto the garden, silent gliding doors, wooden floors, new rugs. They'd go shopping, real shopping, buy glass and china with money she earned. They would have dinner parties like the people she worked with. She hadn't said anything to Luke yet. He didn't like change and novelty.

The nausea was still there. It was unusual for her. She'd felt sick once before when her sugar levels were sky-high but unless there was something wrong with her monitor this was not the case now. She was probably just dehydrated. It was a hot day. She had opened all the windows on arriving home but there was no breeze and the air was heavy in the sun-baked galley kitchen.

Moving was not an unrealisable dream, though she'd need the CPS job. The money from her adoptive father, Ed, would help towards a deposit. But it was nowhere near enough. Still, it was lucky she'd visited him after all before it had been too late. He might have cut her out completely.

She looked at the wall clock. Six twenty. Luke would be in the pub with his workmates for at least another hour. He rarely went out without her and she was usually too busy with work, but this was a Friday ritual: two or three rounds and a visit to the Thai to bring back a curry supper.

Back in the sitting room, she went straight to Jacob's profile page. Just as she hoped, there was another message.

OK. When we meeting?

Next week? she typed.

Cool.

U old enough to get a drink? She knew he wasn't, but it would be interesting to see if he lied.

I'm sixteen. Pub's fine.

His honesty was so sweet. She typed *Waxy O'Connor's? It's in Soho*.

Where in Soho?

She typed the address. She hadn't been there since Ricky. It was her favourite meeting place, big enough for her to see Jacob without him seeing her. She carried on typing *You look FANTASTIC in that photo*.

Tease.

Take off the towel. I'd like to see a bit more of you.

How about we Facetime?

I'd rather meet first. I don't like talking to a screen.

You're a bot.

Come to Waxy's. See for yourself. A public place. If we like each other – fine. If not, you walk away. Nothing to lose.

There was a pause. He would be typing.

Take your top off.

Not online she typed.

His reply came immediately. *What time at Waxy's?*

Two p.m. Thursday next week?

U not working?

Freelance. Main bar at Waxy's

C U then she read.

How wrong he was. She might pop in to get a look at him if she was out of court in the afternoon. But there was no way he would see her.

She took down Lola's Facebook page, logged onto Right-move and browsed half a dozen two- and three-bedroom properties in Dulwich. They were ridiculously expensive but she wasn't going to live in a housing association flat forever.

A cloud cut across the afternoon sun, the light dimmed and the air through the open window felt suddenly chilly. The windows were double-glazed metal sashes. To open them you needed to unclip the latch and slide the inner and outer panes a few inches to the left. They acted as efficient insulation, blocking the sound of the trains and traffic, keeping out the cold in winter. They were safe, Luke explained. Children couldn't fall out; adults couldn't jump. He didn't mention fire risk. Natasha thought about Grenfell Tower. But you didn't need to be in a tower block to die in a fire. You just needed to be trapped.

When she was seven years old, her foster mother had locked her in a cupboard. Natasha couldn't now remember what minor misdemeanour had led to this imprisonment, but she knew she was at an age when she hadn't yet learnt to be devious, when childish frustration emerged as burning fury. She remembered kicking the other foster children, biting them till she drew blood, pulling their hair. Her earliest memories were memories of anger, her own and that of the red-faced adults who sought to control her.

Looking back, she had no idea how long she had been held in that cupboard. An hour, two hours, more? She had never forgotten the stench. Was it filthy water lingering at the bottom of a bucket? Maybe a dead rat under floorboards? It had been so dark that she had to identify her surroundings by touch, the only light a crack around the edge of the door. When her foster mother unlocked it and pulled her into the electric dazzle of the hall, she knew it must never happen again. She would do everything in her power to be good. And if she couldn't be good, she would do everything in her power not to be caught. And if she was caught, she would apologise. Being good was not within her power and she was caught on numerous occasions. She was never confined again, but confinement remained her greatest fear.

Was it the memory of that vile smell that was making her feel queasy now? She closed down Rightmove and brought up Jacob's Facebook page. There was a new message.

Out and about now. Send you another pic soon.

Out and about? What did that mean for a sixteen-year-old boy? She remembered herself at sixteen and hoped he would take care. There were dangerous people out there. She was about to reply with a friendly warning, but she was still feeling strange and as she looked down to the keyboard, the room seemed to be swirling around her. She dropped her head into her hands and waited for the dizziness to pass. But it was getting worse. And now her stomach was heaving. She needed to get to the bathroom. Fast.

Dazed, she pushed herself up, supporting herself on the edge of the table. Her whole body was trembling, and she could feel the sweat dripping between her breasts as she stumbled across the sitting room to the hall and the bathroom. She sank to the floor. Head over the toilet bowl, she waited for the inevitable. Vomit, foul-smelling, bitter-tasting. It was evening, not morning, but as she threw up her sandwich lunch it crossed her mind for the second time that evening that this sickness might have nothing to do with her diabetes.

Afterwards she felt better, though she was still unsteady as she stood up to brush her teeth, then flush and clean the toilet bowl. Her clothing was unmarked, but she felt dirty and was on her way to the bedroom to change her shirt when she heard Luke's voice.

'Tash?' It was obvious from its direction that he was already in the sitting room. And Jacob's profile was still on Lola's Facebook page.

Chapter Twenty

Natasha

He was standing by the sofa staring at her open laptop.

'Who's Jacob Villiers?' His voice was dull and flat, as if he didn't care, but Natasha knew him too well to miss the smothered anger. In the past she had always managed to placate him. Now she could not find the words. She was aware that silence might sound like contrition, but she was far from contrite, merely thinking fast. Before she could speak he continued. 'And who is Lola?'

From where she stood she could see Jacob's profile, his smiling handsome face, his name in the search bar and next to it, the tiny circular picture of herself as Lola. His most recent message was visible in the bottom right-hand corner. 'Out and about now. Send you another pic soon.' The text was small, and Luke was quite short-sighted. It was possible he hadn't read it. The crucial thing was to prevent him reading more. She walked across the room, passed in front of him without meeting his cold stare, closed the Facebook page and shut down the laptop.

'It's not important,' she said, turning to face him.

'I disagree, Tash. I think it's very important. This Lola, she looks like you. Is she you?' He sounded energised, piqued by her dismissal.

She mustn't waver. Her normally placid Luke had scented blood. She would fudge it. He hadn't seen the pictures or the rest of the messages. He might not have read that last one. And he wouldn't be able to restart the laptop without her password, which she changed regularly.

Luke was talking again, sounding increasingly angry. 'What's going on, Tash?'

'Why are you nosing around my stuff? I never look at yours.'

'You don't need to look at mine; I don't lie to you.'

'And I don't lie to you. Lola is just a name I use online.'

'Why would you do that?'

'It's something I used to do before I met you. I haven't used Lola for years, but I've been stressed recently. You know that. Losing the tenancy, worrying about getting another, about getting any kind of job. I come back to an empty flat. I need something to take my mind off things.'

It was all true. Though he was staring at her, shaking his head slowly, like he didn't believe her. She carried on.

'OK, it's not your style. Maybe you didn't do dumb things when you were young. Lola started when I was still at school. You know what it's like when you're a teenager.'

'You're not a teenager. You're a grown woman.'

Something about the way he said it, the way he was looking at her took her back to the nausea, the puking in the bathroom. She could still taste the vomit. What if she was pregnant? It was possible. She had stopped taking the pill when she thought it might be affecting her mood swings. The cap was never 100 per cent reliable. Somehow she'd never believed it would happen to her. She'd taken much bigger risks in the past.

'What's your password?' he demanded.

'I don't give out my password. I don't ask for yours.'

He turned towards her, with a face she had never seen before, a cold stone mask.

'Tell me the truth, Tash. Who is this boy?'

'I already told you. It's just a bit of fun.'

'So, you're doing it to wind him up?'

'Of course not.'

'How old is he?'

'Nineteen.'

'A kid.'

'Nineteen is adult.'

'You're fucked up.'

Something locked in her throat. She would not let him judge her.

'So, how do you know this guy?' he asked.

'I met him online. He's a Facebook friend. That's all.'

'Lola's Facebook friend.'

'I don't use Natasha on Facebook. I don't want people getting too interested and trying to track me down. Listen, Luke, I work flat-out. I missed out on the tenancy. You were out with your mates. I was just messing around.' She paused. He was staring at her, studying her. She tried to read his thoughts and found she couldn't. 'You have to trust me, Luke.'

'Do you meet these people?'

'Of course not. Anyway, it's not like there are lots of them.'

He was scrutinising her face as if he didn't know who or what she was, as if he were working out a puzzle, unsure of the solution. He was a tall man, just over six foot, strongly built. She took a step back.

He said, 'He looks more like fifteen to me.'

'It's possible. It's Facebook.'

'So does Lola prefer children?'

The words cut through her like the slash of a blade. For a moment she stood motionless, clutching her pain. Then she launched herself towards him. She wanted to hurt him physically. 'How dare you!' she screamed, as he gripped her arms and held her firm.

'What am I supposed to think? Can't you see what this is doing to me?'

And though she struggled against his grip she could see it. And she hated what she saw. What she wanted was the old Luke, the easy understanding Luke who loved and trusted her, whose lightest touch could fill every cell of her body with delight. Not this angry combatant. He would never hit her, but if she did not take care, he might come to hate her. He had posed a question she would never stoop to answer, but as she felt the strength of his hands on her arms she knew she needed to break this impasse. His eyes bored into hers. There was still one thing she had not tried, had never tried.

'Please, Luke, I know I'm a mess. Forgive me. I won't do it again. This boy means nothing to me. No one else does. Only you.' She paused. He was looking at her intently. She thought it would be enough, that he would let her go. But he continued to grip her arms and she could not move.

'How can I believe you?' he said.

'Because it's true. Because I love you.' The words hovered in the air, brittle and false.

He said nothing. Just stood there and she sensed the battle inside him. After a long second, he let go of her arms and turned away, alone and silent, shaking. Natasha waited as, still shaking, he tore one of the framed prints from the wall and hurled it onto the floor. The glass smashed around their feet and she jumped back, watching him fall on his knees amidst the fragments.

They slept inches apart. No sex, not even a cuddle. But in the morning he reached for her as he always did, and she responded. To boost his mood, she agreed to walk across the park to his favourite coffee shop. Together, they toured Sainsbury's. Luke loved shopping for food. In the evening she helped him cook, following his detailed instructions to produce an elaborate three course meal which she did her best to eat. After supper they went to the pub to meet some of his social worker mates. No more was said of Lola or her young Facebook friend.

The nausea came and went. On Monday she would book an appointment with the doctor. Later that evening she opened Facebook and checked Messenger. Jacob had sent another photo. She opened it on full screen and as she did so something jumped inside her. He was stretched out on the same old sofa, his eyelids slightly lowered, a half smile curling on his lips. His skin was very pale, almost as white as the bandage on his right arm. And this time she could see all of him. Natasha shivered with pleasure as she took in his young naked body.

She read his message. '*Now take your top off.*' And closed the page.

Chapter Twenty-one

Mel

'You need to tell me, Jacob.'

'You don't know what I need.'

She was standing in the doorway looking down at him sitting on his unmade bed. It was Saturday evening, two days since he had returned to the house with a wound and still he had not told her how it happened. Though he had let her examine the cut which had started to heal into a wide scab that looked like a narrow eye. It would scar. He should have had stitches.

'I'm going out,' he said.

'You can't go out now. You only got back a couple of hours ago. What's going on, Jacob?'

'Why?'

'It's almost eleven.'

'So?'

He was standing now, putting on a cotton jacket, running his fingers through his strange new haircut.

'Where are you going?'

'A party.'

'Whose party?'

'No one you know. Stop interrogating me.'

'Don't talk to me like that, Jacob.'

He swung past her and out of the door. The rest of the evening was a blur of too much red wine, unanswered phone calls to Claude and a smattering of old friends. She was a fool. A total fool.

Dawn streaked around the sitting-room curtains; shapes shifted before her eyes. Irritated with herself for drinking too much and crashing out in her clothes, she pulled herself up and tottered across the floor. Out in the corridor the lights were ablaze. The door of Jacob's room was ajar, his clothes strewn over the floor. Most of him was under the covers, only the mop of hair and half a leg sticking out over the duvet. She could hear him breathing. Thank God. He would have seen her on the sofa with the wine glass and empty bottle on the floor. She wondered what he thought about his mother's undistinguished behaviour. She returned to her own bed and slept.

Around eight a.m. she woke again and lay on her back in a fog of unfocused apprehension. Faces loomed, Jacob, Paul, Natasha. She felt for her phone. Headlines flashed across her screen saver. The news, as usual, was terrifying. She swiped to weather. Sun and showers. The light refracting through the blinds shivered like shot silk on the bedroom wall.

She was due for lunch with her mother and then to meet Natasha at four thirty. To her surprise, as she dried herself off after her shower, she found she was looking forward to both encounters. When the moment was right, she would confront Natasha, who would confess, crumple. Or would she? Nothing about the woman would surprise her.

As for Isabel, she had never been motherly in the conventional sense of protective or nurturing. On big issues such as Mel's choice of career, university or boyfriends, she had remained silent. Her targets were the little things. Advice was forthcoming on hairstyles, choice of dress, accessories and even, repeated several times, how to get in and out of the passenger seat of a sports car. As soon as Mel and Claude had bought the flat, there were curtain fabrics and furnishings to consider. On child rearing she had nothing to say, though she was always delighted to see Jacob.

Isabel had always been the most interesting person in her own world. Conversations were mostly one-sided, reminiscences of past theatrical glory, the days in provincial theatre before she landed the TV part that had supported her towards an unwilling retirement at sixty-seven. Mel let it wash over her. But recently she was finding a new pleasure in their Sunday afternoons in the quiet cul de sac. Earl Grey tea and a gentle monologue in her mother's beautifully modulated contralto, interspersed with desultory deliberations over lethal games of Scrabble or Rummicub.

She would have liked to take Jacob, but it would be a mistake to wake him now. Nor would she want him hanging around during tea with Natasha. She would let him sleep. At least he was safe at home.

She studied her reflection in the mirror by the front door. Not bad. The lines around her mouth were faint. Despite drinking most of the bottle of Merlot, the circles under her eyes were no worse than usual. She dabbed on a little more foundation and stuck a few extra clips in her hair. There never seemed to be time for a haircut. A touch of mascara and lipstick. Was it for Natasha's benefit? Or was the old fear of displeasing her mother still hard to shake off?

The doorbell rang. Mel felt a twinge of irritation. She opened the door and found herself face to face with two strangers.

'Is Jacob Villiers here?'

'He is. I'm his mother. Who wants him?'

The woman and the man both produced police identity cards. For a few moments Mel was on TV, standing in the middle of a police procedural, about to burst into tears. But this wasn't about the death of a loved one. Her loved one was lying in his bed in his room. This must be about something he had done, something wrong. All this spun through her mind as the floor dropped away and the walls began to sway. She put a hand to the doorjamb to steady herself and remained staring at them for what seemed like minutes but must have been seconds. The male officer spoke next. He sounded kind, concerned.

'We need to ask him a few questions. May we come in?'

'Of course,' she said, standing back, letting them through the narrow hall, pointing to the sitting room. Her throat seemed to be closing but she managed to blurt out.

'If you go in there, I'll get him up. He was a bit late last night.' And then she stopped and asked, 'What's it about?'

She heard the words and knew they were her own. But they didn't feel like her words. It was as if she were split in two and the real Mel had left her body and was looking down at the ghost of herself.

'A youth has been hurt.' The female officer was more assertive.

'What youth? How hurt?'

'We'd rather speak to your son, Mrs… er… Mrs…' replied the woman.

'Goddard,' said Mel.

'Of course you can be present, Mrs Goddard,' said the man.

She had known for days that something bad had occurred and though she had worried, she had not pushed him to explain. In truth she had feared to know.

'I'll get him up,' she said. As she entered his room she murmured, 'Jacob,' then leant over him and touched his shoulder. He stirred, opened his eyes, turned to look at her and away again, pulling the duvet over his head.

'It's the police,' she said. For a few seconds there was no movement. Then he threw back the duvet, said, 'OK,' and pulled himself up. He picked up a towel and disappeared out of the door. She heard the water running and went back to the sitting room where the officers were waiting.

'He's in the bathroom,' she told them. 'He won't be long.' She offered them coffee which they both declined.

'I'm DS Williams,' said the woman. 'And this is DC Ali.'

They stood in an awkward triangle, Williams staring at the opposite wall, Ali surveying the books and pictures with interest, smiling when he occasionally caught Mel's eye. Eventually, Jacob walked in, looking presentable in jeans and a dark shirt. He had combed his hair.

'Jacob Villiers,' said the woman officer, 'we are investigating an assault on Nikita Vasiliev. You're named in connection with the offence. We'd like you to come with us to the police station for questioning.'

Jacob looked at Mel. His face was white, and he mumbled, 'Sorry, Mum.' She swallowed. Everything inside her was dissolving; she was the shell of herself. He turned towards the door, standing straight, light shining on his glossy hair. She swallowed again. They would fight this together. She dug her nails into her palms to steady herself. She would stay calm for Jacob. She would stand by him, watch, listen. Jacob's reaction suggested there was no mistake. He was, in some way, involved. For a moment she thought about concealing her profession. Let them get careless, make a mistake. She would spot it and the whole ridiculous charade would be thrown out. She reminded herself: he hadn't been arrested. Possibly never would be. She needed to get a grip. She dug her nails in harder.

'Your mum can stay with you,' said Ali.

'I'd like to call a solicitor,' said Mel.

'Don't worry, Mrs Goddard. There's a duty solicitor at the station.'

'Thank you. But I'd prefer to call a couple of my own contacts. I'm a barrister,' she added. The woman looked unimpressed but nodded her agreement.

Mel tapped in a familiar number. Lauren was good with juveniles and would be able to send someone even if she couldn't make it herself. But there was no reply from the firm's emergency contact number and Lauren's personal phone went straight to voicemail. Mel scrolled through her work contacts. She couldn't represent him herself. Not even at a preliminary interview. Even if she had bothered to attend the police station representation course, it would have been impossible. Professionals needed detachment. Still, she wished she had done the course. She would have been better alert to procedural slip ups. She knew the *Police and Criminal Evidence Act*. She thought she knew the Codes of Practice. But they were changing all the time and at this moment she wished she knew them better.

Jacob stood in silence. The officers waited as she tried a couple more numbers, reached voicemails and asked the speakers to call her on her mobile. She was surprised at how difficult it was to find someone. Didn't solicitors want the work?

'Come on, Jacob,' said DS Williams, after the second call, 'your mum can make calls on our way to the station.' She laid her hand on Jacob's back and ushered him towards his own front door. Mel felt the fury rise in her and, before she could stop herself, shouted. 'How dare you! How dare you touch my son!'

'Easy, Mrs Goddard. No need to get worked up,' said Ali.

'Just don't touch him,' she barked. She might not be able to represent him, but she knew how to stand firm for him. Jacob did not turn. She thought she detected him tremble slightly. For a moment they were, each of them, immobile. Then Williams dropped her hand and Jacob led the way, walking out in front of the two officers. Mel grabbed her bag and followed them out of the flat and into the back of police car, double parked on the road outside. Ali took the driver's seat with Williams beside him. They surged into the heavy traffic. Jacob's pale hand lay on the seat beside her. It looked too big for him. He was staring straight ahead. She laid her own hand on his. It was tiny against his long, curved fingers.

'It'll be all right,' she whispered. 'Just look them straight in the eye.'

He didn't react. She could see a tiny twitch at the side of his face. She hadn't seen it for years. He had grown out of it when he was ten and had stopped biting his fingernails.

On arrival at the station Jacob was immediately arrested. According to Williams, the complainant had made a clear statement naming her son as the assailant. Mel asked about bail and was assured it would be granted, on conditions. While the custody sergeant was logging the arrest, they were told the duty solicitor was available and had agreed to hold a conference with

Jacob and attend the interview. Mel explained she was trying to contact a solicitor she knew and asked for time to make further enquiries. Her intervention seemed to wake something in Jacob. He gave her his penetrating look. The one which meant, 'Why are you the most embarrassing mother in the world?'

'Please, Mum. Let's just get on with it,' he said.

The duty solicitor was called Robert O'Hare. He was a weary-looking middle-aged man with a ruddy complexion, pin-prick eyes and a bulbous nose. There was nothing to suggest he would not be fine. Good looks were no indicator of expertise. Rather the contrary she had often found. The officers handed him an outline of the case. Mel asked to look at it and said she would join them for the conference.

'Better not,' said O'Hare. 'Legal professional privilege. We don't want police putting pressure on you to disclose what Jacob said.'

'They wouldn't succeed. I'm a barrister,' she replied.

'Excellent,' said O'Hare, screwing up his eyes so that they looked like tiny dashes scored into his face. 'That should keep them on their toes. Only what Jacob needs from you now is not knowledge of criminal law or police procedure. What he needs is a mother. Lucky chap. Lots of the kids I see here don't have that. I'll see him alone. What do you think, Jacob?'

'You better stay outside, Mum. It'd be easier, like, for me to talk.'

'Of course, darling, whatever feels right for you.'

The conference lasted half an hour. As Jacob came out the twitch was more pronounced. The police told her she was permitted to attend the interview as an appropriate adult. As if she didn't know that. She took a few deep breaths. She needed to bottle the anger, stay composed for Jacob.

The interview room was a bleak grey box lit with three strip lights. There were no windows. The two police officers sat on one side on the table, Jacob, O'Hare and herself on the other. Williams pressed something on a tablet in front of her and started to speak, introducing them all, explaining each person's name and function, giving the time, date, place and purpose of the interview, stating that they were being recorded, both visually and with sound, by a secured digital network. Mel noted the small shining ball, focused on Jacob, fixed to the ceiling by a short metal bracket. She thought about the network. How clever was it? Did it come complete with lie detection? What did it see, she wondered, as it logged Jacob's hard, clenched expression?

Then Williams said, 'Jacob Villiers, you do not have to say anything. But it may harm your defence if you do not mention, when questioned, something which you later rely on in court. Anything you say may be given in evidence.'

He was not being charged. Not yet. He might never be charged. He had been arrested for the offence of ABH. The caution was merely a preliminary to asking him a few questions. She had not heard the outline of facts that had been given to O'Hare, but she was able to piece things together from the questions he was asked.

'Jacob, can you tell us where you were on Thursday night?'

'Thursday,' he repeated. He was staring at the table, forgetting or perhaps disregarding Mel's whispered advice about eye contact. She knew he was hopeless about days of the week.

'Your last exam,' she prompted.

'Let him answer,' said Williams.

'You don't have to answer, Jacob,' said O'Hare. 'Remember what I told you when we were alone. If you are unsure or want time to reflect, simply say, "no comment". And if you want to talk to me privately or you want a break for any other reason just ask for it.'

'I was in a pub.'

'You're sixteen,' said Williams.

'Drinking Coke. Then a bunch of us went to a party.'

'What happened at the party?'

He paused and pulled up his sleeve. 'I got this.'

'The suspect is removing a bandage from his left forearm,' said Williams.

Jacob unwrapped the bandage and began to remove the lint sticking to the top of the wound.

'Careful,' said Mel, 'you don't want to pull off the scab.'

She started to help him, looking at Williams, who nodded. She removed the bandage to reveal the thick line of hard crust.

'The suspect is disclosing a wound. Short laceration, approximately four centimetres long. The suspect states that the wound is three days old. We'll take close-up photographs after the interview,' said Williams. 'Mrs Goddard, please rewind the bandage. Who did this, Jacob?'

'Some guy. Don't know his name.'

'Can you describe the guy? Age? Appearance? Ethnicity? Any distinguishing features?'

'About my age. Darkish. Not black. Long hair. That's about it.'

'Was there a fight?'

'No.'

'Did you attack this young man?'

'No.'

'Why did he slash you?'

''Cos of Nik.'

'Nikita Vasiliev?'

'Yeah. Nikita.'

'Where was this party?'

Jacob gave an address in Muswell Hill.

'Whose party was it?'

'Guy called Jimmy.'

'How do you know Jimmy?'

'I don't. Like, I didn't then. I just turned up. Nik said it'd be safe.'

'Safe?'

'Cool. OK.'

'Your solicitor has shown you the case statement. You've had time to consider what happened to Nikita, what he said, what his mother said. Did you hit him?'

'I didn't hit him. I pushed him,' said Jacob.

'Why?' asked Ali.

Jacob glanced around the room as if checking whether there might be someone else present who could tell his story.

'Go on,' said Williams.

'Take your time,' said Ali.

'You don't have to answer if you don't want to,' said O'Hare.

''Cos he was bullying them.'

'Them?'

'Don.'

'So, he was bullying Don. Another boy.'

'No. Don's gender neutral. Like, they were born a girl, Donna, only they don't identify as a girl.'

Mel had never heard of Don. She thought the police might be flummoxed but they seemed to have no problem with the idea.

'Go on, Jacob.'

He was staring at the table. His words came in spurts like water from a broken tap. Mel wished she had pressed him earlier. He would have told her. They could have prepared things. Spoken to Nikita's mum, Yelena. Sorted this out privately.

'He's had a few drinks. And he's on at them about their...' he stopped, seeking the right word, '...breasts. You know.' He didn't look up. If the subject matter had been different, she would have reminded him again to look at the person he was speaking to. But what did it matter? The secure digital system was taking in every word and glance.

His audience waited. He continued. 'So Don's not had the op. Like, they're about my age. So, like maybe it's too early. So, Nik says let's see your tits.'

133

'For the purpose of this interview it would be helpful if you referred to Don as she or he. Whichever is most appropriate,' said Williams.

'They won't like that.'

'It would be helpful to you. To everyone. The evidence could become unclear,' she added.

'The police are right,' said O'Hare 'You don't have to answer the questions. But if you do, your answer needs to be easily understood. Of course, you must answer in your own words.'

'They don't mind being ze or zir.'

Williams said, 'That would be clearer. Please continue, Jacob.'

'So Don says no. And Nik's going on about how it's the last chance and he can't bear to say goodbye and he rushes zir like he's going to pull off zir shirt. His mates, they're standing round the door. I grab Don's arm and I'm pulling zir out. Just to get them out of there. And Nik's in the way and I tell him to get out the way only he doesn't, so I give him a shove and he falls back, like, and hits his head. Then this jerk pulls a knife and cuts my arm.'

'Did anyone hit you first?' asked Williams.

'I didn't hit anyone.'

'Describe what you did.'

'I pushed him. He was in the way. In the doorway. Don was trying to get out. We were both trying to get out.'

'Nikita says you hit him,' said Williams.

'He would, wouldn't he?' said Jacob.

'Why would he?' asked Williams.

''Cos he doesn't like me.'

'He invited you to the party,' Ali reminded him.

'Yeah. That was before. Only now I'm standing up to him. Standing up for Don. He doesn't like that.'

'Tell us how you pushed him,' said Ali.

Jacob stood up. 'Want me to show you?'

'If you could just explain, Jacob,' said Williams. 'Please sit down. This is being recorded.'

He sat down again and began to explain, looking up now, gesturing with his arms. He was telling a story. He used to love to tell stories. He and his cousins staged performances with glove puppets in the sitting room, violent Manichean fables of good and evil featuring noble youths, feisty super heroines and dangerous monsters. 'Right... so, like, a hand on his shoulder. Not hard. Like a push 'cos he wouldn't get out of the way. He sort of wobbled over. Fell back. I guess he was drunk.'

'He says he hit the back of his head against a cupboard,' said Williams.

'Yeah. Maybe,' said Jacob.

'Well, did he? You were there. You must have seen.' Williams skewered him with her sharp eyes.

'Remember, Jacob, you don't have to answer every question,' prompted O'Hare.

'If you're not sure, just say you're not sure,' added Mel.

'It was sort of confusing. There were loads of people in the room. The light was dim. I think there was candles and stuff. I just know I pushed him to get him out of the way.'

'Do you remember what you'd had to drink?'

'Two or three beers. Not much,' said Jacob, facing his accusers.

'Go on.'

'One of his mates pulls a knife. Like, I see it gleaming.' He turned to Mel. She remembered her own fear on the ground near the railway line. His fear felt worse. More than anything in the world she wanted him safe. To hold him tight in this horrible room. She wanted everyone else to disappear, to erase this toxic hour like chalk from a blackboard. 'And, like, I don't have a knife so I'm just standing there, and I tell him to put it away only he has a go and I move, and it cuts me. Mum saw it. You seen it.'

'Who cut you, Jacob?'

'Dunno. Don't know his name.'

'And who else was there?'

'Don't know their names. Only know Nik and Don.'

'And Don. Where does she… ze live?'

'Dunno.'

'Are you sure you don't know? She might be able to help, corroborate what you say.'

'I said I don't know. Anyway, ze might not want to.'

'Because it's not true?'

'Because ze might not want to talk to you. People don't. I didn't. You arrested me.'

'Because you hit Nik?'

'I told you I didn't hit him.'

'Isn't the truth of it that you were angry with Nik for harassing this girl? You fancied her yourself, didn't you?'

'That's crap.'

'It's what Nik says.'

'Fuck what he says.'

'Isn't the truth that you fancied this girl and you had a go at Nik? You hit him, and he fell back and hurt himself, hurt himself badly. Because of you.'

Mel's heart was surging in her chest. She thought she would explode. She caught O'Hare's eye. He was shaking his head, indicating to her to stay calm. She had never attended a police station interview though she had read enough transcripts. She couldn't remember every detail of the Code on questioning suspects, but she could remember the prohibition on questions that were oppressive.

'Don't speak to him like that,' she said.

'Mrs Goddard, if you could just allow us to continue,' said Williams. 'The sooner he answers, the sooner this will all be over.'

'This is not an interview; this is an inquisition. My son has been slashed with a knife. Wounded while defending a friend. Are you going to make any effort to find the real criminal?'

'Mrs Goddard, you are not helping Jacob.'

The words were like a lance in her heart. How dare Williams say she was not helping Jacob? Every word, every breath, every action of her life was done to help Jacob. She stood up.

'Mrs Goddard, if you wish to remain present at the interview you will confine your comments to support and advice. Please sit down.'

Mel remained standing. She would not let this woman bully her son. She would not be bullied herself. In her low, calm voice, the one she used in negotiation with difficult opponents, she began to explain.

'This is support and advice. You asked two identical leading questions. My son has made it clear that he did not hit this boy. He has answered all your questions. It's time to stop.'

'She has a point,' said O'Hare. And Mel couldn't help wondering why he hadn't intervened himself.

Williams looked at her with a supercilious smile. She appeared to be contemplating her reply. And though the rage had passed, Mel thought she would like to strangle her. No, she must not go mad. She continued to speak.

'The manner of questioning is oppressive,' she paused a moment and added, 'contrary to Code C.' She couldn't remember whether it was A, B, C, or D. Or possibly F. But it did the trick. Williams looked confused. A bleeper sounded, and Williams put on headphones. Someone must be speaking to her. Mel sat down.

'Are you all right, Jacob?' asked O'Hare, as if it were Mel who had caused the problem.

Jacob nodded. Williams took off the headphones and said, 'I am ending this interview now. The time is 11:56 a.m. Jacob, you will be subject to police bail. The conditions are that you are to live at home and you are not to contact or attempt to contact any prosecution witnesses. That includes Nikita Vasiliev, Donna Seymour and anyone else who was present at the party at Jimmy's that night.'

Mel felt her body slacken with relief. She heard the solicitor's voice. He was saying something to Jacob. The bail conditions were written out and he was taken to have his wound photographed. Afterwards, accompanied by Mel, he was shown mugshots of young men to see if he could recognise his attacker. He couldn't. The boy had come up beside him, the light was dim, and he had seen him for only a fraction of a second. The police didn't seem too troubled about finding the culprit. Mel was enraged. Jacob had been seriously injured. He was lucky it had not been worse. The attacker could have severed an artery. Jacob could have died. The evidence was in front of them. Yet the police treated him as if were the guilty one. She felt sick with fury. At worst he had pushed a boy who was bullying a girl, a young person, standing in his way. He had defended someone vulnerable. He had suffered a serious wound. Surely, they wouldn't charge him? They had twenty-eight days to decide.

She declined the offer of a lift home in the police car. They took the bus. She tried to reassure him.

'It'll be all right. They'll drop it. What did the solicitor say?'

'Not much. He didn't say they'd drop it.'

'Was Nik a friend of the guy with the knife?'

'Dunno. I don't wanna talk about it.'

The bus edged through traffic. It was Sunday, yet the streets were packed. Rumbling buses, cars packed with families and luggage boxes trundling off on their holidays. She had forgotten about holidays. It was years since she'd had one. Claude had been planning to take Jacob away. Now he wouldn't be allowed to go. Not unless they dropped the investigation.

Eventually they reached the stop near the bridge where the boy had jumped her. Something turned inside her as she looked at the place. They still hadn't found GJ. A different police station. Different officers. Initially they had seemed sympathetic. Occasionally they asked her to come in and look at another picture. But they hadn't contacted her for a couple of weeks and last time she spoke to the case officer he seemed uninterested, harassed by other duties. Not like the pair who had picked up Jacob.

Williams would pursue it; Mel was sure. She would try to get him on ABH. Jacob was there, he wouldn't run away. Nikita had named him. They'd pick on the easy one. That way there'd be a tick in the box. Crime solved. Never mind the boy who slashed him. A kid in the shadows who got away with it. Like GJ.

It was a warm bright day; the sky was a clear cobalt blue behind the huge trees. They walked past the corner shop.

'You hungry?' she asked.

'Yeah.'

They stopped and bought croissants, eggs and bacon. Back in the flat she cooked. Jacob gobbled it down.

'You were brilliant,' she said.

'I told the truth. You were a bit extreme.'

'I'm sorry. Did I embarrass you? It won't make any difference. They're not going to charge you just because your mother is a maniac.'

'Guess not.'

She asked, 'Where were you last night? You were really late.'

'I was round Don's.'

'You said you didn't know where she lived.'

'I don't want them hassling. Don's cool.'

'So, it wasn't a party.'

'We play games.'

'What sort of games?'

'Mum…'

'OK, none of my business.'

'Computer games. Board games. Ze's a geek.'

Board games. Sunday afternoon at her mother's. She was due there in less than an hour, but how could she leave Jacob now? While he was finishing his croissant, she dialled her mother's number.

'Where are you, darling? I was expecting you at twelve.'

'I thought it was one.'

'Never mind. So, are you on your way? It's a simple meal. Sardines on toast and a fruit salad.'

'Mum, I'm really sorry. Jacob's not been well. I should have rung.'

'What is the matter with him? Should I be worried?'

'I'll explain. It'll have to be a bit later. I'm meeting someone at the Picture Gallery at four thirty. So maybe sometime after six.'

'There's *Countryfile* and *Fake or Fortune*.'

'We can watch them together.'

'Just go,' muttered Jacob.

'May I call you back, Mum?'

'As you wish.'

Isabel's words were like tiny darts. Mel hung up.

'Mum, will I have a criminal record?'

'Not if they don't charge you. And even if they charge you, well, only if you plead or...' She couldn't get the words out. 'We'll take it one stage at a time.'

'That solicitor didn't say much.'

'He won't know what the police are planning. Anyway he seemed OK; he's got a note of everything. You were good, darling. I'm proud of you.' She threw her arms around him, felt him tense and pull back. He would allow her to hug him, but he would no longer respond. For months he had been like this, throwing up an invisible wall between them. He used to kiss her, even cuddle her. Other parents said it would pass and he would become affectionate again. But everything was happening so fast. What about Don? Was she his girlfriend, his... whatever the word should be?

She said, 'I'm supposed to meet this woman about work. Though I could cancel.'

'Don't cancel her for me. I'll be fine, Mum.'

He looked up at her and his beautiful eyes were alive again, shining, and the last two horrible hours had been a big mistake, and all would be well. She wanted to grasp him and pull him close, but she wouldn't, she would stand back and wait.

'Come with me,' she said.

'Not if you've got a work thing.' His face was face tense with the effort of holding back the tears.

'It'll be fine. She's my pupil. You can just drift around the gallery when we're talking.'

'I'd rather stay here.' He gulped, as if trying to force back whatever was surging inside him. His throat quivered. She noticed for the first time, the hint of an Adam's apple, sign of manhood, symbol of man's fall. He was swallowing again, battling against collapse, a hundred Jacobs warring with each other, the frightened, the angry, the child, the man... She desperately wanted to hug him, to protect him from everything, from the whole world, from himself. But she could not live for him.

'I'm not leaving you alone, Jacob,' she said. 'Not today.'

Chapter Twenty-two

Natasha

Everything was back to normal. Luke wanted to take her for a long bike ride through Epping Forest, but she reminded him she was meeting her supervisor for tea.

'What's she ever done for you?'

'Yeah, well maybe she wants to make amends. Anyway, I'll need a reference for the CPS.'

'When do you think you'll be back?' he asked.

'Not late. Around six. The gallery shuts at five.'

'I'll make a nice supper for you. We'll stay in. Watch a movie.'

'I'd like that.'

She kissed him. He was onside again and she could breathe.

And now the scruffy fringes of Brixton had been left behind and the bus was trundling up Herne Hill. Both the sky and the prospect brightened. The 1930s houses were freshly painted and set back from the road. Natasha felt a smile creep up her face as they swept over the crest of the leafy hill and down towards Dulwich with its cafes and arty shops, tiny fingerposts on every junction. This was where she should be. Mel might have prevented her getting the chambers tenancy she deserved, but she'd get the next best thing, a proper job with the CPS. It might be less exciting, less prestigious than working as a defence barrister, but it made sense. Regular hours, holiday pay, security. She thought about the sickness that had troubled her for the past four days. She was still unsure what she would do. But, if she did decide to keep it, there'd be maternity pay.

It was foolish to discount it as an option. And the thought of prosecuting villains was appealing in a different way. It would turn her life around. She'd satisfied all the criteria so far. She just needed the reference. If Mel was tricky, Natasha would mention Paul. Just a nudge. An unspoken agreement. You help me. I help you. Simple as that. Mel wouldn't want the world knowing her dirty little secret.

It was a beautiful sunny day and a relief to get out of the flat, away from Luke's relentless attention. How would he be if she was pregnant? Well, she would deal with that if it happened. She would take the test and there was still the option of termination. And if she did have the baby she could go straight back to work. Luke could be a house husband. He'd like that.

It was after four when the bus drew to a halt outside the gallery. Natasha walked quickly down the path towards the cafe. Jumping the queue outside she put her head round the door. No sign of Mel.

'Try the pavilion,' said the waitress, pointing across the grass to a wooden and glass structure where the overspill of customers was seated. Natasha scanned the tables for a woman alone. There weren't any. Everyone was in a group or pair. Mel must be late. It was irritating, though not surprising. Natasha headed for one of the empty tables.

Then, just as she was about to sit down, she saw her. Mel was seated only a few yards away, facing Natasha, though her focus was elsewhere. She had made no effort to look presentable for the meeting. Her hair was wild and unkempt and her face pale and devoid of make-up, but for traces of smudged mascara below the lower rim of her eyes. And far from looking about for her expected companion, she was deeply engaged in conversation with the young man sitting opposite her. He had his back to Natasha, but she was close enough to take in the set of his neck and shoulders, the drape of his loose blue T-shirt, the thick chestnut hair, long on top and shaved at the side. He sat very still and her eyes traced the shape of his upright back, his head, his arms. Her throat felt dry, her heart was speeding. Even before he turned his head and she could see his profile, she had no doubt it was him. When he did, she found she was unprepared for his astonishing beauty. Acting came naturally to her, but this was taking it to another level. She breathed deeply and took a step forward.

'Mel?'

Mel looked up.

'Natasha!' She sounded surprised.

'I thought you were expecting me.' Natasha grinned, avoiding Jacob's eyes.

'Of course. Forgive me. My son and I were chatting. Jacob, this is Natasha.'

'Hi, Natasha,'

He turned his face towards her, pronouncing her name slowly, as if to convince himself of the truth of what he saw. And despite the strangeness of his delivery, which might have been enough to alert a more vigilant mother, Natasha was relieved to hear her name. She had feared he might say Lola. His eyes were wide with shock. She was ten years older than the most recent Lola picture, her hair was styled differently, her eyes today were green not blue, and though she was slim, her figure was fuller than that of her slender teenage self. But he knew. And he looked quickly away.

He shifted in his chair, looking as if he was about to stand up. Old-fashioned manners? But no, his shoulders gave a little jerk and he remained seated. She sat down between them.

'Sorry I'm late. My bus was stuck in traffic.'

'Don't worry. It was a good opportunity for Jacob and me to have a heart to heart. He doesn't often come out with his old mum. We're going to meet his granny later. She lives nearby.' Mel appeared not to notice anything unusual about the way her son was looking at Natasha. 'Jacob darling, why don't you get us all coffee and cake?'

Jacob glanced from his mother to Natasha. And for a moment she feared he might say something, blurt an embarrassing question, even tell her he recognised her. But his expression softened, a half-smile dissolved the tension in his features, and he said, 'OK.'

And then she realised that though in many ways he was still a child, he too was an actor. All would be well. He was looking directly at her now and she returned his gaze, studying his long straight nose, arched brows and perfect full lips. The reality was so much better than the photos. Then she remembered what he reminded her of. A painting. Last time she'd been here it was hanging near the gallery entrance, a full-sized portrait of John the Baptist. Only his hair was different. No long Renaissance curls but a sharp contemporary geometry.

Mel had placed a £20 note on the table and her son stood up slowly, lazily, as if being dragged from a bed. As he reached for the note Natasha noticed the bandage on his right arm. She'd already seen it in the selfie.

'What happened?' she asked.

'Accident,' he replied, staring at the table. He didn't elaborate, and she didn't ask more. She would find out later.

'Can you manage alone, darling?' asked Mel.

'Sure.'

'I'll help,' offered Natasha.

'It's fine.'

Another quicksilver change. He reminded her of her teenage self. Yet so much gentler, so much more vulnerable.

'Please. It makes sense for both of us to go. If you don't mind being left alone, Mel?'

'Not at all.' She pulled a paperback out of her bag. 'See you in a bit. No rush.'

It was all going well. There was no way Mel had been snooping into her son's private online world.

They set off, Jacob striding ahead, eyes intent on the path. Natasha had to walk fast to keep up with him, conscious of his long-limbed youthful body beside her. As a teenager, boys of her own age had held no attraction for her. She had been uninterested in anyone under twenty. But the challenge of Jacob's shifting moods intrigued her. It had started as a spot of internet flirting, but as she stood next to him in the queue, the space between them heavy with unspoken words, she found herself wondering where this might lead.

She said, 'Let's go and look at the pictures.'

'We said we'd get coffee.'

'We'll come back for that. There's something I need to show you.'

She held his gaze. His eyes were soft and dark like the painting, but after a few seconds, he blinked and looked away. It was hard to read him. He was holding something back. He was embarrassed, of course. But was he also excited? It was a warm day. She was wearing a sleeveless light green dress and the small implant was visible just below her left shoulder. She no longer worried about covering it up. It was not unattractive, and it marked her out, like a discreet tattoo. Luke liked to stroke it when they made love. The loose pockets at hip level gave access to her pump if necessary, but the bodice was closely fitted and cut low. Jacob's troubled eyes avoided her breasts. In a recent message, he'd asked her to take her top off. Is that what he was thinking now?

'Come on,' she said, a light touch on his left arm. Without waiting for him she turned, setting off down the path towards the gallery, trusting he would follow. He did. But just before the wide portico that framed the entrance he took a long step forward and swivelled round to face her, blocking her path.

'What's going on?' he snapped, his lovely face contorted with anger.

Behind them, visitors were bunched up, eager to get into the gallery. Natasha took a step to one side to get past Jacob, but he stretched out a hand to prevent her, so she stood back to let the group pass. An older woman with a kind face and cropped grey hair glanced back in sympathy. But no one said anything. Jacob looked old for his years, Natasha young. They would appear to be a normal couple in difficulty. Why would anyone interfere?

The path emptied and Natasha turned back to Jacob. His face was different, no more soft edges but a series of hard planes. The intensity of his dark eyes reminded her of Mel.

'Jacob…' She reached for his arm, but he shook her off.

'Why are you doing this?' he demanded. 'Stalking me on the net. Taking me to see pictures. What's it about?'

Natasha could usually read people. Naturally, Jacob would be apprehensive given their previous exchange, possibly regretful at sending her the pictures. But she was taken aback by the force of his reaction. He was taller than she was, standing motionless, inches away, close enough for her to smell the toothpaste on his breath. It was a warm, still day, tiny puffs of white cloud floating on an azure sky. The park was busy, families spread out for picnics on the grass, children skittering about with footballs and frisbees. But they were indistinct figures against a blurred backdrop. Her focus was this boy.

Why hadn't she foreseen this degree of burning outrage? He seemed to have grown several inches and his voice came out rough and urgent.

'So what's it about?' he repeated.

'Keep your voice down,' she murmured. More people were approaching. 'I'm happy to talk but we should move away.' And she headed across the grass towards a spreading lime tree. He followed. When he reached the tree, he stood very close to her, hands in his pockets, breathing hard.

'Well?' he demanded.

'Must you be so confrontational?'

She threw out the tender smile most men found irresistible but which Jacob, it seemed, was able to resist.

'You haven't answered my question.'

'I had no idea she would bring you.'

'You knew who I was when you contacted me?'

'Yes.'

His face which when she first saw him had been very pale had taken on colour and now he was speaking very fast. People continued to pass them on their way to and from the gallery.

'You stalked me. You pretended to be someone called Lola.'

'Please keep your voice down, Jacob,' she said.

'Oh, people might hear. You'd rather they didn't know what you've been up to. I get that.'

She touched his arm. He stared at her hand but did not move away or try to shake her off. 'I saw a picture of you,' she said in a soft voice. 'I thought it would be fun to be Facebook friends. One thing led to another. I think if you reread the whole conversation you'll see who was leading whom.'

'What about those pictures?'

This was uncomfortable. A standing interrogation. He was inches away and there was no yielding, only uncompromising hostility. There was an empty bench nearby. She'd rather they were both seated than have him stand over her like this.

'Let's sit down.' She walked to the bench and sat. He followed but remained standing.

'OK so the Lola pictures were a few years old. I thought it might put you off if you suspected I was nearly thirty. Everyone does it. You know that.'

'Cheats do it. Liars do it.'

His face was screwed up now and she wondered what was coming next. There was an earnest moralism in the outburst that she would never have anticipated from his flirty online manner. He was an innocent. And as an innocent he was shocked at having been exposed, even to himself. Though she hadn't forgotten his other persona, the one that sat with a slip of towel around his loins like some seductive young god. Then that final one, the one without the towel. The seductive god was still there, albeit buried under the guilt and high principles. There was a battle going on. He could walk away but he didn't.

'That's a bit of an exaggeration,' she said, seeking to lighten the tone.

'You made me send you stuff.'

'I didn't make you do anything.'

'What about the photos of me?'

'What about them?'

'Where's your phone? I need to see you delete them. And the chat. All of it.'

'Oh Jacob, you don't think I would do that. I love those photos. Like I said, you look beautiful. Anyway, they're copied on my computer. They're sitting on a cloud now. No way they'll disappear.'

And suddenly he was grabbing her, shaking her.

'Take your hands off me.'

He lessened his grip, but he didn't let go. 'You knew who I was. You looked for me. Deliberately. What the fuck were you doing? What are you doing now?' His eyes were flaming with rage, even as they were pink with tears. 'Anyway, I don't believe you. Where's your phone? In here?'

Her cream leather bag was lying on the seat next to her and he leant forward to pick it up. Furious, she snatched it back.

'Are you crazy? If you touch me or any of my property again, I'll get someone to call the police. Is that what you want?'

At the word 'police' he retreated into himself. For a moment he was quiet. But he wasn't giving up. She could see him take a breath to calm himself as, in a low voice, he said, 'I want to see you delete them.'

A middle-aged couple was walking by across the grass as he spoke.

'Like I said, I've already saved them.'

The couple had stopped now, a man and a woman, and they were standing in front of them. Jacob neither moved nor spoke, but it would have been impossible to miss the fury behind his frozen features.

'Is this young man bothering you?' the woman asked Natasha as the man stood by.

'No, it's fine,' said Natasha mildly. 'We were having a silly argument. I'm sorry if we troubled you.'

But as soon as the couple had moved on the mildness fell away. She struggled to get up off the bench, but Jacob's hand on her arm prevented her, holding her down.

'Let me go,' she said.

'Give me your phone.'

There was a new cold determination in him, and she did not like it. She would not let him bully her. She had shocked him, angered him, teased him. Until now she had not deliberately tried to hurt him. But his attempt to control her touched a nerve and she lashed out.

'You wouldn't want your mum to see those photos, would you?'

He didn't reply but he looked at her with such hatred that she wondered if despite the passers-by, despite the threat of police, he might in fact hurt her. Did he have a knife? Friends with knives?

'Anyway, your mum's got secrets of her own,' she added.

'What secrets?' he stammered, grabbing her arm. There was a tiny twitch at the corner of his mouth.

'I'll tell you if you take your hand away.' His hand dropped. 'You know, the usual sort of secrets, sexual secrets.' She could have stopped there but he was standing very still, waiting for her to continue.

'There's this bloke,' she began. His eyes were locked on hers in furious hostility. The look was familiar. She had seen it before on men she had toyed with. Though never in a boy. It was both horrible and strangely thrilling, a sharp goad, and she couldn't stop.

'Don't you want to know? About your mum's bloke?'

At that he started to back away as if her presence was a disease he needed to avoid on pain of death. When he spoke, it was in a whisper.

'You're evil. Pure evil.'

The words were savage. A snake spitting venom. And they would not go unanswered.

'His name's Paul,' she responded lightly. And with that she stood up, turned away from him and set off for the gallery.

Of course, he wouldn't follow. When she glanced back, he was running off across the grass, not towards his mother, who could shelter him no longer, but to the main park gate and the great, terrible, adult world.

—

She looked at her watch. They had been away almost twenty minutes. Mel would be worried, annoyed. But Natasha was too unsettled to go back to the cafe immediately. She would give herself five minutes in the gallery.

People were making their way out and she squeezed past them, heading for the painting of St John the Baptist. She knew exactly where it was and for a few minutes she stood in front of it, letting the turmoil of the meeting with Jacob subside. She marvelled at the likeness. Even the pose, the outstretched right arm, was a dead ringer for Jacob's half-clothed selfie. And though the sweetness of the face before her was a taunt after the ugliness of Jacob's distress, its seductiveness called out to her. This was how it should have been. But Jacob had run away in anger and distress while this painted boy stood radiant, untouchable. And for the first time she understood why people needed to destroy works of art. How satisfying it would have been to pick up a razor blade and slice the precious canvas from top to the bottom.

She turned away. She had thought the lovely John the Baptist would relax her, but her heart was pounding, and she was weak and dizzy. But it wasn't just Jacob; it wasn't just the painting. She needed sugar.

She walked quickly out of the gallery to the cafe. They were about to close, but she explained she was diabetic and needed food and they agreed to serve her two coffees and a cake. While waiting, she pulled out a cereal bar. Stupid. She had been so preoccupied with her pretty boy, she had forgotten about her blood glucose level. Familiar black dots were already crossing her vision. She swallowed a chunk and waited as her body settled.

The waitress returned with her order and Natasha reached into her bag for the money. Bloody Jacob had gone off with the £20 note. She paid with her own money, and, with renewed strength, set off towards the pavilion with the tray.

Everything would be OK. The kid was mortified by his behaviour. There was no way he would say anything to his mother. It would all die down. As if it had never happened.

Chapter Twenty-three

Mel

Where were they? Mel glanced at her watch. Twenty minutes to buy a coffee was ridiculous. She reverted to her paperback, abandoning it in seconds and calling Jacob for the second time. He wasn't picking up. Perhaps he couldn't hear the ringtone in the clatter of the cafe.

She raised her face to the sky, and for one unthinking moment enjoyed the unfamiliar warmth on her skin. How little time she spent out of doors. Exercise was a quick trip to the gym or the swimming pool. When Jacob was small she used to take him to parks, playgrounds. But you didn't take a sixteen-year-old to a park. Today was different. He was in trouble and had come with her willingly enough. She suspected he didn't want to be home alone. As for Natasha, Mel would talk shop for a bit, get some material for the reference and her supervisor report, and then set off for her mother's. She would have done her duty.

As she sketched out the rest of the afternoon in her mind, her eyes followed the movements of the children playing on the deck of the outdoor cafe, a temporary glass and wood structure that reflected the old brick of the main gallery. Two little girls aged about eight and ten, dark-skinned and with braids pinned around their heads, were teaching an infant to walk, swinging him forwards and backwards. A man was tending to an older boy in a wheelchair, feeding him chunks of cake. On the other side of the table a mother scooped a tiny bundle out of a pram, pulled up her T-shirt and started to breastfeed. Mel watched the lives of these gentle strangers, feeling a stab of loss for the big family she might have had, would have had, if Claude had stayed.

She called Jacob again. Still no answer. Then, just as she was wondering whether to set off to find them, Natasha approached with a tray.

'What happened?' asked Mel. 'You've been ages. Where's Jacob?'

'We've been a bit naughty. The queue at the cafe was so long, we bunked off into the gallery. I wanted to show Jacob my favourite painting. You must know it. The Guido Reni of St John? Spitting image of your son. Anyway, when we set off for the cafe, Jacob told me he needed to get home. Next minute he's stomping off across the grass.'

'Shit.'

Natasha looked surprised by the vehemence of her reaction. 'Said he had a headache and didn't want to be in the way if we were talking shop. Does he normally disappear like this?'

'Not since he was six years old. And he didn't say anything? I mean you've no idea why he went? Did you ask about his arm? He's sensitive about that.'

'No to all those. He said he'd go and see his granny some other time.'

Natasha's airy casualness grated, but what could Mel do? If she returned to the flat, her own mother would be upset. And Jacob might not even be at home. He hated Mel following him, 'tracking' him as he called it. Though given what had happened this morning she had good reason to keep an eye on him. And this sudden disappearance was plain rude. He hadn't even taken the trouble to text. What was it about Natasha? She always seemed to be around when things went wrong, when Mel was in the midst of some crisis.

She reached for her cappuccino, kicking herself for inviting Natasha in the first place. There were a few questions she needed to ask for the reference, but she could easily have dealt with them over the phone. Why had she been so stupid? And now she couldn't think of a word to say to her pupil who sat staring at her with her fake green eyes, their unreal tint glinting in the sunlight. Her pale skin looked like porcelain. Nothing about her seemed real.

Natasha's pupillage would be over in three months. If she stayed at Bridge Court after that she'd be a squatter. Squatters were hard to get rid of. Mel would write a bland reference and get shot of her. She was about to mention the reference when Natasha spoke.

'So you're off to see your mother?'

Why did everything Natasha say feel like it had a double meaning. Was it the voice? The half-smile? The private smirk beneath the breezy surface?

'Yes. I won't linger. Mum will be anxious. She's a worrier.'

'Jess told me she was a famous actress.'

'Not that famous. Unless you're into soaps.'

'Oh, I love soaps. Which one?'

'You won't have seen it. It finished years ago. Canada Row.'

'Canada Row! It was my total favourite when I was a kid. Who did she play?'

'Darcy Black.'

'Darcy Black! Awesome. She was huge.'

The ardour sounded genuine. Darcy Black the powerful, elegant businesswoman whose stilettos strutted through Mel's solitary childhood, who paid for her private school and, Isabel liked to remind her, her Cambridge education, had won the jagged heart of her volatile pupil. The Natasha she was looking at across the table was, for the first time that day, 100 per cent authentic.

'Yeah, she was a big deal for a while. Then they killed her. She never got over it.'

'How awful.'

'Well, that's showbiz. Nothing lasts. But I didn't come here to talk about my mother. There are a few things I need for your reference. I know you've been busy. But I thought if you could give me the names of some of the judges you've been in front of, I could have a word with them about your advocacy. I haven't seen that much of you recently.'

She felt like adding 'and make it snappy'. If Natasha chose to disappear with her son for half an hour it was her decision and Mel wasn't going to hang about for her. Then, for the first time, it crossed her mind that Jacob's disappearance might have something to do with Natasha. Though that was ridiculous. They didn't even know each other. Natasha mentioned a few names. Mel tapped them into her phone, asking casually, 'And out of interest, who's your academic referee?'

'From my crap uni? Waste of time.'

'North Bank? Was it that bad?'

'Not posh enough for the Bar. Not "Oxbridge".' Natasha's voice rose in mock gentility and her fingers mimed quotation marks in the air. Mel was conscious of other people listening, the nice family staring from the next table. But Natasha was not about to stop. It was as if she wanted the whole park to hear.

'I think you know one of the lecturers there. Paul Freedman?'

A cold blast ran through Mel at the mention of Paul's name. How much did Natasha know? Had she read all the emails? Or had she just noticed the name, read a single message and then realised the correspondence was confidential. Any normal person might do as much. And it was quite possible that Mel had left the page open.

'He's an old friend,' she said, unwilling to give away too much information.

'A bit more than that I think.' Natasha's eyes gleamed in excitement. The expression on her face was almost a leer.

'What are you saying?'

'You told me all about him in Daly's. Remember? We went for a drink a couple of months ago. I mean I know he's married and everything, but he's kind of attractive. I don't blame you.'

Mel stared at Natasha who was suddenly as ugly as she was beautiful, hard and cold in her skimpy dress with her manicured fingernails and perfectly streaked hair. She wanted to put her hands around that slender neck and squeeze. Then, with equal intensity, she wanted a cigarette. But she had given up smoking sixteen years ago.

'I've no idea what you're talking about.' She heard her mother's voice in her own, arch, dismissive, false. But it was not a complete lie. She had no memory of any such conversation.

'You must have forgotten. We were at one of the inside tables. You asked where I'd done my law degree and I told you I'd been to North Bank. Then you asked if I knew him. You obviously wanted to talk about him.'

'You're mistaken.'

Could she have said something? She'd probably had a few glasses of wine that evening. Her memory might be hazy.

'I mean I know what it's like when you're keen on somebody. You just want to talk about them all the time.'

'I can't believe I ever spoke to you about Paul.'

Natasha smirked. 'You told me you were shagging him.'

It was as if someone had whacked Mel's chest from the inside with a mallet. She leapt up and grabbed her bag.

'Impossible. I would never use that word.'

Her heart was thumping. Thoughts swirled. Why had she come? She should have gone straight to her mother's. And why had Jacob run off? What if something bad had happened to him? But that was ridiculous. Why should something bad happen to him in a London park on a Sunday afternoon? It was not as if he was in a gang. Or was he? She was spiralling. She took a deep breath and looked back at Natasha whose expression was simultaneously sympathetic and opaque.

'Oh, Mel, you look upset. Listen, it's cool. I don't remember what expression you used – bonking, making out, getting laid, having an affair. I'm not going to judge you. Your bloke pissed off. Why shouldn't you have fun too? It's your business.'

'Please keep your voice down, Natasha.' The sudden assumption of intimacy was unbearable, like having your flesh rubbed down a cheese grater.

Mel's words had no effect. Natasha, usually so controlled and calm, was energised. 'I won't mention it to anyone. I mean, you've done nothing wrong. Not really. You're not the married one.'

The word 'married' bounced off the walls of the pavilion. Only the consciousness of spectators and some deep-seated habit of good conduct prevented Mel throwing the other woman off her chair onto the wooden deck. Her chest was thrumming. She stood, waiting for the sensation to pass. A small cloud drifted across the afternoon sun and was reflected in the mirror beside them. Voices were hushed, people staring.

'Please, sit down, Mel.'

Something in the cool clarity of the instruction cut through Mel's agitation and she sat. The drama was over, the audience members returned to their tea, cake and families, drifting back into conversation. Natasha cut a slice of cake and offered it. Mel shook her head. She couldn't speak. The nice family was packing up to go. Through the fog of her rage against Natasha, she felt a stab of loss at the realisation she would never see them again.

Natasha reached her hand across the table as if to apologise. But what she said was far from an apology. 'Listen, how about you write me a nice reference and...' She paused.

'And what?'

'And I don't say a word.'

At that moment the sun caught the side of Natasha's face and her eyes shone, twin diamonds of light against the startling green of her irises. Her hand was still stretched towards Mel's which was gripping the edge of the table. And for the first time it crossed Mel's mind that her pupil might not just be a troublemaker, not just unfeeling, but a little mad. Mel pulled her hand away as if that madness might be contagious. 'Don't touch me.'

'Cross my heart and hope to die,' said Natasha.

'Are you serious?'

'And if you take me to meet your mum, I'll be your friend forever.'

Natasha was smiling now as if she really believed her words might have influence. Mel jumped up. It was time to be 100 per cent clear.

'Listen, Natasha. I wouldn't let you anywhere near my mother. Or my son for that matter. Oh, I was prepared to hear you out when I came to meet you. I know you had read at least one of my emails, but I was ready to believe you came across it by accident. I could forgive that. But no. It's obvious it was no accident. You had a purpose. You deliberately read my correspondence. You saw your opportunity for meddling and now you want to use your knowledge. And you think I would take you to meet my mother? You're out of your mind. There's no way I would let you near anyone I care about. What's wrong with you?'

And, without waiting for an answer, she stood up and strode away across the grass.

Chapter Twenty-four

Natasha

Natasha aimed an imaginary automatic rifle at Mel's back and let off a volley of bullets. But Mel kept walking. In less than a minute Natasha had leapt up and followed.

The gallery was closing, visitors bunched around the main gate, setting off for buses and cars. Mel disappeared into the throng and Natasha was forced to elbow through to locate her. She pushed past the inevitable complainers.

'Watch out!'

'Where are your manners, young lady?'

'In a rush are we?'

'I'm so sorry,' she explained, 'I need to get to the hospital urgently. My mother's had a bad accident.'

They stood back.

On the main road she looked both ways, spotting Mel about fifty yards ahead, recognisable from her steady gait, broad shoulders and solid hips, advancing down the pavement past the parked cars in the direction of the village.

Natasha's phone was ringing. She pulled it out of her bag, saw Luke's name and put it back. Not now. She didn't want to lose Mel who appeared to be slowing down, practically sauntering, as if her original rapid pace had nothing to do with seeing Isabel and everything to do with getting away from Natasha.

There were no parked cars and few trees on this side of the road and Natasha continued to walk behind her. At one point,

Mel stopped and Natasha leapt over a low wall in front of a large white building by the side of the road. But after a pause to check her phone, Mel set off again, waiting until traffic had stopped at a zebra before crossing the road and moving on in the same direction along the other side. Natasha remained hidden behind the wall until Mel had turned left at a roundabout. Then she ran out and down to the corner.

Peeking around the corner she saw Mel carrying on down the next residential street and turning off into a quieter side road. Making her way to the corner, Natasha next spotted Mel walking along a row of almost identical semi-detached houses, mostly painted white with neatly pointed brickwork. Any one of these would be worth a fortune.

Natasha's phone was ringing again. Luke would have to wait. She wanted to know where Isabel lived. With careful planning she might find a way to get in there and meet her. At that moment Mel stopped, looked in her bag and took something out, swinging slowly around in Natasha's direction. Without hesitating, Natasha walked purposefully into the front garden of the nearest house. She would be instantly recognisable to Mel in her bright green dress, but a quick glance back indicated that Mel was staring at her phone, oblivious to all else.

It was late afternoon but still warm and she remained for a few moments in the pretty garden enjoying the sun on her bare arms. A solitary blackbird was singing its little heart out in one of the trees that lined the road. Other than that, all was quiet. How different from the buzz and hubbub of Brixton. Almost like being in the country. If anyone emerged from the house she would give them a random name and say she was looking for a friend. The garden would serve to conceal her now. Luckily no one came out and she stood for a couple more minutes, admiring the well-tended beds and weed-free gravel, the shining BMW in the driveway, the large pots filled with pink flowering plants and silvery foliage. She could see herself in such a house. With Luke of course.

Mel was off the phone now and was moving on down the pavement. Natasha could see her on the other side of the crescent, eight houses away, entering a garden identical in size and shape to the one Natasha stood in now. But size and shape were the only similarities. The other garden was overgrown and ill tended, Mel's head and shoulders just visible above what looked from a distance like a tangle of brambles. As for the house, it stood out grey and forbidding, its old-fashioned pebbledash dark with age, the paintwork on its windows flaking and cracked.

Mel crossed the garden, took a key out of her bag and let herself in. Natasha was disappointed. She had hoped to get a view of Isabel. Was Darcy Black as neglected and forlorn as the house she lived in? Natasha ventured further down the street for a better look and checked out the number on Isabel's front door. Though she wouldn't need the number to find the house again. The house itself was unmissable, a miniature version of the castle in the Sleeping Beauty, creepers and vines crawling up the walls. Even the curtains were drawn closed.

Then she saw a hand in one of the windows. One of the curtains was being pulled aside. Natasha jumped back, expecting to see Mel's face. But there was no sight of her, and she was able to get one more good look at the house before turning around. It was tantalising. But she had no idea how she would get inside. Every scheme she conceived seemed hopeless. And perhaps it was time to give up mad schemes. They all went wrong. She headed back to the main road and the bus, texting Luke as she walked.

'All good. On my way.'

Natasha stood in the bus shelter waiting for the bus to Brixton. The pursuit of Mel had warmed her but now the evening air had grown cool and with it the excitement of the day. It had all started so well but overall it'd been pretty crap. Jacob had run off, the CPS looked increasingly unlikely, and she hadn't even managed a glimpse of Isabel Goddard. She thought about Jacob. Stupid kid. She would never waste her time with a youngster again. It was meant as a bit of fun. He shouldn't have answered her first message with that flirty text. The last thing she had intended was meeting him. Certainly not with his mum in tow. And now she had followed Mel to her mother's house. For what? She wasn't about to break in. She was feeling sick again. In two months she'd be out of work and then what? She might be allowed to squat, but squatters never lasted long.

Her eyes ranged across the metal and Perspex screen that shielded the shelter from the passing traffic. Coloured posters advertised the usual mix of West End musicals, dreary charities and bus times. They were so familiar she wondered that anyone bothered to read them. But then her eye was caught by a smaller notice, brightly coloured and laminated, the faces of three actors in bubbles floating around a single strapline. She looked again, more carefully this time. There could be no doubt. It was her. The glittering, eloquent eyes. The fine bone structure, the long nose which Jacob had inherited two generations down, the platinum hair swept back and high, the noble head. Darcy Black.

Natasha's bus pulled in at the stop just as she started to read. 'Meet the Stars.' The date was Wednesday this week.

'Door closing,' shouted the driver.

She jumped on the bus. She had enough information to find out the rest later. Darcy Black was making a rare appearance in public. And Natasha would be there to witness it.

Chapter Twenty-five

Mel

The first thing that hit her was the smell. It was sour, musty, with a faint whiff of rotting food. All the windows were closed, as were the two sets of red velvet curtains.

Isabel Goddard was seated in a wing chair, leaning forward, staring at the television. The volume was turned up high.

Mel called out, 'Mum.'

Isabel lifted her head. She wore make-up that did little to disguise the wrinkled remains of years of smoking but gave a clownish definition to the gaunt yet handsome face. Her hair looked different. Swept back and thicker. Had she used a hair piece? And there was a silver gleam in the usual pale grey. It must have been done professionally.

Mel walked over and turned down the sound, then reached for the cord by the window and pulled one of the curtains aside, tucking it behind a large brass hook that had been screwed into the wall for that purpose. Her mother didn't appear to mind. The television commentary was replaced by the buzz of an invisible insect, trapped between the other curtain and the closed window.

'Hello, darling.'

'Hi, Mum.'

'Where's that boy?'

'He couldn't make it.'

'Always so busy. When's he coming to see his gran? I thought his exams were over.'

'He's been a bit hard to pin down recently. You know teenagers.'

'I remember what you were like.'

Mel felt a stab of guilt. She could be kinder to her mother. It was more than a month since her last visit. She used to help her mother with the house and garden, but she'd made little effort this year. Work, Jacob, Paul, there was always something more pressing. But today she could see a new level of chaos. A feathering of dust lay like a second skin across every tired object in the once elegant sitting room. Chipped porcelain figures, silver framed photographs and Chinese ceramics jostled with cups half-full of cold coffee on occasional tables and shelves. Piles of old theatre programmes lay next to unopened post. African violets with faded flower heads and shrivelled leaves drooped in corners. It was curious that her mother could give so much attention to her own appearance and so little to her surroundings.

But she could not disguise all the effects of age. She had always been slim but now she was thin, too thin. She wore a navy wool shift dress that hung from her bony shoulders like a sack. Her bare arms, jutting from the short sleeves, were like sticks wrapped in parchment.

'Are you getting enough to eat, Mum?' Mel asked.

'What a ridiculous question.'

'You're looking rather thin.'

'I've always been slim. You know that. I hope you're not coming here to criticise.'

'Of course not. I was just worried.'

'Why isn't Jacob here?'

'I've said. It's complicated.'

'What's complicated? You haven't given me a proper reason. Doesn't he want to see me? We used to be such pals.'

He did want to see her. In fact, the visit to Gran was the only reason she had been able to persuade him to come out with her today. The more she thought about it, the more she was convinced it was Natasha who had upset him. And now he wasn't picking up his phone. A horrible thought struck her. But it was just a thought. She would set it aside.

'Did you have lunch?' she asked.

'For goodness sake, Melanie. I was waiting for you.'

'It's past five o'clock.'

'Well, you're late, aren't you? I said I'd be watching *Countryfile*.'

'I'll get something ready.'

In the kitchen she wiped down two unmatched cups and saucers. There was no milk. She remembered her mother liked Earl Grey in the afternoon, preferably with a squeeze of lemon. The only lemon she could find was blue and fuzzy. They would do without. But there was a ready meal defrosting on the side so presumably her mother had something planned for this evening. There were ginger biscuits in a tin. She put them on a plate and carried them through with the tea. Then she sat down opposite her mother in the other wing chair.

'What have you been doing?' she asked as she poured the tea.

'The usual. Reading. Watching TV. I meet my friends in the village for coffee. Sometimes I take a walk. And I've been sorting out my old costumes. They're all over the bed in the spare room.'

'What are you planning to do with them?' asked Mel.

'I haven't decided yet. I might organise an exhibition.'

Had her mother lost all touch with reality? She couldn't pick up a duster, and now she was organising an exhibition.

'Maybe you should just take them to the charity shop.'

'Charity shop? I'm shocked you entertain such a thought. They're your inheritance.'

'Sorry, Mum.'

They would have to go of course, like the rest of the clutter. Her mother needed to downsize to somewhere more sensible. It was ridiculous to have four bedrooms and a garden front and back when she lived alone. Mel had never seen the front look so wild. Though it was doubtful whether her mother would agree to leave the house she had lived in for the last fifty years. There was a pause. Mel broke the silence with the thoughts in her head.

'You should get a cleaner. You could afford it.'

'Like the one that stole money from me?'

'It was never proven. Anyway, that was just one. You didn't get on. They won't all be like that. Or you might find a nice lodger. Someone who could give you a bit of help for a reduced rent. People are desperate for accommodation.'

'Ridiculous. I can't have a lodger.'

'Well, you can't go on like this.'

As soon as she said it she wished it unsaid. Why should it matter if her mother lived in mess? It was not Mel's job to run her life. Why hadn't she told her mother she looked nice? It shouldn't be difficult to pay a simple compliment. Just as she was wondering how to temper the mood, Isabel bit back.

'I'll die soon then you'll be happy.'

'For Chrissake, Mum. I won't be happy if you die. Anyway, you're not even eighty. Eighty's the new sixty.'

'Who says?'

Her mother's face darkened. Mel felt the familiar thump of guilt and exasperation.

'Forgive me, Mum. I shouldn't criticise. That's great about the costumes. Good to have a sort out. I'd love to see them again.'

Better to focus on something her mother enjoyed. She had said the right thing at last. 'Pop upstairs.' Isabel gave a thin smile. 'They're all set out on the bed.'

Mel swallowed her tea, ran upstairs and opened the door to the largest of the three spare rooms: her room, though she had moved out the last of her possessions twenty years ago. The walls were still the pastel pink of her childhood. The furniture was unchanged, the small armchair, the chest of drawers painted white and blue, the traditional, kidney-shaped dressing table with the glass top. One of the walls was lined with fitted cupboards whose mirrored doors had been thrown open. Costumes were packed tight along the rail. Others were piled up on the single bed. It was years since Mel had seen them. Evening dresses in satin, chiffon and velvet, some swathed in plastic bags, power dressing suits from the 1980s. High heeled shoes, many in patent leather, were set out on a rack.

Looking at the clothes and shoes, touching them, she was transported back thirty years, the evenings in front of the TV, the visits to the set, the parties, the wet kisses of the men, the chattering confidence of the women. She remembered the words of her mothers' friends, 'You must be so proud of your lovely mother.' And she had been. Then. What had happened to that pride? Now the costumes only saddened her. The faded remnants of a once-glittering surface. She ran downstairs.

'Well done, Mum. It's wonderful to see them.'

Isabel was seated in a low chair. Mel walked towards her, bent down and clasped her hands. Blue veined, age spotted, the knuckles swollen and arthritic, they were nevertheless perfectly manicured. Her mother might have no time or inclination for housework, but she had time to take herself to the beauty shop in the High Street for a spot of pampering. There was something poignant about those pink varnished fingernails which so few people would see. She wore two rings, both gold, a semi-eternity studded with diamonds and emeralds and a ruby set in a circle of diamonds. The rings had belonged to Isabel's own mother.

Mel looked up at her mother's face.

'Your hair's nice. I meant to say.'

'Thank you, darling. I'm making a bit of an effort. In fact there is something I haven't mentioned.'

'What's that?'

'You know that local theatre group, the South London Thespians or whatever they call themselves?'

'You said you'd have nothing to do with them.'

Her mother was a pro. Amateur theatre was anathema.

'Well, this is a bit different.'

A mischievous smile lit up her mother's face. There was an excited glint in her eyes.

'Why didn't you tell me when I arrived?'

'You were too busy criticising my house.'

'So, what is it? Have you learnt your part?' Her mother found memorising difficult. The most recent return to acting, a guest appearance in a pantomime, had been a fiasco, with Isabel calling for a prompt on almost every line.

'There's nothing to learn. I won't be treading the boards. I'll be sitting on a sofa.'

'Interesting.'

'It's a fundraiser. I'm there as a pro. As myself. They're doing an evening on soaps.' Her voice dropped as she repeated the word, 'soaps' rolling it around her still agile mouth in her best RADA drawl. 'Horrible word. Canada Row was pure drama. A reflection of life. For many people, it was their life.'

Isabel was sitting up straight now. She appeared to have grown by several inches.

'Don't stop. I need to hear the lot,' said Mel.

Mel was delighted for her mother, though apprehensive lest everything should go wrong again.

'It's in that new Community Hall. Hardly my venue of choice but it's for charity of course, so needs must. Not far from here. Just the wrong side of Dulwich. They're sending a taxi to pick me up. They'll do my hair and make-up, though I'll be wearing my own clothes. I thought I'd dig out something suitable from the collection. They'll show a few clips from Canada Row and a couple of other dramas. There'll be a compère chappie interviewing three of us. I've no idea who the others are.'

'What are they interviewing you about?'

'Mostly our telly roles. Maybe a bit about our lives now. Then the audience clap and we all go home.'

'That's amazing. How did they find you?' Mel was sitting down now, settling into this, pleased for her mother and amused by her rapid mood shift.

'Darling, I still have an agent.'

What would Isabel say when asked what she was doing now? Would she make something up?

'Mum, that's brilliant. When is it?'

'Wednesday evening.'

Her heart sank. She was out of London. 'I'm so sorry, Mum. I'm in Canterbury.' A three-day trial. The money would be good. There was no way she could forfeit it for her mother's fifteen-minute performance.

'All evening?' Isabel sounded plaintive.

'I don't know. It's an hour and half on the train. I'm not sure when I'll be able to get away from court.' She would need to wait for the verdict. Courts often sat late rather than sending the jury away for the night.

'Up to you, darling,' snapped Isabel.

'I'll do my best.'

She would. She wanted to be there for her mother now. As much as she had wanted her mother to be there for her in the past. And she had longed for it. Still did. But, there seemed to be taboos on every subject of importance. She had never been able to share a problem. And Isabel would be horrified if she knew what the problems were: the affair with Paul, Jacob's arrest, Natasha's troublemaking. She hadn't even told her about the mugging for fear of upsetting her. A mother–daughter friendship had never been part of the picture.

But Isabel was an old woman now. Mel could at least give her more of her time. She would do her best to get to 'Meet the Stars'.

Chapter Twenty-six

Mel

Mel stared through the train window at the houses, parks and warehouses of south London. The slow rumble of the overground helped calm her thoughts. Jacob had texted. He was home and safe and they would talk later. The visit to Dulwich had been a nightmare but the visit to her mother had turned out better than expected. At least Isabel had something to look forward to.

As for Natasha, there was nothing left in Mel but a bullet-hard determination to erase the woman from her life. Mel would talk to the members of the pupillage committee. Someone else could take over Natasha's supervision for the final two months of her pupillage. Mel would cite personal differences. After that she would avoid all contact. If Natasha tried to squat or get a third six, Mel would do everything in her power to stop it. With careful management, she would never have to see her again.

She glanced at her phone, opening Jacob's message for the third time that evening.

I'm home. CU l8ter.

She smiled inwardly. The silly code they still used. Textspeak had moved on but it was good enough for them.

Her mood lightened and she felt stronger, more hopeful, as she alighted from the train at Finsbury Park and set off down the tunnel towards the bus.

There was a queue for the W3 and it was only three stops from the station to her home, but she decided to wait. It wasn't yet wholly dark, but in the half-light of a summer evening, Mel preferred to avoid passing too close to the place where she'd been assaulted two months previously. There had been nothing more from the police. She wondered if the case was closed.

The flat was quiet, only the usual muffled thud of music from the floor above. She threw down her bag and pushed open the door to Jacob's room. Her boy was staring into his computer screen, oversized headphones wrapped around his asymmetrical haircut like a pair of plastic earmuffs. His right hand was draped over a mouse, scudding around a worn-out mat. Mel pushed a jumble of clothing to one side and plonked herself on the large bean bag she had given him for his thirteenth birthday. A nod of his head indicated he had seen her but there was no lull in the gaming.

Scanning the room for something to write on and with, she spotted a biro on the floor and a notebook full of illegible scribbles on the edge of his computer table. Turning up a clean page, she wrote, 'Talk to me.' She was about to add 'when you've killed enough baddies,' but it sounded patronising and she wanted the mood to be right. Ripping off the page, she left it on the table next to his computer, voices ringing in her head: You spoil him. You let him dominate you. The voices had a point, but tonight she needed to approach him on his terms.

There was soup in the fridge. She popped it in the microwave. A drink would be welcome but in her eagerness to get back she had omitted to pick up wine at the corner shop. And she needed a clear head for work.

After the soup, she opened the Canterbury brief and laid out the papers on the table. Her client had stabbed her lover with a fruit knife. The evidence against her was strong. Mel would need to be at her focused best to get the woman off on self-defence. Cross-examination of the lover would be key. For a good hour she was oblivious to her own concerns, losing herself in preparation.

Shortly before midnight Jacob walked in. Mel was deep in work and didn't look up immediately. When she did, her son seemed different, more solid, with a new confidence. Over the last few weeks he'd grown tall and lanky, but when did his shoulders become so broad? It was not as if he worked out.

'I'm going to bed,' he said.

'Don't keep avoiding me, Jacob.'

'I'm not avoiding you. I'm here, aren't I?'

Even as she heard him speak she was conscious that half her mind was on tomorrow's case. Was she, too, guilty of avoidance? She shut her notebook and held his gaze. It was late, but she needed to know.

'Listen, darling, you walked off this afternoon. You didn't tell me you were going or why. You know I'm anxious because of the assault thing. You might at least have texted.'

'I did text.'

'Two hours later.'

'One hour.'

'One hour, two hours, what's it matter? The thing is you pissed off. Why?'

'I wanted to come home.'

As a single mother Mel had yearned for a companion. Was that why she had treated Jacob as mature beyond his years? Why she had assumed an understanding and experience he was too young to possess? She should have been a better parent, a better guide. He was sixteen now, but it was not too late. He might think he was almost a man, but he was on police bail on an assault charge and she needed to protect him.

'What happened? Did Natasha say something to upset you?'

His body gave a little jerk. His features looked tight and hard and his eyes lost their dreamy softness. Mel waited, the walls of the room pressing in on her. The electric overhead light felt harsh and cruel.

'You won't like this, Mum.'

'Tell me.'

'Natasha told me. About you and this bloke Paul.'

And though she had suspected what he might say, she was unprepared for the physicality of her reaction. A bitter taste flooded her mouth; her stomach seemed to curdle. Was it revulsion at the lies she had told him? The days she had called to say she was stuck at work when she'd been resting in Paul's arms in a hotel bed? Had she felt even a slither of guilt? No, more like a running strain of mild discomfort, mostly ignored. Because no one would get hurt, would they?

Hearing it from Jacob changed everything. It was hard to know which was worse. The exposure itself or the way it had happened, that her pupil Natasha should divulge her secret out of sheer malice. Mel was grateful she had followed her instinct and prevented her meeting her mother. Though God knows why she had invited Natasha for coffee in Dulwich in the first place. Was it some deep fascination, hard to shake off? Was Natasha's charm a spell, even when you could see its falsity? Was that why she had deceived so many in chambers? Well, Mel was shot of her now. There would be no reference. No more supervision. Natasha could do no more damage.

Her son was fixing her with his big eyes, 'So, you're always on at me for keeping silent. But I don't have secrets like that. It's true, isn't it? The guy's married.'

Mel would lie no longer. 'I've been seeing Paul, yes. He's married, yes. And no, he's not leaving his wife if that's what you were wondering. And yes, I've decided to stop seeing him.'

Had she? This was not the first time she had made such a decision, only to respond with humiliating alacrity to Paul's pleading after a break of a few weeks when he called to say he missed her.

A son could never understand how the mother he relied on might need support of her own. She could not explain to Jacob how Claude's departure had floored her. How difficult it had been to pull herself upright, to have the confidence to start meeting other men. How none of them had been right. How introducing another man into their flat felt like a travesty. How she could never trust they would not hurt her or Jacob. How being with Paul, keeping that part of her life separate, enabled her to feel safe with her son. Paul would never be a step-father, would never intrude on the most important person in her life who was standing in front of her now with a cracked heart.

But there was something she needed to know.

'So, did she just come out with it? I mean you don't even know Natasha. You never met her before.'

'Not really.'

'What does "not really" mean?'

'Mum, if I tell you, promise me you won't ask me any more questions.'

The music upstairs had stopped, and now there was only the occasional rumble of a tube train deep below them. City nights were full of growls and rumbles.

'Jacob, I can't promise anything like that. But you don't have to answer everything. Just tell me what you can.'

'OK.'

He paused and his expression softened. He spoke slowly, haltingly and she could sense the mingled relief and awkwardness of his unburdening. 'Me and...' He paused again. 'Natasha's got another name. Lola. Me and Lola. We've been Facebook friends.'

Lola? A Facebook friend? It was one shock too many. All she could say was, 'I thought you didn't use Facebook.'

'I don't. Mostly. But I've got a profile. Everyone has. That's how she found me.'

So, she had looked for him. Why? And what made him respond?

'And she just asked to be your friend? Out of the blue?'

Like most people she knew, Mel had toyed with Facebook for a while, until she became bored with the exotic holidays and ranting political pronouncements of people she would barely class as acquaintances. Scrolling Facebook could send you to sleep on a wakeful night. But did any sane person actually look for friendship there?

'More or less.'

'And you accepted? You didn't even know this Lola!'

'Like you said, Mum, I don't have to answer everything.'

'But what did she say? What did she want?'

'It doesn't matter. It's stupid. I've no idea why she contacted me. Maybe it was a coincidence.'

'That's absurd. How could it be?'

'Or, like, maybe she was curious.' He was speaking faster now. 'Or maybe she was pissed off with you. I don't know, Mum, and I don't care and I don't want to talk about it. OK?'

His expression was fierce and she knew he would not back down. Instead it was she who backed down.

'OK. I get it. I won't ask you more now. It's late anyway. I'm going to bed. We're both too tired. We'll talk tomorrow evening after court. Thank you for being so open with me.'

It sounded strange and formal. He nodded. The blazing eyes looked calmer now. His body was no longer poised for action.

'There's one thing, Mum.'

'What?'

'I don't want you saying anything. To anyone. Especially not Lola... Natasha..., whoever she is.'

'You haven't told me much. Did she ask to meet? What did you talk about?'

'Please, Mum. It's private. Like, I know it was stupid. I was messing around.'

'She wasn't. She deliberately targeted you.'

'Yeah maybe, but I don't want it coming out. I don't want you winding her up.'

'What did she make you do, Jacob?'

He looked like he was about to explode. 'Nothing. You've got to promise, Mum.'

'How can I promise when I don't know what I'm promising?'

He walked out without answering. She heard the tap running in the bathroom as he cleaned his teeth. Minutes later she followed and, after another too long day, went to her room and climbed into her pyjamas. It was then she remembered she hadn't mentioned Meet the Stars. Perhaps Jacob would go alone. He was still on police bail, but no one seemed to be checking up on him and there was nothing to stop him travelling down to south London for an evening.

For half an hour she lay listening to an audiobook to calm her mind. It was only when something jolted her awake that she realised she had drifted off. She pulled herself out of bed. She needed one more look at him.

The LED glimmered red at the side of his computer screen. He was in bed, asleep, curled on his side beneath the duvet, facing the wall. As she drew close she could hear his breathing, soft and regular. She placed a kiss lightly on the top of his head. His hair felt silky on her lips. He stirred but did not wake.

Chapter Twenty-seven

Natasha

It only took a bit of googling to find out the details she'd missed. It was a fundraising event for the local theatre group and Isabel Goddard had star billing. Luke took a little persuading.

'Not my thing.'

'Come on, Luke. When do we ever go out?'

'It's a week night.'

He was finishing the Sudoku in his free newspaper. 'Wake up, buddy. You sound about fifty years old. Get living. It'll be fun.'

The entrance hall was bleak and unpromising with brutalist concrete walls and a small corner table serving as a ticket office. Drinks were sold over a kitchen counter in plastic glasses which could be taken into the show. Luke bought a fruit juice for Natasha and a beer for himself and carried them into the auditorium. And now expectations were raised. The walls were adorned with blown up photographs of the stars in their former glory, the spaces between them adorned with satin drapes.

Soundtracks to the old soaps were playing on a loop. A huge screen took up most of the stage, while in front of it, to one side, a red velvet armchair and a long sofa were strategically placed. Natasha and Luke edged their way down an aisle packed with grey-haired women in their sixties and seventies and beyond, interspersed with a few ancient men.

'Not your usual scene, Tash,' muttered Luke.

'Just wait,' she whispered, surprised by the degree of her excitement. The soaring orchestra was a memory jogger for the twice weekly fix that had lifted her out of the gloom of her early teenage years. She owned several box sets but this was taking her passion to another level. The sound system was brilliant, a cascade of strings taking her back fifteen years, filling her body with thrilling apprehension.

And not just the music, not just the big screen, but the chance to see her idol in the flesh. So what if the rest of the audience were forty years older? Canada Row had been special and still was.

She hadn't explained the connection with her pupil supervisor whom Luke simply knew as Mel. And indeed, Mel was far from her mind as Natasha sat waiting for the lights to go down. It was Darcy Black she had come to see. Darcy with her brilliant repartee, her effortless charm, her ruthless ambition, had been a role model to the young Natasha. There was one moment when she wondered if Mel would turn up to see her mother, whether Jacob would saunter in. Too bad if they did. It was a public event. She had every right to be here. And having Luke beside her was a reassurance. Gentle soul as he was, she knew he would lay down his life for her if necessary.

The presenter introduced himself, cracked a few lame jokes, and promised them a night of nostalgic wonder. The lights went down, the music soared again, and they were into Canada Row. Immediately Natasha was back in the glittering world of cut-throat fashion. The designers, the buyers, the models, the financiers and directors. It was dated of course, a pre-internet dream of retail success. But the struggle for the top, the ruthless pursuit of money and fame were as timeless as ever. And through it all strode Darcy Black, arch manipulator, trampling her male admirers, outshining all the women.

The clips were of the most famous encounters. Natasha was relieved they didn't show the terrifying episode when Darcy got killed in a car accident. But when the lights went up and Isabel Goddard walked in, Natasha's first reaction was disappointment. How old she looked. Her long-sleeved purple suit would once have been a glamourous outfit, but its flowing lines were now slack on the shrunken body. However, disappointment faded as Isabel Goddard moved slowly across the stage. She trembled a little, the old swagger was gone, but the gait was stately, the presence undeniable. Isabel had the indestructible majesty of a true star.

And as she sat down on the sofa, head high, back straight, legs crossed, as she smiled to the audience, Darcy Black was reborn.

Natasha glanced at Luke who was staring into space. Not his thing.

The content of the interview was unremarkable. Yet Isabel was riveting. It was not what she said, but the way she said it. The deep tones, the full-throated consonants and purring vowels, the perfectly timed pauses. She used her hands with graceful emphasis and, from her seat near the front, Natasha could make out sparks of colour as the spotlights caught the precious stones on the rings that adorned her idol's long thin fingers.

'Tell us more about those amazing costumes,' urged the presenter.

'In Canada Row we lived and breathed elegance,' replied Isabel. 'Do I mourn the decline of true sophistication? Of course I do. It's a concept that seems of little interest to the young these days.' She paused and looked out across the audience. 'With notable exceptions of course.' Then she smiled. Was it Natasha's imagination or was that smile aimed at her? Impossible. From the brightly lit stage Isabel wouldn't be able to see Natasha's perfect French plait, nor the neat blue dress that matched tonight's azure eyes.

When Isabel spoke of the car accident which ended Darcy's career Natasha was sure she could detect a tear.

'Shall we sneak off?' asked Luke when the presenter introduced the next clips. 'You're not interested in these other two are you?'

'No, but I want Isabel Goddard's autograph. And he'll give her the last word. You'll see. We have to stay.'

Luke didn't complain. Natasha suspected he was amused by what he saw as her childish enthusiasms. Well, she put up with his football and political protests.

Isabel was sitting on the sofa, smiling blandly as other actors joined her, a villain from EastEnders, a beloved matriarch from a Liverpool soap which Natasha had not bothered to watch. The smile didn't falter. Yet it never failed to appear genuine. There was nothing obviously fixed or false. Isabel Goddard was a true professional.

–

'It may sound daft to you,' Natasha whispered to Luke as they waited at the stage door. 'But this show kept me alive. It's like my life was totally grey. And there was this flash of scarlet and gold twice a week.'

Other fans were standing by, programmes ready, pens poised.

Isabel emerged, her purple outfit hidden under a light summer coat of mauve silk. A matching scarf was draped loosely around her long neck. Natasha waited for the others to have their programmes signed. She would go last. That way they might linger.

'Who shall I say it's to?' asked Isabel in her warm contralto.

'Natasha.'

'That's a pretty name,' said Isabel. Leaning against the edge of the stage door, her writing hand a little shaky, she wrote: To Natasha, with kind regards Isabel Goddard.

They hovered at the door a little longer. Isabel's glance darted from side to side as if she were looking for someone.

'I was expecting my daughter to come. She said she might be late, but I hoped she'd be here by now.'

'She'll be sorry to have missed it,' said Natasha.

'Can we give you a lift anywhere?' asked Luke.

Darling Luke. He was brilliant.

'Please don't trouble yourselves. I'm sure I can find a taxi,' said Isabel.

'Oh, you can't rely on taxis,' said Natasha quickly. 'You could wait all night. We'll give you a lift.'

'That's very kind. But I don't want you to go out of your way.'

'No problem at all,' said Luke. 'We'd be happy to help. Where do you need to get to?'

Her Luke. So tactful. Not even, 'Where do you live?' but 'Where do you need to get to?' As if Isabel were spending the night in a hotel with a youthful lover. The old lady's anxious expression melted as she took in Luke's movie star looks, his cool assurance.

'How very kind.'

'I'll get the car. You wait with Tash.'

They waited at the back of the building. Isabel was easy to talk to. All Natasha had to do was tell her how much she had enjoyed the show, how she had watch Canada Row as a child, and she was unstoppable. Natasha asked about her fellow actors, her co-star. There was so much to tell. When Natasha admired the purple outfit, Isabel told her she had a near complete set of costumes in her house.

'I'm thinking of organising an exhibition,' she announced.

'That sounds amazing!'

When Luke turned up with the car, Natasha suggested sitting in the back with Isabel so they could carry on chatting. Luke was happy to act as taxi driver and they set off for Dulwich. He asked for Isabel's address and tapped it into Google maps.

Natasha had to hold back telling Luke where to stop as he drove slowly around the crescent looking for the house. Isabel herself seemed uncertain, but eventually she told him to pull up outside the unlit dark house with the overgrown garden. It was some distance to the nearest street light and remembering the state of the garden Natasha was worried Isabel might trip over in the dark.

'I'll see you to the door,' said Natasha. 'There's a light on my phone.'

As they approached the house, Isabel's confidence appeared to falter. For the past few hours she had relived her years as Darcy Black. Natasha could sense that the role of Isabel Goddard might be much harder to play. The woman was a curious mixture of confidence and vagary. Natasha held her arm as they negotiated the narrow path to the front door and there was momentary panic as Isabel tried to locate her key in the bottom of her handbag. Natasha decided that if she got to know her better she would suggest tying the key to one of the zips with a long piece of string. It was such a simple tip she was surprised Mel hadn't suggested it. At the sudden thought of Mel, she felt a surge of rage. Not only had this cheating woman gone out of her way to make trouble for Natasha, she clearly neglected her mother. She hadn't even bothered to come to her show. As for Jacob, he obviously couldn't care less.

The key was found. The door pushed open. It was time to say goodbye, always a difficult moment. Natasha was thinking about the possible costume exhibition. Might she offer to help? Just as she was wondering what to say, she felt the touch of Isabel's hand on her arm. The long thin fingers felt cold. Two lovely rings glittered in the hard, artificial light of Natasha's mobile phone.

'Come and see me. Any time,' Isabel's voice was breathy, a stage whisper.

'Oh thank you. That would be lovely.'

'You might like to look at the rest of the costumes.'

'Please. And I could help you sort them out. When should I come?' Work was busy but she could always find an afternoon or evening.

'Whenever you like, dear. I'm always here.'

Natasha wondered about a phone number, but it wasn't offered. Isabel was of a generation when people simply called at the front door. Well, she would do just that.

Chapter Twenty-eight

Mel

The trial went well. To Mel's amazement and her solicitor's delight, her client was acquitted. Her advocacy had never been better, and she strode out of Canterbury Court Centre at 5:30 p.m. with a light heart. If she took the fast train she might make it in time for Isabel's performance. But on reaching the station, the platform indicator informed her there would be delays on all London trains. Her train, when it arrived, was more than twenty minutes late and when they pulled into Clapham Junction it was already half an hour past the show's start time. Mel could visualise her mother's sour expression as her unreliable daughter walked in. It was not what she needed after a brutally early start and a long and draining session in court.

What she did need was to be home with Jacob. Preferably on the sofa with a large glass of red. They needed to talk. She remained on the train until they reached Victoria and jumped on the tube.

Music thrummed out from the kitchen as she entered the flat. Jacob was sitting at the kitchen table staring at his laptop, a packet of biscuits on the side. The room was filled with the sticky aroma of supermarket pizza.

'Hi, Mum. I've been waiting for you.' A wave of appreciation washed over her. He had bothered to read her texts about the train delays, had taken the initiative and put the pizza in the oven himself, even remembering to lower the temperature to stop it burning.

'You're a star,' she said. At the word 'star' she realised she had forgotten to tell him about Gran's comeback. When she told him now, he laughed and said he reckoned Gran would slay any audience. He promised to go and visit her soon. There was a lightness in his tone, but as Mel caught his eye he looked quickly away.

He stood up and put cutlery and plates on a tray, still not looking at her. Yet he was here, he was safe, and he had thought of her. That was enough. Usually Mel would insist on salad or at least something green on the side, but tonight she wouldn't criticise. She opened the tap on the wine box. So much cheaper than bottles and no waste. Jacob was still hooked on Coca Cola. No amount of sugar seemed to add an extra pound to his long thin body. But as she filled her glass he opened the fridge and took out a can of beer. She couldn't remember buying it. Did his pocket money stretch to alcohol? He had mentioned a couple of older friends. Might they have bought it for him? She decided not to say anything. The last thing she wanted now was an argument about underage drinking. If he wanted alcohol he would get it somehow. At least he was home. A can of beer wouldn't kill him.

Not bothering with a glass, he yanked off the tab and took a swig, picked up a tea towel and removed the pizza from the oven, dividing it into quarters and carrying the tray into the sitting room without a word. It was an unspoken under-standing. They would eat in front of the telly, watching the drama together at nine.

But he didn't join her on the sofa as usual. And as the dark tale unfolded and she began to unwind, she never lost the uneasy consciousness of her son's silent presence on a separate chair. At ten o'clock, without commenting on the thriller, he stood up and carried the tray to the kitchen. Mel had wanted to ask again about Lola but she'd missed the moment. Why was it so hard to say what you wanted to say to the person you most loved? Jacob said nothing about Paul.

As she sat watching the news, barely hearing what was said, he came back in and told her he was going to his dad's tomorrow night and would stay for a week. He was earning holiday money painting their spare bedroom and newly extended basement. The announcement came like a punch in the stomach.

'I didn't know you could paint,' she said. It sounded pathetic. Ridiculous. A caricature of a needy mother. Like her own, she thought.

'I'm teaching myself.' He grinned broadly. 'New skill. Like you always recommend.'

'What about your bail?'

'Dad reckons they'll drop the case.'

If Dad said it, Jacob would believe it. He had a touching faith in his father's wisdom. Despite her pain, she attempted to tell herself how lucky she was. Claude may have abandoned her, but he would never abandon Jacob. All sons needed to separate from their mothers. At least hers had somewhere safe to go and something constructive to do. He interrupted her thoughts.

'Goodnight, Mum.'

'Goodnight, Jacob.' This was the moment. But she couldn't speak.

'You're not cross, are you?' he asked.

'No. I'm not cross,' she said. Then she asked, 'Are you all right, Jacob?'

'About what?'

'About everything. The charge. The Lola business.'

'I told you Dad said they'll drop it.'

'And Lola?'

'I told you about that too. And yes, I'm all right. I'm not a kid.'

He was clamming up now. But he had not moved from the door and she stood up, walked across the room, opened her arms and hugged him. He stood very still, neither pulling away nor moving towards her.

'If you ever want to speak, darling,' she said.

'I know, Mum.'

She let her arms drop. This was not the time for him. Would there ever be time? He turned towards his room. And now it was as if an unknown hand was reaching deep inside her and was tugging at her guts. Jacob had sought a promise from her. But he had not told her everything. And she hadn't felt able to give it. Even so, confronting Natasha would feel like a betrayal.

The following evening, she rang her mother.

'How did the show go, Mum?'

'Very well indeed thank you, darling.'

Isabel made no reference to Mel's absence, but Mel could tell from her clipped tones that she was hurt.

'I'm really sorry. I was stuck on a train. I didn't want to walk in an hour late. I'd love to hear about it. Shall I come over at the weekend?'

There was a pause.

'I may be a little busy.'

Mel was stunned. Her mother could be peevish, martyred, even unwelcoming. But it was many years since she had been busy. Before she could respond, Isabel continued, 'I met such a charming couple at the show. The young woman's coming over to help with the costumes on Saturday and then we're going out to lunch. Sunday's Bridge Club as you well know.'

Mel had forgotten. Bridge Club met once a month. Usually it was a relief. An activity to keep her mother, if not happy, at least occupied. But today the news unsettled her. Isabel was still talking.

'And you're quite right about the cleaner. I took a fresh look at the place after the show and rang the agency this morning. They're sending someone over.'

At seventy-eight, Isabel was embarking on a new life. Mel knew she should be pleased. Instead she felt confused, even bereft. The ground felt a little less stable.

She called Georgie.

'Mel, sweetie. What you up to? We never see you these days. It's all rush–rush in chambers.'

'That's what I was thinking. It'd be great to get together. How are you fixed at the weekend?'

'Oh, shame. You should have rung earlier. We've got stuff on. But come for supper next Saturday. Farouk and I promised ourselves a night alone. Just us.'

'I'd be gate crashing.'

'Of course not. You're family. You don't count.'

'I'll take that as a compliment. Thanks, Georgie.'

The ground was firm again. It was always a pleasure to spend an evening with Georgie and his partner, Farouk. That left tonight. And tomorrow. There were other friends, people she could ring. But you needed confidence to call people at the last minute to see if they were free on a Saturday night. And she didn't need any more rejections.

She tried several novels but couldn't concentrate beyond a single paragraph. Eventually she picked up a new book on Family Law reform which she'd been meaning to read for some time. It was dry, consisting mostly of suggestions for a new procedural framework. Yet tonight, its very dryness appealed, reminding her of one of the reasons she had taken up law. It provided a structure by which you could manage unruly emotions. People had the mistaken notion that law was difficult. It was so much easier than the emotions themselves.

Chapter Twenty-nine

Natasha

It was Sunday and she was ready for her second outing with Isabel.

'You've really taken to the old dear,' Luke laughed.

'Please don't call her "old dear". It's patronising. She's a friend.'

Friend was not a word she often used. She wasn't sure she had any. But she and Isabel were good together. Isabel liked to have an admirer. And it was easy to be a fan.

'Or the mother you never had.'

'Cut the psychobabble, Luke. We just get on. We've a lot in common. Anyway, you're off to footie. I'm due at hers at ten. We're going to lunch at a museum. I'm hoping she'll let me wear one of the costumes. I'm a perfect fit for Darcy Black. Even the shoes.'

'Don't overdo it, darling.'

She wasn't sure what he meant.

'For fucksake, I'm not the seventy-eight-year-old.'

Had he noticed that she was more tired than normal? That she had eaten half her usual breakfast? Of course. Luke noticed everything. Though he had not seen what she saw in the Ladies' toilet yesterday. The clear blue ring.

'Just saying. Take care.'

He wore his anxious look. As if he feared something terrible might happen to her. She smiled at his concern, brushing her hand up his arm as she leant to kiss him goodbye, jumping quickly away towards the door before he could stop her leaving. If he had seen what she had seen in the toilet he would have looked even more anxious. Might even have suggested joining them. But she would not let him suffocate her. No, she would not have this baby.

When she arrived at the Dulwich house Isabel was in her dressing gown.

'Oh, am I too early?'

'Not at all. I thought we might choose our outfits together. Come in. I'm making coffee.'

The water was boiling. Isabel spooned fresh coffee into mugs, apparently forgetting you didn't just pour hot water on the grounds. Natasha thanked her and they carried their gritty drinks upstairs into the spare room where the cupboard doors were open to reveal a tightly packed rail of dresses and suits. They dated back to the Eighties and Nineties and last weekend she and Isabel had sorted them all according to function or occasion.

'Pick one,' said Isabel.

'You mean…?'

'Choose one you'd like to wear today. If you're happy with it you can take it home. With the right shoes of course. You'll find Schiaparelli, Prada, Gucci, most of them only worn once.'

Natasha chose a brilliant green suit with a floppy Thatcher bow. There was a hint of power dressing in the discreetly padded shoulders and nipped in waist and it was perfect with black and gold platform shoes. She twisted her hair high into neat bun like a ballet dancer and gazed into the mirror at the stylish stranger. The stranger's carefully made-up lips returned her gentle smile. What would Luke think?

'The designers used to give me everything. Apparently I boosted sales. Of course, I'm not the woman I was. One shrinks you know. None of this is any use to me now.' Isabel looked wistful, pulling herself upright as if to dismiss a painful thought. 'I could get a tailor to take in the seams, but it would feel all wrong. Like destroying a beautiful artwork. Mel says I should get rid of it all. Dump it at a charity shop.'

'That would be a pity.'

Natasha calculated. She might get £100 or more for any one of these on eBay. And there were plenty of them.

'Maybe I could help you sell them? After the exhibition of course. Come on, let's find something for you.'

They moved into Isabel's room and rifled through the jumble of garments in her own cupboards. Natasha pulled out a black silk shift. It was simple and elegant. The only problem was that the lack of colour drained all life from Isabel's complexion.

'Make-up!' declared Natasha, settling Isabel in a chair in front of the mirror. She used her own pallet to add subtlety to Isabel's foundation, lipstick, rouge and mascara, standing back to admire her efforts. There was something missing. Apparently reading her mind, Isabel pointed to the two inlaid wood and gilt boxes on the table in front of them. Natasha opened them both and picked out a flamboyant diamond brooch that transformed Isabel's outfit from ordinary to exceptional.

'Now you,' said Isabel.

'Me?'

'Pick something for yourself.'

'From your boxes?' Natasha endeavoured to sound more surprised than keen.

'That's what I said, isn't it? Anything you like. I've got far too much. Mel won't want it. I might as well give it to someone who appreciates it.'

'Well, maybe just for today.'

Natasha studied the contents of both boxes and chose a leaping emerald leopard encrusted in diamonds, or possibly glass, and a pair of matching earrings. It was extravagant and outlandish, but it looked cool on the vintage suit.

Finally, she presented Isabel with her own gift, a silver feathered fascinator she had picked up at Harvey Nichols ten years ago. She had never worn it herself and never would, but it was perfect for the old lady.

Isabel stood up and, taking Natasha's hand, led her back into the spare room so they could both look at themselves in the full-length wardrobe mirror. They made a striking pair. Natasha tall and polished in her figure-hugging suit and platform shoes, Isabel inches smaller in low heeled pumps but still with the commanding presence of an ageing star. Her eyes gleamed with excitement.

At the front door she stopped, turned back to Natasha and tugged a large ring off her finger. It was another emerald setting, and this time it was obvious the diamonds were real.

'Try it,' she insisted.

'I couldn't possibly wear your ring.'

'Nonsense. It will look wonderful on your long slim fingers. And ideal with the outfit. Anyway, it's too big for me now. I'm worried it might fall off.'

'Well, just for today.'

The ring fitted perfectly. To Natasha at that moment it felt that not only had she met Darcy Black, she was Darcy Black.

They took a taxi to the station where they sat in the bright morning sunshine, waiting for the train. It was already hot, and Natasha felt overdressed and sweaty in her suit. What had looked stunning in the privacy of Isabel's spare bedroom might not look so stunning in the outside world where people wore shorts and jeans. It was a bit Margaret Thatcher. Did she look ridiculous? Were people staring?

Then came a twinge of hunger. She had forgotten to bring a snack. There was nothing to buy on the platform and there would be nothing on the train. What a fool she was. She had felt too sick to eat much breakfast and since then she'd been preoccupied with Isabel, allowing herself to focus on someone else, losing her grip on her own needs. Even when working she was better organised than this.

The train was due in a minute. If there were no delays they'd be in Victoria by eleven forty-five. She would buy something there. Her reader was in her bag and she took it out. It worked through her clothes and she was practised at running it over her upper arm without drawing attention to herself. But this morning she felt self-conscious. Yes, people were staring. She not only looked absurd but was behaving strangely. More importantly, the blood glucose level was dropping fast. She would need to eat soon.

A crowded train pulled in. They were forced to sit separately. Added worry. She'd need to be sure not to lose Isabel in the crowds when they got to the station.

Through the window the low houses and warehouses of south London gave way to the glassy office blocks and apartments of the centre. She continued to feel both sick and ravenous. Could it be the pregnancy? Was that why she was hungrier? Why her blood sugar had dropped more than usual? She hadn't been able to eat much at breakfast. It was a cruel irony that just when you needed food you couldn't swallow it. Was that what pregnancy would be like? Despite the heat of the carriage she felt cold inside at the thought. She couldn't have a baby. It was impossible. It would interfere with everything. Her phone was ringing. Luke of course.

'Hi, babe,' she said. 'I thought you were off to the pub.'

'Not yet. It's hours till kick off. I just rang to check you were OK.'

'Why wouldn't I be?'

'You were a bit funny at breakfast.'

'I'm fine.'

'When are you back?'

'Five-ish. Listen. I can't talk now. We're just pulling into Victoria.'

In fact, they were held at signals. She put away her phone. She wouldn't tell him. She would have an abortion. He would never know.

Passengers were already getting up and moving towards the doors. She joined them, stopping next to Isabel and leaning down so that she could hear.

'I need to get some food at Victoria,' she told her.

Isabel looked unhappy. It was obvious she was a woman who didn't like her carefully made plans to go awry. 'But we've booked a table at the restaurant.'

'Just a snack. I told you. I've got type 1 diabetes.'

'Goodness. Is it serious?'

'It's fine. I just need something to eat.'

'You don't look diabetic. I mean, not fat or anything.'

'Or a drink. Then we can go to lunch.'

The explanation seemed to satisfy her, and she replied, 'Of course, darling. Don't you worry. I'll look after you.'

The train was pulling into Victoria. Brakes squealed, carriages shuddered, slowed down, stopped. Passengers were rushing to get up, heaving luggage from overhead racks, pushing their way to the door. Isabel stood up to join them. Natasha was about to follow her when two young women on the other side of the aisle jumped up and shoved themselves forward. More people joined the queue to get out and soon the only sign of Isabel was the occasional glimpse of the silver fascinator bobbing in the gap between their heads. Natasha edged down the aisle steadying herself on the little knobs on the top of the train seats. Her platform heels made her feel enormous. She was practised on stilettos, but these were weird, like walking on stilts.

She was shaking as she stepped down from the train to the platform and the clatter and chaos of London crashed over her. Sweat poured from her body dampening the silky fibre of the stupid Eighties suit which clung to her back, her breasts, her stomach. She must reach the concourse. Must find food or drink. If only she'd worn something sensible, jeans, trainers. There were cafes in the distance but there was no way she could run in these useless shoes. And anyway, she hadn't the strength.

The symptoms were familiar; the fog where thoughts started and faded like unfinished sentences. Stray notions flared up like flames in embers. She would make an appointment with the doctor tomorrow. She would get rid of this baby. She couldn't look after it. She was not fit to be a mother.

Then, through the crowd and the fog she spotted Isabel waiting at the barrier. Memory clicked in and she located the tickets in the side pocket of her bag, handing one to Isabel who passed through the gate with ease. When she tried to insert her own into the slot, it stuck. Travellers were surging past through the other exits. The dizziness was getting worse, the fog drawing in again. Beyond her on the concourse, standing out like a lighted window on a dark night, she could see a Whistle Stop shop. She called to Isabel.

'Get me a Coke. Or a Pepsi,' adding, 'not Diet Coke.' But the thud of feet and rush of bodies drowned her voice and she wasn't sure if the words had got out.

If she didn't eat soon, she would pass out. Isabel was no use and Luke was far away. Her legs were too weak to take her much further, but diabetics didn't wear placards announcing their condition. All she had was a wrist band, too discreet for anyone to notice until it was too late. The only thing she could do was wait, leaning on the barrier, hoping a railway employee would find her and let her through. Eventually a young man in a Hi-Viz jacket took her ticket, and the gate slid open. She staggered through, looking for Isabel who seemed to have been swallowed by the crowd.

The fog was thickening. People rushed past her in the other direction trying to get to their train. By now sweat was streaming from every pore. She needed to sit down but there was nowhere. Just as she thought she would collapse onto the concourse a young man stopped and asked, 'Are you all right?'

Natasha tried to speak but nothing came out. Everything inside her crumpled and she fell against him.

Chapter Thirty

Mel

It was Sunday, a week after her dinner with Georgie and Farouk. Jacob was still with Claude and Jo, though he'd texted he'd be back tonight. Mel had spent the week blotting out her loneliness by returning to chambers after court every afternoon, visiting the pub with colleagues in the evening. Was she a coward to keep avoiding Natasha? A couple of times she'd seen her disappearing down the corridor ahead of her. But Jacob's pleading echoed in her mind. He didn't want Mel mentioning the connection. He was a child in some ways but not in others. Was it her duty to warn people about Natasha? Or was it just a bit of silly mischief-making? Worst of all, she had no idea what Jacob had done.

No one seemed concerned that the pupil–supervisor relationship had broken down. Natasha had her own work. What if she had missed out on a tenancy this time around? She was competent, building connections. Everyone assumed she would find something somewhere else.

By midday, tired of the weekend silence, Mel bundled some papers and her laptop into a bag, threw the bag into her car and set off for Dulwich. Isabel had explained she was going out to the V&A with her new friend. They were having lunch at the museum and would be back around teatime. That suited Mel. She would work on tomorrow's case in the quiet of her mother's sitting room. She would put out the tea things and be nice and daughterly when Isabel arrived home. And she would be intrigued to meet the new friend.

Isabel had mentioned a cleaner, but Mel was unprepared for the transformation. The smell had gone; papers were in neat piles; there was no trace of a dirty glass or cup. There was even a bunch of huge pink lilies in a glass vase, filling the room with that sickening scent that always reminded her of funerals. The house was hushed, only the sound of the occasional car entering or leaving the crescent, the buzz of muffled talk from a radio on the other side of the adjoining wall. A lawnmower broke the stillness and she was transported back more than thirty years to summer afternoons, lying on the landing, waiting for her mother's return.

It had been more than twenty years since she had waited for her mother. After they had killed her off in Canada Row, Isabel had always been the one to wait for Mel, irritable, demanding, her affection tinged with a hint of resentment. The resentment might be aimed at the world at large, but Mel was often the recipient of her not-so-subtle barbs.

'Maybe you should visit her less often,' Claude had suggested. But visiting her mother had been more than just a duty. Her mother's life was meshed with her own; you could no more pull them apart than you could pull stitches from a garment. And when Isabel's face lit up on seeing Jacob, her daughter could forgive her anything.

Not long after she had settled on the sofa with her laptop and papers, she heard the crunch of a key and the swing and clunk of an opening and closing door. Then her mother's voice, calm and solicitous. The muffled reply was monosyllabic, subdued. But Mel knew that voice. Her skin felt suddenly tight on her body. She jumped out of her chair. It could not be true.

But it was. Standing behind her mother, wearing an old-fashioned green suit and looking more dishevelled and confused than Mel had ever seen her, was Natasha. Without acknowledging Mel, she moved unsteadily across the room to an empty armchair and flopped down.

'She's had an accident. A hyper,' said her mother, who appeared younger and more confident than she had for years.

She might have been off to an elegant drinks party. She wore a sleek black dress, a diamond brooch and an oversized hair ornament perched on the top of her head like a turkey's crest.

'Hypo,' murmured Natasha, looking up briefly, though still not acknowledging Mel. 'But I'm OK. It was stupid. I was stupid.'

'No, you're not, darling.' And then, looking at Mel, she added, 'She fainted in Victoria Station. Just imagine. The place was packed. No one gave a damn.'

'The young man was nice,' said Natasha.

'At last. When you were nearly dead,' said Isabel.

'I'm fine now, Isabel. You saved me. And like I said, it was my own silly fault.'

'Stop blaming yourself, sweetheart.'

Mel still could not speak.

'Well, aren't you going to say anything?' said her mother. 'Natasha dear, this is my daughter Melanie.'

'Hi, Melanie.' Natasha's lip curled halfway between smile and smirk. Mel's body felt very cold. Her head was bursting. Knowing she needed to stay calm, she tried slow breathing, avoiding Natasha's narrowed eyes. But she couldn't avoid Natasha herself, sitting in front of her with her Cheshire cat grin. She turned and walked into the kitchen.

'What's the matter with you?' asked Isabel, following her in.

'Why didn't you tell me?' asked Mel.

'Tell you what?'

'About Natasha.'

'I'm telling you now. The poor girl collapsed. We got a taxi back and picked up a sandwich en route. She looks better now. I certainly hope so.'

'She's my pupil. The one I told you about. The one that's been so difficult. Didn't you recognise the name?'

'Oh, I never remember names these days. But what a coincidence.' Isabel looked troubled. 'She told me she was training to be a lawyer. I don't think she said barrister. I don't recall.'

'She knew you were my mother.'

'Why would she know that? Oh, the photograph.' There was a graduation photograph of Mel on one of the bookcases. 'She must have missed it. You've changed a bit. Most of the family pictures are Jacob.'

'She knows Jacob too. And she knows you're my mother, because I told her.'

'Goodness, I wonder why she didn't say.'

Because she's a scheming bitch, thought Mel. Though what she said was, 'We'll find out.'

She took a deep breath, gathered her thoughts and went back into the sitting room. Natasha was still in the armchair, though she seemed to have recovered and was leafing through a copy of Vogue from the coffee table.

'So?' Mel's question sounded accusing. It was meant to.

'Yes?'

'What's going on?'

Natasha put down the magazine. Her smile was gentler now. 'Silly isn't it? I had intended to tell your mother, but it just didn't come up. We got on so well. To tell the truth I knew you'd taken against me and I was worried you might try to put her off me.'

'How did you get in here?'

'Get in?'

'Yes, get in this house, inveigle yourself inside, invade my mother's life? More importantly why did you do it? But I guess I don't need to ask that. It's what you do isn't it. Some people would call it stirring. Personally, I think it's more serious than that.'

Before Natasha could reply her mother intervened.

'Mel, that's ridiculous. I invited her. Natasha and her nice young man came to my show. I asked her to call and she called. Simple as that.'

This was worse. Mel's blood was rising, dark and furious. Not only a cheat and a liar, but a manipulator, deliberately fooling Isabel into inviting her in. And all the time Natasha was sitting in the chair as if she owned the place. Mel had intended to give her a chance, to wait to hear what she had to say. But now all she could think was that Natasha needed to go and the sooner she left the better.

'Get out,' she said.

Natasha stood up. As she stood Mel noticed for the first time that she was wearing her mother's ring. 'And before you do that, you better give my mother back her ring. And anything else you've tried to filch.'

'I'll go and change, Isabel,' said Natasha, ignoring the accusation about the ring. And she left the room, walking too close to Mel who pulled back swiftly, unwilling to breathe the same perfume filled air.

'Poor girl. She's not at all well,' murmured Isabel.

Mel wondered about the diabetes. Was that too a lie, fabricated to provoke attention and sympathy? How could you be sure? She remembered the calloused fingertips. But she hadn't noticed them since that first occasion.

'Why is she wearing your ring?'

'I gave it to her. It matches the outfit.'

'You gave it to her?' Mel was incredulous.

'Just for today.'

'Mum, I'll tell you everything later. Natasha is not what she seems. I need to go upstairs and make sure she isn't taking anything else.'

There was more she needed to say to Natasha and she didn't want her mother to hear. Whatever Natasha did now, Mel wouldn't let her get away without knowing the damage she had caused.

Mel ran upstairs and into the spare bedroom.

'Don't worry, Mel, I'm going.' said Natasha. She was standing in her stockinged feet and her own clothes. The green suit was on the bed. The platform shoes were lined up on the carpet with the rest of Darcy Black's footwear. She looked tired, but her expression was calm, and she gazed at Mel as if she were a mild irritant, a traffic warden or an over-zealous ticket inspector. She was still wearing the ring.

'Take off the ring,' ordered Mel.

Slowly Natasha pulled off the ring, laying it on the dressing table next to a leopard brooch and the earrings she'd been wearing. Mel had been so appalled to see her that she had not even noticed till now that every piece of jewellery she had on belonged to her mother.

Natasha spoke. 'Mel, please don't concern yourself. I'll go.'

It was important to stay calm. Professionalism was kicking in. So far there had been nothing criminal. But she needed to know. Jacob was sixteen. It was the age of consent. But he was still a child. 'There's one more thing,' said Mel. And try as she might to remain controlled, she could not stem the anger. 'What the fuck were you doing messing with Jacob?' Natasha didn't reply. The smile which looked like a smirk returned. Mel continued. 'Oh I know you're a crazy bitch. I know you're a thief and a liar. I know you like to meddle in other people's lives. I could forgive all that. I could even forgive you telling the world about my private life. What I can never do is forgive you interfering with my son.'

'Interfering's a loaded word,' said Natasha. The smile had disappeared and now she was looking hard at Mel as she took a step towards her and whispered, 'You want to keep an eye on that kid.'

'What are you implying?'

'Though there's not much you can do to stop him. The internet's a freeway to the world. You won't be able to hold him back if he wants to put himself about. The pictures are out now. Nothing anyone can do. I could show you if you like.'

Mel stood transfixed. So, there were pictures. She had feared as much. And though she didn't want to see, she needed to know what Jacob had done. Her insides were churning as Natasha reached in her bag for her phone.

'You might as well learn what your boy's up to.' Natasha held up the screen. Unable to prevent herself, Mel took a step forward for a better view. Jacob was lounging on the old coffee stained sofa in his room. He wore no clothes, but one of their family bath towels was draped around his narrow hips. He must have been holding the phone with his other arm on that selfie stick his dad had given him. Part of her wanted to laugh. It was so absurd. Her child pretending to be an adult. But it was also horrifying. He was so vulnerable. She looked quickly away.

'Course there's plenty more. I'm sure Jacob wouldn't want you to see those, but since you seem so interested I'll dig them out for you. I've tucked them away. Didn't want my boyfriend finding them. Like I explained to Jacob, I've saved them on a cloud too.' Natasha was still holding up the phone, still smiling. Behind the smile was something frightening, an inhuman light in those brilliant green eyes.

And now she was swiping through the pictures as casually as if she were about to show a holiday snap to a friend. Then she stopped and turned to face Mel.

'Nice body', she murmured, as she held up the phone for a second time.

The pose was the same, languid, provocative, though the facial expression was different. The innocence had vanished. The eyelids were lowered, the mouth was slightly open. But that was not the only change. The small towel, that modest covering, had been removed.

Mel squeezed her eyes shut, unable to believe what she was seeing. She took a deep breath before opening them again, forcing herself to look at what she had already seen but had been powerless to absorb. It was true. The smile was one she had never seen in him. Her son had done what she had most feared and she could no longer protect him. She quickly averted her eyes again.

At that moment her mother's voice rang through the air, echoing round Mel's head, 'No, no, she's not well.'

But there was only one way Mel could respond to what she had seen.

She hurled herself at Natasha, pushing her backwards, causing her to lose her footing and trip across the rows of shoes which had been left on the floor. Natasha's body, which had been falling back, twisted sideways. And in that moment Mel thought she heard her mother's voice, but the words were inaudible and interrupted by a terrible smashing sound as Natasha's head struck the glass edge of the kidney-shaped dressing table.

Mel's pupil lay on her side on the floor. Her hair had fallen over her face. Mel stared. Anger was churning inside her, urging her to lash out again, hurt her properly, silence her forever. Part of her had expected Natasha to fight back. Then she heard her mother's voice again. 'No, Mel.'

She turned towards the sound. Isabel was standing in the doorway, supporting herself on the door jamb, eyes wide in her wrinkled handsome face. What had she seen? And what was she asking Mel to do? Not to hurt Natasha or not to help her? Whatever it was, Mel was frozen into obedience as she looked away from her mother to Natasha's body lying motionless on the floor.

Isabel let go of the door jamb and moved slowly to where Natasha lay. Out of the corner of her eye Mel saw her lower herself with difficulty to her knees and lift several strands of blonde hair from the pale, expressionless face. Natasha's eyes were closed, one side of her face was perfect and unharmed, but blood was pooling on her crown, dripping onto her forehead, meandering in slow rivulets down her left cheek.

Chapter Thirty-one

Mel

The Uber driver, told this was an emergency, raced down Half Moon Lane and across the Herne Hill roundabout, narrowly missing law-abiding drivers who were keeping to the appropriate lane. Mel would have driven but Isabel had insisted.

'You're too shaken up, darling...'

Natasha was strapped into the back seat, leaning against the door. She was conscious, though her face was ashen, and she made no sound other than the occasional low moan. Isabel, sitting next to her, was holding what had been a clean tea towel against the wound. The driver took a rat run, mounting the kerb at one point to avoid an approaching lorry, descending with a crash, making the car rock on its springs.

'Watch out,' squealed Isabel. 'How are you, darling?' she asked Natasha, replacing the bloody tea towel against her face.

'Bit sick,' whispered Natasha, her head lolling from side to side. Mel was aware that mild concussion would work in her favour: Natasha sounded confused.

'Sorry, love. Didn't see that, I'll get you there nice and quick. Two minutes now.'

Mel turned back to Natasha. 'How's your head?'

'Hurts.'

'You'll need stitches,' she replied as if in sympathy, hearing the tension in her own voice.

'You don't want a scar,' said Isabel. 'Still, I expect your hair will cover it.'

'What happened?' Natasha muttered drowsily. Had she really forgotten?

'You fell over,' said Mel quickly. And as she spoke a memory surfaced: grey walls, a metal table, a foxy-faced young man wheedling his way around a charge of assault. Conrad Stevens had lied to her, changed his story, lied to the court. And she had got him off.

'Dreadful bang. Right on the dressing table,' Isabel added, speaking straight ahead as if addressing an audience.

The minicab dropped them off by the automatic doors leading into the reception area and triage station of King's College Hospital's A&E. Mel helped Natasha onto the pavement and held her pupil's arm as they shuffled together through the automatic doors. Natasha was wearing a pair of Isabel's slippers. Her mother, behind them, walked unaided on low heeled pumps. The hospital was warm, but Mel felt cold inside. She must focus on the present. The important thing was to get help for Natasha. She felt herself wobbling, heard her mother call out, 'Do be careful, Melanie, you'll pull her over.'

Minutes later all three of them were leaning on the counter that separated the triage desk from the waiting area. Natasha was still holding the tea towel to her head.

'Can she speak?' asked the receptionist.

'I can speak,' murmured Natasha, through half-closed lips. She sounded drunk.

'Good. In that case, I'll just take a few details. Don't worry, love, we'll sort you out.'

'I'll find my mother somewhere to sit,' said Mel. And she left Natasha leaning on the counter.

Isabel allowed herself to be guided away. She was uncharacteristically silent. They walked through a maze of corridors until they reached Costa. Mel settled her mother at a corner table with a magazine and a latte.

'I'll come and check on you in half an hour.'

Isabel looked exhausted. Make-up was smudged around her eyes; her hair had unravelled. Mel picked up a few strands and tucked them into the clips.

'Don't fuss me,' snapped Isabel. Then, before Mel could speak she added, shaking her head slowly from side to side, 'All those shoes on the floor. She seemed such a tidy little person. I'm surprised she didn't put them back in the cupboard.'

'I'm sorry, Mum. You don't need this.'

—

Natasha was sitting among the other patients, head flopped against the wall, eyes closed. Mel went up to the counter. Eventually one of the nurses came forward to speak to her.

'We've given her some painkillers. Keep an eye on her. Don't let her sleep.'

'How long will it be?'

'Two or three hours? She could be lucky. She had a nasty bang. The doctor may want to see her sooner.'

There was no vacant seat near Natasha, so Mel sat down at the other end of the waiting area opposite a tank of tropical fish. She stared at the tiny darts of colour. They did nothing to still her thoughts.

Natasha would not let this lie. She would inform the Bar Standards Board, the police. Mel felt the breath catch in her throat as her imagination spiralled. Others would make the decisions now. Her career would be ruined. Any career.

Every half hour she went to check on Isabel who had perked up, having found a gentleman admirer to keep her company. Even when looking her worst, Darcy Black never failed to attract elderly fans. She was on her third coffee when Mel returned to the waiting area to see Natasha being led away by one of the nurses through some double doors. She turned back to the tropical fish.

Isabel's evidence would be key; Mel's shocked recognition of her pupil, the accusation about the ring, about Jacob, the shoes on the floor, Natasha toppling. How much did her mother see? How much did she hear? A mother would support her daughter. Of course, she would. Mel shivered.

Twenty minutes later, Natasha reappeared on the arm of a nurse. She was limping slightly. Had she tripped on one of the shoes as she fell? If so she might have twisted an ankle. Mel flashed back to the scene in the bedroom. One minute she'd seemed to be toppling backwards, the next slipping sideways. How much had Isabel witnessed? She'd been standing in the doorway with a clear view. Looking at Natasha now, Mel could see that the blood had been washed off the wound, a small area of hair shaved, and a dressing applied. Four stitches, the nurse told them. It was a nasty cut, crossing the hairline just above the temple. She had been given paracetamol. There was visible, faint bruising stretching down her forehead below the dressing. She was no longer swaying, but she still seemed confused.

'Can she take Ibuprofen?' asked Mel.

'We don't advise it,' said the nurse, 'It can increase the risk of bleeding.'

'I can speak,' murmured Natasha. Her speech was slow and slurred.

'She needs someone to keep an eye on her for the next couple of days,' continued the nurse briskly. 'Any vomiting or bad headaches, bring her back. Are you next of kin?'

'No. Just a… just a work colleague.'

'Is there someone?'

'She lives with her boyfriend. We'll drop her off there.'

'Make sure she has her proper kit. If it wasn't for the ID bracelet, we'd never have known she was type 1. So how did this happen?' asked the nurse.

'Hasn't she told you?'

'She's confused. That's why we're worried. Were you in the room at the time?'

'She fell against a glass dressing table. She tripped. Probably on a shoe. They were lined up on the floor…'

The nurse was listening hard. Mel knew it was important to get this right.

'We've given her a letter,' the nurse continued. 'We'll see her again soon. She may need a scan. We'll have to run tests. There could be some balance issues.'

'Thank you,' said Mel. She turned to Natasha, 'How are you feeling now?'

'Weird. Can you get me something to eat?'

Of course, the diabetes. Would that be a complication?

'What do you want?'

'Cheese sandwich.'

Mel returned to the coffee bar, bought the sandwich and told a reluctant Isabel it was time to go.

'And I was just beginning to enjoy myself.' She smiled at her new devotee who politely shook her hand and said what a pleasure it was to meet her.

'I'll get you home. Then I'll take Natasha back to her boyfriend,' said Mel as they were returning to A&E.

'Such a nice young man.'

'Excellent. Then she'll be well looked after.'

Mel heard the edge in her own voice. It was not excellent. Luke would not accept the accident theory. He was a social worker and would examine his girlfriend with a social worker's forensic suspicion.

'You'll have to give me the address. Can you walk OK?' she asked Natasha.

'I can walk.'

Mel took her arm.

'I said I can walk,' barked Natasha, snatching her arm away. The antagonism felt like a punch in the gut. No, Natasha was not a woman to let this go. And provocation was no defence.

She called Uber from triage. Natasha was once again installed in the back next to Isabel. They hurtled off up Denmark Hill.

Back at Isabel's house, she settled her mother in an armchair, turned on the TV, organised tea and toast and left her, curiously calm, in front of *Flog It*. Mel still hadn't asked what Isabel had seen. For years there had been areas of silence between them. Most of her mother's life had been a performance. This could just be another one. Isabel would need time to work out what role she would play.

Mel turned to Natasha who was slumped on the sofa, staring into space. There was a plastic NHS bag on the floor beside her containing medication.

'Are you OK? I mean, with your diabetes and everything.'

'They checked at the hospital. It's fine.' She was more lucid by the moment. 'I need my handbag,' she added, pushing herself up.

'Don't try to move. I'll get it.'

Mel ran up the stairs and into the spare bedroom. A cream handbag was open on the bed, its contents spilling over the quilted flowery counterpane: wallet, make-up, comb, some medical gadget. Nothing belonging to her mother. But where was Natasha's phone? The image was sharp in her mind, Natasha standing a few feet away, brandishing the picture of Jacob like a trophy. She fell on her knees amidst the shoes and scanned the floor, lying down to look under the bed. And there it was, a white iPhone, just out of reach. It must have skidded across the carpet when Natasha fell.

Stretched out on her front, Mel managed to squeeze part of her shoulder under the base of the bed, allowing her to touch the phone and nudge it towards her. The sound of the TV floated upstairs. With luck Natasha would have fallen asleep.

The phone kept slipping away but eventually Mel managed to coax it out. She pushed herself back from the bed, clasped hold of the smooth object, stood up and stuffed it into her back pocket. Then she pulled her own phone from her other pocket and took several pictures of the shoes strewn around the floor where Natasha had fallen. There was blood on the carpet. Should she wash it out? But she was desperate to get rid of Natasha, needed her out of the house. And if there was any issue about the injury, a large bloodstain just below the dressing table could do no harm to Mel's case. She stood motionless, thinking. What case? Nothing would happen. But the sight of the red brown patch unnerved her. She went to the bathroom, picked out a towel and soaked it in cold water. Back in the bedroom she wiped the stain ineffectually for a few seconds, merely transforming a small dark puddle into something more like a thunder cloud.

She took the towel to the bathroom and left it to soak in the sink. Her mother had arranged a cleaner. There was no need to do more.

Downstairs, she handed Natasha her bag.

'I'll take you home,' said Mel starting to help Natasha up. As soon as she was upright Natasha jerked away. 'Don't touch me,' she snapped.

'OK,' said Mel.

Natasha was walking slowly towards the front door. Mel turned and crossed the room to where her mother sat.

'I'll call you, Mum.' Mel lent over and kissed her mother's cheek. It felt cool and powdery. 'Don't worry. She'll be all right.'

'Goodbye, darling. Look after her.' Her mother's words sounded neutral, neither warm nor cold. Nor did she turn from the television as she spoke.

Natasha was waiting by the front door. Mel held it open and they both stepped across the ill-tended garden to the pavement and Mel's parked car. Mel held open the passenger door and Natasha slid into the seat, gave Mel the address and sat in silence as the car navigated the dark streets to the Brixton estate.

'This one,' said Natasha. Mel pulled up outside a low-rise concrete block. It looked bleak and forbidding with tiny windows and snaking walkways. Mel was surprised her pupil should live in such a place. Natasha was rummaging through her bag.

'Where's my phone?' she said.

'I've no idea. Maybe it fell on the bedroom floor.'

'Did you take it?'

'Of course not.' She could feel the phone pressing on her right buttock.

'I need it back.' Natasha's face was hard with anger and her eyes were narrow. One of them was almost closed, beginning to puff up. But Mel could still see the colour of the other one. Earlier that day it had been a sharp green. Now it was a pale grey blue.

'Don't worry. I'll find it. It must be in the bedroom. I'll go back now and look.'

Natasha's good eye signalled her fury, but she said nothing. Mel sensed it was only pain and weakness that stopped Natasha from attacking her from the passenger seat of the car. And when she opened the door to let her out, Natasha did not budge. Was she about to insist on coming back for the phone? Neither woman spoke. Eventually Natasha heaved herself out and walked slowly towards her front door, pressed an intercom and waited, leaning against the wall of the cheerless building.

After a couple of minutes, a tall man appeared in the doorway and embraced her. Mel looked on as they stood together, locked tight. Then the man drew back and stared at Mel. For a moment she thought he was about to come towards her, but after a couple of seconds he turned away, put his arm around Natasha and disappeared with her inside the flats.

Mel got back in the car and set off for north London. She still had Natasha's phone in her pocket.

Chapter Thirty-two

Natasha

Luke was leaning over her. His features were fuzzy. The room behind him was blurred. He was speaking but she couldn't follow what he was saying. Working out what had happened was too difficult. Mel had been driving her around and had left her at the front door. And now she was in her own bed, but she couldn't remember how she had got there. Her head was thumping, and her own words sounded slurred and broken.

'Not now. I need to sleep.'

The next morning her head was still hammering. And the pain from her wound felt worse. But her mind was clearing. The pictures were growing sharper by the minute: Isabel's house, the clothes in the wardrobe, the shoes on the floor. And Mel, charging towards her, her face twisted in fury. Luke brought her a cup of tea.

'You still haven't told me what happened.'

'I'm trying to piece things together. You better call chambers. I should be in court.'

'I'll ring them, explain you were injured.'

Natasha nodded agreement, listening as he spoke to one of the clerks.

'Badly hurt... yes hospital... it's hard to say... concussion... yes, some memory loss... maybe... I'll get her to call you when she's up to it.'

She felt strong enough to take a bath, taking comfort from the heat of the water. There was a burning pain behind her right eye. Someone had taken out her contact lenses at the hospital. She couldn't remember it happening, but Luke had found them stored in a small plastic case in the bag with her medication. Would she ever wear them again? She doubted it. It was as if those glittering colours belonged to a different self. And there was something else.

She ran her hands down her tummy, a slight depression between her narrow hips. Memory was seeping back. A tiny creature was growing inside her. And with that memory came the decision she thought she had made. But as she soaped her aching body she knew that what had happened last night changed everything. She had been hurled against a glass dressing table by a woman who hated her, and it was as if she had been thrown onto a different course. The creature was little more than a speck, a comma. But it was hers. Natasha couldn't stop herself wondering if it had survived. And as she wondered, she realised she was hoping. And as she hoped, her anger was taking shape.

The details were drifting back. Isabel had been standing in the doorway. How long had she been there? But it would be crazy to rely on Isabel.

She needed to tell Luke what had happened. At least as much as he needed to know. If she did decide to go to the police, his account would be crucial. The evidence would be hearsay, but it would be her first report of what had happened and therefore admissible. The sooner she spoke, the better. Mel would have been careful to exonerate herself.

Natasha stepped carefully out of the bath, still a little dizzy, wrapped herself in a towel and stared in the mirror. Her right eye was almost closed and through it she could detect only a crack of light, the faintest hint of shapes. The eyelids had begun to puff up like a ripe plum. The main wound was across the hairline and a patch of her hair had been shaved. There were greenish yellow blotches across her eyebrow and the top of her cheek. A selfie would be a good idea. But where was her phone?

And then it came back to her. She had been holding it up when Mel rushed her. It must have fallen to the floor. And instead of giving it back with her bag, Mel had kept it. Through the wooziness and continuing pain, she felt a stiffening of resolve. Mel would pay for this.

Luke had insisted on taking the day off work, and was sitting on the sofa, looking at his tablet when Natasha sat down next to him. He had left a bowl of cereal on the coffee table for her, but she knew she should check her blood glucose before eating. As she reached for her monitor his fingers closed gently around her wrist.

'Shall I check for you?'

Apart from a nurse, no one had ever done this for her before. It would have been an intrusion, a step too far. But today, with Luke, it felt natural.

'Yes. Thanks.'

He picked up the monitor, holding it over the small button-sized implant in her upper arm, reading out the numbers on the graph. The reading was slightly low, but she would be fine after the cereal. She reached for his hand, squeezed it and started to eat. When she had finished, he moved the plate aside and said, 'So?'

She started to talk. She told him about Isabel, her kindness, her loneliness, how she, Natasha, had wanted to help, how she had enjoyed taking her out, cleaning up the lovely house in Dulwich.

'We'll have a house like that one day,' she said.

'Dream on,' laughed Luke.

She told him about the costumes, the loan of a vintage outfit and jewellery, the trip to the V&A, cut short by her hypo. Then she spoke about Mel, her distrust and false accusations, the sudden outburst, the brutal shove that sent Natasha flying onto the glass edge of the dressing table. After that, the mist, the faces, someone helping her up, the drive to the hospital, the sense of displacement, as if she was both present and absent.

Luke listened intently, taking everything in. She knew he would remember, just as if he had written it down. She omitted her own rage, her own instinct to hurt the other woman in the way she knew best, spitting out words like poison darts. She made no mention of Jacob.

Luke was puzzled. 'But why would she do that? Even her mother said she'd lent you the jewellery. And didn't she say you could have the outfit?'

'Some people are like that.'

'There must be a reason.'

'You mean I must have behaved badly?'

She knew what he was thinking. Amsterdam. The one time he had caught her thieving. Since then he had noticed whenever she wore new earrings and, once, a silver necklace. 'Cheap tat!' She had laughed when he asked how she could afford it. 'It doesn't look cheap,' he had commented. And now he was studying her wounded face and she feared he might accuse her. But instead he protested gently. 'I don't mean that. I mean in Mel herself, something in her background.'

'I dunno. You're the expert on psychology. Isabel's kind of self-absorbed. I've no idea about Mel's father. But Mel's got this paranoid streak. Someone in chambers told me she was prickly. She's prickly all right. Like a barbed-wire fence.'

'But why turn on you?'

If she couldn't get Luke on side, what hope was there?

'I can only tell you how it was. From the start she didn't like me, didn't want me around, like I was an irritant. She was supposed to train me, but she never taught me anything. I taught myself, watching her stupid mistakes. When I tried to help, she accused me of interfering. Once I sent her a note in court and she never forgave me. She said I interrupted in conferences. I'm an adult, for God's sake, a qualified lawyer. I may have made suggestions once or twice. But apparently pupils are supposed to sit in total silence. We're like ladies in waiting, in case madam needs a bit of photocopying or the name of a case. My previous supervisor wasn't like that. I should have had Georgie. He's a nice guy. I might charm him for a reference.'

A shadow fell across Luke's face.

'Don't worry, he's gay,' she said, with the hint of a smile. 'Oh, and one time she forgets to log off the computer in chambers. She rings from the tube and asks me to do it. I sort it for her, and she then accuses me of destroying her documents. She's a nightmare.'

He nodded, and she knew what was happening. He was weighing things up. Trying to be fair. He might love her, but he was trained not to rush to judgement. She needed a different tack.

'To be fair, things were going badly for her. She was mugged; her son was causing trouble; she was finding work hard. She made mistakes, lost things, got confused. She needed a scapegoat. Plus, she was having an affair.'

'How did you know?'

'She told me.'

'Wow. That suggests she must have trusted you.'

'She was drinking at the time. We were in the wine bar after work. It just came out. She asked if I knew the guy. He was one of my tutors at North Bank. Married. Bit of a creep. Then when I mentioned it again, she was furious.'

'Hmm.'

'She's a control freak. If I got a brief, she thought I was stealing her solicitors. Georgie warned me about that. She's got a reputation. Thinks everyone's out to get her.'

'Still, hitting out like that.'

'You sound like you don't believe me.' His eyebrows were lowered in a frown. 'Luke, I know I'm not perfect. But I'm not lying about this.'

'So, what are you going to do? Are you going to the police?'

She shrugged. 'I don't know. I haven't decided. I'd have to give evidence. I don't know if I can face that.'

'I'll take some photos, just in case. Your eye's a hell of a colour.'

He picked up his phone and took a range of shots from different angles. Then he said, 'So, what shall we do today? There's no way you're well enough to go out.' He looked into her good eye and traced his hand around the contour of her wound. 'Let's go back to bed,' he said.

'I'm a bit…' She was afraid she might shatter.

'I won't hurt you. I only want to hold you.'

He stood up and stretched out his arm for her. She took it.

–

They lay together in the grey light, the curtains half closed. Through the mid-morning stillness, she could hear the rumble of buses from the road below, overground trains in the near distance. London was at work; she and Luke were at peace in their private world. They faced each other, inches apart. Her head was throbbing more slowly now, but the pain was raw, and she was conscious of her damaged face. Yet he looked at her as if she were the loveliest creature he had ever seen. She longed for him, yet she was afraid that if he touched her, she might scream. After a few moments, he began to stroke her arms, her shoulders, then her breasts, her thighs. His desire met hers, coursing through her like an electric current. She pulled away.

'No, please, I can't. I'm sorry.'

'It's OK. You had a shock.'

Then he leant over her, held her face between his hands and kissed her good eye, her forehead and then, with a feather-light touch, her bad eye. The sheets were warm and the mattress soft against her nakedness, and his body beside her was her bulwark against the world. She remembered once telling another woman why she liked big men: that sense of being protected. And the other woman had replied that sometimes it's the big man you need to be protected from. But no, not with Luke.

He murmured, 'I'm sorry I was angry – about the boy's profile.'

'You were right. I deserved it.'

'I should have at least given you a chance to explain.'

'Shall I explain now?'

'No, not now. I just want to be close to you.'

He held her. One day she might have to tell him about Jacob, or some of it. But this was a special moment and she would not tell him now. His body was warm and comforting against her skin. They had never lain like this for so long without having sex and there was something soothing and sweet to her now in this simple affection. Like coming in from a long run, lying in a hot bath, only better. She was loved and safe. From now on she would take care. She couldn't afford to lose Luke.

'I'm sorry,' she said.

'For what?'

'For everything. For being difficult. You don't want to talk about it now and I get that. Only...' she snuggled into his neck, breathing the deep animal scent of his strong body, 'sometimes I'm afraid you'll throw me out.'

'You're crazy. I'm the one who should be afraid.'

'Afraid of what?'

'Afraid I'll bore you. Afraid I'll try to hold you down, put you in a box. Afraid you'll run away.'

'You'll never bore me. And I'd like that. A little box, just you and me and...'

She hesitated. This time yesterday she had been sure she would have an abortion, had persuaded herself it would be a kindness to destroy this baby before it had a chance to suffer, as suffer it surely would with such a mother. But everything had changed when Mel attacked her. She had attacked both Natasha and the child she was carrying. Natasha took a deep breath. If she told him now, she could never go back on that decision.

'And?' he nudged.

She let the breath out and as she did so, she knew that Mel had made the decision for her.

'There's something I've been meaning to tell you. I'm... we're... going to have a baby.'

Chapter Thirty-three

Mel

As she entered the flat, she could hear her son's voice drifting out from his room. Her body settled in relief. Whatever crazy things he might have done, at least he was home. And though she needed to confront him, she needed to support him too. He was young. Thoughtless. He meant no harm. But the anguish at what she had seen was churning inside her.

In the kitchen, an empty pizza box had been squeezed into the top of the bin. There were beer cans in the recycling. And now she heard the unfamiliar voice of a girl. This was a new development. Jacob rarely invited friends back to the flat and any girls that did come were in large chattering groups, picking him up on the way to somewhere else.

She stood by his door, listening. The words were unclear, the tone suggesting conversation rather than the excitement of teenage sex. She knocked.

'Hang on,' called Jacob. He opened the door a crack and his face appeared. His hair was tousled, but no more than normal.

'Hi, Mum.'

'Are you going to introduce me to your friend?'

He turned his head. 'Don, come and meet my mum.'

A bright pixie face framed in short black spiky hair appeared around Jacob's elbow. A small area around the ear had been shaved, drawing Mel's attention to three silver stud earrings and a feathery tattoo which ran down the side of the neck.

'Hello, I'm Don.'

'Good to meet you, Don. I'm Mel,' she said. There was an openness and confidence about the girl that was unusual among Jacob's gang. Then it hit her. Don. Donna. The girl who was not a girl. Her son was breaking his bail conditions.

'Don from the party?' she said, trying to sound calm.

'I go to lots of parties,' said Don and a huge smile broke across her delicate features. She was pretty, with a small nose and fierce dark eyes. The loose grey shirt failed to disguise her slim female form.

'It's OK,' said Jacob.

He was standing in the doorway, blocking his mother's path into the bedroom. Mel remained in the hall, less than a couple of feet away, aware that even a tiny step forward would feel to him like an invasion.

'What do you mean, OK? You're breaching your bail. You could go to prison. What the hell were you thinking?'

'Mum, it's OK. Nik's gone. Left the country. He and his mum are in Moscow. They're dropping the case. I'm going to the station to sign something tomorrow.'

Her heartbeat slowed.

'How do you know all this?'

'The policewoman rang me. The stroppy one. She said the witnesses weren't testifying so the CPS was dropping it. I rang round some of the guys. Turns out Nik's left the school. Something to do with his dad and Putin.'

'State secrets,' added Don with a cheery grin.

'The police should have told me,' said Mel.

'You weren't around. She said they'd write.'

'Good, innit,' said Don. 'Our Jake's a hero.'

'And the knife attack?'

'Mum, we don't know who it was. Anyway, it wasn't an attack, it was a scratch.'

Her body softened and she leant back against the wall for support.

'You all right, Mum?'

'I'm just relieved. So relieved.'

'Don's disappointed,' he said, turning to his friend.

Don punched Jacob playfully in the arm and said, 'Course not. I'm glad for you. Only I was kind of looking forward to the court bit. Good chance to speak out.'

'I'm sure you'll have the chance to speak out on another occasion,' said Mel, straightening up, 'maybe in a more sympathetic venue.'

'We're not looking for sympathy. People have got to understand. But you're right. There'll be another time. A better time.'

Mel could believe it. There was an assurance about this girl, this child, this person. It would be interesting to talk to her. But right now, she needed to speak to Jacob alone.

'Don, I have to talk to Jacob. It's important. Can I give you a lift home? Where do you live?'

'Not far. I can walk. No problem. You stay and talk to Jacob. Nice meeting you.' Mel took the offered hand, pleased and surprised by the unusual display of manners. They exchanged smiles.

Jacob walked slowly with Don towards the door. There was none of the verbal banter Mel had witnessed when he was with a member of his own sex. She realised she had never seen him alone with a girl, apart from one of his cousins, since he was in primary school. She withdrew to the sitting room, trying not to listen to their murmured goodbyes. The front door opened and shut and she could hear Jacob returning to his room. The sitting-room door was ajar and she called out, 'I need to speak to you.'

He stopped in the doorway. 'Speak.'

'Come and sit down. You're making me uncomfortable standing over me like that.'

He walked in, threw himself into an armchair, stretching out his long legs, resting them on the coffee table. One of his socks had a hole in it.

'I like Don,' she said. He said nothing and she added, 'Good about the case.'

'Yeah.'

'I need to talk to you. About Natasha.'

'What about her? I'm not contacting her again if that's what you mean. No way.'

'It's more complicated than that.'

She longed to tell him. But it would have to be an edited version. The version she was working on. And yet. There were things she needed to know. She pulled Natasha's phone out of her bag.

'I've got her phone.'

'What the f—' he stopped. He was sitting up straight now. She had taught him not to swear, taught him well. 'Why?' he asked.

'Are you any good at hacking a password?'

'What's this about?'

'You sent her photos.'

'How d'you know?' His troubled eyes were fixed on hers.

'She showed me.'

'For fucks sake.' The teaching had fallen away; the voice was angry. He jumped up as if to go and she sensed his internal struggle, the need to get away from her wrestling with the need to know what this was about.

'Please don't walk away, Jacob.' She kept her voice steady. It was important to stay in control. 'Natasha and I had a row. I almost lost it.' She had lost it. But she could never admit that to her son. 'So, you see, darling. I need to know exactly what you sent her. I'm assuming you took the pictures yourself.'

He sat down. 'So how come you got the phone?'

'She fell over. Dropped it. Jacob, we need to decide what to do.'

'You still haven't told me what this row was about.'

'I'll tell you. I promise. Just not tonight. Please, darling, trust me in this. Right now I need to know about the photos. I've seen a couple. I got the impression there were more. I could take the phone to a shop but...' She knew he could crack the password. He had told her, boasted about how easy it was. It was all on YouTube.

'I could do it but…' He hesitated. 'It won't help. She's already copied them. They could be anywhere now. You might as well just give this back.' He spoke in a low calm voice. It sounded strange to Mel, not like the son she knew. Then whatever was controlling him snapped and he exploded. 'Why d'you want to wind her up? She's a fucking nutcase.'

'Who said I wound her up?'

'You just told me you lost it.'

And she realised it was not only Natasha who had incensed him, but also his mother. It was Mel who had shown Natasha his photograph, she who had insisted he come to the park. His eyes were on hers, challenging her to answer with the truth and she couldn't help thinking of sons who turned against their mothers. She didn't reply and he lent back in his chair with an air of resignation and said, 'The phone's irrelevant. She doesn't need it. She can still post her crap all over the internet.'

'That's not what I meant.' And then, when he said nothing, she continued. 'Are there more?' They were bad enough. Could there be worse? 'You didn't actually, you know, do anything with her?'

'Fuck off, Mum. What do you think I am?'

'I don't know. That's the problem. I thought I did but I don't know any more.'

He slumped forward, head in his hands. Then he raised his head a little and fixed her hard with his dark eyes.

'No. I didn't, as you say, do anything with her. When I saw her in the park I freaked. That's why I came home. I already told you that. Only…'

'Only what?'

'There were texts.' Her head was already full. There was no space to process all this. 'Listen, Mum, give back the phone. There's no point in riling her. No point in breaking the password, no point in deleting anything. She'll have everything on her computer.'

She paused, waiting for her breath to still. 'OK. But keep what you've got.'

'What for?'

'If anything happens… I don't say it will… but if it does… if Natasha tries to make things difficult for me, for you, we need something to get back with. You're sixteen. She's twenty-nine. What she's been doing is not exactly a crime, particularly if you're OK, but it's a grey area. She'll say she never intended to meet you in person. But if it comes out, it'll do more harm to her than to you. Listen, darling, I'm not going to ask you to show me anything. I've seen enough. But whatever is there, I'm asking you to keep it. Just in case.'

'I don't want anyone seeing it. Any of it. I don't want anyone knowing about this.'

She refrained from asking why he had sent her the photo of his naked body in the first place. The answer was obvious. He was young. Young people were reckless. And she could see that he regretted what he had done. For a moment, as she looked at his pained expression, she forgot her own actions. But his next question cut through her thoughts.

'What have you done, Mum?'

'Nothing wrong.' What could she say? He would dig and dig. He was his parents' child. 'Like I said. We had a row. She fell over and hurt herself. Gran and I took her to hospital. She might try to blame me. That's all.'

She reached out and touched his hand as a wave of exhaustion crashed over her. Jacob didn't move but his eyes were searching. She drew back her hand as he began to speak.

'Was it about me? I told you not to say anything.'

'Please Jacob. I can't talk about it now. Yes, you came into it. But it wasn't just about you. There was a lot of stuff. I need to sleep on it. It's all a bit of a muddle in my head. But darling, don't worry. You've done nothing wrong. I mean you've been stupid but… I guess… we're all stupid at times.'

'Like you and that bloke.'

'Like me and that bloke. And I'm not seeing him anymore.' She couldn't meet his eyes, prayed he would let this drop.

After a moment's silence he asked, 'So are you giving back the phone?'

'Yes. I'll leave it in chambers.'

She wished she could tell him everything. There were many things she wished. She wished she had never shown Natasha the photo of her beautiful son, never offered her that coffee in Dulwich, never mentioned Paul. She wished she had not left her car in East Finchley, never asked Natasha to log off her computer, never taken a week off work. Jacob looked deflated and she sensed he didn't want to talk any longer. At least not now. All she could count on was that Natasha would not want her mischief-making publicised. But how could you count on anything with Natasha?

Through the swirl of thoughts, she heard her own mitigation: her good character, her successful career, her son. Then she heard the words of an imaginary prosecutor, 'Miss Goddard, you of all people should understand the consequences of your actions.'

She poured herself a glass of red wine and pulled back the curtains to look at the city at rest. On clear nights you could see stars beyond the light-polluted air, the faintest hint of infinity, though not tonight.

Tonight, the only visible lights were human, street lamps, splinters of brightness around the blinds and curtains in the houses opposite. She gulped her wine and, as it swam down her throat, she thought of Paul. For the last week he had been texting again. She had ignored the messages, but she wondered how long she could withstand the pressure. Despite the awkwardness of their last meeting, her body longed to be close to his once more, simply, without complication, as it had been in those early days, when secrecy went unmentioned and only added to the excitement.

Tomorrow she was due at Wood Green Crown Court to defend Vicky Brightman in her prosecution for assault of her ex-wife's partner. She should have been working on the case this afternoon. If only she had. But what happened in Dulwich had happened, and the only thing to do now was wait.

It was almost eleven. She would need to be up at six to go over the statements and refine her cross-examination. She should go to bed, but the events of the day had transformed exhaustion to a manic wakefulness, and she wouldn't sleep for at least an hour. She pulled out her phone to check the time. Another message from Paul.

I'm sorry about last time. Can we speak?

She stood up, walked to the bedroom, began to undress, putting out her court gear to speed her progress in the morning. The thought of what she had done was growing inside her, spreading like a bruise. She could see Natasha's edgy, troubling beauty. Both had sought confrontation, but it had been Mel who lost control. And she couldn't banish from her mind the panic on Natasha's face as she fell backwards, twisting, crashing the side of her head against the sharp edge of the dressing table. Mel had wanted to hurt her. She might be horrified at her own violence, but while she had, at the time, felt shock, and now felt both fear and regret, at no stage had she felt remorse.

She lay in bed staring at the crack of grey between the curtains. Her head swirled. Natasha on the floor, limp as a rag doll, Isabel, frightened and stunned to silence, the breakneck drive to the hospital, the clatter of trolleys, the scent of bodies and disinfectant in the waiting area.

Then in her mind it was morning and she was in one of the courts at Wood Green, the high-ceilinged Victorian space she had stood in so many times to represent feckless clients. Tomorrow it would be Vicky Brightman, but as Mel imagined the scene it wasn't Vicky in the dock, but herself, alone, friendless, and pleading for her life.

Chapter Thirty-four

Mel

Vicky Brightman was acquitted. For the four days of the trial the details of another person's struggle had blanked out Mel's own concerns. But as she packed up her wig and gown in the robing room, sounds and pictures looped through her head: angry words, jumbled objects on the floor, the glass edge of the dressing table, a pool of blood. She pulled out her phone. Two missed calls from Paul and a text asking her to ring. Ignoring other barristers chatting about their cases, she called him. The week's tension unravelled as she heard his warm, low voice asking her to come to Barnes. Now.

'Now?'

'I miss you. Caro's in Spain. On a yoga course.' He explained. 'You've always been curious about where I lived.'

Her heart was pumping fast. He had missed her. Despite the frostiness of their last encounter he still wanted her. What they had was special. They were good together. And now, more than ever, she longed for his touch as if it could weave the tangled strands of her life into a single fabric. Just once. And if it was to say goodbye, so be it. After three years together they both deserved something better than that awkward parting outside the Premier Inn.

'OK,' she said.

She set off for the station, wondering why he had suggested meeting at his house. Was there some perverse additional pleasure for him in bringing his other woman onto home territory?

Mel dispelled the thought as she imagined their lovemaking and what she hoped would be its gentle aftermath, those precious, companionable moments of easy talk. There was so much to tell him. The mugging, Jacob's arrest, Natasha's pursuit of her son, her own actions. Not all of it. But some. Enough to lighten the load.

He picked her up from the station in his battered Mercedes, the back of which looked like an extension of his office, piled high with boxes and papers. As they drove off, she sensed him glancing at her thighs. He knew every inch of her. But his look unsettled her, and she wished she were wearing trousers.

They turned into a quiet side road lined with pollarded lime trees. It was late afternoon, and the street was almost empty under the clear sky. A couple of women were pushing buggies along the narrow pavement. He slowed down and drove into a small brick parking area in front of a large semi-detached house.

'Here we are,' he said with uncharacteristic brightness.

Mel stepped out onto the path which ran alongside the neat garden. They were only twenty minutes from the centre of London, but the air was sweet with the scent of flowers. The silver and blue planting would be Caro's work.

The house was painted white and had bow windows, edged with dusty brick. Fifty years ago, it would have been considered a very ordinary house. Today it was a house to kill for. Millions of pounds of suburban understatement. Paul was right, she had been curious to see it. And she had suspected she might feel uncomfortable here. But she hadn't been prepared for the ripping pain that tore through her stomach as Paul unlocked the front door.

He walked ahead of her into an open-plan kitchen and sitting room. Huge sliding windows looked out over the garden and, as he stood waiting for her in the still bright afternoon light, he appeared shattered. His complexion was drained and blotchy. There were dark rings under his grey green eyes. He seemed smaller too and older, shoulders slightly hunched under his blue shirt.

'So,' he said, in the same bright tone, 'the matrimonial home.' They had not yet touched.

It was one of those cool interiors that featured in design magazines. A big, splashy, red and yellow abstract painting gave a touch of warmth, but the prevailing sense was neutral, a setting rather than a home. Framed photographs were ranged along the lower shelf of a wall bookcase, the young brown-haired Paul standing close to a smiling blonde woman with a full, open face; graduation portraits of the twin girls in academic gowns, clutching their degree certificates, wide-eyed and grinning under their improbable mortar boards. A few academic journals were scattered on the coffee table. A vase of dying yellow roses lent a mournful air. This was where Paul lived, where he slept and ate and prepared his lectures. It felt unreal.

'Sit down,' he said, brightness softening into something closer to friendliness as he indicated the wide sofa. 'Tea?'

'Thanks.'

He busied himself with water and teabags while she looked out to the garden.

To one side of a pond and beds there was a weeping birch casting an inviting pool of shade across a wooden bench. If this had been any other visit she would have suggested sitting outside. But this was not that sort of visit. She was no longer sure what sort of visit it was. At least her stomach was beginning to relax.

He came back with the tea and sat down on the armchair near her.

'It's been a few weeks,' he said.

'Eight,' she said, immediately regretting it. Counting weeks smacked of desperation.

'You been OK?'

'OK.'

She longed to spill it out, had thought she would. How she had lost all self-control, lashed out at her pupil, causing her to crash against a glass dressing table. But now that he was sitting in front of her she couldn't speak.

'You?' she asked.

'It's been tough,' he said. There had been difficulties at work, a female student accusing him of sexual impropriety. The accusation was bollocks, but the university had to go through the motions. She was about to ask what had happened when he explained.

'Her father died. She came to my office to explain why her dissertation was late. Wept all over me. Her middle-aged tutor. A perfect father substitute. Not much I could do about that.'

'So, what *did* you do?'

'I just stood there. I mean I could hardly hurl her off. The poor girl was distraught.'

'You didn't respond or anything?'

He winced. 'Fuck, no. I'm no saint but I'm not totally stupid. Still, it looks bad. She's made an official complaint. I could lose my job. Worse.'

'Did anyone see you? I mean when she... I mean what evidence does she have?'

'Who needs evidence? Her word against mine. Lovely young girl against lecherous old goat. Who they going to believe?'

'Why would she make it up?' She was pushing him. The habit was ingrained. Yet he seemed untroubled by her questioning, probably expected it.

'She was needy. Breaking down. About to fuck up her degree. I guess she wanted someone to blame. Maybe she believed her own lies. People do.'

She swallowed her tea. He had left the teabag in the cup and the taste was strong and bitter. 'And you wanted me to come over, so you could tell me about it?'

He stood up. 'I thought you would understand,' He took his teacup to the kitchen area, stared into the sink and said, 'You of all people.'

'Me of all people?' She heard her voice, brittle and sharp. It was not what she meant to say, not how she wanted this conversation to develop.

'I only meant that as a barrister; you don't jump to conclusions. Anyway, there's bugger all in it, but as you can see, I'm pretty steamed up about it.'

She asked, more gently this time, 'Did you tell anyone else. Caro? The girls?' In their three years together, she had never mentioned Caro's name.

'Of course not. Caro hates secrets. She wouldn't have been able to keep it from the girls. I don't want them to know. Not unless it's unavoidable.'

'Surely they wouldn't think…'

He walked to a low cupboard, pulled out a bottle of whisky and placed it on the kitchen counter. From another cupboard he took out two tumblers and a small water jug. He filled the jug from the tap and poured himself a whisky. A cloud crossed the sun outside and the air in the pale painted room was suddenly melancholy and cold. He said, 'Fuck knows what they think. Whisky?' She nodded. He poured the whisky.

'I trust you, Mel.'

'I was surprised when you contacted me. I mean, I thought maybe you'd had enough.'

He gave a weary smile. How well she knew that smile. It spoke of a life lived to the full, an understanding of the complexities of this crazy world, an understanding free of passion and illusion, shot through with a streak of determined selfishness that was curiously seductive. It was a smile that made women vulnerable, that won over his students and had probably seduced the young girl with the dead father. She still didn't know whether the smile was true or false, whether he practised it in the mirror to get the perfect curve of that well-defined mouth. But the eyes must be true. Only the most consummate actor can transform the message of his eyes and she doubted Paul was that. He came towards her with the whisky. 'I thought it was you who'd had enough.'

'It's been difficult. Work's been tough…' She might speak of Jacob and Natasha eventually, but not now. Both subjects were too big. He slugged his drink and sat down beside her. She sipped hers.

'I haven't had enough, Mel.'

She had taken off her court jacket and was sitting in her cream silk blouse and the skirt that was too short for a woman her age. He shifted closer, reached out and touched her arm, as if acknowledging that conversation was too complicated, too loaded, and that this was the language they understood. The touch was tentative. She wondered if he would suggest one of the bedrooms. Would he show her round the house and ask her to choose? But he made no such suggestions, only studied her face, continuing to stroke her arm. He looked younger now, energised. The sun had emerged from the clouds and the skin that had looked so worn and grey was glowing in the afternoon light. She didn't move, even when his hand began to trace the swell of her breast.

'Do you want me to stop?' he whispered.

'No,' she murmured. She wanted him to go on and on, stroking her body through the film of her clothes forever. Nothing more, only this. But she heard herself say, 'Kiss me.' And everything changed.

His lips met hers as they had a hundred times before, but within seconds he was pushing hard against her, his breathe sour with whisky, his large tongue filling her mouth. Her heart went cold, but she didn't stop him. He had always been a wonderful lover, slow, careful, considerate. Never like this. At times his desire had been fierce, but this urgency was closer to anger.

He stopped kissing her and pulled away. She shifted to the edge of the cushion and lowered her feet to the floor, about to stand up, gather her things, walk out. But his eyes were locked on hers, gluing her to the sofa. It was as if she'd been hypnotised, split in two. Part of her wanted to leave but the other part, the part that prevailed, could not move. Paul was looking at her, smiling, waiting for her to act. Without speaking she started to undress. Soon he was down on her with his firm lips and strong tongue.

He pushed himself inside her, burying his face in the cushions. She was staring past the side of his head to the ceiling as he plunged into her. His curly grey hair tickled her cheek. Her mind was drifting. She should never have come. She needed to get home. She no longer knew this man in this bland house that looked like something out of a TV property show. He needed a woman and she could have been anyone. She'd responded from habit and because she didn't know what else to do. It was too late, but it would soon be over. It was. He slid off her, reaching for the Kleenex on the coffee table. She heard strange gulping sounds, and when she looked up at him, he was sitting with his head bowed over his knees, heaving with sobs. 'Forgive me, Mel.'

'It's all right,' she heard herself say. And then. 'I wanted it too.'

'Not like that.'

'What is it, Paul?'

He didn't answer but handed her a bundle of Kleenex, turning away from her as she wiped herself and pulled up her knickers and tights.

'Do you want to shower?' he asked. She looked up. His eyes were pink and puffed with tears.

'No, I'll do it at home.' Not here. Not in this house.

'I'll take you to the tube.'

'This minute?'

'You won't want to hang around here. I'm no use to anyone.'

'Christ, Paul, it's not just about fucking. You're upset. It happens. It doesn't matter. I know you're not like that.'

'It doesn't matter?' He sounded incredulous.

'No.' It did, of course. Everything mattered. But he was no longer weeping. That was a relief. She said, 'I'll make more tea.' She stood up and moved to the spotless kitchen area, glanced about her and switched on the kettle. Inside one of the cupboards she found a row of teas, herbal, China, English breakfast. Choosing English breakfast, she put two teabags in cups, poured on boiling water and found milk in the fridge. When she turned around, he was dressed.

They sat with their tea, the air heavy with silence. She stood up. 'You're right. We're both upset. We both have stuff in our lives. It's not going to work. I shouldn't have come.'

And he murmured with unexpected tenderness, 'What stuff?' When she didn't reply he added, 'I've been a selfish shit. The least I can do is listen to your stuff.'

She sensed the effort it cost him to speak like this. Whatever he had done, this was an old friend who knew her better than anyone else and she needed a friend. The man with the puffy face who had just fucked her on the family sofa was not the whole man. That was an aberration. What if he had gone a step too far with this student? What if his whole career was on the brink of ruin? Should they not be partners in iniquity? At the very least she could give him time. She asked, 'Did you hear anything more from Natasha Baker?'

'No. Why?'

'Only she's had an accident. She's off work.'

'What sort of accident? Is she OK?'

'I think so. Sort of. I mean, it was serious, but she seemed OK when we left the hospital.'

'Hospital?' He sounded alarmed.

And she told him. Not what she had wanted to tell him. The version she offered him did not bring the sweet unburdening she had longed for, but it was the version that would become increasingly familiar over the next few weeks.

'So, are you all right?'

'I'm fine. She didn't hurt me. She tried to, but she fell. She was totally out of control. Doesn't like being challenged.'

'Still… going behind your back like that… I mean if she wanted to meet your mother she could have just asked you.'

'She did. It's a long story, Paul. She lost my trust months ago, soon after she started. You remember the email. She likes to stir it up.'

'Lucky she didn't get the tenancy then. But… did she say anything else?' A slither of fear ran through his voice. She knew what he was alluding to. Had Natasha mentioned his name? But no, she reassured him, Paul had not featured in the quarrel.

He looked unconvinced, abandoned his tea and stood up to pour himself another whisky. She had been unable to finish her own. It tasted like their last kiss. The distance between them had never felt so vast. How could she tell him about Jacob? She was mad to even consider it.

'Listen, I ought to go. Jacob will be home and I've got to prepare for tomorrow.'

'I'll take you to the tube.'

'I can walk. It's a nice afternoon.' She needed to get out of this house.

'I'll take you.' His expression was set, determined and she sensed that he would have her do what was required, and that if she tried to leave now, he would stop her. He handed over her jacket. The crying man had vanished. She was edgy and unsatisfied, and the ludicrous thought came into her head that they might try again. Then she asked herself how and why she could think such a thing. She was beginning to hate him, but she hated herself more.

And she knew why he didn't want her to walk out alone. It wasn't worth a confrontation. She'd had enough of confrontations. She followed him to the car. He opened the door and she dropped onto the passenger seat.

He drove quickly away in the comfortable knowledge that none of his neighbours, nor the women on the street with buggies, would have noticed a lone woman in her early forties turning up at his door with a large bag, spending an hour in his house in the middle of the afternoon when his wife was away.

They reached the station car park. He turned off the engine and waited for her to get out. She sensed he was not going to kiss her, not going to suggest another meeting. She sat for a moment, turned and pecked him on an unresponsive cheek. Would he say sorry again? He said nothing.

'Goodbye, Paul.'

'Bye, Mel. Let me know how you get on.'

'You too.'

She opened the passenger door and stepped out onto the pavement. Paul drove off and she stood alone for a few minutes. Commuters scurried out of the tube, jostling past her. The long summer evening rolled out before her.

There was a letter on her doormat when she arrived home. A letter inviting her to attend Tolpuddle Road Police Station at ten a.m. the following Tuesday. Miss Natasha Baker had made a complaint.

Chapter Thirty-five

Mel

Everything about the room was horribly familiar, the grey metal table and chairs, the flickering strip-light, the hard acoustic.

Two male officers introduced themselves; Mel immediately forgot their names. One, sandy-haired, pasty-faced, not much more than twenty years old, made no contribution to the inter-view other than turning the tape on and off. The other was a coarse-featured man in his thirties whose flat vowels rasped across Mel's nerves like nails on a blackboard. She forced herself to focus as he outlined the case against her. Neither of the two friends she had called was available and she wasn't going to accept any old duty solicitor. Better to manage alone.

'Aren't I going to see Natasha's statement?' Mel asked.

'In time,' said the older man. 'We've told you the main points. The examining doctor takes the view there must have been a degree of force to have resulted in the wound sustained. There is one other thing Miss Baker wanted us to tell you. She's pregnant. Fortunately, it seems that there is no damage to the baby.'

Pregnant. The word was a slap across the face. What chance did Mel have? Pregnant women were believed. Pregnant women were untouchable. Pregnant women didn't spit out bitter words. Mel felt the officer's small eyes boring through her.

'We'll be speaking to your mother, Mrs Isabel Goddard.'

'Please don't involve her. She won't cope.'

'We understand she was an eyewitness.'

'I don't know what she saw.' True. You could never know what another person had seen. But she did remember her mother standing in the doorway, did remember the warning, 'No, Mel,' in the moment before the attack. What would Isabel say? Mel felt hot and cold at once as she heard the familiar words: 'You do not have to say anything. But it may hurt your defence if you do not mention when questioned something which you rely on in court. Anything you do say may be given in evidence.'

'So, I'm being charged?'

'We'll hear what you have to say.'

This was the moment. She should confess all. Explain everything. Provocation was no defence, but it was strong mitigation. An early plea meant a lighter sentence. Do it now. Do what you believe in. Bursts of anger were wrong. Violence was wrong. But, worst of all was anger coupled with violence, followed by the relentless drip of dishonesty. For that there could be no redemption.

No damage, the officer had said. How could they be sure? She prayed he was right, though she couldn't help wondering about the hapless child.

Her story bounced off the hard walls, her language articulate and practised. After a lifetime of public speaking she didn't know how to sound genuinely troubled. In front of an audience, she was cool, prepared, confident. The worst way to proceed now. But it was all she could do. She had decided before arriving that she would give a broad outline of her actions. Not too much detail. She could refine it later if necessary. She prayed it would not be necessary.

She admitted that she and her pupil were no kindred spirits. There was nothing she could put her finger on. The pupil–supervisor relationship was delicate, particularly when the pupil was older, more experienced than usual. Mel had tried to be fair, but things had not worked out. It happened. Two women who simply didn't like each other. Different backgrounds. The inherently competitive nature of the Bar.

She held back on the Attendance Note, the email to Paul. With luck she would never need them. If ever she did, a jury would understand why she had kept them back, her desire not to bring up confidential correspondence or unfounded suspicion. A jury. She was already imagining a trial and she hadn't even been charged. As for Jacob, she couldn't even utter his name in this vile place. It would be sacrilege. She took a deep breath and continued.

She had met Natasha for coffee in the Dulwich Picture Gallery. Her pupil needed a reference and there were a few matters she, Mel, wished to discuss. During the conversation Mel had referred to her mother, Isabel Goddard, a retired actress who had appeared in a long running soap. It turned out that Natasha was a fan and was eager to meet Isabel. But Isabel had become somewhat reclusive in her old age and Mel was reluctant to arrive with an uninvited guest. Natasha seemed disappointed but Mel thought no more about it until two weeks later.

She had let herself into her mother's house and was waiting for Isabel to return from an outing. It was hard to describe her feelings when Isabel walked in with Natasha. Mel had been stunned. Not simply that Natasha had chosen to befriend her mother independently. But that she had failed to mention to Isabel that she was her daughter's pupil. It was duplicitous, inexplicable.

They had been standing in the spare bedroom. An argument arose. As the argument grew heated Natasha had rushed towards her, whether to grab her or hit her it was impossible to say. Natasha was so unpredictable she might even have been intending a conciliatory hug. With appalling luck the poor girl had tripped, probably on one of the many high heeled shoes that were lined up across the carpet. And so, she fell, crashing against the glass edge of the dressing table.

The man's eyes tunnelled through her. The technique was routine, intended to intimidate. There were rules about what the police could say and do, but there were no rules about their facial expression. It was their final weapon. When he asked for the second time about the relationship with Natasha, she told him she had nothing to add. She had already been open and honest about the difficulties. Anyway, the relationship was irrelevant. What mattered was what had happened in her mother's spare room last Sunday afternoon and she had already told them what she had witnessed. There was nothing more she could say.

Privately she told herself she would need the support of a good solicitor if the police wished to take this further. She had said too much already. The older officer repeated the date, stated the precise time and declared that he was terminating the interview. The younger man turned off the tape. Mel was free to go.

–

She went straight to chambers and handed in Natasha's phone. She emptied her pigeonhole and went home to prepare her next case. For the next week she threw herself into work, focusing on other lives. At home, at night, her own crashed in, images of blood, of falling, the bleak, grey interview room, swirling panic about the future. Jacob avoided conversation and for once she was glad that he was wrapped up in his separate world. She could only speak in pleasantries, her voice and body in the room with him, her mind elsewhere, circling, ruminating. Just as she was considering whether to ring the police to see how they were progressing with Natasha's complaint, she was invited to attend the station again.

She was charged with Assault Occasioning Actual Bodily Harm and given police bail with a condition not to have contact with the complainant Miss Natasha Baker. Nor should she speak to any potential witnesses about the case. This included her mother, Mrs Isabel Goddard.

'I'll have to speak to my mother. She lives alone. She's frail, elderly. She depends on me.'

'You may see her. But you should not speak to her about the events that led to Miss Baker's injuries.'

She had no choice but to agree and sign the conditions. In a daze she walked out into the busy street, narrowly avoiding a cyclist hurtling across a zebra crossing. She could no longer keep her secret from Jacob but how could she tell him? She might call Claude. He would maintain a barrister's detachment, clicking into professional mode, even when dealing with the mother of his son. She carried on walking in the direction of chambers. It was almost noon. Perfect. Most of the tenants would be in court or working from home. Her heart was thumping as she entered the clerks' room.

'Hi, Andy.'

'Hi, Mel,' said Andy. 'Everything OK? Haven't seen you for a bit.'

'Sort of. It's kind of complicated. I'll need a couple of days off court. I hope that's not too inconvenient for you. I just wanted to pick up a few things and check my pigeonhole.'

'Sure. Two new care cases came in for you yesterday. Natasha had an injury. Did you hear?'

'Yes. I did. Poor girl.' He looked as if he wanted a chat. She smiled and said, 'Catch up later?' as she headed to the computer room, the room where three months ago, Natasha had scanned her emails. It was empty. She sat down. Voices clamoured in her head.

'*Plead not guilty. You need to keep working.*'

'*Plead guilty. How can you stand up in court again?*'

'*Everyone in chambers will know about the charge.*'

'*The media will love it.*'

'*What will you tell Jacob?*'

Just as she felt as if her head would explode, she remembered the advice her own pupil supervisor had given her more than twenty years ago. Take it slowly. Stage by stage. Law is only a form of common sense. No magic in it. It's problem solving. Like life. And don't forget to breathe.

For long minutes she sat alone, breathing, trying to empty her mind. Then she opened her eyes, picked up the phone and asked the receptionist to put her through to her head of chambers, Jeremy Troughton, QC. It was time to go public.

Chapter Thirty-six

Mel

Bridge Court was not a wealthy set of chambers and even its head, a busy QC with a large murder practice, had only a small room to himself. The window looked out over a tiny sunken courtyard. Its very modesty brought up a tangle of emotions.

Jeremy Troughton QC stood up when Mel entered, inviting her to sit in the leather upholstered chair facing him, the one usually occupied by clients. She felt herself trembling as she sat down.

He was the only member of chambers who met the public's fantasy of what a barrister should look and sound like: the stern gaze, the head of thick grey hair swept back from a high forehead, the deep public-school voice. He asked how he could help, and she outlined her edited version of what had occurred.

He listened attentively and, as she spoke, the enormity of her possible loss punched her heart. She had been a tenant in this place for twenty years, a pupil here when a small group of high-minded criminal and family barristers had broken away from another set to focus on Legal Aid work. Some of those people were now taking on private work to survive and, like most chambers, it had grown. At that stage there had been only eight of them. Now there were more than fifty.

Bridge Court was her second home, her other family. After Claude left her, it had been a comfort to walk in from the hurly burly of London courts to meet fellow tenants in the scruffy communal kitchen for a cup of tea. They would compare notes about judges, opponents, solicitors. When everything had changed at home, it was a place holding some sense of continuity. Increasingly her colleagues worked remotely, and she missed the chambers' companionship. But it was still there if you looked for it. There was usually someone around to bounce off the latest case law or, more likely, court gossip.

'Speak to the Bar Standards Board,' said Jeremy. 'Self-report before anyone else passes it on. Natasha's solicitor might have contacted them already. They'll want details immediately but they're unlikely to act while there's a trial pending. As to work, unless and until they say otherwise, it's up to you.'

'I don't see how I can carry on. Natasha's still here. I'm not allowed any contact with her. She's got another two months of pupillage to complete. After that she might want to squat.'

'Paula's offered to take her on as a pupil. And there's no need for you to meet. I'll speak to the clerks. Just let them know if you're planning to come in. As for squatting, I don't think that would be wise.'

'She might have a job with CPS. I wasn't prepared to write a reference but I expect someone will.'

Jeremy lowered his eyebrows. His thin mouth tightened. It was impossible to read his thoughts.

'I'll have a word with Donald.'

'Tresiger?'

Donald Tresiger was Director of Public Prosecutions and had overall responsibility for the CPS. A word in his ear would surely assist Natasha's recruitment. It crossed Mel's mind that in several other countries a word in Tresiger's ear could lead to the CPS dropping the charge, but this was the English legal system, revered throughout the world for its honesty and integrity.

'The same. We were at Magdalen together. I'm sure he can sort it.'

Difficult as it was to accept that Natasha might get away with her sickening behaviour, Mel couldn't help feeling that a job with the CPS might be the best way to shut her up, the best way to put a brake on her reckless conduct. The image of Jacob's naked body rose in her mind. Natasha must know that Mel would not hold back if the photos were posted to the world. For the first time in her life, Mel was grateful for the old boys' network.

'No point in you leaving immediately. It'll be months till trial.'

'They may want to expedite matters because of the pregnancy.'

'Well, we're not going to ask you to go. As far as Bridge Court is concerned, you're innocent until proved guilty. I won't go into Natasha's motivations. That's a matter for your legal representative. Mel, you know as well as I do that a barrister's trained to keep calm in a storm. When the going gets tough the tough get going and so forth. Apply it to yourself and you'll be fine. I'd be surprised if it goes as far as trial. Any witnesses?'

'My mother.'

'Perfect. She'll back you up. They'll drop it.'

'I'm not sure.'

'Have you thought who you'll use if it gets that far?'

'Maybe Alisha.'

'Good choice. I imagine she'll do it pro bono.'

'I hope so.'

Alisha Mehta had recently left Bridge Court for a more prestigious, human rights set. She was highly regarded and, having moved on from Bridge Court, she would be able to represent Mel without any suggestion of special interest.

'You've a son, haven't you?' As Jeremy asked about Jacob, she saw another, softer, side to her head of chambers and remembered that Jeremy too had a son, a wayward lad with drug problems.

'Yes, Jacob. He's just sixteen.'

'You'll need to keep working.'

'If it's all right with you I'll do what's in my diary for the next two months. After that I'd prefer to take a sabbatical till it's all over.'

'Your decision. If it helps, I'm on the board of the Barristers' Benevolent. You could always apply for funds to tide you over.'

'I'll be OK.'

'You should prepare a statement for your solicitors. I'll happily look it over for you. Natasha might have put something on social media.'

'I expect she has. I don't intend to hide anything. I'll do what you advise. Whatever happens I'll lose work.'

'You'd be surprised. Solicitors and clients like a bit of excitement. After an acquittal your practice will bounce back. You'll soon make up for the lost time.' He stood up, ending the interview. 'Thank you for coming to see me, Mel. I know we barristers can seem wrapped up in our own work. But Bridge Court has always had a heart. We all support you. Stay strong.'

He held out his hand. She took it and he placed his other hand on top of hers. The eyes that had seemed stern were now warm and kind. A lump rose in her throat. It occurred to her that if Bridge Court was her second family, Jeremy was the father she had lost.

Part Three

February

Chapter Thirty-seven

Mel

'Good to see you again, Mel,' said Alisha, smiling, her lovely dark eyes glinting through her heavy spectacles. It was February. There were two weeks to go before the trial and Mel hadn't seen Alisha since the previous September. A fortnight's window was nothing unusual, but the trial felt terrifyingly close. Alisha was busy with a successful practice and this was the first date that could be arranged. Mel's savings were dwindling fast, but there was no way she would be granted Legal Aid. She was profoundly grateful to Alisha for agreeing to represent her for no fee.

'You're very kind to do this.'

'You'd do the same for me.'

Mel smiled, unable to imagine the tables turned. She looked about her. Alisha had done well. Much as Mel loved her own chambers, Kings Bench Walk was in a different league. She thought about the threadbare carpets on the upper floors of Bridge Court, the ancient fittings in the kitchen and toilets, the references to premises at chambers' committee meetings and the inevitable conclusion that refurbishment was more than they could afford. By contrast, King's Bench Walk had an air of understated prosperity with its polished wood panelling, soft grey carpet, and recently painted walls.

From her seat next to Alisha's desk, Mel could see through a window to the tops of plane trees, jagged fingers against a winter sky. If she walked over to the window, she guessed she would have been able to pick out the roofs and chimney pots of Middle Temple Lane, the distant outline of the London Eye and the curve of the muddy river as it swept towards Waterloo and Westminster. But the view was for the benefit of the barristers who worked here. She was a client now, waiting for the difficult questions.

On the few occasions they had defended together, Mel had studied Alisha's measured court manner. Her own style was, she suspected, more animated. It was difficult to gauge. Colleagues would not necessarily tell the truth if asked for a critique. The chambers' website published a few reviews. She had checked yesterday and the reviews were still there:

'Melanie Goddard manages to combine professional detachment with a deep compassion for the family client.'

'If you want a barrister who cares, go for Mel Goddard.'

'Sharp on the law, and sharp on her opponent, Mel Goddard is much more than a safe pair of hands.'

As agreed with Jeremy, she had completed the important cases in her diary, avoided going into chambers and ceased working in early October. It had been four months now and solicitors who asked for her were told she was on 'sabbatical'. It was the first time since her maternity break after Jacob's birth that she had taken more than two weeks off work.

Alisha started with the background, the relationship with Natasha, the meeting in Dulwich, Natasha's interest in Darcy Black. The Attendance Note allegation was common knowledge since the tenancy interview, but Mel chose not to dwell on that. Her story would focus on Natasha's surprise infiltration into her mother's life, Mel's suspicion about the designer shoes, the costumes and jewellery. Whether she was right or wrong was not the issue. Indeed, being in the wrong with regard to Natasha's intentions could only assist her. It would give Natasha a motive for lashing out.

A slender young man with eyes as lovely as Alisha's was tapping away beside them on his laptop. Alisha had introduced him as her pupil, Ilias. Apart from smiling and standing up as she entered, he had said not a word.

After about twenty minutes, Alisha asked Ilias to make them all some tea and he left the room with a quiet grace. Mel wondered whether he would object after she had gone. She remembered Natasha taking a stand on making tea.

In his absence, Alisha asked what Mel had been doing since she stopped working.

'Helping Mum mostly. Looking after Jacob.'

'Must be nice to have a bit of time off.'

'In a way, yes.'

She'd had no choice. The Bar Standards Board had told her they would delay any regulatory proceedings until after the outcome of the trial, but the charge had hit both the legal and the national press. One satirical legal website called it the 'clash of the barrister babes' using provocative photoshopped pictures of her and Natasha in court wigs, boxing gear and gloves. At the pre-trial review of R v Goddard, the judge warned that further comment whether in traditional print, online or social media could lead to charges of contempt of court. Traditional print and online media ceased speculation, but social media swirled with anonymous comments.

Mel was astonished at the level of interest and flurry of attacks. Georgie suggested they were probably disgruntled trainee barristers who had failed to get tenancies. After one particularly vicious Tweet, Paul called her. He apologised for his long silence, explained he had been preoccupied himself with the student allegations he had told her about and asked if she'd like to meet for lunch. She was polite but cool, telling him she didn't feel like talking to anyone at the moment. It was hard to imagine that their bodies had once been entwined in ardour, soaked in each other's sweat, that she had experienced an ache of separation when he stood up to go to the bathroom. After the call she uninstalled Facebook, Twitter and Instagram from her phone, wondering why she hadn't done it long ago.

But though Jeremy had asked her to remain absent from chambers while the charge hung over her, in private a few of her colleagues were supportive. She was particularly touched by her clerk, Andy, who called her once a week to see how she was getting on. Georgie's support she had expected, though he was always careful not to slag off Natasha. Most of the tenants were wary about taking sides publicly, but after Natasha's pupillage had come to an end, Jess had rung and suggested a walk on Hampstead Heath. They had crunched through dead leaves, talking generally about their children, their elderly parents, the grim happenings in the wider world, anything but the forthcoming trial. Their conversation was unremarkable, but Mel felt as if she had been invited in from a storm and wrapped in a warm rug.

There were other friends, women she had neglected in the flurry of work, and over a drink or a coffee she could focus on their concerns and almost forget her own. She took up swimming again. Ploughing through cold water gave her some relief from seemingly endless rumination. But these were merely temporary respites. She considered contacting her solicitor friend Lauren who had taken on her case and instructed Alisha. Mel would tell her what had really happened. That it was she who had lunged towards Natasha. But as she moved to bring up Lauren's number, she hesitated then put away her phone. A guilty plea might ease her conscience. With luck she would get a suspended sentence or even just a fine. But it would mean the end of her career. A conviction would not automatically disbar her from practising. Barristers had been involved in brawls before. But no chambers would take on a woman who was convicted of assaulting her own pupil.

She had spoken to Jacob, told him what she planned to tell the court. Natasha had rushed her. Mel had held up her hands to protect herself, an act of self-defence that had led to Natasha tripping and banging her head. He appeared to believe her and as the weeks passed, she began to believe her own story. When she tried to raise the issue of the photographs he refused to discuss it.

'Leave off, Mum. Nothing anyone can do now. I was a fool. I know that.'

But he looked anxious and she needed to reassure him, 'She won't post them online. I'm sure of that. But promise...'

He interrupted. 'Of course I won't fucking do it again. I'm not a complete idiot.'

Though she sounded more sure than she felt. Natasha had a reckless streak. She was capable of anything. And if she wanted to give the jury a motive for Mel's attack, the photos would be perfect. Her pupil's thirst for revenge might well be stronger than any instinct of self-preservation.

She told Alisha some of this, commented on the media frenzy, her relief as it died down. What she didn't tell her, what she told no one, was her sense of being cut loose, the blank mornings after Jacob left for his new sixth form college, the unlooked-for leisure time. It was not clear whether the work gave meaning to her life or simply disguised her life's lack of meaning. What did it matter? It had kept her away from a black hole. The edge, the hurry, had disappeared. Perhaps forever. If she had known it was to be forever it might have been easier to bear. She could mourn. Put her career behind her. But this was like losing a loved one without knowing how they had died.

Ilias came back with the tea. They had already covered Mel's relationship with Natasha, the difficulties, some of which Mel had explained, some of which she chose to ignore. Once Ilias was settled with his laptop, they moved on.

'Why did you go to your mother's house that Sunday when you knew she would be out with her new friend?'

'I needed to get out of the flat. I was struggling with an Advice. Plus, I was worried about Mum. Last time I saw her the house was a mess and I was sure she wasn't eating properly. I had a key. I just thought I'd go over. Check that everything was as it should be.'

'In what way?'

'Mum mentioned a new cleaner. I wondered how she had managed. The house was a disaster zone when I last went round. I thought I might do a bit of cleaning.'

Alisha looked unconvinced, possibly remembering the chaos of Mel's desk when they shared a room, 'And did you? Clear up? Clean?'

'I didn't need to. The place was spotless. Never seen it so tidy.'

'So, you waited for your mother and her new friend.'

'Yes.'

'Did you have any idea this new friend was Natasha?'

'None whatsoever. Why is that significant?'

'Only that Digger might try to suggest you were waiting to confront Natasha, possibly even harm her.'

At the mention of Digger her heart thumped.

'Digger?'

'Diggory-Brown, yes. He's prosecuting.'

'All I can say is, I'm glad I've got you. He's a pit bull.'

'Tough yes, but of course as a prosecuting counsel he will need to be even-handed.'

'I'll believe that when I see it. If I wasn't in the dock, I'd say this could be fun.'

'You haven't answered my question.'

'I had no idea Natasha had met my mother.'

That at least was the truth. They moved on. Mel described her edited version of what happened that afternoon. Her irritation that Natasha had befriended her mother behind her back, her suspicion as to her motives prompted by seeing her in her mother's clothes and jewellery. Her insistence that Natasha leave, followed by Natasha's sudden outburst. Natasha had accused Mel of failing to support her, of ensuring she didn't get the tenancy. They had argued, voices were raised then Natasha had rushed at her. Mel instinctively raised a hand to protect herself. Natasha, still unsteady after her hypo, had toppled backwards. As far as she could recall Natasha was still wearing high heels. Mel could remember her body twisting as she fell onto the edge of the dressing table.

As soon as Mel had finished, she remembered the shoes on the floor. Hadn't she already told someone it had been the shoes which caused Natasha to trip? The police? Lauren? She needed to get her story straight. Her other potential problem was her mother. Isabel was a prosecution witness. Her statement emphasised the ill-feeling between Mel and Natasha, referred to raised voices, accusations. But there was no mention of an assault by either woman. One minute Natasha was shouting at Mel, the next minute she was flying across the room.

'I won't be challenging your mother,' said Alisha. 'Your versions differ in tiny details but not fundamentally. I've told the CPS her statement could be read. I'm not sure why they want her.'

'I don't trust Digger. What's he playing at?'

'Don't worry, Mel. I'll make sure he sticks to the rules.' Ilias was still tapping. Alisha stopped and wrote something in her own notebook.

The conference was going as well as she could have hoped, but Mel knew how quickly things could turn in court. She was firming up her story. She might have forgotten about the shoes but that was hardly surprising. Everything had happened fast. Some details were precise, others vague. A hint of muddle wasn't necessarily a bad thing. She didn't want to sound too rehearsed.

An hour had passed. She was describing the trip to the hospital, Natasha's continued confusion, the stilted parting outside her flat. Alisha was no longer prompting her but was looking hard into her eyes and at that moment Mel knew why Alisha was so good in court, why she had a reputation for destroying the prosecution case. She could see when someone was lying, knew exactly where to aim her darts.

'You could plead guilty,' she said.

Mel's heart stopped. 'I'm not guilty.'

'I'm only pointing it out. You would, as you know, get a lighter sentence than if you were found guilty after a trial.'

'Alisha, you don't believe I'm guilty, do you?'

'I shouldn't need to remind you, Mel, that what I believe is irrelevant. I am here to follow your instructions and give you advice.'

'And you're advising me to plead guilty?'

'Not at all. Your plea is your decision.'

'I'm not changing my plea.'

'Fine. Now is there anything else? Anything you haven't told me that might be relevant, even faintly relevant to the case? Anything about Natasha?'

'I don't think so.'

'Did you know she was pregnant?'

'I had no idea.'

'You're aware of course it's still an aggravating factor. Hitting a pregnant woman.'

'I've already said I didn't hit her. And, of course, I'm aware.' Mel could feel the irritation rising. She gripped the side of her chair with one hand, forcing herself to stay seated, reminding herself that Alisha was just doing her job.

'It's important to be open with me, Mel. If there is anything more that can explain Natasha's behaviour prior to the events in question it may help you, if only to sway the sympathies of the jury. You know the rules. You can tell me anything you want. Leave me to decide if it's relevant. If you then instruct me not to mention it, it will go no further. But I can't mislead the court.'

Mel thought fast. The Jacob story. The email to Paul. Both shed a bad light on Natasha but neither of them helped Mel. Both offered a motive for the assault and the last thing she wanted was the court hearing about her affair. Jacob had made her promise to say nothing. The thought of his name being raised in evidence caused a physical pain to rip through her insides. To her relief there was nothing about him in Natasha's witness statement. There was no reason for him to be dragged into this unless Isabel had heard the taunt or seen the photo. Her mother's statement was silent on both points, but anything might come out under cross-examination. Should Mel pre-empt trouble by telling Alisha now?

'Mel?' Alisha's voice cut through her racing thoughts. 'Is there anything else?'

'No. Nothing.'

Her editing had been extreme. A jury would sense there was a lot more going on in this relationship. But as she had reminded herself, as she anticipated any judge would tell a jury, the verdict must depend on one discrete set of facts, the actions that occurred in Isabel Goddard's spare room that afternoon last summer. Mel would keep it simple and hope her mother did the same.

'Thanks so much, Alisha. I can't tell you how grateful I am.'

'See you Monday week then. Can you be there at nine a.m.?'

Mel nodded and stood up. She wanted to go to the window to look out. Had she simply been visiting an ex-colleague she would have stepped across the room to admire the view. But everything had changed. She and Alisha were no longer on the same level.

'Ilias will show you out,' said Alisha as they stood together at the door of the conference room. Alisha held out her hand and Mel shook it. It felt strange to shake this woman's hand. She was no longer a friend but a client.

Ilias walked with her to the clerks' room and the outer lobby, pushing open the heavy door that led to the stone staircase.

'There's a lift if you want.'

'Happy to walk. Thanks again,' said Mel, turning to walk slowly down the familiar stone staircase. Twenty years ago, she had climbed these stairs to attend a tenancy interview in the set of chambers on the opposite side of the landing. She had been asked difficult points of law and procedure and failed to reach the second stage. How different it had been at Bridge Court.

She'd already had a couple of friends there, one of whom had indicated what questions she was likely to be asked at interview. The questions had come up. Mel had been granted the tenancy along with a bad case of impostor syndrome.

She reached the bottom step. As she walked out into afternoon sun she was thinking about Digger. How he would enjoy ripping her to shreds. She turned left beside the car park towards the elegant terrace of Crown Office Row. There had been an interview here too. Once again, complicated law and procedure. Once again, a failure to reach the shortlist.

Voices battled in her head. One told her she was strong; she was prepared. She was fighting for her son as well as her career. A minor deception was nothing compared to the destruction of his security.

The other, quieter, voice reminded her of the barrister's duty of honesty and integrity, the duty not to mislead the court. Whatever she had done, she should plead guilty, explain. Her mitigation was strong. Any sentence would be suspended. Wouldn't it? The murmur faded to a whisper so tiny it was no longer distinguishable from the sound of the slight breeze wafting across the Temple. A third voice, deeper, louder, thrumming through her body with the persistence of a drumbeat, told her the impostor was about to be revealed.

Chapter Thirty-eight

Mel

Through habit, she had taken the more familiar but less popular route, passing the back windows of her chambers, walking where her feet took her. Now, as she stopped beside a low wall, she realised they had taken her to Kath's bench.

The air was mild for winter and she put down her bag, pulled her coat across her legs and sat. Here in the empty garden, wrapped in the grey stone and faded brick of the fine buildings, she sensed, as always in this spot, the presence of her old friend. Kath would not have allowed herself to get into this mess. She would have confronted Natasha at the first hint of her pupil's transgression, would never have allowed Natasha to infiltrate her private life as Mel had done. Until recently she had been able to hear Kath's voice. But the distinctive tone had faded with the years as colour fades in the evening. She had photographs: Kath balanced on top of a rock in Cornwall, laughing, characteristically fearless, ready to dive into the sea. And though the voice was indistinct, she could still hear the words, calling to Mel to be gentle with herself, to trust in her strength. Kath could feel it. Mel should feel it too.

Spots of rain splattered her coat and dotted the flag stones, but she had no wish to move on. Jacob would not be home yet. He had taken to coming back late, working till five or six in the library, or going around to Don's. Mel had grown fond of Don. It was still difficult to get used to the new language, but she had stopped calling her his girlfriend. 'Special friend' was apparently acceptable. She listened and sympathised with the arguments for gender neutrality, while still wishing the traditional female roles were broad enough to encompass whatever variations Don might wish to adopt. It was not as if Don was convinced she was a man, in the way Vicky Brightman was convinced she was a woman. Moving beyond masculinity or femininity was an interesting theory. Mel just hoped Don wouldn't allow a surgeon to slice into her young body.

It was not something any of them mentioned. When she had touched on it with Jacob, he had turned on her angrily and said it was not her business and he didn't wish to discuss it in Don's absence. Mel conceded. The important thing was that Jacob and Don should be happy. It appeared they were. They laughed a lot, chattering in incomprehensible teen-speak, romping like puppies over the sofa. They shut themselves into Jacob's room and hung a KEEP OUT notice on the door. Mel was relieved it was not her son who had the gender doubts. At least, she believed he hadn't. She reminded herself how little she knew of him. Love and guidance. The essentials of parenthood. She had been good on the love, less good on the guidance. Sometimes it felt as if she had simply watched him grow, hoping it would be in the right direction.

Since his outbreak in the summer, she had not spoken to him about Paul, except to tell him the affair was over. His eyes had clenched, as if by shutting out the light, he could shut out what she was saying. As soon as she had finished, he pivoted on his foot and walked away. It was clear he didn't want to know. As for Natasha, he had said all he was prepared to say.

But gradually, instant by instant, the breach between them was mending. He was more considerate, washing up his cups, offering to make her tea and toast. His room was tidier. She sensed from the way his books and papers were arranged that he was taking work more seriously. But he rarely told her where he was going, occasionally staying out all night. She wished she could put a tracker on his phone, though she knew his agreement would never be forthcoming. She consulted Claude whose unhelpful view was that a seventeen-year-old boy should be allowed to stay out all night if he so chose. And so, she and Jacob walked a fine line. If Mel demonstrated too much anxiety he would bite back, telling her she was trying to control him, staying out even longer, sending the occasional brief text to let her know he was still alive.

Sometimes, when they were sitting companionably on the sofa, watching TV, she imagined telling him the truth about Natasha, how his own mother had lashed out. But it was a fantasy. Impossible. He could never know.

On her weekly visits to see Isabel she avoided mention of Natasha. They spoke of domestic matters, the old days, celebrity gossip, continuing plans for the costume exhibition.

'We'll do it when this wretched court thing is out of the way,' said Isabel.

'I'm sorry, Mum.'

'I don't know why they want me as a witness. Everything happened so fast. What shall I say?'

'Mum, we're not supposed to talk about it.'

Mel had read her mother's statement. It was uncontentious. But how would she fare under cross-examination?

Having resolved nothing, she stood up and set off for the tube, through the arch that led into Middle Temple Lane. A man swung around onto the path in front of her, blocking her route. She waited for him to stand aside, annoyed by the thoughtless way he had rushed into the narrow alleyway. But he stood firm, a couple of feet from her, his broad face cracking into the huge smile she knew so well. Of all her fellow tenants, this was the one she was happiest to see. Ten minutes later she and Georgie were seated in a small cafe in Holborn.

Georgie liked to talk, particularly about his pet hates: certain politicians, a few irascible judges, the iniquities of the Home Office. But he also liked to listen. He knew how to pump information from witnesses, relaxing his technique with friends and acquaintances. If he liked someone, he wanted to know them. He liked Mel, and this afternoon, over cappuccino and a slice of rich chocolate cake, he listened.

He asked about the prosecution, and she told him the now well-rehearsed version she intended to tell the court. But her words seemed to come from somewhere beyond her body and as his questions grew more precise, more focused, they began to feel like a line of tiny wedges slowly splitting her in two. Was this what he did to witnesses? She looked away and then down, picking up her coffee cup.

'Please, Georgie, I'm not your client, I've just come from a conference with Alisha. My head's full of it. I'd rather have a break.'

She swallowed her coffee. She had wanted to spend this time with him. But now she wanted to be somewhere else. It seemed to happen in every encounter with anyone she cared for.

Georgie looked concerned. 'I get that. Force of habit. Rebuke taken. What else have you been up to?' His concern warmed her, and it was her own voice that answered.

'Looking after Mum, feeding Jacob, painting the kitchen, watching Netflix.'

'Sounds wonderful.' There was a tired sadness behind his smile and she could see he meant it. The Criminal Bar might appear romantic to outsiders, but unless you were defending murderers and fraudsters in the Old Bailey, it was poorly paid, the hours were unpredictable, and it could take a terrible toll on your private life. His partner Farouk was several years younger and worked in the music business. Mel wondered how much time they had together. She knew they had considered adoption. It seemed improbable, given their work patterns.

'You're exhausted,' she said.

'Has nobody told you, Mel, that the one thing exhausted people hate is to be reminded they are exhausted?'

'Well, if we can't talk about you either...' She grinned.

'OK.' he said. 'How about your love life? You seeing anyone?'

Mel laughed. 'Christ, Georgie. That's the last thing I'm thinking of right now.' Another lie. On several evenings, when Jacob was out, she had interspersed TV drama with Tinder surfing. A brief flirtation with fantasy which only aggravated the loneliness.

'You need support,' he urged.

'You're my support. You and everyone in chambers.'

A quiver of uncertainty in his eyes lit a fuse paper and another anxiety flared in her. Mel could be sure of him but what of the others? Natasha had been a pupil. It was she who had suffered injury. Safeguarding. Wellbeing at the Bar. These were hot issues. Bridge Court's reputation had already been dented by the incident. If Mel was found guilty she'd be thrown to the wolves. Even if she was acquitted, some of her colleagues might have doubts. She gripped the slippery handle of her coffee cup. She must focus on the moment. Not the past. Not the future. Only now.

'You know what I mean, Mel. You're a beautiful woman; you're young…'

'Ish,' she interrupted quickly.

'Forty's the new thirty. But life's short. Jacob's growing up. You don't want to…'

At that something snapped in her. He was sounding like a parent in a Victorian novel.

'Can we drop it, Georgie?' She didn't need him to tell her what she wanted.

He pushed his chair back and raised a hand off the table. 'Badly phrased. But it's only because I care. Just tell me you're not still seeing that married guy?'

What was it to him? She loved Georgie, but his concern for her well-being made her feel as if her heart were being ripped open to public view. Was that how Jacob felt? Was that what prompted her child to stay away from her?

'I haven't seen him for months.' That at least was true.

'Good. You deserve better than that. If I knew any nice heterosexual men I'd introduce you like a shot.'

'Thanks, Georgie. Not really your field of operation but if you do… And before you ask I'm not interested in anyone under thirty-five.'

At his reference to nice heterosexual men, the image of the Palestinian dentist surfaced in her mind. Sami had rescued her once. Could he rescue her again? But the timing had been wrong. He had rung a few times since the incident on the railway path. They had even met for coffee. But after what she had come to call 'the Dulwich afternoon' she had stopped answering his calls. What kind of relationship starts with a lie? And now he had stopped ringing her. She was sorry she had not come to know him better.

'Tricky. They're mostly spoken for. I'll keep an eye open.'

She felt herself smiling as she stood up. Georgie followed her to the cash desk to pay. He offered to pay for her coffee, she offered to pay for his and they agreed to share it.

'Have you got a trial date?'

'Monday week.'

'Would you like me to be there?'

'Professional interest?'

'Don't be daft.'

'You always liked Natasha.'

'I hardly know her. She seemed OK. But you're my friend, Mel. Don't forget it. Who else will be there for you on the day?'

'Mum. She's a prosecution witness. Maybe Jacob. I'm not sure.'

'I had better come then. You'll need someone to break the neck on the Bollinger.'

'Don't be too confident.'

'Mel. You're not going to lose.'

'CPS must think so. Why else would they have brought it?'

'God only knows. How many days is it listed for?'

'Three.'

'I'll try to get there on Wednesday.'

They walked out into the crowds and tumult of Kingsway. He would leave her here to walk back to his flat near Waterloo. She looked up into his rough, compassionate face and flung her arms around him. His strong arms embraced her in return, and she was held, grounded, and in that moment, safe. It had been too long since she had felt the strength of a man's body against hers.

Chapter Thirty-nine

Natasha

The waiting room was stifling. On the wall by the door there was a display panel indicating a temperature of 24 degrees, a line of metal buttons and what looked like a circular thermostat. Natasha fiddled with the thermostat and pressed a few buttons. The figure displayed did not budge.

'Centrally controlled,' said Luke. 'Stops arguments. We've got the same thing in Social Services.'

'What if it's too hot for the baby?'

'I'll go and see if I can find someone.'

'Get me a bottle of water.'

'I'll do what I can. Will you be all right?'

'I'll have to be, won't I?'

He gave her his beseeching look and left her alone. His obsessive attention was beginning to irritate her. Less than two weeks to go. The hospital had fixed a date for induction because of possible risks to the mother and the baby which was likely to be bigger than usual. She preferred not to think too hard about that, hoping the birth would be over quickly. A Caesarean was an option, though she didn't like the idea of a scar and a flabby stomach. She would take all the drugs on offer. Luke had arranged time off work and she would start her new job as soon as possible after the birth. At least that was the hope. The Crown Prosecution Service still hadn't been given a date.

She was seated on one of the low plastic benches, which lined two of the walls. Ranged down the middle of the long room were three sets of chairs and tables, one of which was occupied by a noisy Asian family, mother and father, an older woman and a cluster of little ones. The two women both wore the hijab and they were chatting to each other in what sounded like Urdu. The man had a wailing toddler on his lap and tried to calm the older child, a boy of about seven, with something on his tablet. The baby in the pushchair was asleep. Natasha was surprised the parents had been allowed to bring the children to court, but no one seemed to be checking or paying them attention. Like Natasha and Luke, they had presumably turned up at the appointed time, been directed to the Witness Service desk and told to come into this horrible waiting area.

She walked over to one of the two windows which faced the brick façade of another part of the court building. If you twisted your head to the left, you could just spot a slip of sky. Daylight was insufficient, so the room was lit by fluorescent strips in the ceiling. The windows were impossible to open. There appeared to be no handles. Luke had said the small holes in the lower corners were part of the opening mechanism. You just needed the appropriate key to slot into them.

She looked again at the Asian family who were now picking food out of Tupperware boxes. The younger woman caught her eye and smiled. The food seemed to be doing the trick and the children calmed down.

Luke returned with the water and told her there was nothing he could do about the heating. The technical team was short-staffed. The temperature could be changed but had been fixed at 24 degrees after there were too many disputes between waiting witnesses. It was 11:30 a.m. The trial was due to have started at 10:30 a.m. Natasha knew she would not be permitted to sit in court during the prosecution opening, and she felt a rising anger. She was the one who had suffered. It was all about her and yet she was stuck in this hideous room to wait and do nothing. Luke was scanning the news on his phone. She pulled out her own and checked her pregnancy fitness app. No way was she going to do 10,000 steps today.

Then she heard a voice she recognised, female, with conventional BBC pronunciation, and an actor's throaty resonance.

'Do I really have to wait in here?' it asked, emphasising the 'really'.

Natasha looked up. Isabel was wearing a faux leopard skin coat, at least Natasha assumed it was faux, and her hair was pinned in elaborate swirls on the top of her head. There seemed to be more of it than before. She must be wearing a hairpiece. She was scanning the room as if she were a prospective hotel guest inspecting inferior accommodation.

'There's the corridor, if you prefer,' said the young woman beside her, wearily. She looked bored. Natasha recognised her from the Witness Service desk in the court foyer.

'May I not sit with my daughter?'

'I'm sorry, Mrs Goddard. You're daughter's the defendant. She's not allowed to chat to prosecution witnesses. Miss Baker is here too, but we do advise you not to confer before the case.'

'Hello, Isabel,' said Natasha, hauling her bulk off the plastic bench and making her way across the room. 'Nice to see you again. I believe you've met my partner, Luke.'

Luke walked over. Natasha felt a quiver of pride. He had put on a shirt and tie for court. Tall and well built, he looked like a film star. The Witness Service woman brightened up. Most women did when they encountered Luke.

'Hello, Isabel. Nice to see you again,' he said, stretching out a hand. 'It's good of you to do this for Natasha.'

Isabel looked surprised at the comment though she took his hand. 'I'm simply doing my civic duty,' she replied with a cold smile. Luke let the hand drop and Isabel sat down and took a paperback from her bag.

He and Natasha returned to their seats. The baby started crying. The mother picked it up and jiggled it around until it stopped. Eight months of pregnancy had done nothing to alter Natasha's distaste for babies, their uncontrollable bawling, their dribbles and smells. Yet her antenatal nurse spoke as if this servitude was the perfect compensation for months of discomfort and tedious antenatal appointments. It was bad enough being type 1 without pregnancy. Now the blood glucose graph was even more erratic, margins were tighter, and she'd had a couple of near-miss hypos at awkward moments in court. 'It's different when it's your own,' the nurse had told her. Natasha doubted it. Even so, she had started to think about names.

A voice from nowhere announced that Mrs Fatima Bhatti was required in Court 4. The young woman handed over the squalling bundle to the older one, threw her shoulders back and, with an air of defiance, disappeared through the door to the foyer. Natasha would like to have followed her and watched her case. The heat in this enclosed space was making her feel faint. She would much rather be in the public gallery, following someone else's drama.

But watching was nothing compared with appearing in court herself and the last three months had been frustrating. She'd hoped to squat at Bridge Court after her pupillage ended in October, but Mel's outbreak had put a stop to that.

'I know it seems unfair,' Paula had told her, 'but the view of the committee is that it's just too awkward now there's a charge against Mel.'

'So, what was I supposed to do? Sit quiet after she smashed my head in?'

'It's tough on you, I get that. But squatting's never automatic. It's no reflection on your work. I'm sorry. But won't you be starting at the CPS soon? I sent a glowing reference.'

'I'm still waiting for a date. They said it wouldn't be till next year.' They'd told her they needed to make other enquiries. What kind of enquiries? (There was the caution for shoplifting, years ago. But she'd been using the fake identity. They'd never track that down.)

Over the last three months she'd picked up some part time paralegal work but, after running her own cases, it was frustrating sitting behind other barristers, taking notes on their work. And money was tight. Her flash glucose monitor was

£100 a month. It was supposed to be available on the NHS by now but she was still waiting. There was no way she was going back to pricked fingers and test strips. She'd be looking for compensation immediately after the verdict.

As the trial approached she'd hoped to be more involved in the case against Mel, expecting to attend meetings and conferences with the prosecution team. Instead she was just a fat victim, passive and drowsy in a hot waiting room. In another time, another culture, she would have taken her own revenge or paid someone to do it for her.

At noon the Witness Service person returned.

'You can all take a break till two thirty. Judge McDermid has a couple of outstanding matters and Miss Goddard's trial's been put back.'

It was a relief to be in open air, even cold, fume-filled London air. Though walking was becoming difficult. Sciatica was shooting down her thigh and she found herself leaning on Luke as they crossed the road in front of the court building.

'I've never liked the criminal courts. Desperate places,' said Luke as they stood on the central island between the rushing traffic. 'Are you sure you want to work for the CPS?'

'You want me to stay at home and be a mum?' said Natasha.

'Whatever makes you happy, Tash. Come on, there's a gap.'

'Hey, I can't walk that fast.'

It amazed her that someone so caring could sometimes be so insensitive. A car screeched to a stop as she lumbered to the opposite pavement.

'What about a proper lunch?' he said. 'We've got plenty of time.'

'There's an Italian on the corner. People usually go there.'

She and Luke ordered two spaghetti carbonara from the counter and sat down. Natasha, with her back to the wall, looked out across the tables which were beginning to fill with early diners. Then she saw them: Melanie, ushering her family to a table on the other side of the restaurant; the boy, Jacob, thin as a reed, pale as paper and a foot taller than she remembered him; grandmother Isabel in her leopard skin coat, eyeing the restaurant patrons with stately disdain. Jacob was staring into his phone. He'd changed his hairstyle since last summer and with a bit of luck Luke would miss the resemblance to the young man on her computer. She was in no mood for more explanations.

'Shit,' she muttered.

Luke turned. 'Don't worry, we don't need to speak to them.'

'Only problem is I need the loo.' She would have to pass their table on the way to the Ladies.

'You just went,' said Luke.

'I'm pregnant. My bladder is about to explode all of the time.' He was beginning to annoy her.

'Don't get dragged into anything.'

'I won't say a word.'

But as she walked past the table, avoiding eye contact, Isabel muttered something which sounded like 'witch', or even 'bitch'.

'Mum, please don't,' said Mel, adding. 'I'm sorry, Natasha.'

'Sorry? Is that what you're going to tell the court? "Sorry I nearly killed my pupil." You'll need to change your plea.'

Without waiting for an answer, she walked into the Ladies. When she came out a few moments later Luke had walked over, followed by the waiter. She heard him addressing the little gang. 'Please don't upset my wife. This is a difficult day for all of us.'

Wife? Since when had she become his wife? Jacob stood, squaring up against Luke like a bodyguard, as if he were about to punch him in the face.

'Jacob,' murmured Mel, reaching for his hand, indicating he should sit. But he remained standing. 'Leave us alone,' he said, in a firm voice, looking and sounding much older than he was.

He turned away from Luke and caught Natasha's eye. The look was penetrating and a little frightening, as if he could see through the veneer to the core of her, thoughts and feelings she would rather not disclose. She held his gaze for a second then threw out a seductive grin. He grimaced. She wanted to grab his arms and shake him. This was the kid who had sent her suggestive messages and naked photos. Who'd invited her to take her top off. And now he was looking at her with disdain as if she were dirt.

It was easy to imagine the kind of man he would become. The kind of man who despised any woman who enjoyed sex. Her skin was prickling, whether with some new irritation of late pregnancy or simple exasperation that she couldn't expose his devious behaviour before the court. It was Jacob's name that had set Mel off, giving her a motive. And it was maddening that mentioning his name could rebound on Natasha, bring Mel more support than disapproval.

He was still eyeing her as if he would like to hurt her. Luke, beside her, appeared troubled. By now he must have recognised Jacob as the face on her computer all those months ago. It was time to move on. Just as she was about to return to her seat Isabel's ringing voice cut through the clatter of eating and conversation that filled the restaurant.

'I'd like a small salad and a large glass of Orvieto. Jacob, darling, will your mum permit you a glass of wine?'

Jacob sat down. His reply was inaudible. Natasha smiled inwardly as she picked up his embarrassment. His grandmother had turned him into a child again.

'Come on, Tash,' said Luke, laying a guiding hand on her back. She thought of pointing out in a loud voice that Isabel wasn't supposed to hang around with her daughter before the trial. But who would check? The best she could do was tell Digger when they got back. If Isabel turned hostile, he might find it useful to let the jury know that she had joined her daughter for lunch.

After the large lunch she felt exhausted. The waiting room temperature had been adjusted but it was still warm, and she sank onto the plastic bench, leant against Luke's arm and closed her eyes.

A disembodied voice was calling her name and she shook herself awake. As an advocate before a case she was used to feeling excited rather than nervous. But now, preparing to take the witness stand, her heart was pounding in a way she did not like. She was accustomed to being looked at, but this would be different. There were no charges against her. Yet she would be judged. And she needed to be judged as good. Acting was second nature to her and for the role of victim she was wearing a simple blue dress, bland without being drab. And she would wear it every day of this trial. Let no one accuse her of vanity. A pity the scar just below the hairline was too small to be visible across a courtroom.

'Don't appear proud,' Digger had said. 'Ask for a chair, another glass of water, a break. Be vulnerable. If you're not sure how to answer, ask for time.'

'I hate being vulnerable.'

'You want to win this, don't you?'

'Of course.'

'Then use what you've got.'

She walked into the courtroom. The witness box was raised slightly from the floor, like a small stage. She could feel the eyes of the jury members as she hoisted herself up the three steps and turned to face them, making a quick assessment. Eight women, four men. Three of them black, two Asian, the others white or part white. Most of them looked old, though there were two women about her age. At first their expressions were stern and impassive but then she caught a glimmer of a smile from one of the men, a big, handsome guy in smart clothes. She remembered Digger's advice. 'Don't smile too much. Look at the jury when you answer the questions. Don't miss anyone out, even if they appear unsympathetic. You need to get them on your side. In a case like this it often boils down to who they like. Sell your story, but don't be too confident. Take your time. Remember you're a victim, not an advocate.'

Digger questioned her for an hour. Natasha spoke about the relationship with Isabel. How they had met by chance at a fundraising event. How she'd been a long-standing fan of the actress and how thrilled she'd been when Isabel invited her to visit her at home. She explained about her diabetes, the hypo on the way to the V&A, Mel's ridiculous suspicion that she had some ulterior motive in befriending Isabel, the equally ridiculous claim that Natasha intended to steal her mother's jewellery. Naturally, after being confronted by Mel, Natasha had wanted to leave the house as soon as possible. She had been changing into her own clothes, putting Isabel's outfit in the wardrobe, when Mel followed her into the spare room. Her violent outbreak had been totally unexpected.

'You have said she just attacked you. Can you think back, Miss Baker – is there anything you said that might have motivated her to do that?'

'It's hard to say. Melanie's on a short fuse. Takes offence easily.'

'I repeat, Miss Baker: is there anything you said that might have provoked her?'

'There might've been.'

'You might have said something? Or something you said might have provoked her?'

'Something I said might have provoked her.'

She turned to Mel who sat in the dock, her expression uncharacteristically blank and hard to read. Then she looked towards the public gallery. Jacob was staring at her, wide-eyed. Mel would have lied to him about what happened that afternoon in his grandmother's spare room. And at that moment she had an urge to tell the court everything, to cast shame not only on Mel but her self-important son. But any mention of Jacob would be self-defeating. It would give Mel a reason for attacking her, but Natasha would lose what sympathy she had with the jury. She remembered Digger's words. In a case like this, each person's word against the other, it could boil down to which of you the jury liked best.

'Please tell the jury what you said.'

'She accused me of stealing. I was pretty annoyed. I was only trying to help her mother. I guess I bit back. I think I called her a cheat and a liar.'

'This is not in your statement.'

'No. It's not.'

He was not expecting this, but Natasha trusted him to deal with it. She knew the rule for advocates. Never ask a question when you don't know the answer. But sometimes you need to break the rule. Digger was about to ask several such questions.

'Why is that?'

'I didn't want to upset people. There are others involved.'

'Please explain, Miss Baker.'

'It's a private thing.'

'Private for you?'

'No, private for Mel. There are people who'll be hurt by what she's done.'

The jury was transfixed. Natasha was beginning to enjoy this.

'The thing is, she was having an affair. With a married man.'

'How did you know?'

'I read an email from her lover.'

Sell your story to the jury, Digger had said. Well, she was selling it.

'Why did you read the email, Miss Baker?'

'Melanie had forgotten to log off one of the computers in chambers. She rang me on her way home to ask me to do it for her. She also wanted me to print off an Attendance Note. When I rebooted the computer, it was open on an email. I didn't mean to read it, but I saw a few words before I shut it down. The words were, well, you know... suggestive.'

'How did you know the writer was a married man?'

'I recognised the address.'

'How was that?'

'It was one of the lecturers at North Bank University. North Bank was my university, so it jumped out at me.'

'Please go on.'

'I knew the guy. He was one of my tutors. Listen, I should have ignored it, shouldn't have said anything. It was private stuff. Only when she accused me of being a thief, I just snapped. I regret it now. I wish I'd kept cool. She wouldn't have lashed out. I wouldn't have this scar.'

'It may be put to you that you started this. That you rushed at her, you wanted to hurt her. What would you say to that?'

'No way.'

'You agree that there were angry words.'

'Yes.'

'Miss Goddard states that she didn't hurt you in any way. She says that she only touched you in self-defence.'

'She grabbed me and threw me against the dressing table. You saw the medical report.'

'She will say that in fact you charged at her, she held up a hand to protect herself and you slipped and fell. Is there any truth in that?'

'Absolutely not. I didn't move. I was just standing there. I accused her of the affair. I may have mentioned his name. Paul Freedman.' There were faces Natasha recognised in the public gallery. Members of chambers. Other barristers. Let them see their esteemed colleague in a different light. Word would spread quickly on social media. And wasn't that a reporter tapping furiously on a laptop on the press bench? 'OK, it was provocative. I expected her to argue. I didn't expect her to respond like that. It was terrifying. She looked like she wanted to kill me.'

Natasha turned from the jury towards Mel who sat facing the court room behind the glass panel of the dock. Her hitherto inscrutable expression betrayed a hint of emotion, a tiny tremble around the mouth as she lowered her eyes from the courtroom to the shelf in front of her. She was holding a pen or pencil and bent forward to write something on a notepad. Natasha knew Mel well enough to be sure she would be churning inside at the public mention of Paul's name. Good. Whatever decision the jury took, at least Mel was suffering now.

Her glance shifted to Jacob. He was staring at her with the hard aggression of an aggrieved young man. Natasha suspected he had no idea how lucky he was not to have his own character ripped to shreds in court. His hostility burnt through her and she felt her anger rise. So far he had not been mentioned. But Alisha was bound to put a few background questions: the reference request, the trip to Dulwich. What if Natasha told the court that Jacob had been present that day? What if she put a different spin on his behaviour? What if she told the court that he had tried to kiss her outsider the gallery? That she had told Mel as much. Telling Mel would have given her another reason to lose her rag. After the way Jacob had turned on Natasha outside the gallery, the way he had tried to outface her just now in the restaurant, it would be good to see him squirm. If asked why she was mentioning it at this late stage she would say she was just trying to spare the boy.

'Thank you, Miss Baker. I have no further questions. If you would just wait there.'

Judge McDermid broke in. They would adjourn for the evening. Miss Baker needed a rest. She must remember she was still on oath and should not speak to anyone about her evidence, not even her partner Luke Gearing who was due to give evidence tomorrow. Digger reminded the judge that Miss Baker lived with Mr Gearing.

'My order is unchanged. They may speak of course. But not about the case.'

'I'm grateful, Your Honour.'

'The hearing will resume at ten a.m. tomorrow morning.'

Chapter Forty

Natasha

Luke was in the lobby outside the court. He wanted to know everything.

'I'm still on oath,' she said. 'Can't speak to you.'

'Not at all?'

'Not about the case. Don't worry. I'll tell you everything later. Let's get out. I need some air.'

They made their way down the stairs to the automatic doors, stepping out onto the pavement and the fading afternoon light.

'We'll get a taxi,' said Luke.

'I don't mind the bus. I've still got 5,000 steps to do.'

'Can't you give it a rest? Only two weeks to go.'

'I'm not going to become one of those great flabby women. You'll see; I'll be super fit.'

'A yummy mummy.'

'Exactly.'

They took the bus. Natasha graciously accepted the seat she was offered and stared through the window as they wound their way through the traffic towards Brixton. The bus stopped by the tube station, opposite the department store.

'Tell you what, I'll cross over and have a snoop around Morley's. That way I'll do my steps and buy myself a treat at the same time.' Luke made a face. 'You don't need to come.'

'Why d'you want to go traipsing round a busy shop? Don't you want to get home?'

'Stop fussing. A spot of retail therapy is exactly what I need. I'll look at baby stuff. You can pick up something at Sainsbury's and make us a delicious dinner.'

He looked unhappy. But she knew he wouldn't follow her. Luke hated shopping for anything but food.

'What do you fancy?'

'Whatever you like. Everything you cook is brilliant.'

He'd said nothing about Jacob. Though she was sure he had recognised him. He kissed her and held her a little too tight. Something was digging into her lungs. She heard herself squeal. 'Sorry,' he said. 'Overenthusiastic. You OK?'

'Fine.' She pecked him on the cheek, 'I'll be back in half an hour or so.'

They separated. It was a relief to be away from him. He was a good man and she needed him, but he was beginning to crowd her. She entered Morley's. Babywear was on the first floor but there was no pull in that direction, and she drifted towards the cosmetics counters where she was drawn to a sign announcing: Pregnancy Body Care.

'May I help?' asked a willowy young woman, dressed like a doctor in a neat white jacket. Her face was a pale mask, the heavily made-up eyes shadowed in dusty pink and grey.

'Just browsing, thanks,' said Natasha.

Pregnancy was supposed to be good for the complexion. Her adoptive sister Eleanor had told her she was 'blooming'. But Natasha hated the flushed look and there were some unattractive red splotches on her cheeks. What she needed was a decent concealer. She noted a line of testers at the front of the counter, tried out three and made a mental note to pick up the expensive one if she had an opportunity. Now was not the moment. The assistant was watching, and she would need to be careful.

She approached the perfume counter. The air was rich with scents, the shelves a picture gallery of crisp packaging and jewel-coloured liquids.

It had been weeks since she had lifted anything. Since the beginning of her pupillage she had resolved to stop, but the urge to appropriate was powerful. The symptoms were familiar, the lightly fluttering heart, the rapid breathing, the restlessness, like unslaked thirst. Voices competed inside her, one, the clearer, telling her to walk out of the shop, the other, low and insistent, telling her she was good at this, she could do it. Pregnancy had given her an advantage. She was more conspicuous but less likely to arouse suspicion. And she wanted the best.

Customers took their time. It was essential to test before you decided. Under the white and gold logo a young woman with black-fringed green eyes, scarlet lips and a blonde bob, and wearing a badge marked 'Chloe', was occupied with two middle-aged Indian women in bulky red and green saris. Both had grey hair twisted into buns at the back of their heads. One was overweight, the other skinny and neither of them looked the type to sport expensive French perfume. Perhaps they were buying for a daughter or niece. Chloe was giving them her full attention, setting out the products on the glass counter, letting them use the testers, explaining the relative merits of Eau de Toilette and Eau de Parfum.

Natasha hovered behind them, waiting to try the tester. If nothing else, she would leave the shop in a cloud of seductive Chanel. But the women were taking their time and she drifted to the next counter, sweeter modern fragrances, which were much less appealing.

After about five minutes the Indian women thanked Chloe and ambled away, chattering in their own language. Chloe started to replace the packages she had so carefully laid out on the counter. Natasha glanced at a clock on the wall. It was just after five. The shop would be open for another three hours. Luke would wait. There was no need to rush.

A woman wearing the standard Morley black, with an ID card dangling round her neck, walked over and led Chloe away to the back of the shop where Natasha noted a gathering crowd. Much later she learnt that a customer had collapsed with a heart attack. The perfume department was empty, apart from the two

Indian women dithering over another display about five yards away. Natasha turned back to the Chanel counter, brushed her bulk against its glass edge and slipped the Eau de Parfum in its white and gold cellophane wrapper into her open bag.

There was a rush inside her body as if something had caught fire. She managed to tamp the flames, walking more slowly than she would have liked towards the exit, aware of the heart thumping below the cool exterior, adopting a calm, neutral gaze. As a child she had played at being invisible and some tiny part of her still believed that if she concentrated hard, avoided anyone's eye, looked straight ahead, though not too fixedly, she could disappear. Her reactions were so finely attuned that, without looking about her, she could sense if she was being watched, even from behind. All was clear. She continued to walk slowly. It had happened more suddenly than she would have liked, and she had omitted to make the single legitimate purchase which would have provided her with a store bag. She needed to get out.

The front of the shop was quiet. The consternation around the collapsed customer at the back had deflected interest away from the entrance and there was no security guard by the exit doors.

As she approached the automatic glass door, it slid open. She stepped out onto the pavement and was thrust into the thunder of rush-hour traffic and fume-filled air. Two buses had stopped outside the shop. She was about to run between them, to zigzag through the stationary cars and disappear into the evening throng. But some sense of self-preservation stopped her, and she waited as a woman with a toddler in a pushchair strolled past. Clutching her bag tightly against her chest, Natasha swung left towards the pedestrian crossing when she felt a hand on her shoulder, a tight grasp. It was the fat woman in the green and red sari. Her eyes were bulging and excited and Natasha's first thought was that the woman was mad, about to ask for money or talk gibberish. She struggled to release herself. But then she felt another hand on her opposite arm and she realised this was not madness but intentional restraint and the two women in saris were preventing her from walking away.

'Madam,' said the fat one, 'I'd like to look in your bag.'

'I'm sorry. I don't understand.'

'I have reason to believe you have store merchandise in your bag.'

'You must be mistaken. Now if you will let me leave. Please. I have an appointment.'

A man appeared from the heart of the shop. He was tall, broad, unmistakably security. She had not noticed him before. The woman produced a card. It showed her name and then in clear dark letters: Store Detective.

In a gentler voice the thin woman said, 'We'll go somewhere private.' They began to lead her away, a woman on each side, the security man in front. Where a moment before there had been empty space, a crowd had gathered.

Thoughts whirled through her mind, explanations, excuses: confusion, exhaustion, the trial, pregnancy, exhaustion, diabetes. She would hand back the Chanel and talk her way out of this. There came a stirring inside her. He, for she was sure it would be a 'he', no longer kicked; he was too close pressed for that. Instead he shifted and squirmed and pushed and she sensed that any moment he would try to break out. Why not now? They would all forget about the Eau de Parfum if she was hurled into labour on the shop floor. But the squirming stopped, and the two women were still holding her, one on each arm.

'We'll take her into the office,' said the security guard. They walked her through the store. She swallowed hard and held up her head, sensing a growing resolve. She had been in worse situations and come out unscathed. She would not be defeated.

Chapter Forty-one

Mel

'Supper's on the table,' she shouted through his bedroom door.

'What is it?'

'Rice and vegetables.'

'Boring.'

'Not much else on your list. If you were prepared to eat sensibly...'

'And fuck up the planet eating animals.'

'Plus cheese, eggs, mushrooms, raisins. Catering's increasingly complicated...' But she felt herself smiling as she spoke.

'I came with you today, didn't I?'

Before she could reply, he appeared in the doorway, took a step towards her, stretched out his arms and hugged her. Her cheek met his shoulder and she wanted to fall on him and weep. But she swallowed her tears, straightened her head and hugged him back, feeling his strength through his old T-shirt. Never mind the demanding diet. The least she could do was look after him.

'You'll be all right, Mum.'

'I'm not sure.'

'They won't believe Natasha. You wouldn't hit anyone. You never even hit me, and I bloody deserved it.'

'They're not saying hit. They're saying I hurled her against the dressing table. But it's just as bad.'

As for hitting him, he was wrong. He'd been screaming in a swimming pool changing room – he was four years old. She couldn't remember what it was about. He'd probably refused to put on his socks. He'd been standing on the changing bench, so his eyes were level with hers, challenging her as Natasha had challenged her, only his way was to stare into her face and howl.

Other mothers were organising their well-behaved offspring, casting disapproving glances at the woman with the undisciplined child. Mel needed Jacob to stop, but he was beyond listening and she had smacked him hard across the cheek. She still remembered his silence, the look of shock and surprise, the red mark. And now she felt sick with self-hatred as she took in his trusting face.

In court that afternoon Natasha had spoken fluently, telling the jury how hard she had tried with Mel, how the hostility of her pupil supervisor had taken her by surprise. Though she recognised how Mel had been affected by the attack in the street. She knew only too well the destabilising effect of physical violence. When Digger asked her if she could elaborate, she began to speak about her adoptive father until Judge McDermid intervened and told Digger to stick to the essentials. While the defendant's background might be relevant, he could see no relevance in the complainant's.

More tactics. Digger wanted the jury to fall in love with his witness. Mel had watched the judge who was looking intently at Natasha. Surely, he was not going to fall for her as well?

'Thanks for today, Jacob.'

'She's a bitch.'

'She's troubled.'

'No fucking excuse. That stuff about your... thingy.'

'Paul.' She wanted to tell him off for swearing. But right now, a telling off felt out of place.

'What's it got to do with anything? Why'd she want to chuck that shit around? I reckon she fancies him herself.'

'I'm sorry you had to hear it in court.'

'No worries. It just makes her look like a bully.'

But it gave Mel a motive. Not the most powerful motive and at least Natasha hadn't mentioned Jacob. But a motive, nonetheless. Mel prayed Jacob would be left out of this. Despite his confident words she could tell he was shaken, could see through the surface outrage to something struggling inside him. His need to protect his mother was strong. Her eyes had pricked with tears when he stood up to face Natasha in the restaurant and now there was a swelling ache in her throat. He was too young for this. Not yet an adult, he already saw himself as her defender. And he could never know the truth of what she had done. She turned away from him to the kitchen.

They did not speak as she took the food out of the oven and placed the dish in the centre of the table. She ladled out Jacob's share, thinking of the lies she would tell tomorrow. There was no choice. ABH carried a maximum five-year sentence. If she was found guilty, prison was possible, even probable. Mel had a clean record, but the pupil–supervisor relationship was a relationship of trust. There was public interest in the outcome and the judge would not want a member of the Bar to be seen to receive preferential treatment. It was unlikely to be the full five years but it would be a sentence and a sentence would strip her of everything, her place in chambers, her right to practice, her reputation, her home.

She had managed to keep up mortgage payments, but she couldn't stay off work much longer. And Jacob? Would she lose him too? He would move in with Claude. He might visit her in prison. But what would she tell him? Another lie? That the jury had got it wrong? Or what was about to become the truth. That she had lied to her barrister, lied in court. Lie upon lie. Lies created a wall around you. How could you ever be close to anyone again?

He was sitting now, staring at his plate. It was unlike him not to tuck in as soon as the food was served. Perhaps like her he had no appetite. As she waited he looked up and met her gaze.

'I wish I could help you, Mum.'

'You do help me. Just being here. Only don't come tomorrow. Go to college. You've already missed a day.'

Tomorrow she would step out of the horrible glass cage of the dock and stand in the witness box in front of judge and jury. How could she bear her son to be present when she gave her evidence?

'I've got a class in the morning. But I'll try to come later.'

She couldn't stop him. Any more than she had been able to stop him staying out all night. And who else would be there for her? Georgie had promised to come. But even his trust in her might falter as he heard the evidence against her. There had been about ten people yesterday in the public gallery, more than she had expected, members of her chambers, other faces she did not recognise. Might they be friends of Natasha? She'd heard nothing from Paul. He knew her trial date. She hadn't expected or wanted a meeting. But a good luck text would have been nice.

What would Isabel say? Despite her mother's occasional vagueness, she had been adamant about her duty not to discuss the case and it was still unclear to Mel how much she had seen.

She watched Jacob picking at his supper and tried to eat something herself. But there was nowhere for the food to go. It was as if a huge boulder had been lodged in the space that should be her throat. Months of treading water. Now everything was about to change. And fast. Old friends might wish her well, but the weight of reality was crashing in on her and she needed to carry that weight alone.

Chapter Forty-two

Natasha

The shooting pains had started again and the great weight she carried felt as if it would crush her. There was no movement. It was warm in the custody suite but she felt suddenly cold. What if the baby were dead? She thought she might be sick.

'Miss Baker, if you would just read this through and sign it. The PC will take you through for fingerprints. Then DI Clark and DS Singer will have a word with you in the interview room.'

'I want to ring my husband. You've taken my phone.'

'We can organise that later. Just check this and sign. We'll sort the fingerprints and you can give him a ring.'

Voices echoed around the walls. They had found the pump when they searched her and had allowed her to hang on to the BG meter and the flash glucose reader, though they looked at each item with suspicion before putting them in a sealed plastic bag. Through a glass door she could see people moving between desks, staring into computer screens. A tall slim woman in a belted green jacket clacked by with a clipboard. Two uniformed officers sauntered past, chatting, ignoring her. Natasha reminded herself that their indifference was cause for optimism. These people had real work to do. She was a petty shoplifter, of no serious interest to them.

'If you're going to ask questions, I'll need a solicitor.'

'You'll have to wait. There's no one around right now.'

'That's ridiculous. You have no right to arrest me anyway. I haven't done anything wrong.'

The man pursed his lips and opened his piggy eyes as wide as they would go, which was not very wide. He was young, about Natasha's age, with a pink face like the moon. He walked out from behind the counter and leant towards her. 'Forgive me, madam, but I was under the impression that theft was usually considered to be a crime.' His breath smelt acrid. 'You said you were a barrister?'

She gave him the scary look, the one she'd been practising on witnesses and he backed off a little as she replied, 'Theft requires the intention permanently to deprive. There was no such intention.'

'Tell that to my superiors. I won't argue with one of your noble profession. If you'll just sign this, we'll go and sort the fingerprints.'

Natasha heaved herself up and swayed to the counter. She scanned the form which set out details of the alleged offence, the time and place of arrest, her name and address and the contents of her handbag.

She scanned the page. Some of the type was large, some tiny, the stuff about your rights, the stuff they didn't want you to read. The sergeant offered her a pen and she leant over the counter and signed, accepting that she had been arrested on suspicion of the theft of a bottle of Chanel perfume. She fell back onto the hard seat.

The light was hot, blinding white and one of the strips was flickering. The nausea was fading but now she had a headache coupled with an urge to hurl something hard and heavy across the counter at Piggy Eyes who was fiddling about with more bits of paper, trying to look interested in his dull job.

After fingerprinting, she was invited to follow a young, stony-faced policewoman down another cream-painted corridor. 'We'll take you to a place where you can wait for the duty solicitor.'

'I've changed my mind about the solicitor. I've got nothing to hide. It was all a stupid mistake. I just want to get this over with and go home.'

'Too late. He's on his way. Follow me, Miss Baker.'

'What about the phone call?' she called after the young woman who was striding ahead.

'Give us his number. We'll call him for you.' The woman didn't turn but stopped at a heavy door which she opened, standing back to allow Natasha to enter. Something stuck in her throat.

'You're not putting me in here?'

'Only till the solicitor gets here.'

'Why can't I wait in reception?'

'Sergeant makes the decision,' said the woman.

In front of Natasha was a low, narrow bed. No bedding. Just a mattress covered in grey and white ticking and a folded blanket. Natasha didn't want to go near it, but she was exhausted. She sat down heavily, leaning against the wall. 'I need something to eat.'

'We'll see what we can do.'

'You saw the pump. I'm type 1 diabetic. It's not optional. You want me to go into a coma?'

'No need to get excited.'

'And my husband, you'll ring him?'

She was amazed at the ease with which she used the word 'husband'. She had been irritated by Luke's reference to her as his 'wife', but since her arrival in the police station, the status of marriage had come to seem strangely desirable.

'Give me the number then.' The police officer wrote it down and walked out, slamming the metal door.

The cell was stuffy, smelling of someone else's sweat. There was no window, only a couple of airbricks high in the wall. Were they expecting her to spend the night here? There was a toilet in the corner, about a metre away from the bed, a toilet roll on a holder attached to the wall. Even a dog would leave more distance between the place it slept in and the place in which it chose to defecate. There was a small sink with a plastic bottle of handwash and a towel. Above the sink was a sign:

NOT DRINKING WATER. A plastic pitcher of water and a mug had been placed on a small table.

How dare they do this to her? She would sue them for false imprisonment. They hadn't even listened to her explanation. The bed was low, and her thighs were wedged up against her swollen belly. The only way to begin to be comfortable would be to lie down. She stretched out on her side. The headache was bad, but the shooting pains had ceased. What if she went into labour? There was no bell. They would forget about her. She would die in here. There was no guarantee they would contact Luke. She looked at her watch. 6:45 p.m. He would be worrying, ringing her mobile. She could hear sounds, banging, shouts. Other prisoners, real prisoners, were thumping the doors of their cells. The woman with the hard face came back with a sandwich: sliced white bread and processed cheese filling.

'All I could find.'

She put it down on a small metal table and left, slamming the door behind her.

Natasha took a reading. Her levels were haywire. She pumped in the required amount of insulin and bolted down the horrible sandwich. Afterwards she felt calmer, though her head still ached. She lay down on the bed and fell asleep.

–

Someone was shaking her shoulder. It was the woman who had brought the sandwich.

'Your solicitor's here.'

'Did you ring Luke?'

'He's coming down.'

Natasha pulled herself up and let herself be led back down the corridor to a room with a glass door. Her mouth tasted foul.

'May I have my bag, please?' There was a roll of peppermints in the side pocket.

'Not yet.'

'What time is it?'

'A few minutes after eight. You've been asleep just over an hour.'

'I need to go home. You can't keep me here.'

'You'll have to wait a bit longer. We're doing our best to organise the interview tonight.'

The woman walked out, banging the door behind her. And it came back to her, the overheated rooms, the plastic chairs, the smell of sweat, the heavy doors. She had bitten her foster mother and been returned to the children's home. For twenty-four hours she had been placed in secure accommodation. Once again, she heard the clang of the door and the rasp of the key in the lock.

It was a memory, nothing more. Memories could do this. Could take you to a place of horror you thought you had left behind. She would never go back there. She would never again be locked up. The police seemed determined to go through with this farce. Maybe they had to achieve a certain number of arrests. But she would break free as she had always broken free. Soon she would be home with Luke. Tomorrow she would return to the court and speak out against the woman who had attacked her.

–

The interview room was as hot as the corridor, with the same brown metal and plastic chairs. The solicitor looked too young to know what he was doing, and her first thought was that he would be no use to her. But she felt calmer as he gripped her hand, looked firmly into her eyes and said, 'Don't worry. We'll get you out of here.'

His own eyes were a startling blue and he had the childish good looks of a singer in a boy band. They had five minutes together before the start of the interview. She told him what she planned to say. She was very clear. He nodded and said, 'Right then, over to you.'

A man and a woman in plain clothes arrived. The man turned on a tape and gave his name and rank and that of his colleague, explaining that Natasha Baker had been arrested at 5:30 p.m. that day and that they were asking her questions about an allegation of shoplifting. What time had Natasha entered Morley's department store?

'About five p.m.'

'Why did you go there?'

'To buy stuff of course. Why else would I go to Morley's?'

'To steal?'

'No way.'

'What was in your mind as you entered the store?'

'I needed a treat. Luke and I spent the most of the day hanging around South London Criminal Court waiting to give evidence. I was beaten up six months ago and the case was listed for today, only some other stuff overran and we got on late. We were on our way home when I decided to pop into Morley's, buy something nice to cheer myself up. I couldn't talk to Luke anyway 'cos I was in the middle of giving evidence. He went home to start the supper.'

'Go on.'

'I should have gone straight home. When I got into the store I started to feel woozy. I told you, I'm type 1 diabetic. I need to eat regularly. Pregnancy only makes it worse. I picked up the perfume, meaning to pay, only I stopped to have a cereal bar. I carry them round with me. Next thing there's some emergency, one of the customers collapsed and everyone starts rushing about. My memory's a bit vague after that. On my way out, this Indian woman stopped me and made me turn out my bag.'

'The store detective gives a slightly different version. She says you waited to see if anyone was looking and slipped the perfume into your bag. You didn't eat a cereal bar. You went straight to the exit. You had left the store and were about to cross the road when she stopped you.'

'That could be partly true. Like I said, I was woozy. My memories are not that clear. What I can say is I had no intention of going off without paying for something. That would be crazy. I'm a barrister, for Christ's sake. You think I'd risk my career for a bottle of perfume?'

'It certainly seems surprising.'

'I wanted to go back and pay for the stuff, only the stupid woman wouldn't let me. So now I'm here wasting everyone's time.'

The male officer announced the time and said he was turning off the tape.

'Wait here with your solicitor, Mrs Baker. We need to check a couple of things.'

He and his sidekick left the room.

'What d'you reckon?' Natasha asked the baby solicitor.

'I reckon they'll shelve it. They can't afford the personnel. I'm surprised they even brought you in. They're not bothering with shoplifters these days. Shootings, terrorism, hate crime, cyber-crime, they've got enough to deal with. There's been another knifing on Moorlands today.'

Something quivered inside her. It was a huge estate. There was often trouble there. The chance of Luke getting caught up were minimal. The shooting pains came back, and she needed to stand and walk about.

'We live on Moorlands,' she said, pacing the tiny room, thinking ahead. When all this was over, when she started the CPS job, they would move. She wasn't bringing up her child on a south London council estate.

'I wouldn't worry. These things blow up and die down. Drug gangs. You must be used to it.'

'I'll never get used to it,' she said. She could hear the officers approaching. She stood straight and tall to give herself strength. The door opened, and the two officers walked slowly back in, looking grave.

'Please sit down, Mrs Baker.'

Her heart lurched. What now? Had something happened to Luke?

'We've just received a report regarding your prints. It seems there's a match.'

A chill ran through her and she reached for the edge of the chair. Her solicitor held it steady as she sat down. Then he sat down himself. Once again, she was glad of his presence.

'But that's absurd.'

'Leicester. 2013. Name of Lola Tondowski.' The officer smiled as if he were delighted to have found something concrete at last.

The police in Leicester had given her a caution. When she joined Lincoln's Inn, just before being called to Bar, she had signed a declaration to say that she had no criminal record. It was true. A caution was not a record. And she was Natasha now. Lola was someone else. She turned to the solicitor, not because he could do anything to help but because there was no one else to turn to. He addressed the officers.

'May I speak to my client?'

'Couple of minutes. We'll wait outside.' The officers stood up and left the room.

'I can deal with this,' said Natasha.

'Give a no comment interview. We can discuss tactics later.'

'No. I'll tell them the truth.'

'Which is?'

'It'll be fine. You'll see.'

He raised his eyebrows but did not contradict her, only reached for the door handle, opened the door and invited the police officers back in. They set up the tape with the new timing and she launched into her story before they had a chance to question her. Better to set the mood, give her version of events before they could twist things.

'I was just starting my law course. My father – my adoptive father, that is – was very ill. To be honest, I was a bit of a mess. The course was tough. I was working all hours to support myself, so I never got to know the other students. Taking the dress was a spur of the moment thing. I had so little money. I was depressed, worried about the course, worried about Dad. I was living in student accommodation. I was lonely. That's no excuse. I know. I knew it then. But I couldn't stop myself. I don't know why.'

She could talk herself out of this. She made her voice shake, not too much, but enough to convince them she was genuine, which, in a way, she was.

'It was wrong. I absolutely know that. Only I so wanted to go the Bar. When I got picked up I was terrified. I knew if I got in trouble that would blow everything. So, I gave another name. Lola's my birth name.'

'So. Who is Natasha Baker?'

'That was the name I was given when I was adopted.'

'How did you persuade the Leicester police that you were Lola?'

'I had an International Student Card. A fake. I had it made when I was seventeen to help get into clubs.'

'You were twenty-three when you were arrested. You didn't need a fake ID.'

'I kept it. Like a sort of memento of who I used to be. You think that's pathetic?' There was no obvious reaction. She carried on, 'Tondowski's a Polish name. I like it. I was never a real Baker.'

Enough. Better not overdo the unhappy childhood.

She'd been in Leicester for the weekend. A business conference, only it wasn't her business. Her business was pleasuring the wealthy Bulgarian who attended. She had been set up by the escort firm. It was well paid. Lenko was at a meeting and she'd been dropped off at a department store. She had found an amazing, figure-hugging crimson dress which had lost its security device and taken it to the fitting room. The woman at the gate hadn't bothered to count the items. Or so it seemed. Natasha had come out with the scarlet dress under her own and stepped quickly to the exit. But the woman had called security and she was stopped at the main door, taken back in and searched.

'I don't know why I did it. I've not done it since. Getting that caution scared the hell out of me. It was the only time. I swear.'

The two officers were looking at her intently and she suspected they didn't believe her. If they decided to charge her for today's incident, she would have to give up the all hope of the CPS.

'It was five years ago. I'm a different person now. Please let me go. I'm worried about Luke.'

'He's waiting in reception.'

Something loosened inside her. Her headache had gone. She had told the truth, almost the truth and she had landed. The floor was solid. He was there. She felt her bump and thought she detected a slight shift inside.

The solicitor spoke. 'You can see my client is distressed. She's eight months pregnant, not to mention the diabetes. You know the case law on diabetes and automatism.' Natasha doubted whether they did. It was contradictory and illogical, but she knew enough to know she could use it to her advantage if things got that far. The solicitor continued. 'Even if the caution goes before the court, there won't be enough evidence to convict. Haven't you got better things to do?'

'Wait here a minute, please.'

The officers left again.

'Thanks,' said Natasha.

'No problem. They're going through the motions. You'll be out of her in five minutes.'

He really was rather cute. She noticed a wedding ring. Suddenly she felt naked without one and wished Luke had given her an engagement ring. Then she recalled her reaction when he had first mentioned marriage. She had been horrified, frightened. But that was how she had felt then. Life with Luke was different now. It would have to be different. A ring would be the symbol of that difference.

The woman came back alone. 'You're in luck.' She handed Natasha a leaflet and a typed letter. 'Give them this letter and this reference and you could jump the waiting list.'

Natasha scanned the leaflet. Seven smiling faces – young, old, male, female, black, brown and white – all testified to the success of their treatment at Action on Addiction. The list of problems tackled included drugs, alcohol, gambling and shoplifting. She read through the quotes. The participants sounded like happy tourists on a package tour.

'Thank you. This looks really interesting.'

'The initial consultation is free. They've had some great results. They really helped me,' said the woman, her face softening.

'Come on,' said the solicitor, 'Let's get you signed out.' By now Natasha was so exhausted she could barely walk. He held her arm as they went to the reception desk where she signed a receipt and was given her bag. The peppermints had gone.

'Natasha. Lola. Whoever you are,' said the woman. 'Don't let us see you again.'

The solicitor stood so close Natasha could smell him, the familiar smell of fresh male sweat. She had already forgotten his name. He hadn't said much but what he had said was good. His presence had helped her. Without thinking she threw her arms around his neck. He stood unmoving, accepting though not responding to her burst of affection.

'Thanks. You were great.'

'Good luck, Natasha.'

She spotted Luke on the other side of the glass wall in the waiting area. He would believe or wish to believe her tale of forgetfulness. There was no need to mention the caution. Just the sight of him felt like fresh air through an open window. The news of the stabbing had unsettled her. There was always a fear of losing the person you loved.

He had never asked her whether she loved him. She had always behaved as the recipient of his love and she wondered whether he preferred it that way. He knew she needed him and perhaps need was easier for him to bear than love. But now as he stood there beaming on the other side of the reception desk, she realised that if anyone tried to hurt him she would want to kill them.

'Who's the kid?'

'My solicitor.'

'A bit friendly.'

'He was good. I was scared you were dead.'

'Oh that. Yeah there's been trouble on the estate. Some nutcase.' He paused and looked hard at her with his dark eyes. 'What've you been doing, Tash?'

'I was stupid. I didn't mean to take anything. It was a dumb mistake. I just wasn't thinking.'

'Let's get home. I brought the car. You look shattered.'

'I'm feeling pretty weird.'

'In what way weird?' He sounded anxious.

'Just tired. Hungry.'

She needed food and sleep. And love and shelter and warmth. Tomorrow she would need all her strength. Alisha would be cross-examining, doing everything she could to try to blacken Natasha's character. But Natasha knew about cross-examination. It could destroy a case or strengthen it. And there was no doubt in her mind about what would happen in hers. By tomorrow evening the jury would be 100 per cent sure which of them was the villain, which the victim.

She sank with relief into the passenger seat. It was almost midnight, but the city was still heavy with traffic as Luke negotiated the short drive home. Sirens pierced the air. Horns blared. Mad cyclists without lights swerved in front of them. She looked at Luke's hands on the wheel – large, strong hands which brought on a twitch of desire.

When they reached Moorlands, the police were still milling about behind strips of tape. But the nightmare of her arrest had disappeared, and they were going back to their tiny flat which, for the moment, was home. She laid her hands across her bump. The baby would be fine. The shooting pains were nothing but a reminder that someone was there, waiting to come out. She glanced down at the leaflet from the clinic.

'What's that?' said Luke.

'Some therapy bumf.'

She thought he would say 'you should go', but he didn't. His hand slid up the steering wheel, as he steered the car to the left and backed into parking place.

Chapter Forty-three

Mel

'All parties in the case of Goddard to Court Four.'

Mel's heart lurched. She and Georgie were sitting in the crowded coffee bar in the reception area. His proximity warmed her, and she dreaded exchanging that warmth for the stifling atmosphere of the court room. He would be her only support today. Alisha was running the case without a solicitor. Jacob was in college. She hadn't known who else to ask. The disembodied voice resumed.

'All parties in the case of Goddard to Court Four.'

Georgie stood and stretched out an arm towards her. She reached for him. A memory surfaced, a tiny, terrified child, clutching her mother's firm hand on her first day at nursery school. And now, forty years on, just as then, her throat was dry, her stuttered words hoarse and painful.

'I'm worried about my mother. How will she cope? She's too old for this.'

'She's certainly made an effort.'

It was true. Isabel looked splendid in a scarlet silk dress and jacket. Her hair was swept up and she was wearing a platinum and ruby brooch. She appeared to sense their scrutiny for she looked up, smiled and then turned back to her companion, a woman from the Witness Service who had brought her a cup of tea.

'She's enjoying the drama,' said Georgie.

'If only I knew what she was going to say.'

'She's not going to rat on her daughter.'

'Digger's clever. He can't lead of course, but he can lure. I've seen him before with a reluctant witness.'

'Don't go that way, Mel. You can't control him. You can't control her. You're not running this show. The only thing you're running is your own story.'

She studied his face. What did he mean, 'story'? Had he seen through her? Something inside her wobbled and she asked, 'Will I have to give evidence today?'

'Why are you asking me? You know how it works.'

'I won't be able to speak. I can hardly walk.'

'You'll be fine. No one could ever believe you were capable of violence. No one. You'll be great.'

They walked into Court Four, Georgie turning into the public seating area, Mel acknowledging the usher and making her way to the glass-panelled dock at the back of the court. The panels were spaced inches apart so a defendant would be able to hear the proceedings. Yesterday had been tough, but she'd felt curiously detached. The first day of a trial was often like this, even her own trial. A novelty, a spectacle, not yet real. By day two the jury would have settled in, allegiances would be formed, sympathies established. Like a cinema audience they would move from critical detachment to total immersion. And sympathies could switch in a flicker. The usher closed the heavy door. There was no handle on the inside. The door on the other side of the dock led to the cells.

Beyond the low hum of the air conditioning, Mel could hear the occasional cough and shuffle of feet as the prosecution team settled themselves. Still no sign of Alisha.

She took her seat, staring ahead of her to the coat of arms above the Bench, remembering the advice she gave her own criminal clients. Sit up straight. Don't smile or laugh. Try not to weep. Follow the evidence. Watch the witnesses carefully. Take notes if you like, but not too many. When giving evidence, be as nice to everyone as you can. Answer the questions put. Don't try too hard to control your face but remember, every reaction you give will be noted by the jury. Tell the truth but don't say more than necessary. Could she really have given such advice? How could any sane person follow it?

Alisha had given her no advice, only an attempt at reassurance. 'You'll be fine, don't worry.' It was unsatisfactory. She would have expected more from her representative. She would also have expected her to be in court in good time, to have another chat with her before Natasha's cross-examination.

'Court rise.'

Judge McDermid took his seat. He was considered both fair and robust, his interventions sparse and measured. It was impossible to read much in his ragged Scottish countenance.

Seconds later, Alisha raced in, uncharacteristically frazzled, a few strands of long black hair escaping from the wig which sat slightly askew on her forehead. McDermid said nothing. His facial expression was enough.

'Your Honour, I apologise for my late arrival,' spluttered Alisha. 'Shortly before we were called into court, a police officer acquaintance spoke to me. He passed on some information which will be relevant to today's proceedings.'

McDermid remained impassive. 'Do you wish to address me on that information?'

'If I may take instructions?'

'Very well, Miss Mehta, you may speak to the defendant. Usher, please inform the jury there will be a further slight delay.'

Alisha stepped into the dock and spoke quietly to Mel. 'Natasha was arrested last night. For shoplifting. She gave fingerprints and they traced them to someone called Lola Tondowski. I'm going to ask about Lola.'

'No. I don't want to go into that.'

'Why not? It goes to credibility. Casts doubts on Natasha's character.'

'I said NO,' Mel retorted, her voice rising in pitch, unable to quell her agitation.

'What is it, Mel?'

'What's what?'

'There's something else. Something you haven't told me. This Lola. What about her? If Natasha's hiding something that can only help us.'

'I've already said, Alisha, I can't talk about it. OK?'

'Mel, if you want me to represent you properly you need to be open with me.'

Mel shuddered. Everything could blow open. Her son had refused to show her the texts. How bad could they be? What if there were more pictures? And how could she be sure of Jacob's story? He had closed down pretty fast and she had no idea how far he had gone. Natasha must have made the first move. But she was not on trial today. Her behaviour would only reinforce Mel's motive for hurting her.

'You'll have to trust me on this, Alisha. There's stuff about Lola, about Jacob, I don't want it coming out. They were texting, sharing photographs. I can't even bear to talk about it. Mention the shoplifting if you like, if the judge lets you. But nothing else.'

'But that's serious, Mel. Are you saying she was grooming him?'

'I don't think I would use that word. From what I gathered from Jacob he was pretty keen to go along with it.'

'But that's just the point. Sexual predators...'

'For Christ sake, Alisha, I said I don't want to go there. God knows what Jacob might have done or said. I don't want it mentioned. Anyway, he's all right now. That's the main thing.'

'What if Digger raises it?'

'Why would he blacken his own client?'

'If it gives you a motive for hurting Natasha, she might agree to it. It depends what she did. Did you see her texts?'

'No. He wouldn't let me see them. Made me give her back her phone.'

'So you only have Jacob's word for what happened?'

'For Christ's sake, Alisha! I saw the fucking photographs!'

It was hard to breathe. Something in her chest was fluttering as if a tiny bird had been caught between her ribs.

'OK, Mel. Stay cool. I'll follow your instructions. You know that. I only wish you'd told me all this before.'

Mel remembered how often she had said or thought that about her own clients who kept things back. But all she could say was, 'I couldn't.'

Through the glass of the dock she could see Digger conferring with someone from the Crown Prosecution Service. There were three people on the public benches: Georgie; a young woman with a notebook who might be a law student; and an elderly man who Mel guessed was one of those full-time court room spectators, a self-appointed expert who filled his days with other people's catastrophes. Her mother wouldn't be allowed in until she had given her own evidence. At least Jacob had agreed not to come. On another set of benches closer to the judge she noted the reporter she had seen yesterday. Alisha was sitting close, waiting for her to continue.

'Was Natasha charged?' *Mel asked.*

'No, they let her go. So that won't get us very far. We'll see what McDermid says. But Lola – that's another story. Lola was guilty. She was cautioned five years ago in Leicester.'

'What for?'

'Same thing. Shoplifting. The main thing is the fake name. It goes to credibility. She told the Bar Standards Board she had no convictions. Strictly speaking true. But she should have mentioned the caution. Remember the little box where you're supposed to put anything else that might be relevant? You were right all along. Not what she seems.'

'She's waiting to start work at the CPS,' said Mel.

Alisha made a face. 'Could be tricky for her. They'll be looking into her background pretty carefully after last night.' She paused. 'So, what about this Lola?'

'OK. But not a word about Jacob.'

Mel heard movement from beyond the dock and she looked through the glass to see the usher standing beside the judge's bench.

'Court rise.'

Their short break was over. In seconds the judge was back, and Alisha had left the dock. From her place at the front of the court, she explained about the arrest.

'Has Miss Baker been charged?'

'No, Your Honour.'

McDermid peered down from the Bench; his voice was tinged with irritation. 'So, a young woman is picked up for shoplifting. She fails to pay for some items. The young woman happens to be pregnant, and in a heightened nervous state. I do not propose to delve into allegations when the police themselves chose not to take the matter further.'

'Your Honour, the issue relates to credibility. Miss Baker has another name. Lola Tondowski. Unlike Miss Natasha Baker, Miss Lola Tondowski was charged with an offence of shoplifting five years ago. There was no trial. She accepted a caution.'

'And on what basis do you say this Lola Tondowski and the prosecution witness are the same person?' queried McDermid.

'They have the same fingerprints.'

Digger bounced up. 'Your Honour, this has absolutely no relevance to what happened to Miss Baker six months ago in Dulwich. She was attacked. She was hurt. These are the matters on the Indictment. What she may or may not have done five years ago is not in issue here.'

'Well, Miss Mehta. I will allow some questioning on the use of the name. If the questioning proves to be unnecessarily prejudicial it will of course be stopped. As to the caution, the usual rules apply. Mr Diggory-Brown, you may wish to re-examine your client.'

The jury was called. Natasha walked slowly across the court-room, using her right arm to lever herself up the step into the witness box. She wore the same outfit as yesterday, a long-sleeved blue dress that caressed her bump. She looked tired but lovely, an exhausted Madonna.

Alisha began with uncontested matters, aiming to put Natasha at ease by referring to her achievements, how she had worked her way through law school, landed a sought-for pupillage. A sketch for the jury. Not the victim portrait offered by the prosecution. But an ambitious woman. Strong-willed. Tenacious. A woman who might take a step too far to gain her ends. A woman who could be motivated by revenge.

'Miss Baker, it's true, isn't it, that you sometimes use another name?'

Most witnesses would have been rattled, but Natasha kept her cool. 'Occasionally.'

'Lola Tondowski?'

'Lola Tondowski is my birth name. I was adopted at ten. That's when I became Natasha.'

'But you still use Lola?'

'Sometimes. Lola has a Facebook page. I don't want to lose touch with where I came from. My father was Polish. I never knew him but the name is special to me.'

Mel could tell Alisha was itching to take it further, longing to get stuck in, to expose Natasha as a liar and a predator. But, good barrister that she was, she would not veer from her client's instructions.

She put Mel's case, Natasha's failure to get the tenancy and consequent determination to injure her pupil supervisor in whatever way she could. By slow careful questioning she attempted to shift the jury's viewpoint. Natasha would no longer be a woman wronged, but a woman ready to cause damage.

Following Mel's instructions Alisha accused Natasha of plotting her way into Mel's mother's house, of planning to pocket her jewellery and sell the vintage costumes for her own benefit. But there was no hard evidence to rely on. When she accused

Natasha of blackmail, threatening to expose Mel's affair if she refused to write the reference, Natasha shook her head slowly.

'That's absurd.'

'But correct, is it not Miss Baker?' urged Alisha.

'Absolutely not.'

Apart from that one exchange, Natasha's demeanour remained calm and unruffled. When it came to the assault itself and Mel listened to the story she had rehearsed in her mind so many times, the scenario sounded horribly unlikely. According to Alisha, Natasha had lost her temper and rushed at Mel who had attempted to defend herself by holding up her arms. Natasha had been wearing high heels and had stumbled, tripping on one of the other shoes scattered across the carpet. Initially she had fallen backwards but hitting the shoe caused her to twist and crash against the dressing table. It had been a horrible accident and had led to serious injury. Natasha's accusation of assault was simply an attempt at revenge for what she saw as Mel's lack of professional support.

Natasha denied it all.

Having failed to see her witness crumple in response to direct challenge, Alisha tried a different tack. 'The Bar is a competitive profession, isn't it, Miss Baker?'

'Yes, very.'

'Things can get difficult in chambers.'

'I don't know what you mean.'

'You were expecting to get a tenancy at Bridge Court.'

'Hoping.'

'And when you didn't, you blamed Miss Goddard.'

'I've no idea how the voting went. Anyway, she's entitled to her opinion.'

'You were angry with her?'

'Not at all.'

'Looking for revenge?'

'No.'

'And the best revenge would be to blacken her name and ruin her career?'

'I've already said no.'

'Indeed, you invented this complaint after the event.'

'I don't know what you mean.'

'When you fell against the dressing table you were concussed?'

'Slightly.'

'It's in the medical record.'

'Yes. That's what they said.'

'So, you don't actually remember what happened that afternoon?'

'That's not true. She grabbed hold of me and threw me against the dressing table. I might have blacked out for a few minutes afterwards, but I remember exactly what she did. I never laid a finger on her. I told them at the hospital. You saw the evidence. The defendant didn't even challenge it. And I told Luke when I got back from the hospital. Every word of it is true.'

'Thank you, Miss Baker,' said Alisha.

There was no re-examination. At least no one had mentioned Jacob. But for all her years of experience there was not much Alisha could do with a clever, determined witness, particularly one who was telling truth. It was looking bad.

Chapter Forty-four

Mel

Isabel appeared unsteady as she approached the witness box, turning to smile at the judge and then the jury. Mel had no idea whether the unsteadiness was authentic or part of today's role-play, nor how far she could count on her mother.

Isabel's written statement emphasised the antagonism between her daughter and her guest. There had been a disagreement. The disagreement had led to a scuffle. But Isabel could not say precisely what had caused Natasha to fall with such force against the dressing table. During the long months of waiting, her mother had refused to speak of the incident.

'I'm not allowed to talk to you, darling. You've seen my statement. I'll do what I've been asked to do.'

In the witness box Isabel confirmed that she had looked again at the statement which was prepared last year. Yes, the contents were true.

Digger led her through the events of that day, the outing to the museum, the early return to Dulwich, Mel's attitude to Natasha, the unexpected outburst.

'Please describe the outburst, Mrs Goddard.'

'Melanie was in the house when we returned. She announced that Natasha should leave immediately. Quite out of the blue.'

'What happened then?'

'Natasha went upstairs to change.'

'Did your daughter explain why she wanted Natasha to leave?'

'Something to do with Natasha being not what she seemed.'

'In what way?'

'I don't recall. It was all very confusing.'

The judge intervened. 'Mrs Goddard. You cannot be compelled to answer every question. But you were an eyewitness to what occurred that day. Anything you can remember about what preceded the events that led to this charge will be helpful to the jury in reaching its verdict.'

'I understand, Your Honour.'

'What did you do next?' asked Digger.

It was as Mel had anticipated. Digger didn't want Isabel to divulge too much about the causes of the argument, didn't want to risk the jury members asking themselves questions about Natasha's character. Maybe her mother had forgotten the main cause of the clash between the two women. Or maybe, like Mel, she didn't want Jacob's name brought into this. Alisha had promised not to mention him. If Mel was to get off, the jury must never know the full story. But as Digger moved on, Mel was aware of a weight in her chest. She had been growing used to a variety of inexplicable symptoms, aching limbs, a fluttering stomach, a tightness in the jaw, pains around the eyes. This one was new, a slow persistent thudding as if her heart had become suddenly heavy.

And now Digger was asking Isabel to describe the spare bedroom.

'The bed's on the right as you walk in. There's a fitted cupboard down one wall, a chest of drawers against the other and a dressing table in front of the bay window.'

'Did you enter the room?'

'No. I stood in the doorway.'

'Where was Miss Baker?'

'She was standing near the dressing table.'

'In your statement you mention shoes on the floor.'

'Yes. Natasha had been trying them on before we went out.'

Mel glanced from her mother to the jury. There was only one point they needed to decide. Did she fall or was she pushed?

But Digger wouldn't ask that. Wouldn't chance it. He didn't need to put Natasha's case to Isabel. She was there to set the scene for the prosecution. No more, no less.

'You've told us you followed your daughter into the room. What was the atmosphere like at that point?'

'Very unpleasant.'

'Please explain.'

Isabel paused and looked at Mel. It wasn't a compassionate look, not a look the jury would expect from a mother to a daughter. And at that moment Mel wished she had been nicer to her mother. She remembered the times she had been irritated by Isabel, had shouted at her, argued with her. She tried to remember what the arguments were about. Nothing important. Isabel's habit of opting out when discussion became difficult, her insistence that she was too stupid to understand law or politics, her love of the superficial, her obsession with style and celebrity. Once Isabel had accused Mel of trying to make her feel small. Was this it? Isabel's revenge?

'I felt frightened.'

'Why?'

'Mel was angry. I know what she's like when she's angry.'

'What is she like?'

'Loud, out of control. Aggressive.'

'Violent?'

'She can be.'

Mel felt her throat closing, her breath quickening.

'Can you describe instances when you have witnessed her violence?'

'I prefer not to say.'

The jury appeared attentive. Digger fiddled with his spectacles and looked down at his notes, letting the answer sink in, a familiar tactic. Then he raised his head. 'We'll come back to that, Mrs Goddard. Can you describe the conversation in the bedroom between Natasha and your daughter?'

'I wouldn't call it conversation. More like a row.'

'What did you hear?'

'It's in my statement.'

'Please tell the jury.'

'My daughter believed Natasha was planning to steal my jewellery and sell my costumes.'

'Did you believe Miss Baker would do this?'

'Certainly not. She and I had been organising an exhibition.'

'Was there anything else that might have made Melanie angry?'

'Natasha said something about Jacob. That's what set Mel off.'

At the sound of her son's name a shockwave tore through her. As the aftershocks died down, she was conscious once again of the weight in her chest.

'You haven't mentioned Jacob in your statement.'

'I didn't want him dragged into this. Melanie doesn't either, I'm sure of that. But I've sworn to tell the whole truth.'

'What did Natasha say about Jacob?'

'I don't remember the exact words. Something about him being a good-looking boy.'

'Why would that make her angry?'

'It was more than that. Almost as if, you know, Natasha might have had an interest in the lad. That would have upset Melanie. It upset me.'

Mel tried to read her mother's face. The features were taut; the eyes narrowed in what might have been pain. Physical or emotional? It was impossible to say. The words 'Please, Mum,' looped silently in her mind.

'Is there any other reason why there's nothing about Jacob in your statement?'

'After everything that happened, I was distraught. I still am. I didn't want my grandson bandied about in police statements.'

'Yet you mention him now.'

'When the police interviewed me, I answered their questions. They only asked about the jewellery and costumes. But I've taken an oath. The whole truth.'

'Can we go back to the scene in the bedroom? Where was Melanie when you arrived in the doorway?'

'Close to Natasha. They were both by the dressing table.'

'How was Natasha's mood? As far as you could judge?'

'Calm at first, even when Melanie accused her. Then she grew animated, as if she was enjoying herself. I think she might have laughed.'

'Mrs Goddard, you say in your statement there was a scuffle but that you don't know who started it.'

'That's right.'

'Yet you have just told us that Miss Baker was calm, Melanie angry.'

'Everything happened so fast. One minute they were standing there arguing. The next minute the poor girl was on the floor covered in blood.'

Digger changed tack. 'Can you describe Miss Baker's character? What sort of person is she?'

Isabel glanced quickly at Natasha, sitting behind the CPS representative.

'A nice person. Organised. Helpful. She cleaned my house, took me out. She gave me a new interest. I was becoming fond of her.'

'Yet you have told us that your daughter found Miss Baker difficult.'

This was safer ground. But the reply was a shock.

'Melanie finds lots of people difficult. Lots of people find Melanie difficult.'

'In what way do they find her difficult?'

Judge McDermid intervened again. 'Mr Diggory-Brown, Mrs Goddard cannot give evidence as to what other people might think or feel.'

'My apology, Your Honour. I'll rephrase that. In your experience as a mother, Mrs Goddard, is there anything you have seen by way of behaviour in your daughter that you would call difficult.'

'She can be touchy, hot-tempered, opinionated. I suppose we all can.'

'Mrs Goddard, I will ask you for the second time, have you ever witnessed your daughter being physically violent?'

'I prefer not to answer that.'

Judge McDermid spoke. 'Mrs Goddard, you cannot be forced to answer a question. But you should be aware that the jury may draw an inference from your silence.'

'I understand.'

'Your Honour, I have no further questions.'

An usher walked to the witness box with a fresh carafe of water. The judge asked, 'Mrs Goddard, would you like to sit down to give your evidence?'

'That's very kind, Your Honour, but no, I prefer to remain standing.'

When the Isabel's examination was completed Alisha asked permission to speak to her client.

'So Jacob's in it now. How do you want me to deal with it?'

'Don't challenge her,' said Mel. 'I'll sort it.' Though she had no idea how.

Alisha went through Isabel's first meeting with Natasha, the new friendship, the shared interest in fashion and jewellery.

'In a short time you grew very fond of Miss Baker, didn't you?'

'That's true.'

Then she turned to Isabel's relationship with her daughter. Whatever she asked there would be risk.

'Mrs Goddard, you have never witnessed your daughter being physically violent, have you?'

Isabel looked at Mel and then back to Alisha. 'She was a rough little thing at school. Scrapping in the playground. Once she bit another child.'

'And as an adult?'

Mel felt herself trembling. Could the jury see her hands gripping the ledge in front of her? Why hadn't Alisha checked with her client first? The fundamental rule of advocacy. Alisha had asked a question to which she did not know the answer, going way beyond what they had agreed at the conference.

What Isabel said next was so unexpected Mel almost laughed.

'I had a little cat. Peanuts. One day he tried to jump on Melanie's lap. I'll never forget it. She hurled him to the floor. If that wasn't violence, I don't know what was.'

Out of the corner of her eye Mel could see two of the jury members smiling. One woman looked upset.

'Any other time?'

'Yes. Melanie was at my house. Worrying about her work as usual. She found it very stressful. I remember darling Peanuts slinking up beside her. She kicked him away across the floor. Dreadful behaviour. I told her to leave the house. We didn't speak for weeks after that.'

Now the jury really would hate her. Hurling herself at a pregnant woman was bad enough. But kicking a defenceless cat would be unforgiveable. Alisha moved on to the defence case.

'Returning to the day in question, the prosecution say that your daughter pushed Miss Baker against the dressing table.'

'That's what they say.'

'You saw Miss Baker fall.'

'I did. She went flying.'

'But you don't know why she fell?'

'No.'

'You saw a scuffle.'

'Yes.'

'But you did not, at any time, see your daughter push Miss Baker?'

Isabel paused. The pause felt very long. Mel's heart was banging in her chest. Her mother had presented her as heartless, cruel and violent. Would she lie for her now?

'No. I didn't.'

Isabel stepped from the witness box and walked slowly towards the public seats, exhausted by her efforts, avoiding the eyes of her daughter. Mel's heart was still pounding. That bloody cat. The jury would hate her. But as Isabel turned towards the almost empty benches of the public gallery it occurred to her that Alisha had played a clever game. She had allowed Isabel to become a credible witness. Most mothers would support their daughter. But a mother who had issues with her daughter would be less likely to do so. Isabel had written her own script and acted her own part. It had been a brilliant performance.

Bail was refused over lunch. Mel was offered a sandwich on a tray in the cell behind the dock. The dock officer held onto her phone, bringing her yesterday's Metro to read. She asked for a pencil and for half an hour she succeeded in blocking out the world with a Sudoku. Her heart had grown quieter though the weight was still there. In this second day she was beginning to feel more detached. Trial by jury was a form of theatre and she was still offstage. There was nothing she could do to change anyone else's part and she had already learnt her own.

For months she had thought of little but of how she was to get off this charge. Now, as she set aside her Sudoku, a new awareness was surfacing. Beside the instinct for self-preservation was another instinct, equally solid, equally powerful. It was the desire that the jury, here to administer justice, should know what Natasha was really like.

Luke Gearing was next on the stand. After sitting transfixed through Isabel's account, the members of the jury now gave their full attention to the young man with the film-star looks. What he said concurred closely with what they had already heard from Natasha. He had been at home when Miss Goddard brought Natasha back from the hospital. Natasha had been woozy at first and slept. But the following day she was more alert and had told him everything. His speech was hesitant, and though the words were well chosen and articulate, the voice

315

seemed to come from elsewhere. At times it shook and wavered in pitch, there was even an occasional stammer. He repeated Natasha's story almost word for word.

Alisha got nowhere in cross-examination.

It was 3:45 p.m. Mel was preparing to give evidence herself when Digger addressed the judge.

'Your Honour, allegations concerning the defendant's son, Jacob Villiers, have been made in court this afternoon by our witness, Mrs Isabel Goddard.'

'I think I know what's coming next, Mr Diggory-Brown.' The judge who had been tapping notes on his laptop looked down over his spectacles.

'The allegations were not included in Mrs Goddard's statement and were therefore unexpected. With Your Honour's permission I should like to recall our principal witness Miss Natasha Baker.'

'And how long will that take?' McDermid sounded weary.

'No more than fifteen minutes, Your Honour.'

'Very well.'

Natasha, who had been sitting behind the prosecution team, was recalled and sworn in again. As she placed her hand on the New Testament she gazed towards the high window of the courtroom. More theatre, thought Mel. When it came to her own evidence she would affirm.

'Miss Baker, immediately prior to the assault in Mrs Goddard's spare room, did you mention the defendant's son, Jacob?'

'Briefly, yes.'

'In what context?'

'I was telling the defendant I enjoyed meeting him. He was with Mel at the Dulwich Picture Gallery when we met for a coffee a couple of weeks previously.'

'Why did you mention him?'

'I wanted to find out if he was OK. He and I went off to buy the coffees and he just ran off. It was a bit odd.'

'Did you tell her he was a good-looking boy?'

'Not on that occasion.'

'So did you say he was good-looking on some other occasion?'

'It's possible. Weeks before. When she showed me a photo of her son.'

'Mrs Goddard suggested you had an interest in him, that you found him attractive.'

'That's ridiculous. I was just being friendly.'

'So, if I can take you back to the moment in the bedroom. How did Miss Goddard react to your query about her son?'

'She went berserk. Like I'd been trying to seduce him. Totally over the top. But I told you. She's like that. Prickly. Paranoid I'd say.'

'Why didn't you mention this in your evidence before, Miss Baker?'

'To be honest I didn't want to upset his grandmother. Anyway, it didn't seem important. I'm used to Mel overreacting. She does it all the time. What really tipped her over the edge was me mentioning Paul Freedman. Maybe I shouldn't have said anything. But when she called me a cheat and a liar I was furious. It was so unjust.'

'Thank you, Miss Baker. If you would stay there, Miss Mehta may have some questions for you.'

Alisha obtained permission to take instructions.

'I'll have to challenge her,' she told Mel once the door of the dock was shut behind her.

'I've already told you I don't want Jacob brought into this.'

'I'll need to contest what she said about your reaction. As for the allegations in detail...'

'Absolutely not.'

'OK. We'll keep it low key.'

Natasha was waiting in the witness box, looking bored.

'Miss Baker, I have two points to put to you. My first is this. You have stated that Miss Goddard was upset by the mention of her son and later by the mention of Mr Freedman.'

'More than upset. She was out of control.'

'That's not correct, is it, Miss Baker?'

'It certainly is.'

'Throughout your confrontation in the bedroom, Miss Goddard remained calm.'

Natasha started to laugh.

'Answer the question, Miss Baker,' insisted McDermid.

'With respect, Your Honour, it's not a question. She's just said something which is wrong. It's so wrong it's laughable.'

McDermid simply raised his eyebrows, indicating Alisha should continue.

'In fact Miss Goddard accused you of deception and that is what sparked you to rush towards her and fall.'

'Bullshit. Apologies, Your Honour.'

Alisha sat down. There was no re-examination.

When the jury was dismissed Mel was granted bail. She stepped out of the dock to where Alisha was waiting.

'Don't worry, Alisha. I understand your difficulty.'

'It could go either way. There's a lot under the carpet here. Get a good night's sleep. I'll see you tomorrow.'

Without waiting for an answer, Alisha pulled off her wig and left the court room.

The room was emptying but as the backs of spectators moved towards the door Mel spotted Georgie heading towards her. When close he opened his arms and for a few seconds she rested her head against his shoulder.

'Want to talk about it?' he murmured.

'I prefer not to, Georgie,' she said, pulling back. They set off together for the exit.

'I get that.'

'But thanks for being here.'

They walked in silence to the front of the court building. One of the assistants from the Witness Service was helping Isabel into a taxi. A relief. If she wasn't prepared to speak to Alisha or Georgie, she certainly wasn't ready to face her mother.

Chapter Forty-five

Mel

Back home, Mel threw off her clothes and fell into a hot bath with a glass of Merlot for company. Never had wine tasted so good. The day's evidence swirled in her head. She imagined the scene tomorrow, spiralling into the horror of a guilty verdict. McDermid would delay sentence. Alisha would ask for reports. More waiting. Swigging back the wine, she wondered whether prison might be better than a suspended sentence. She could continue to protest her innocence, write a bestselling book on conditions inside. It would change her life but that might be no bad thing. Someone, somewhere, would employ her when she came out. She might become a cleaner, long quiet days, dusting and vacuuming the houses of the rich, free to think, dream, perhaps even feel remorse.

Jacob would move in with Claude's gang. He would survive, might even thrive away from the claustrophobia of the mother-son connection, though she would have to lie to him for the rest of her life. Whatever happened she would have to lie.

She took another swig, luxuriating in the deep, scented warmth of the water. No baths, no wine in prison. But as she turned on the tap for more blistering heat against her skin, she dreamt of a different touch, one she had not known since that painful afternoon in Barnes last summer. She and Paul had once seemed perfect, wrapped in their cocoon of private delight, untainted by the fevers of the world. Finally, the world had clattered down upon them, as it had always threatened to do.

She stepped out, reached for her towel, conscious of the sway of her buttocks, the spread of her hips which she had always thought too wide, the breasts which she had thought too large, but which had shrunk in the sixteen years since she had fed Jacob. Now that they were no longer of use to anyone, they were beginning to feel about right. She stood in front of the full-length mirror, examining her reflection. The gloss of youth was long gone. How cruel that in all those years of obsessive male attention, only Claude had touched her heart. Claude who had never truly wanted her. And now, as male attention faltered, the longing for connection had grown, the need for physical contact at times unbearable.

She rubbed herself dry. The longing became an ache. Would she ever love or be loved again?

Jacob was preparing her dinner. It was his friend Don's birthday, but he had chosen to stay in to cook for his mother on what might be her last night at home. Neither had mentioned the possibility that she could be locked away.

As the wine swam down her gullet, she saw again Paul's angular features. His grey blue eyes looked sad, and his skin had the pallor of a man who had spent too much time hunched over his books and computer. She pictured his long hands with the heavily jointed fingers. As she yanked up her trousers, smelling the garlic, onions and tomato wafting through from the kitchen, she could feel those hands running across her waist, over her hips and buttocks. No, she wouldn't see him again.

Jacob's voice rang out down the corridor.

'Mum!'

'Five minutes,' she replied.

They had barely spoken since she got back from court and she longed to hug him for his kindness in staying home for her, cooking for her. But hugs with Jacob were still awkward, still self-conscious. He was struggling. He needed space and time. If only she had the time.

She was finishing dressing when, in her mind, she heard again Paul's name, sounded out in court for all to hear. As she tugged a comb through her wet, tangled hair she felt the familiar hot surge of anger: at Natasha, at Paul, even, it now seemed, at herself. And there was something else, another less familiar emotion. For years she had seen herself as an innocent party. It was Paul who had betrayed his wife. Mel had betrayed no one. But as she waved the dryer around her damp hair a persistent inner voice was telling her otherwise. Mel had been complicit in the deception. Natasha might be a bitch and a troublemaker, but she had told the truth about Paul. There was a sour edge to Mel's anger. It felt more like shame. The jury would know Mel as a woman who was prepared to lie. She ran a comb through her hair, looked in the mirror then quickly looked away.

'Are you coming?' called Jacob.

'Coming,' she said.

She picked up her empty glass and walked through to the kitchen, praying this would not be their last night together.

Chapter Forty-six

Mel

Light flickered around her curtains. She showered and put on the short-sleeved brown dress and jacket she had worn for the last three days, the only smart outfit she had that was not barrister gear. Foundation, lipstick, eye-liner, mascara. Make-up would help her face her accuser.

At breakfast Jacob was taut and taciturn. He was off to college, but they had agreed that he would try to get to court in the afternoon. Mel forced down two slices of toast and they both had large strong coffees. Everything would be fine, she told him. She would see him later.

–

In the witness box, Alisha let her take wing and she told the story she had rehearsed so often in her head. When Digger pounced, she was ready with that surge of energy that arises on the brink of disaster.

'There was a degree of professional jealousy in your attitude to Miss Baker?'

'Not at all. I was pleased she picked up work so quickly.'

'Surprised too?'

'A little. It's unusual to get that much work in your second six.'

'On one occasion she took one of your returns after you had been the victim of a mugging?'

'That's true too.'

'You were suffering from a degree of Post-Traumatic Stress Disorder.'

'I was pretty shaken up. Anyone would be. I was never diagnosed.'

Judge McDermid intervened. 'Mr Diggory-Brown, no expert evidence has been adduced attesting to Miss Goddard's psychological state.'

'Apologies, Your Honour. I'll rephrase the question. After the assault you took a week off work.'

'That's right.'

'And when you returned, you found, to your surprise, that Miss Baker already had the beginnings of an independent practice.'

'You can do better than that, Digger,' said Mel.

To her amazement, Digger looked flustered, two members of the jury tittered and there was no intervention from the judge.

When it came to the nub of the narrative, the afternoon in Isabel's house, she was well rehearsed. 'I don't deny there was irritation, even antagonism between us. I was uneasy about this new friendship.'

He didn't ask why. The old rule which Alisha had broken so defiantly and successfully yesterday. Never ask a question if you don't know the answer. But he didn't stop her when she carried on.

'I had a hunch and I was proved right. Not only was Natasha wearing one of my mother's vintage designer outfits, she also had on some of my mother's valuable jewellery. A ring, a brooch and earrings. I asked her to leave and she went upstairs to change. I followed her. I needed to be sure she was leaving empty handed.'

'And Miss Baker took off the jewellery.'

'Yes.'

'But the jewellery, the vintage costumes, they weren't the main cause of the row were they?'

'I wouldn't call it a row. More of a spat.'

'You had never liked Miss Baker.'

'Liking is not the issue. I was cross with her for inveigling her way into my mother's house.'

'Despite entering at your mother's invitation?'

'Natasha sought her out. She never told my mother she was my pupil. That sounds pretty duplicitous to me.'

'The truth is you were envious of Miss Baker.'

'Not at all.'

'She was clever, popular, she had been attracting work from your solicitors.'

'That's ridiculous. Why would I be envious of her? She didn't even get the tenancy.' As soon as she had said it she wished it unsaid. It sounded arrogant. And which was worse? Envy or arrogance?

'Miss Baker met your son at the Dulwich Picture Gallery, didn't she?'

'Yes.'

'When you met again at your mother's house, she asked if he was OK?'

'That's not true.'

'She said she had enjoyed meeting him.'

'I don't remember her saying that.'

A couple of jury members were taking notes. Mel looked over to where Natasha was sitting behind the CPS solicitor. Their eyes met but Natasha's gave no hint of acknowledgement. She wore the same blue pinafore dress, this time with a cream silk blouse, buttoned to the neck. Her hair was tied back neatly. There was no sign of a scar. She reminded Mel of an antique doll. And at that moment Mel realised that despite everything she had said to Alisha, despite her horror at hearing her son's name tossed around in court, she could no longer stay silent. The jury needed to know what kind of woman had brought this complaint.

Digger paused to look at his notes. Mel was conscious of the low buzz of the air conditioning, the occasional scrape of feet on the wooden floor, bodies shifting on benches, fingers tapping on devices. The wordless sounds were soothing, and she leant against the side of the witness box. Then, quickly, she pulled herself straight, needing to call on what buried strength remained. Before Digger could lob another question, she turned to face the jury and spoke.

'She said he had a nice body.'

'Miss Goddard, she did not say that. She merely asked if he was all right,' interrupted Digger.

'My son was sixteen years old at the time.'

'Miss Goddard, there was no mention of Jacob in your defence statement.'

'No. Because he has nothing to do with my defence.'

'And so you mention him now in an attempt to malign the character of the complainant, Miss Baker?'

'My sole intention is to tell the truth about her. Natasha is a thirty-year-old woman. She flirted with Jacob online. Got him to send her pictures. Texts. I didn't want to mention him but my mother did, so you might as well know the whole story.'

McDermid was staring at her. Mel was amazed he hadn't stopped her. Her glance shifted from the Bench to the public seating area. On this final day of the hearing it was almost full. Alongside the law student and the self-appointed court expert, were Georgie and Farouk and several members of her own chambers and others she had no time to register because her attention was drawn to her mother, upright, elegant, perfectly turned out and sitting in the back row. Next to her, to Mel's amazement, sat Claude, looking stern, and next to him, his face bleached white, dark eyes wide, sat Jacob. Mel clutched the side of the witness box.

'None of this was put to Miss Baker,' said Digger.

'No.'

'Even though she was called back and Miss Mehta had the opportunity of cross-examining her once more.'

'I didn't want my son brought into it.'

'Yet you bring him into it now. Isn't the truth of the matter, Miss Goddard, that you have made up this allegation?'

'Why would I make it up? It only gives me a motive for hurting her.'

'She made an innocent remark about your son and you have twisted it for your own purposes.'

'I don't see how it helps me. On the contrary.'

'It wasn't put because it didn't happen.'

'That's not true.'

'Is all this relevant, Mr Diggory-Brown?' asked the judge. 'It is, as Miss Goddard herself concedes, relevant as to motive.'

'Yet these purported photographs and text messages have not been put in evidence.'

'No, Your Honour. Because they don't exist.'

The judge turned to Mel. 'Miss Goddard. You have raised certain allegations concerning the complainant. If you wish to pursue these allegations, the jury will need to see the documentary evidence to which you refer.'

'I understand, Your Honour.'

'And do you propose to disclose this evidence?'

'Your Honour, I cannot do that. My son has deleted the texts and photographs.'

Mel glanced at Natasha. Her expression was unchanged. Though she must be relieved, must have realised the risk she had taken in bringing this prosecution. In some perverse way, Mel found herself admiring her enemy.

'I think that answers your question, Mr Diggory-Brown. I will address the jury on the issue in my summing up. Please proceed.'

'So, Miss Goddard, you admit you felt aggressive towards Miss Baker.'

'I didn't feel aggressive. I'm not an aggressive person. I was upset. I may have felt angry. That's not the same as aggressive.'

Wasn't it? When she hurled herself at Natasha it had felt more instinctive than aggressive. Could anyone hear the blood pulsing through her veins as she spoke? Was this what they picked up on lie detectors?

'That's not what your own mother said.'

'We've had our difficulties.'

'This is not the first time you've been violent.'

'You mean the cat. It was awful. I know how much my mother loved that little creature. I told her how sorry I was...'

'You have been violent towards people too.'

'I deny that.'

'You used to be married to a member of the Bar. Your son's father, Claude Villiers.'

'What has he got to do with anything?'

Alisha jumped up. 'Your Honour, the defendant's relationship with Mr Villiers is not in issue here.'

'Continue, Mr Diggory-Brown,' said McDermid.

'Miss Goddard, did you not, on at least one occasion, hit your husband?'

It was clear in her memory, sharp as a well-defined etching. Claude was shouting. She could see his face, heavy-featured, broad and unshaven, contorted with anger, bellowing. Jacob had been a baby. His cries resonated from the next room, as loud as his father's. What had the row been about? She couldn't recall. But she could recall hating Claude at that moment, wanting to hurt him, slapping him hard across the face. And now he was sitting in the public gallery. Here to support her.

'I hit Claude once. I regret it.'

Where had Digger got hold of this? Claude wouldn't have said anything. Or would he? They were friends now, but it had not always been friendly. She might even have told someone herself, confessed it drunkenly over too many drinks in Daly's. The Bar was a small place. Word got around. Digger carried on questioning.

'Anyone else?'

She couldn't lie about Jacob. Not with his eyes burrowing through her.

'I once smacked my child. I regret that too.'

'Where did you smack him?'

'In a swimming pool changing room.'

'Where on his body?'

'His face.'

Digger waited. There was an aching silence. A woman in the front row of the jury coughed. After that, only the hum of air conditioning.

'How old was Jacob at the time?'

'About four.'

She stared at the jury, avoiding individual faces, allowing her vision to blur, conscious of Jacob's silent presence on the other side of the court room.

'You have a short temper.'

'Sometimes. I mean, if provoked.'

Bugger. Why use that word? Provocation. She might as well dig her own grave.

'You were provoked on that Sunday in Dulwich.'

'No.'

'You believed Miss Baker was stealing from your mother.'

'Yes.'

'Betraying her trust as your mother's guest.'

'Yes.'

'You accused her of deception, and she countered with your affair with a married man, Paul Freedman.'

It was not a question. And it was impossible to speak.

'You also decided, either wilfully or mistakenly, that Miss Baker, a woman of almost thirty, was stalking your teenage son.'

'I wasn't mistaken.'

'You were furious with Natasha.'

'Yes.'

'Without thinking, just as you lashed out at your husband, your son, a defenceless cat, you grabbed hold of Miss Baker's arms and threw her backwards.'

328

She must deny it. For Jacob's sake she had to deny it.

'That's not true.'

'Causing her to hit her head on the glass edge of the dressing table.'

'No.'

Mel was shaking. She looked at Alisha, seeking rescue, but Alisha could not rescue her from her own untruth.

Digger looked satisfied with his morning's work. 'Thank you, Miss Goddard.'

'Any re-examination, Miss Mehta?' asked the judge.

'No, Your Honour.'

It was time for speeches. Digger went first. He set out the background, the difficult relationship, Mel's resentment of her successful pupil, the allegations of theft and lying. He seemed about to wind up when to Mel's surprise he referred to the online stalking.

'Members of jury, I ask you to consider the defendant's allegations regarding Miss Baker's purported contact with her son. The evidence itself is not in issue. That has been made clear by the judge. There are no photographs or texts for you to consider. So what are you to make of these groundless allegations? Ladies and gentlemen, they are but a ploy to besmirch the good character of the complainant. Moreover, even if they were true, which is denied, how could they possibly help the defendant's case? All they could do would be to paint the complainant in an unattractive light. Indeed, as the judge will no doubt out confirm in his summing up, even if true, they would not give rise to a criminal offence. No, members of the jury. You are not here to give a judgement on the character of the complainant on hearsay evidence. You are here to decide on how Miss Baker sustained serious injury on that summer afternoon. The defendant relies on self-defence. But even her own mother was unable to give evidence of any hostile action on the part of the complainant. The medical evidence is uncontested. Miss Baker could only have sustained injury as a result of an aggressive push on the part of the defendant. For those reasons, members of the jury, I ask you to find the defendant guilty of this offence.'

Alisha came next. She focused on the layout of the room, the shoes on the floor, Natasha's antagonism towards her supervisor. Mel felt herself drifting off. Alisha had not impressed her. Was it because she had not believed her from the outset? When Alisha had finished all Mel could hope for was that there must be a doubt. But the climate was changing in the justice system. The defendant-led culture was shifting to focus on the victim. Juries had become readier to convict.

They reached a suitable moment. The judge would address the jury after lunch. Mel was granted bail. Alisha came over and suggested they have a snack in the coffee bar. She looked for Jacob, Claude and Isabel. They had disappeared. As Alisha went up to buy the sandwiches Mel took out her phone to text Jacob. There was a message from Paul.

Hi Mel. I'm in London for a couple of days. Fancy lunch? Paul x.

Mel felt a lurch of distress or anger, she could not tell which. He had forgotten her trial date. She deleted the message and texted Jacob.

I'm sorry, darling. Forgive me.

The judge spoke from two p.m. to two thirty. The words rose and faded as if someone were fiddling with an amplifier, raising and lowering the volume. He outlined the medical evidence, the details of the alleged assault, the lack of evidence to support the contention of self-defence, the geography of the room, the shoes on the floor, the breakdown of a relationship of trust. Mel heard the words 'ancillary matters' and it was as if the volume had been turned up as he mentioned Jacob, the photographs, the texts, only to dismiss them as irrelevant. The jury were reminded of the need to reach their verdict on evidence, not on speculation or inference. McDermid told them they needed to be satisfied so they were sure of the defendant's guilt. His tone was grave. And though he avoided clear obvious bias, his emphasis on the pupil–supervisor relationship left her with a powerful sense that he was asking them to convict.

As if she were on the brink of death, her life spooled before her. The quiet, dull days in Dulwich which now seemed days of peace and even joy, her mother's lack of interference offering a freedom for which she was now grateful. She re-imagined those long afternoons, stretched across the carpet, reading magazines, comics, romantic novels. It had been a safe place. There was little control, but neither was there threat nor fear. It had not been an unhappy childhood.

Her teenage years had been turbulent, but whose had not? Then came the joy of study when she had learnt to love the order and symmetry of law. It gave shape to a life otherwise undisciplined, and after she had befriended Kath, they were ready to take on the world.

Everything went wrong after Kath's death. The relationship with Claude was turbulent; baby Jacob was difficult. He had health problems, minor, but enough to make him scratchy and discontented: ear infections, eczema, asthma. Work had carried her through. And now Jacob's love, and her love for him, was carrying her through this trial. She had messed up. Given another chance she would act differently, she would hold back, learn to wait.

The jury went out and bail was granted again. Mel was to stay in the precincts of the court. She looked back and saw Jacob, Claude and Isabel, but did not feel she able to join them. Alisha gave her a copy of *The Times* and she studied each page assiduously, though she would not have remembered anything she'd read if asked. At 3:30 p.m. they were called back into court. A verdict in an hour would be unlikely. They would be asking for a direction, perhaps looking for a majority verdict or querying some point of evidence. The forewoman stood up, the one who had coughed when she mentioned slapping Jacob.

McDermid spoke. 'Members of the jury have you reached your verdict?'

'We have.'

'What is your verdict?'

Mel gripped the ledge at the front of the dock. If she could hold on tight, all would be well. She closed her eyes. A voice rang out across the courtroom.

'Not guilty.'

She was rigid, unable to move or breathe. It was too much to take in. She must have misheard. Something wound tight inside her began to unwind. There was air in her lungs, and she opened her eyes. Through the glass of the dock she saw people moving. Alisha was standing, asking something of the judge. And now what had been taut grew soft, her bones were jelly and she was falling into herself, melting. The jury were standing up, walking slowly out of the back of the courtroom. One of the men turned to look at her. She caught his glance. Reasonable doubt. Not enough to convict.

The usher was standing next to her, taking her arm, raising her up, leading her back into the world. Like an old woman she steadied herself on the ledge as she walked towards the door of the dock. She heard the words, 'Court Rise' and a clatter of bodies pulling themselves up as the judge left the courtroom.

Familiar voices reverberated around her as she stepped into the well of the court. Through them all one stood out, Isabel's perfectly modulated 'Darling!' There were pats on her back, chatter she could not follow, congratulations from friends: Georgie, Jess, even Jeremy. Then she heard the deep, resonant tone she knew so well.

'Well done, Mel. Spot on.' It could only be Claude.

It was overwhelming. It was what she had longed for, but now it was happening she felt shaken, troubled, torn inside. She had done wrong and these people should know. But they were smiling, oblivious to the truth. She wanted to hug Jacob, but he had disappeared. Panic hit. Her breathing became rapid. Where was he? Had he been devastated by what he heard? Briefly she wondered about Natasha and Luke, smothering some mad instinct to apologise. They were nowhere to be seen.

The usher was asking the public to leave the court so that the next case could be brought on. Mel was hovering, uncertain where to turn, when she felt a pressure on her arm, gentle but determined. It was Georgie, and he was leading her out of the court room. She should be ecstatic, but everything felt unreal. Had they made a mistake? Then she heard the gleeful voice she longed to hear.

'Mum!' Jacob was waiting by the door. Relief tore through her as the tears broke and she fell against him, uncertain if she was sobbing or laughing.

Chapter Forty-seven

Natasha

Natasha had been unable to settle all evening. Her skin felt as if it were crawling with mites. After dinner, which she struggled to eat, Luke stood behind her chair and started to massage her neck. His touch made her wince and she stood up and walked to the sofa, craving movement, too heavy and exhausted to move. The only thing that might pacify the turmoil inside her was a run. Would she ever run again? She lay down, shifting to her side to ease her aching back.

Then, heaving herself up, she walked to the hall, picking up the car keys from the hook. As she turned for the door, she sensed him behind her. His hands were on her shoulders, pressing into her flesh and bones. She twisted to face him, met his blazing eyes.

'You can't stop me,' she snapped. But he continued to grip her tightly. 'Let me go,' she said, 'I need to do a finger-prick test. I'm taking the car.'

It worked. He stepped back. She opened her kit bag and took out her meter. He watched in silence as she inserted the strip, pricked her finger and smeared on the drop of blood. The reading was high, but within bounds. She needed to get out of the flat.

'Where are you going?' he asked.

'Just for a drive.'

'It's past ten o'clock.'

'I'm restless. I need to get out.'

'I'll come with you.'

'No.'

'You're eight months pregnant; you're in a state; your blood sugar's all over the place. I don't want you going.'

'What the fuck do you know about my blood sugar?'

'I've lived with it for two years.'

She met his anxious eyes. 'Don't go there, Luke.'

'We tried, Tash. Guilty people get off all the time. You need to accept it.'

'I can't.'

'It must have been tough for her too.'

'What the fuck?'

'Being on trial. Imagine how she must have felt.'

'For Chrissake.'

His eyes narrowed. 'And then there's her son. Jacob. He was the one on your computer, wasn't he? I recognised him in the restaurant. It was the same guy.'

'I told you it meant nothing.'

'You denied it in court. Your barrister said there were no photos.'

'What did you expect? Anyway, it's over now. Finished. Done.'

'What did you say to her?' He wore his pained look, the one where his handsome features became sharp and tight.

'What does it matter now? You heard Melanie. She made Jacob delete everything.'

'That's not the point, is it, Tash? The point is Jacob's photo was on your computer. I saw it. Was that why she hit you?'

'For fucksake, Luke. Why you raising this now? We lost the case. I'm about to have your baby.'

'Tash, we talked about it after your arrest. It's not just the shoplifting. There's other stuff. Please, don't go out. Not tonight.'

'Let go of me.'

'You know I'll always be here for you. You need help. Especially now.'

'I don't want to talk about it. You have no idea what I've been through listening to that lying cow.'

'Stay here. Have a nice hot bath.'

Bloody Luke. He thought a nice hot bath was the answer to everything. That or therapy. But he wasn't going to stop her. Nothing would stop her. Let him think what he wanted about Jacob. She wasn't going to explain anything. It was not like she'd done anything criminal. And she'd been in the witness box long enough. She snatched up her keys, grabbed her jacket and walked out before he could stop her, slamming the door behind her.

Rain splattered her windscreen as she set off towards the river. It was hard to see the route through the swishing wipers, but she knew the address from previous research and the satnav led her there through crowded streets. Even at this hour the traffic was bad, with road works and detours, and it was an hour before she arrived in the quiet north London street with its solid Edwardian red-brick homes. 57a. She parked near the front door. There was no umbrella in the car, and she had only her short jacket. Too bad. She crossed the pavement in the pouring rain, walked up the path to the porch and rang the bell marked 'Goddard'. Wet and cold, she waited. No one came. She rang again. Mel's voice drifted out through a grille.

'Who is it?'

'Your pupil.'

'What do you want?'

'I want to talk to you.'

The Entryphone clicked and there was silence. Natasha pressed the bell again. No reply. Of course. Mel would not open the door to a visitor at eleven thirty at night, particularly this visitor. In her mistaken imagination, Mel had opened the door and would be standing before her, vulnerable, in her nightdress. Instead Natasha was the vulnerable one, a fat helpless cow, dog-tired, sopping wet, on the wrong side of London, with nothing to show for her ridiculous journey. She tried to console herself. At least she had interrupted Mel's evening, hinted that life might not be exactly as it once was when you got away with a serious assault charge.

She rang one more time and was about to leave. It had not been a complete success, but something had yielded. Getting out of the flat had helped. The itch was partially relieved. She'd had the last word. Then, as she was turning towards the car, the front door opened. Jacob stood in the doorway. His round eyes were tired. His hair was rumpled and his T-shirt half out of the jeans which hung so well on his slender hips. She ran her eyes over his body. Defeated, weary, angry and pregnant as she was, it still gave her pleasure to look at him.

'Leave us alone,' he said.

'I came to see Mel.'

'Please go.'

'But it's nice to see you.' She felt a smile creep up towards her eyes.

His expression was steely, but she would not turn away.

'Must have been a shock to hear all that stuff in court,' she said.

'I said go. Now.'

'Not just the photos, but the violence. And you only four years old. That's horrible.'

'Fuck off, Natasha.'

She had her hands in the doorway. If he slammed the door he would break her fingers and she knew he wouldn't do that.

'She's guilty, you know that, don't you? She bloody threw me down and got away with it. That's why I've got this.' And she pulled back her hair to expose her scar. It was small, not much more than a centimetre beyond her hairline. But it was a visible reminder of what his mother had done.

The change in his face was miniscule, an eyelid flickered, there was a quiver in his lip. It was enough for Natasha to detect the shift from certainty. Something in her words had dented the mask of his assurance. It was hardly a triumph. But it was a seed. With luck he would lose faith in this woman who had hit him as a child, taken a married lover, lied in court. What was a bit of Facebook flirtation compared with all that? But he only said, 'Go'. And when she didn't move, he grasped her shoulders, squeezed them and pushed her away back from the door. And as he squeezed her she remembered this was how Luke had held her before she left under an hour ago. There were only so many ways you could take control of a heavily pregnant woman.

'You're hurting me,' she squealed.

'Good,' he said, moving back inside.

'Little shit,' she countered. And he shut the door in her face.

The moment she switched on the ignition, her phone started ringing. Luke.

'Where the hell are you?'

'I'm coming home.'

'What are you doing?'

'Driving around. I feel better now. I'll be back soon. I love you, Luke.'

It was not what she had imagined, Mel distraught, begging forgiveness, but it was something, telling the boy, who seemed to hear her. She felt calmer, relieved, physically soothed, as if she had cleaned the house and thrown away the rubbish. Her world was tidier now. There was space to think and move. She could look forward. Even the rain had eased. Yet as she tried to reassure herself, edging through the traffic on Blackstock Road towards Islington and Holborn, she felt her body tense. Pain shot through her groin. Surely it could not start now? Over the last two weeks it had stopped kicking and there were times when she found herself wondering if it were dead.

She had an appointment at the hospital in two days' time. Her bag was already packed, and they'd told her they might have to induce early. Luke had wanted to buy a cot and baby things, but Natasha had refused. She felt superstitious about making plans. It was still hard to believe she could ever be a mother. Some part of her felt she never would, that this thing was happening to someone else, another Natasha who inhabited the same body and was ready to step onto the stage of motherhood, while the real Natasha waited in the wings in disbelief. She was beginning to feel faint. Her blood sugar might have dropped but she wasn't going to stop and check it now. She was probably just tired. The shooting pain ceased.

The car rolled on towards Holborn. Lights gleamed confusingly through the night air. London felt too big, too threatening. But she would be home soon. Luke would have waited up for her and they would fall into bed and snuggle up. She needed to be close to him. No sex these days, but that was fine. She was too enormous to enjoy it and Luke was always worried about the baby.

She turned into Gray's Inn Road. It was quiet here at night. No clubs, few pubs, everything closed by eight p.m. But this was a special place and she loved it. It had been a struggle to get here. She had so nearly made it: the good degree, the tricky Bar exams, call to the Bar, the precious pupillage, clearing every hurdle but the last, the tenancy. As she thought about all she had nearly won, she pictured the woman who should have helped her but instead had stood in her way like a locked door, keeping her from everything she had fought for.

'Forget it. Put it behind you,' Luke had said. 'You're still a barrister; she can't take that away. You'll be great in the CPS, prosecuting criminals. Don't say that isn't important.'

It wasn't the same. Who remembered the great prosecutors? And she was worried. There had been no action on the arrest but the CPS representative in court had noted down everything she said. She owned up to the caution because if it hadn't come from her, Mel's barrister would have raised it. But she had failed to mention it on her application. What if the job was taken from her?

The traffic was light now, and the rain was easing as she approached the river. She drove onto Blackfriars Bridge and headed south for Brixton.

Her phone was ringing. It would be Luke again, still fretting. But she couldn't stop on the bridge and when she got to the other side there was no safe place to pull in. She'd forgotten to plug in the hands-free. He would have to wait. If he was going to sound off about her staying out late, she would rather hear it at home than in the car.

She was negotiating the enormous Elephant and Castle roundabout when the pain returned. Like period cramps, only worse. Not the stabbing pain they had warned her about, but tough, intense, lingering. Headlights were coming at her from all directions. She carried on driving, breathing deeply as she'd been taught. After a few seconds the pain subsided.

She wouldn't ring Luke. Not unless it got too bad for her concentrate. But as she set off down Walworth Road it returned, rising and falling in waves. She carried on, speeding up a little, never mind the speed limit. Suddenly there was a cool wetness between her legs. The seat felt slippery and cold. She was already wet from the rain, but this was different. This was coming from inside her. Alone in the car she heard herself shouting, 'Stop. Stop.'

She hardly knew how she reached Moorlands. It seemed that some benign force took her there. As she drove onto the estate, something twisted inside her, her guts were being wound around a corkscrew. What she had thought of as pain was nothing in comparison to this.

Their flat was in the first block. She managed to stop the car, opening the door and scrambling out, falling forward against the wing and the wet bonnet. It seemed she would die from this agony, and that she would welcome that sweet oblivion. Then as suddenly as it had arisen, it ceased and there was only exhaustion. She straightened, looked about her. The car park was empty, the rain had stopped, the black tarmac was shiny with puddles under the floodlights. A new puddle was forming beneath her, water still trickling down her thighs. Their block was a few steps away. She turned towards it and pressed the buzzer.

'Haven't you got a key?' he called.

'Help me,' she cried into the intercom.

Chapter Forty-eight

Mel

'I told her to go away,' said Jacob.

He ran a hand through his hair which was greasy, needing a wash.

'What did she want?' asked Mel. She had been unable to stop him going to the door.

'She's angry. Says you got away with it. Plus, I reckon she wanted to see how I took it.'

Natasha had done her a favour. It was the opening she needed. 'And how have you taken it?'

'I'm really happy for you, Mum.'

She studied his tired face. Whatever he had done or not done in the past, whatever teenage lies he had offered her, she was convinced he now spoke the truth. There were a thousand Jacobs and she would never know them all. But she knew the son that mattered to her. Just as he knew the mother that mattered to him.

'I'm sorry about all that stuff,' she said.

'Gran told me about the cat.' He chuckled, opening the fridge for another beer. She sat over the single glass of wine she had been nursing all evening, wondering why she found it so hard to drink. Contrary to Georgie's proposal, they had come straight home. There had been no champagne. Not tonight. There would be time for that.

'I didn't realise you were there. You weren't there when I started in the witness box.'

'I couldn't face going to college. I just turned around on the way and got the tube to court. You were giving evidence, only the usher let me sneak in. So, like, you'd have said something different if you'd known I was there?'

'Of course not.'

He stood looking at her as if waiting for her to speak and she said, 'You did nothing wrong, Jacob.'

He shook his head. 'I fucked up.'

'I don't think she'll do anything with the photos. Not now her barrister has denied they exist.'

He sat down at the table and stared at his beer.

She said, 'We should go to bed. You've got college in the morning.'

Still staring into his beer, he said, 'You're not seeing that Paul bloke again, are you?' She wanted to say 'no', but the word took too long to come out and he carried on. 'Only that, you're too nice. Like, if he's married to someone else, that sucks. I mean, like, I know it didn't work with Dad but you'll... Shit. I mean, if you want, when I go to university. If you want to get married again. I won't mind.'

Something in the way he spoke reminded her of his protest in the police station, some deep struggle to say the right thing. Where did that come from? Surely not from her.

'So you're going to university?' Last week he had threatened to give up college and work in a bar.

'I guess so. It's what people do isn't it. Like getting married.'

He was deadly serious, and she reminded herself that Jacob didn't do irony. Like getting married, she thought.

'I've finished with Paul,' she said.

He continued to stare into his beer.

–

The next morning, she went into chambers for the first time for four months.

'Hi, Mel,' said Andy as if she had never been away. 'A few of your solicitors have been asking for you. There's a big care case at the Principal Registry next week if you're up for it.'

'Great. Thanks, Andy.'

He handed her a bundle of papers. 'I'll send the rest over by email.'

She drifted along the corridor and made tea in the galley kitchen, noting the coffee grounds and lipstick blotches on the unwashed cups that had been left after the morning rush for the High Court. She had eaten no breakfast and the biscuit tin was empty, as usual. A couple of colleagues dashed past her with quick nods of greeting as she took her tea and climbed the stairs to her room.

The desk she used to think of as her own was piled high with other people's papers. She walked to the window and looked out over Temple Gardens. The sky was a pale grey and the false starts of an early spring lay under a melting film of sleet. There was a lump in her throat, her eyes pricked with tears and suddenly she could not hold back and she wept for her love of this place and the colleagues who had trusted her when she didn't deserve their trust and who welcomed her now as if she had never left. She had been drawn back in the easy, offhand way she might have expected. Soon there would be work in the diary and, in that sense, everything was just as it was. But something fundamental had changed and it could never again be as it was.

On Sunday she would go down to Dulwich to see Isabel. Jacob had promised to come along and had asked to bring Don.

Chapter Forty-nine

Mel

In Isabel's kitchen Don and Jacob were arguing over the rules of some incomprehensible strategy game. Jacob had his hands deep in hot soapy water. Don was wiping a plate with a tea towel; she looked up to smile at Mel standing in the doorway then reverted to her discussion with Jacob.

'If you two are OK here, I'll head off home and get some work done. Gran's having a snooze.'

'OK. See you later, Mum.'

'Bye, darling.' They hugged. Jacob smelt of sweat. He probably should wash more, but she loved that smell. Don looked on, smiling. Mel had feared how it would be when Jacob found a girlfriend. Would she take him away? In some curious way Don seemed to be bringing him back.

She went into the sitting room and whispered to her mother who was sitting in an armchair. Her eyes were shut.

'Mum, I'm off home, I hope you don't mind. I've got a bit of work.'

'You and your work,' muttered Isabel. But she opened her eyes and smiled. 'Of course, darling. Thank you for coming.'

'It was a pleasure. Lovely lunch. Look after yourself. I'll call you in the week. And, Mum – thanks for everything.'

'It was nothing. Any mother would do what I did.'

Mel pressed her lips against her mother's cool, powdery cheek. Briefly she held the fragile bony hand which felt as if it would break at the slightest pressure. There was so much she wished she knew. So much she had never asked.

It was mild for the time of year, rain spitting from an overcast sky, as she walked out of the cul de sac, heading for Herne Hill Station. When she reached the park, some impulse drew her over the busy road to the wave of green unrolling up the gentle hill.

She had once seen an imaginary map of the city after the collapse of the Thames Barrier. Much of north London stood high above the flood. Most of south London was submerged. She was heading up one of its few islands.

A message pinged. She glanced at her phone, wondering if it might be Sami. But it was from Natasha's phone.

Ned Thomas Baker Gearing 3.4 kilos. Mother and baby doing well. Luke.

She was surprised they had thought to inform her. But perhaps Natasha didn't know about the message. Perhaps Luke didn't believe Natasha. Perhaps, as had happened with the jury, it was Mel who had convinced him. It was hard to imagine Natasha as a mother, though she was glad the baby was doing well.

She walked on. The rain had stopped, and a weak sun glimmered beyond the thin cloud. Winter had been short, and the branches of the huge trees already rippled with the yellowy tinge of new growth. A couple of runners streamed past her. Dogs scuffled under shrubs or chased random scents across the grass. A group of young women with pushchairs were heading for the cafe. A single optimistic kite flyer stood near the top of the slope, waiting for the wind to rise. It was many years since Mel had come here. As a small child she and her mother had visited this park for dull, dutiful Sunday walks. The two of them. She remembered staring longingly at the large rowdy families. She had never flown a kite, never been allowed to keep a dog. As soon as she was old enough to come to the park alone, she had stopped coming. Her school was on the other side of the borough.

As she walked on towards the top of the hill she thought of her tears of joy at the window in chambers, the cheery chaos of the clerks' room, the deep ties that bound her to her colleagues. However little she knew of their private lives, they could share in the lives of others, treading a fine line on the brink of client confidentiality to compare and compete in love and loss, rape, ruin, even murder. Jacob came first, but he would leave her soon. Lovers would assuage her hunger for intimacy. She hoped there would always be lovers. But Bridge Court was her family and she had been given a second chance.

At the top of the hill she turned back to look down over the city. The sun was breaking through the cloud now, enough to touch the urban landscape with a pale gold shimmer. Colours were sharper, lines more distinct. Beyond and below her she could make out the glittering towers of the City. If she twisted her head to the right, she could see the Surrey hills.

She ought to turn back. There were papers she needed to study for Monday. She was due to represent the father of an eight-year-old boy who had been starved and tortured by his mother. It had happened in Haringey, in a street not far from her own. The child had been beaten, tied to a bed. When he was found, his belly was swollen from malnutrition. The mother was in prison and the father was asking for the child to live with him, though he had never cared for him nor protected him from his dangerous mother. At their worst, families were brutal, tore each other apart. Yet each of them needed good representation. She would be well prepared.

Acknowledgements

My profound thanks to my dear friend Chris Peachment who read all my early drafts. Without you I would never have become a publishable writer. Thanks to my other readers, Susie Graham-Jones, who believed in my characters, and Sue Gwilliam, who took endless trouble to instruct me in the complications of type 1 diabetes.

Thanks also to Diane Nixon and James Wood QC for taking the time to discuss aspects of criminal procedure.

Above all I owe a huge debt to my wonderful agent, Anne Marie Doulton, who saw potential in my baggy monster of a first draft and to my editor at Canelo, Louise Cullen, whose brilliant ideas and sensitive responses led to the finished book.